Joseph O'Neill was born in Ireland a̶̶̶̶̶̶̶̶̶̶̶̶̶̶
and the Netherlands. After working in ̶̶̶̶̶̶̶̶̶̶̶̶̶̶
New York, where he lives with his fam̶̶̶̶̶̶̶̶̶̶̶̶̶̶
and *Netherland*, were longlisted for th̶̶̶̶̶̶̶̶̶̶̶̶̶̶
the PEN/Faulkner Award and the K̶̶̶̶̶̶̶̶̶̶̶̶̶̶
short stories appear regularly in the *N̶̶̶̶̶̶̶̶̶̶̶̶̶*
published in the *Guardian*, the *Irish Times* and the ̶̶̶̶̶̶̶̶̶̶̶̶̶̶

Praise for *Godwin*:

'I didn't want it to end … What an achievement. Among the best novels I've read in a long time' Bill Buford, author of *Among the Thugs*

'At once a minute, hilariously observed and poignant workplace novel about Pittsburgh, and a sweeping postcolonial picaresque novel about the grim fringes of the global soccer industry, replete with laugh-out-loud observations, gorgeously turned phrases and exhilarating dialogue, pervaded by a winning sense of exasperated humanism. The whole time I was reading, I was thinking "I wish there were more books like this"' Elif Batuman, author of *Either/Or*

'A fantastic novel, brilliantly crafted, using such a clever lens to explore the world of football … I loved it' Marcus du Sautoy, author of *Around the World in 80 Games*

'O'Neill has a gift for finding humour in emotional stress, and it shines … An astonishing marathon of storytelling … that highlights the avarice of sports recruitment and the legacy of colonialism … Another exceptional entry in the O'Neill corpus' *Kirkus Reviews*

'No one will exit this pinwheeling novel unmoved by its tender and terrible surprises … Every sentence is suffused with O'Neill's capacious intelligence, humour and care' Karen Russell, author of *Swamplandia!*

'*Godwin* is a miracle: a gripping novel refracting in clear and poetic language the seemingly incompatible elements of today's world … *Godwin* is a champion book' Aleksandar Hemon, author of *The World and All That It Holds*

'An exceptional tale of desire and betrayal … O'Neill's storytelling here has an enthralling fireside quality, ushering us with deceptive simplicity into a labyrinth of motive and desire, breathtaking betrayals and artfully twined threads. A book to sink into, in other words, and one not to be missed' *Guardian*

'A meticulously constructed marvel … Nobody else's fiction tears up the ground quite like O'Neill's profoundly introspective novels … In their careful braiding of anxiety and aspiration, his stories are marvels of narrative magic and stylistic panache … Like Godwin, this novelist is a player whose charges and feints will leave you amazed – and defeated' *Washington Post*

'Populous, lively and intellectually challenging … *Godwin* uses sports as a window on global realities that might otherwise be too vast or too abstract to perceive' *New York Times Book Review*

'Absorbing … picaresque' *Vogue*

'Crystalline prose and keen observations on family and postcolonialism as seen through the seedier side of the global soccer industry make this a winner' *Boston Globe*

'An exercise in realism by one of its finer contemporary disciples' *Vulture*

'O'Neill combines the brothers' exploits with sharp observations about international business and issues like greenwashing and corruption that have tarnished the world's game' *Los Angeles Times*

'Exciting and incisive … As O'Neill artfully pairs the thrill of the hunt for Godwin with the complex politics of cooperative work, the driving force that connects the twinned narratives is the corruptive power of capitalism. This has all the velocity and swerve of an unstoppable free kick' *Publishers Weekly*

ALSO BY JOSEPH O'NEILL

FICTION

Good Trouble
The Dog
Netherland
The Breezes
This Is the Life

NONFICTION

Blood-Dark Track: A Family History

GODWIN

JOSEPH O'NEILL

4th ESTATE • London

4th Estate
An imprint of HarperCollins*Publishers*
1 London Bridge Street
London SE1 9GF

www.4thestate.co.uk

HarperCollins*Publishers*
Macken House, 39/40 Mayor Street Upper,
Dublin 1, D01 C9W8, Ireland

First published in Great Britain in 2024 by 4th Estate
First published in the US in 2024 by Pantheon Books
This 4th Estate paperback published in 2025

1

Copyright © Joseph O'Neill 2024

Joseph O'Neill asserts the moral right to be identified as the author of this work
in accordance with the Copyright, Designs and Patents Act 1988

A catalogue record for this book is available from the British Library

ISBN 978-0-00-828408-4

This novel is entirely a work of fiction. The names, characters and incidents portrayed
in it are the work of the author's imagination. Any resemblance to actual persons,
living or dead, events or localities is entirely coincidental.

All rights reserved. No part of this publication may be reproduced, stored in a
retrieval system, or transmitted, in any form or by any means, electronic, mechanical,
photocopying, recording or otherwise, without the prior permission of the publishers.

Without limiting the author's and publisher's exclusive rights, any unauthorised use
of this publication to train generative artificial intelligence (AI) technologies is
expressly prohibited. HarperCollins also exercise their rights under Article 4(3) of
the Digital Single Market Directive 2019/790 and expressly reserve this publication
from the text and data mining exception.

This book is sold subject to the condition that it shall not, by way of trade or
otherwise, be lent, re-sold, hired out or otherwise circulated without the publisher's
prior consent in any form of binding or cover other than that in which it is published
and without a similar condition including this condition being imposed on the
subsequent purchaser.

Typeset in Janson Text LT Std

Printed and bound in the UK using 100% renewable electricity
at CPI Group (UK) Ltd

MIX
Paper | Supporting
responsible forestry
FSC™ C007454

This book contains FSC™ certified paper and other controlled sources to ensure
responsible forest management.

For more information visit: www.harpercollins.co.uk/green

For R

GODWIN

L

Wolfe was behaving strangely with clients and co-workers. Annie, my Co-Lead, thought we should give him a written warning, in accordance with our *Guidelines*. In her opinion, a recent incident 'crossed a line'.

I was more cautious. A written warning was a big step. I felt it would be more constructive, and less destabilizing to our community, to offer Wolfe a measure of support. He was a long-standing member of the Group. This was the first time that he'd had any real issues with his workplace deportment. I suspected he was having the kind of difficulties that all of us face at one time or another.

I told Annie I'd meet him for a coffee and try to find out what was going on.

I had no deep feelings about Wolfe. I wished him well, of course, but I barely knew him, even though we'd been colleagues for seven years. Like many of our more experienced members, he worked from home and came to the office only for the occasional meeting. He'd say very little and leave at the first opportunity. That was fine. Members were under no obligation to get involved in the Group's internal administration.

The Group (officially, the P4 Group) was founded in 2004 as a technical-writing co-operative. The co-operators were known as 'members'. Each member paid the Group a flat monthly subscription, plus an annual contribution that was calculated as a percentage of their earnings. In return, the Group managed members' client relations (including fee negotiation and billing), provided them an office where they could meet colleagues and clients, and gave them a stronger brand presence. It's more professional for a technical writer to be identified as a part of an organization with an impressive website. A collective like the Group is attractive to someone who wants to stay self-employed but doesn't want the risk, hassle and isolation associated with being a sole trader or freelancer. The term 'freelance' sounds good, but most folks find the reality stressful and not at all 'free'.

To become a member, a writer had to demonstrate their personal and professional suitability. That wasn't as forbidding as it sounded. If you were a technical writer who did OK during the three-month probationary period, you would very likely be offered membership. We were always looking to take on new people. Our turnover was significant. Technical writing is hard and not for everyone.

Annie and I were the Group's Co-Leads. If a prospective client contacted the Group, it was the Co-Lead's job to handle the approach on behalf of the membership. If a member asked for help with their practice, it was our job to handle that, too. Annie managed one half of the members, I took care of the other half. None of it was easy. When the Group's membership increased, our responsibilities as Co-Leads also increased. Meanwhile, our compensation stayed flat at around twenty thousand dollars p.a. Annie and I did not make an issue of it. We were ready to accept part-time pay for a full-time job, out of idealism. Idealism, if it's real, means extra work.

When we started out, our ideals were foggy. The four founders – Annie and I plus two others – were women, but we did not attach importance to that fact. We did not see ourselves as feminists. We saw ourselves as a quartet of competent women. If anything, we were embarrassed by the absence of men, and we made a push to recruit them. They were needed, because we were busy right away. There are countless medical-scientific entities based in Greater Pittsburgh, and they all could use help with their technical and commercial literature. We were much more success-ful than we'd anticipated. Soon we needed to be more systematic, more institutional. In 2006, Annie and I produced the Group's *Constitution, Rules and Guidelines for Co-Operators*. It took a year to put it together, but what fun we had. We learned so much.

The truth is, we had not thought deeply about what we were doing. We'd started the co-operative not because we'd read his-tory books or gone to political meetings but because we needed to make a living, and a setup like the Group's struck us as obviously good. We were not ideological. But I found it very interesting to learn about the Rochdale Society and the history of co-operatives. Annie and I agreed that the co-operative movement's traditional principles should be affirmed in the *Guidelines* and put at the center of the Group's identity. It worked very well.

As our reputation grew, assignments arrived from clients all over the country. Medical writing had been our core business, but now we took on installation manuals, feasibility studies and techni-cal reference guides. We also began to offer grant-writing services. That's where Mark Wolfe came in.

Everyone knew him as Wolfe, as if he were a TV detective. He had charisma. The younger newcomers to the Group were intrigued by this blond, rangy man in his late thirties who was often sighted with his dog and, less often, with his beautiful part-ner and their young child. Men esteemed Wolfe on account of the rumors that he'd spent two years in Antarctica. Even cooler, it was said that he was friends with the professional skateboarder Heath Kirchart: years ago, the two of them had reportedly been spotted fooling around in the little skatepark in Polish Hill in the middle of the night. The Antarctica rumor wasn't true – I'd seen Wolfe's Human Resources file – but I kept this knowledge to myself. It's nice to believe that we have admirable workmates. What I saw, when I looked at Wolfe, was a member with output issues. His gross earnings hovered around thirty-seven thousand dollars a year. This wasn't due to any lack of ability. Our 'fees generated' metric had identified him as the Group's most efficient grant writer – the writer most likely to write a successful grant. Other metrics contra-dicted this status, but this isn't the place to go into the problem of how best to measure a worker's overall productivity, a problem that becomes even more interesting in a collective such as the Group, where we had our own ideas about what constitutes value.

The detail of Wolfe's curriculum vitae that spoke to me, as his contemporary, was that as an undergrad he'd studied (at Carnegie Mellon, like so many of us at the Group) molecular biology. It was a thrilling field back then, in the first half of the 1990s; everyone was excited by Kary Mullis and his work on the polymerase chain reaction. Mullis tried to be a fiction writer and a baker before finally dedicating himself to science. He became famous not only as a Nobelist but also, unfortunately, as a crackpot.

I arranged to see Wolfe away from the office. He suggested Lili Café, around the corner from his home in Polish Hill. The neighborhoods of Pittsburgh have a proud and competitive character, and Polish Hill is one of the proudest – the kind where *For Sale* signs are vandalized.

Our meeting took place on a worryingly warm January morning. To signal that the usual formalities didn't apply, I wore a cotton dress with blue checks that I would never wear to the office. I arrived punctually. Fifteen minutes went by before Wolfe, wearing torn-up blue jeans and a white undershirt, turned up with a big old brown-and-black mutt named Pearson. Pearson wore a red bandana in place of a collar. He lay down without a tether at the perimeter railing of the terrace.

Wolfe seemed agitated when he sat down. I wondered if I had done something wrong. Would I mind, Wolfe said, if we moved outside? He did not want to leave Pearson alone.

'Good idea,' I said.

We relocated to a table in the sunlight. Wolfe immediately began to interact with his dog. Pearson responded with remarkable obedience to his human's highly specific commands – in fact, there was no possibility of a conversation as we waited for our breakfast, because Wolfe was so busy signaling and mouthing orders, many of which struck me as unnecessary. 'What a good dog,' I said. He answered with an explanation of his dog-training philosophy, apparently inspired by Benedictine monks. A central tenet of this philosophy, Wolfe told me, was that dogs were happiest when they were clear about their subordinate relation to their master. He went on at such length that I was forced to interrupt with a direct reference to our reason for meeting – his erratic workplace behavior. 'Yeah,' he said. 'Go ahead.'

The first problem – the one that had most concerned Annie – arose when Pete, the building's front-desk agent, stopped Wolfe in the lobby. Pete had been in his job for a month and did not remember seeing this visitor before. Wolfe now told me that it was Pete's rudeness, rather than the request to stop, that upset him. Instead of quickly verifying Wolfe's ID, Pete made Wolfe stand around while he, Pete, had an 'intentionally drawn-out' conversation with a delivery person. Pete's whole demeanor, the way he totally ignored Wolfe, was intended to make Wolfe feel powerless. 'He was exactly like a cop,' Wolfe said. 'Like the law is *him*. I wait a while. And I wait a while longer. And then – you know what? – I go to work. I go into the office that I pay for.'

This was the moment (the security-camera footage showed) when Wolfe walked toward the elevator with his middle finger raised in the direction of Pete. Pete's reaction was to grab Wolfe's backpack. There was a scuffle. A piece of wall art got knocked down. Wolfe's backpack was torn open and its contents flew about the lobby. Pete's shirtsleeve got ripped. It was a somewhat shocking disturbance, observed by several witnesses. Pete later reported that he was shorthanded at the front desk and had multiple visitors to deal with, and he'd asked Wolfe to hold on a minute. When Wolfe decided to walk past him, Pete felt that he had to intervene. That was his job. Pete stated that he would be lying if he said that Wolfe's obscene gesture didn't bother him.

Wolfe said, 'Look, maybe I was a little bit brittle. I wish I hadn't been. In an ideal world, nobody's brittle. But Pete was being a dick. And you know what? Once in a million years, you push back. This was the day I pushed back.' Wolfe snapped his fingers at his dog. 'Do I regret the whole episode? Of course. Would I take a do-over? Sure. But only for prudential reasons.' He added, maybe because he thought I might not understand the word 'prudential', 'Not because I was in the wrong.' Then he was back to snapping his fingers at Pearson.

I brought up the second problematic incident. After a client's grant proposal had failed, they decided to review their entire funding process, including the grant writer's role. They sent Wolfe an e-mail, a questionnaire essentially, asking for his input. Wolfe – who actually had a history of being a little unmoved by clients, a little too indifferent to both their praise and criticism – responded:

> I'm very happy to participate in this review and fully agree that it should be 'thorough and honest'. My true opinion, as someone with years of practice in this expert field, is that my work on your behalf fully optimized the merits of your proposal. If anything, it added merit. Ergo my grantsmanship is not the issue here. As to what the problem might have been, I suggest that you ponder your organization's credibility as a potential grantee of a six-figure sum. Hiring just one person with a meaningful professional track record would be a good start.

The Group received a complaint from the client. They described Wolfe as 'amazingly discourteous and unhelpful'.

Wolfe told me that if you read the correspondence fairly, you'd see that he offered the client thorough and honest advice. It wasn't his problem that the client didn't like the advice. The client, Wolfe said, was a startup operated by assholes in their twenties who from the beginning of the project had made one stupid and disrespectful demand after another. Their claim to funding was worthless. It didn't surprise him, once they'd fallen on their faces, that their next move had been to turn on him. He had seen it coming, in fact.

I pointed out that we often dealt with demanding clients.

'That's very true,' Wolfe said.

I was already fighting a prejudice about what was ailing Wolfe – namely, that he was suffering from a crisis of dignity. This was a common problem at the Group. More than a few of our members were gifted individuals who became technical writers as a stopgap. Time passes. *Torschlusspanik* – closing-door panic – sets in. In masculine cases, especially, its symptom can be a kind of ongoing indignation – a tendency to take offense. Wolfe's occupation, his earnings, maybe did not accord with his sense of being successful.

He had a partner and a young child. I suspected that his financial responsibilities were burdensome, even humiliating. His tattoos were at least a decade old. Heath Kirchart had retired. Soon that beautiful blond hair would start turning white. As he accepted his breakfast from the server, I saw it had already started whitening.

•

I said, 'I guess my question is, is everything all right?' Between taking mouthfuls of vegan ratatouille and black coffee and gesticulating at his dog and fiddling with the carabiner keychain attached to his belt, Wolfe tried to answer my question. It was very confusing. From what I could gather, his worries were connected to a concern about 'the commons' in the context of 'collapse' (of human civilization, possibly, or maybe capitalism). He had some theory about 'inversion' – i.e., about turning a predator-prey social system into a prey-predator system. Somehow this was connected to jihadism – not in the sense of violent religious fanaticism, he said, but in the sense of 'ecopolitical' struggle and perseverance. Before long I gave up trying to follow him. The meeting was out of control. I concentrated on managing my frustration. The café emptied out and filled up; the day grew colder; Pearson slept, woke and slept again; the tab arrived and was settled by me; and all the while Wolfe went on with his monologue. An hour had gone by when I realized he'd come to a stop. I got to my feet right away.

'That's very interesting,' I said. 'You should think about writing it down.'

He said, 'Yeah, maybe I should do that. Write it down. Leave my mark.'

I'd hurt him. I should have been more sensitive.

I hastened home. I have a dog of my own, Cutie.

The next day, I went to see Annie.

'The pith, please,' Annie said. It was her catchphrase. It arose from motherhood and its effect on her time.

The pith was that my meeting with Wolfe, though chaotic, had been useful. He was now fully aware of the Group's level of concern. He had been given the opportunity to tell his side of the story.

And I'd learned something about his state of mind: for whatever reason, Wolfe was going through a period of emotional instability and poor self-awareness.

Annie said, 'Now what?'

There was no obvious answer. Neither Pete nor Wolfe had lodged an official complaint, and the alternative – a proactive, top-down disciplinary investigation – was undesirable in our organization, which had a strongly horizontal ethos. We embraced the concept of decision latitude: as far as possible, individuals decided for themselves how to deal with the demands of Group membership, including social conflicts. A conflict involving a physical altercation, however, was an extreme case. My feeling was that, when push came to shove, we were in Wolfe's corner. We had to be. Pete was an employee of the building, whereas Wolfe was a co-operator. He was one of ours.

'Let's wait a week,' Annie said. 'Then revisit.'

It was exactly what I had in mind. Things can blow over.

But later that same day, Wolfe paid me a surprise visit.

The Group's offices were open-plan. My desk was in a nook called a 'think pod'. The think pod had a pleasant view of treetops, but it wasn't suitable for a private conversation. We found a conference room.

The office was originally a can factory. It was big and spacious. It always gave me pleasure to walk through the reception area, where the large, bright windows were subdivided into squares. The reception area was designed to be a space for anyone who wanted to noodle on a laptop or hang out. Clients responded well to its contemporary 'cool' vibe. Because open-plan settings can adversely affect workers' blood pressure, attentiveness and so on, we installed a long bench on which they could 'wall-ride' – sit with their backs to the white-brick wall, with their screens visible only to them. Wall-riding was popular with our younger people. Often they'd use headphones to create the auditory 'bubble' that can help with a focused mental effort.

I have mixed feelings about these bubbles. In my first real job, with a corporation, earbuds were the norm among the junior employees. It was the dawn of the iPod, and we took pride in our playlists. Then I noticed, as we separately labored in our musically customized headspaces, that the managers didn't wear earbuds. They had bubbles of their own – their offices. Roars of laughter frequently came out of these rooms, especially when their doors were closed. One of the leading laughers was my boss, Dave. His office was a kind of dwelling – not only because of its size but also because of the quantity of personal possessions he hoarded there. When Dave retired, I was drafted to help him pack. In one cabinet I found a colander, which apparently Dave used when washing the fruit that he liked to buy from street vendors; in another, a sleeping bag; and in another, an unusual-looking pair of black gloves. They were climbing gloves, Dave told me, pulling them on. 'Climbing gloves?' I said, and his reply was to open a drawer from which he produced a length of new orange rope. I knew Dave to be a kind boss, but it was nauseating to be in a room with a man wearing black gloves and holding a rope. It was a rappel rope, he said. If ever there was a catastrophic event, his plan was to exit through the window and rappel the five floors down to the street. That was why the gloves had cowhide palms. I must have been wearing a funny expression, because Dave laughed loudly. He was kidding me: the rope was for his son, who was a rock climber. Then I also laughed loudly, and I guess at that point I became one of the laughers. It felt good. We continued to box up Dave's things. Later that day, he left the building through the front door, to more laughter, and after that I never saw him again. My point is that earbuds or headphones are productive, but they detract from the communality of the workplace. The Group was a quiet place, and sometimes I thought that it would be good to hear Dave's laughter. Dave died, though.

In the conference room, Wolfe and I could be seen but not heard.

He wanted to apologize, he said, for 'being an idiot', both to Pete and to me, at our recent meeting. He said, 'I can't explain it. It's not who I am. I'm very sorry.' He stated that he'd be happy to speak with Pete if that would help. He seemed to be fighting tears.

I agreed that it would be a great idea to make up with Pete. I told him that Pete was very anxious about the incident, too, and would be just as relieved to move forward and put a line under the whole business.

Afterward, I went straight to Annie.

She said, 'He has two weeks of accrued leave.'

There was no need to say more. I wrote Wolfe an e-mail thanking him for meeting with me twice. I also wrote:

> Annie tells me that you have two weeks of accrued leave. Would this be a good moment to take a well-deserved break?

'Leave' designated an absence during which a member's monthly dues were suspended. A 'vacation', by contrast, referred to an absence during which the obligation to pay dues continued. I had long advocated for the creation of a sabbatical – a yearlong leave, in effect, for which members of six years' standing would be eligible – but this was never approved. Mistakenly, I believe.

Everybody needs a break sometimes. Occasionally, when my spirits were low, I would glance around the office and be shocked to see human beings forcing themselves to concentrate, and I would be filled with doubts about our purpose. But who doesn't sometimes question the project of labor? That was when I felt even more committed to the ideals of co-operation. If alienation could not be extinguished, surely it could be reduced. Surely a positive solidarity was possible.

Wolfe responded to my e-mail on the following Monday morning. He stated that he would take his accrued leave effective immediately.

The lack of notice wasn't ideal, but in the circumstances it was for the best.

If anyone noticed he was gone, they didn't mention it to me.

How easily a person can disappear.

Sometimes, when everyone else had gone home, I poured myself a cup of coffee and got down to my writing workload. I'd reached that stage of experience where I had a real specialization – biotech compliance – and my writing felt like an exercise in competence. Whereas for years it had felt like I was pushing against the limits of my capacities, not to mention the skepticism, even suspiciousness, of clients. At any rate, at the Group I worked most efficiently in the evening. The feeling of detention associated with the phrase 'working late' rarely arose; and even if the writing would sometimes frustrate me, this did not convert into the thought that I had lost my way in life and should be elsewhere, doing something else. And yet there always came a moment when the quiet would get to me, and I'd become conscious of the melancholy of a deserted office. It was rationally true that the office had been only temporarily vacated and in a very few hours would once again be filled with life; and yet it felt spooky. To be clear, I don't believe in ghosts and nonphysical beings. But there was a sense, at such moments, that I was imperceptibly working alongside the women in bonnets and ankle-length dresses who had once operated crimping machines in this very space. It was not my favorite feeling. It usually led to another uneasy thought: that everything we had worked for at the Group was impermanent, that everything hung by a thread that could not be seen. I always took courage from the arrival, at eight o'clock, of the nightly cleaning crew.

We co-operators did our own office cleaning. There was no getting out of it. We had a roster. Everyone had to muck in about twice a month. Some argued that our time could be more profitably allocated and that an inexpensive contractor should do the cleaning work. Maybe so, but I always felt that the other benefits made the scheme worthwhile. There is nothing like an egalitarian donation of time and labor to enhance team spirit. I played basketball in high school. I did not get many minutes on the court, but the experience was very rewarding. My coach once said to me, 'Lakesha Williams, you are a real team player,' and I have not forgotten how proud that made me.

During the second week of Wolfe's leave, I was scheduled to office-clean with Edil. I wasn't looking forward to it. Edil joined the Group soon after it was founded, and other than Annie and me, she had been around longer than anyone. My relationship with her had always been one of outward cheerfulness but inward anxiety. Over the preceding decade, Edil had billed about $64,000. That was not enough to remain financially viable as a co-operator. Edil retained her Group membership because she always paid her subscription.

She had no pressing need for work income – her parents were in the movie business in Los Angeles, as she liked to mention – and she stayed with the Group because it gave her a socially identifiable occupation and a place to hang out during the day. That was fine, in principle. We all had our reasons for being at the Group, and many of us contributed in ways that were not financially calculable. But Edil made no incalculable contribution, unless it was negative. She involved herself in other folks' business. She passed the time with intrigue. It was mostly harmless, but I didn't like it – and I didn't like her. That was a feeling I had to acknowledge if I was ever going to overcome it.

Our cleaning calendar specified what had to be accomplished on a given day. Cleaning the kitchenette and taking out the trash and wet-mopping our handsome concrete floor was a daily chore. On this occasion, the special assignment was to clean the steel ceiling fans, which revolved constantly during office hours and collected a sticky black coating of dust, soot and whatnot. Pittsburgh has the worst air of any city east of the Mississippi. Cleaning a fan necessitated climbing to the top of a stepladder and keeping your balance as you manipulated a long-handled duster. It was a job that required care and concentration. My hope was that this would deter Edil, who was mopping the floor, from talking to me. It didn't. As soon as I reached the top of the ladder, that chatterbox decided to mop the area where I was dusting – an inefficient decision, because after every swipe of her mop my duster would send more flecks of black dust to the floor, requiring her to swipe again.

She said, 'So what's the story with Wolfe? Is he OK?'

I said nothing. I was trying not to fall off the stepladder.

'I'm very worried about Pete,' Edil said. 'He has three kids, you know.'

'Uh-huh,' I said. I considered it unlikely that Edil was worried about Pete or Pete's children. As the person responsible for collecting the Christmas tips for the building workers, I (and only I) was aware of precisely how much Edil had given.

'Is it true,' I heard Edil say, 'that Wolfe's been given a special vacation?' She had a deep, sonically impressive voice. Maybe that was what enabled her to talk such nonsense. 'I'm not saying it's wrong or right. But I guess some people aren't too happy about it. Because, you know, is there a bylaw in the *Rules* that allows for special vacations? And, you know, why are we rewarding someone for getting into a fight?'

I climbed down the ladder. It was satisfying to see the three-foot blades gleaming. When I dragged the ladder over to the next fan – there were six fans in total – Edil slowly followed me with her bucket. I was perspiring as I climbed the ladder again. I started dusting. I said, 'He took accrued leave. Not a special vacation. Accrued leave.'

The only sounds in the room were the ones being made by me. Edil was leaning on her mop, staring into space. I said, making sure to laugh in a friendly way, 'You going to start mopping, Edil?'

'I was just thinking, Kesha,' she said, sweetly. She extracted the dripping mop from the bucket.

We worked without talking after that. At eight-forty, Edil went home. Then I cleaned the floor properly.

M

I connect the recent unusual occurrences to a very small prior incident. In December, I was walking down a street, lost in an aeon
of my own making, when I looked up and noticed, through the
windowpane of a restaurant, an old lady devouring an ice cream.
I'm not sure what caused me to stop. I can only guess it was the fact
that it was Christmas Eve and the temperature was sixty degrees,
and someone eating gelato on a warm winter's day in Pittsburgh
was some kind of last straw. For several seconds I stared at her
lively blue tongue, seemingly a creature that sprang in and out of
its grotto. I was staring, too, at the middle-aged male reflected in
the window. Apparently, it was intolerable to him that a woman in
her nineties should enjoy ice cream. I walked on, in every sense
disgusted. My only cause for disgust, need it be said, was my own
blackheartedness.

So: I was more than a little sick of the taste of life – not of my
own life, which was touched by love – but of human life as such.
The year that was coming to an end, 2014, had been a dark one. I
will not describe the dark; I refuse its dominion. I'll say only that I
took comfort – to be honest, still take comfort, in spite of the aforementioned touch of love – from fantasizing about the time, surely
less than one thousand years away, when our kind no longer roams
Earth and we shall at last have some peace. (This estimate may

seem short: *H. sapiens* is, after all, listed by the International Union for the Conservation of Nature as the species of least concern. But things are going downhill fast, and humanity is a lowly hillock, as paleontology teaches.) This happy future could be glimpsed, it seemed to me, in the wilderness of the Korean DMZ, where an extraordinary fauna newly thrived in the absence of man; and also in the irradiated forests of the Chernobyl Exclusion Zone, which sheltered ever-increasing populations of wolf, bear, wild horse, elk, eagle and lynx. To my darkened mind, these magnificent natural nouns functioned as the antonyms of words such as 'beheading', 'suicide bombing', 'mass displacement', 'mass abduction', 'mass enslavement', 'mass extinction event'.

I must explain what I mean by the dark. I don't mean a malevolent unseen force – a great controversialist. I mean stupidity, and not the simpleness and brute dullness of old, the yokel hearing the thunder of the divine voice. I mean modern stupidity, which is to say, stupidity that's purposeful and communicable and strangely greedy, and is everywhere rising at such a rate that I sometimes think that it's not only our glacial poles that are thawing but also some undetectable continent of frozen idiocy. This isn't to suggest that I considered myself above it all. The opposite is true. I had a strong, hopeless feeling that I was going under. In this sense, it becomes accurate to speak of an emergency.

On the final day of 2014, when a wintry cold has at last arrived, Sushila and Fizzy come home in the afternoon to find me sitting in the armchair. I am reading for my own diversion a book I got for Fizzy, who is three – William Steig's *Rotten Island*.

Something in my face must alarm my wife. 'What's happened? Mark?'

She unbuckles Fizzy, then looks over my shoulder at my laptop, which is open next to my copy of *Rotten Island*. The article on the screen concerns – I can hardly bring myself to accept it – the last male northern white rhinoceros on Earth. This rhinoceros passes its days in a Kenyan conservancy under the protection of armed guards, because without such protection poachers would certainly kill the animal. A defense system involving guard dogs, watchtowers, fences and drones has been put in place. Also held in custody are the rhinoceros's daughter and granddaughter. It is hoped that the old bull will inseminate one or both of them and keep northern white rhinoceroses going for a little while longer. But this hope has not yet been realized, nor is the outlook good. The bull is more than forty years old – older even than me. His sperm count is low. He lacks the strength to mount the females forcefully, as is the reproductive habit of these beautiful giant herbivores.

Sushila softly kisses my left eye. She says, 'Why don't I make us some tea,' and I say, 'Thank you, that would be wonderful,' and she answers, 'You're not the last rhino.' Then off she goes, to the kettle, on one of those tiny domestic expeditions that, when combined and viewed as a single journey, constitute the great trek of love.

I am about to protest – I wasn't identifying myself with the rhinoceros; I was identifying only the rhinoceros with the rhinoceros – when I grasp what she really means. She is referring, not for the first time, to my sense of our home as an island and of everything outside it as a barbarous ocean. This negative idea of the world, Sushila has suggested, is 'maybe a little unrealistic'.

My wife is someone who reads Zbigniew Herbert for pleasure, and her insights are precious to me; but on this point I'm not to be influenced. The world *is* rotten. To step outside *is* to enter a vicious element. Of course, I also understand that to stay indoors all day, every day, however safely and happily, is hardly salvation. The outside world inevitably seeps in, and there is no end to the mopping and the pumping and the bailing. The rhinoceros percolates.

When Sushila returns with the tea, she tells me that she's received another e-mail from Faye.

My biological mother and I are – there's no better term for it – estranged. She has taken to e-mailing Sushila, ostensibly about her granddaughter, Fizzy. Sushila e-mails Faye back. All of which is fine by me. It's a free country, as we used to say.

The tea is excellent, as always. I never drank tea until I met Sushila. We only drink stuff from Sri Lanka: Sushila buys it out of some romantic feeling of connection to her ancestral land, which she has yet to visit. She is descended from one of those basket-carrying women in the postcards who brilliantly smile for the camera as they labor on a steep hillside of tea bushes; or so we're assured by Sushila's mother, who remembers bringing drinking water to her own mother as she picked leaves on just such a tea plantation. The planters' bungalows now serve as luxurious tourist lodgings. This fills me with an anger that I do my best not to give voice to. It's humiliating at my age to be enraged and confused by history, and in any case Sushila has stated that she doesn't want Fizzy to grow up in an angry house. I couldn't agree more.

Sushila continues, 'It's about Geoff.'

She is referring to my younger (half) brother, Geoffrey Anibal. Faye is his mother, too. Geoff has always lived on the other side of the Atlantic and currently resides in England. Geoff's father is a French gentleman named Antoine Anibal, now deceased. According to my dad, 'old man Anibal' was a terrifically ancient guy, a Methuselah Romeo who married Faye out of a sense of honor after he'd 'knocked her up' with Geoff. Faye lives in England, in a town called Winchester.

'I think it's best if you read it,' Sushila says.

'No, thanks.'

She forwards me Faye's e-mail.

'What's this?'

Sushila answers, 'Read it, delete it, whatever. You decide. He's your brother.'

•

To repeat, this comes at a dark and brittle time. The brittleness, I must assume, is the result of the usual shocks and wallops received in the usual way over the course of four decades, with the usual hardening and enfeebling effect perhaps made worse by a peculiar fragility on my part. Who knows? Who wants to know? If one thing repels me more than the gloom without, it is the gloom within. After years of blundering introspection, I accidentally tripped on private happiness – Sushila – and my feeling ever since has been that the great purpose of my life is to preserve and defend this marvelous fortune like a treasure guardian, and at all costs to avoid squandering it by excessive rumination. That is my mission: to accept a living gift without suspicion; to not screw up. It's not as easy as it looks.

Soon after the rhinoceros episode, on 5 January 2015, I get into a scuffle.

Unless it is unavoidable, I work from home. I don't like spending my day under the surveillance of others, however friendly the surveyors may imagine themselves to be. When I do go into the office, I'm tense. On the morning in question, I have a problematic encounter with lobby security. The fine details of what happened are beside the point and debatable, but, whichever way you look at it, it is a very regrettable, very uncharacteristic incident involving raised voices and raised hands. In my defense, I am not the only one who hasn't covered himself in glory. There is a second guilty party. It takes two to tango, to quote my dad.

When I tell her about the regrettable episode, Sushila chooses to say, 'Honey, you're very anxious right now. Be aware of that and try to protect yourself.' Then she mutters, 'I should never have sent you that e-mail.'

This last statement arrives as an astounding illumination. She's right: Faye's e-mail, which sits unopened in my mailbox, has put me in an intolerable position. To read it would be to break my rule, established at no small emotional cost, of absolute non-contact; and yet to delete the e-mail unread, as would be my normal practice, would break another rule – that brothers must look out for each other.

The subject line contains only the word 'Geoffrey'. The content preview reads:

> Darling Sushila, there have been some worrying developments regarding Geoffrey that

I decline to rehash the history of my dealings with Faye. But it is my conviction that her latest communiqué is strategically enticing, the strategy being to lure me, under color of a family crisis, inside her striking distance. This is a person who cannot be understood without reference to the techniques of animal predation. I have researched the topic. Animal assassins may be roughly separated into two groups: ambush predators and pursuit predators. Faye belongs in the first group, specifically in the subcategory of aggressive mimics that includes the humpback anglerfish and the alligator snapping turtle. The mimetic signal, in Faye's case, promotes her resemblance to the classic maternal figure. If it isn't already clear, the term 'mother' is applicable to her only in the narrowest genetic sense.

As a matter of self-protection as well as of fraternal obligation, I decide on a halfway course: I delete Faye's e-mail but I also ask Sushila what was in it. We are in bed.

'She says she's worried about Geoff.'

'What's the matter with him?'

'She doesn't say why, exactly.'

I make a triumphant sound. 'What did I tell you? She's dangling the bait.'

Sushila says, 'Let me handle it. I'll let you know if anything important happens. I don't want you to think about it anymore.'

I feel bad for my wife. She already bears a thousand and one responsibilities, and now she's assuming the role of the buffer. But I accept her proposal. If there's one thing I'll never turn down at this point in my life, it's a buffer.

Sushila does things efficiently. In the morning, she calls Faye. It comes out that my brother has been in an accident. He won't tell Faye what kind of accident or how seriously he's been hurt. He has been evasive with his mother for months, Faye alleges to Sushila, and has been acting all furtive about a business opportunity that he won't discuss. He won't even reveal his whereabouts. 'All we know,' Sushila tells me, 'is that he's convalescing.'

'Convalescing?' I have a vision of my brother in a wicker wheel-chair, a tartan blanket on his lap, with the white and brilliant Alps looming behind him.

'Oh – and he asked her for money.'

I perk up. 'How much?'

'Fifteen thousand pounds. For his secret project.'

Now I'm laughing. If Faye is inseparable from anything, it's her loot. Not for one day in her life has she worked in the conventional sense, but somehow she has made her fortune. When Geoff's dad, Monsieur Anibal, died, Faye inherited 'millions'. This was according to Dad, who started to call Faye 'the merry widow'. She soon got married a third time, my dad claimed, 'a brief but no doubt lucrative liaison' with an unnamed Greek. The irony is that after Dad died, Faye helped herself to his wealth, too – wealth that should have been mine. With Sushila's help, I've taught myself not to dwell on it. Dad is buried at Calvary Cemetery in Flagstaff, Arizona, in a grave that was decorated, when I last laid eyes on it, with a cheerfully spinning silver-and-purple pinwheel. Who placed the pinwheel there, I cannot say.

There is no point my calling my brother, even if I wanted to (which I don't). Geoff doesn't answer his phone, not when I'm the caller. So I text him:

Hey. Everything good? I'm hearing rumors.

I leave it at that. To be pushy would be useless. Geoff has never been a compliant informant about Geoff. His finances, his romances, his work, his exact location – all were foggy in the years after he dropped out of college (at Loughborough, England) and moved to Paris, kept afloat by unidentifiable financial buoys. During that time, we would exchange the occasional text message – jokes, memes – and, at Christmas, voice messages. I last saw Geoff in the flesh nearly five years ago, in the summer of 2010, when as a twenty-four-year-old he bicycled across America and made a stop here in Pittsburgh. The prospect of his visit brought me a lot of joy – and apprehension. A solo transcontinental bicycle ride wasn't per se crazy, but it wasn't exactly normal, to my mind, even for a young guy without responsibilities. It signaled a disturbance, a disorientation. I was worried that a Forrest Gump type would turn up at our door. And why hadn't he accepted our invitation to stay longer than a single night? What was the rush? I asked Sushila for her opinion. Tell me more about him, she said. We had just moved in together, after six months of dating. She didn't yet know everything about me.

My poor brother! For the first five years of his life, he was carted by Faye from one European city to another. Postcards in her handwriting purporting to be from 'Geoffrey' arrived for me from Monte Carlo, Positano, Kitzbühel, Santorini. Was she trying to torment my father? When Geoff turned six, she placed him into the custody of his seventy-four-year-old father. The boy and the old guy lived together in Paris in luxurious disarray, an arrangement that was practicable only because of the around-the-clock work of a live-in Cameroonian housemaid, Dad told me. He somehow got acquainted with Anibal and took a shine to 'the old hound dog', and I imagine that they formed a bond over their common experience of looking after a son whom Faye had abandoned. Anibal fell victim to dementia, though. When Geoff was eleven or twelve, Faye had no option but to retrieve him and house him with her, in London. Soon after, I flew to England to see them. It was Dad's idea, not mine. I had decided to celebrate my college graduation with a trip to Prague, and he said, Why don't you go see Geoff? And say hi to your mom?

I like the sound of your dad, Sushila said. I wish I'd had the chance to meet him.

What happened during my London visit was something I had not yet disclosed to her. I was worried that too much evidence of family craziness might scare her off. But now that I'd moved in with her, I came clean: my so-called mother, who had not laid eyes on me for more than a decade, took off within an hour of my arrival. She showed me around the house and then, putting on her coat, announced that she had a very important meeting to go to. She looked like a news anchor, with makeup and blond hair and expensive-looking rings and earrings. My impression was that she would be back shortly. Her meeting lasted four days and nights, which was exactly the duration of my visit. Geoff was left in my care. We made it, my brother and I; we survived. We ate bread and cheese and cereals, which I bought at the nearby gas station, and watched a lot of soccer on TV. I had played the game in high school, and I vaguely kept track of English Premier League. Geoff wore the same Manchester United replica shirt – the number 16 shirt of Roy Keane – every day and every night. If at any point he changed his underwear or brushed his teeth or took a shower, I didn't see it.

He hardly said a word – it took me a day or two to figure out that English was a foreign language to him. The whole thing left me feeling ashamed. When I told my dad about it, he made no comment. He, too, felt ashamed.

He was still fascinated by her, Sushila said.

Geoff cycled into Pittsburgh a day and a half late. We had a barbecue in our dark little yard, where even arugula fails to grow. My brother told us that after years of playing semiprofessional soccer in Paris, he had finally accepted that he wasn't good enough to make it as a player. The experience, he went on, had deepened his knowledge of the game, and, most important, had gained him the trust of the Parisian soccer community. His plan was to deploy these assets to make a career as a 'football intermediary'. There were different kinds of intermediaries, he said – players' agents, club representatives, talent-agency guys, brokers and so on – and he wasn't yet sure which kind he wanted to be. But he was confident it would all work out. He was excited and optimistic. It was true that he was young and that the business was dominated by guys in their forties and fifties. But in Geoff's opinion his youth would work in his favor.

While Geoff was telling us this, he was wolfing down a lot of food. The three hamburgers I'd cooked for all of us he'd piled onto his plate right away, along with a corn on the cob. I had to make a run to the fridge and get out the chicken sausages earmarked for breakfast. In the middle of the night, we were woken up by noises: it was my brother crashing around in the kitchen, feeding himself all over again. In the morning, our blackberries, all of our cheese, and two packets of crackers were gone.

It made us laugh. My kid brother was cycling fifty miles a day: he had every right to a huge appetite. There was something charismatic about his athleticism, and he was very likable and guileless, as well as strangely impressive: we overheard him taking a call in fluent-sounding French.

We stayed in touch after his Pittsburgh visit. The news eventually came that he had indeed embarked on a career as an agent for soccer players, based in London. From time to time we spoke on the phone, and I noticed that his bland, neutral English was being replaced by a London-Jamaican argot. That struck me as a bit strange, because Geoff was a white guy, but what did I care? If he wanted to make hyperactive use of the vocative case, who was I to object? How Geoff spoke was up to him. Meanwhile, his wandering persisted: whenever we heard from him, he seemed to have just returned from Africa or Asia, presumably for business. The details of these trips Geoff kept to himself. Good luck to him, was my attitude. Keep the fuckers guessing. Almost certainly they do not mean well.

My expectation is that Geoff will answer my text with a laughter emoticon and thereby confirm that he is basically fine. But Geoff doesn't answer my text.

I don't think about it. I have other stuff on my mind. Things at work have taken a complicated turn.

The scuffle in the office lobby, not of my making but nonetheless a source of self-reproach, became the subject of an informal management inquiry. Without going into the exhausting, extraneous particulars, the upshot is that no disciplinary action was officially taken. Unofficially, it was suggested that I use some of my accrued leave, like Dirty Harry. I held my peace. I bit my tongue.

In my immaturity, I would not have. Oh no – a stand would have been taken, and to hell with the consequences. It wasn't a question of recklessness or high-mindedness. It was a question of my unique immunity, as I must have perceived it, from the ordinary rules of fate. The present difficulty was a temporary and miragelike state of affairs. Time had not yet disclosed its bounty. My day would come.

Sometimes I catch sight of this selfsame notion in the faces of my younger colleagues. With that mild psychopathy of youth, they can't help viewing the world, and the people in it, as a kind of ironic, semifictional entertainment; and it may even be that in their bones they sense the presence of a discriminating god alert to their secret virtues. The men, especially, view me with an expression at once merciless and pitying. No way, they figure, will they end up like me, grinding out grant applications for the medical-pharmacological complex. They could well be right, of course – and it should be said that I'm rooting for all of them. I have a good notion of their struggle, and I certainly don't judge them. I'm the last person to say anything about self-aggrandizing cognitive distortions.

Over the course of a weekend, I absorb my workplace setback and stew in it – undergo cooking by simmering. I crash on the couch with my dog, Pearson, and, my hand on his loyal head, share with him thoughts too rueful for human ears, even Sushila's. Sushila nonetheless notices. You don't read Zbigniew Herbert and fail to perceive a soul in pain.

'Perhaps taking a little break isn't such a bad idea,' she says.

'I just took a break.' I don't have to spell out to her that I work in a technical-writing co-operative and am not a salaried employee with paid vacations. My compensation consists of project fees (half payable on signing, half upon completion), plus success bonuses. It's piecework, essentially. If I'm not working, I'm not earning.

'We can afford it,' says Sushila. She has long maintained that my perspective on our finances fluctuates between the too euphoric and the overly negative. 'You've been under a lot of pressure. Cut yourself some slack.'

Have I been under a lot of pressure? No more than usual. Although it must be said that I am not taking the news of the world well. In Paris they have just gunned down a roomful of cartoonists. Our new year seems as rotten as the one gone by. How long can this go on for? When will it end?

Just when I've completely forgotten about him, Geoff phones. It's been four days since I texted him.

When I don't answer (I don't recognize the number), he leaves a voice message: 'Yeah, hi, Markie. It's me, bro. Could you call me back when you get a chance? That'd be great, bruv.'

I say to Sushila, 'You're right. Something's up.'

•

A few years ago, my phone turned into a device for strangers and robots to butt in between me and whatever I'm doing. Any given caller was very likely a financial-verbal intruder. The simple buzzing of a phone began to frighten me. I decided to shun phone calls systematically, with an exception being of course made for Sushila – and even Sushila knows that, unless it's urgent, a text is optimal. This decision was overdue. The general history of the telephone call, it can safely be said, is a grim one. Who can begin to measure or even grasp the volume of the calamities reported or produced by this sound-transmission system? It was with very good reason, I now understand, that my father invariably commanded me to ignore the ringing beige gadget stationed in the living-room bookcase. Together he and I would wait, all activity put on hold, for the shrill to stop, an interlude of suspense that could last a minute or more, because in those landline days there was nothing to stop a caller from sticking at it indefinitely, and often the house would be filled with that eerie, seemingly infinite electronic cry, and often this cry would be followed by a second, appellate cry undertaken in the hope, perhaps, that the first call had been misdialed or that my father had just stepped through the door or climbed out of the bathtub. Dad refused to get an answering machine. As a concession to me – I was a high school freshman; it was newly important for me and my friends to be in constant discussion – he permitted me to pick up the phone, but only on the condition that, should the caller ask for him, I would declare him to be 'not presently available'. This was the formulation he insisted on.

The point is that I've developed my father's aversion to the phone. It's two days before I get back to Geoff.

'Hey, Markie,' he says. 'Thanks for calling, fam. Sorry to barge in on you.'

'Don't be crazy,' I say.

I will say that I love my brother's voice, which I hear so rarely. It is a voice from a complementary, more summery world that once was or could never be. It's the voice of love long lost or long impossible. That is where things stand in the matter of me and my brother's voice.

He informs me that he finds himself 'in a bit of a tight corner'. He wonders if I might be able to set aside a few days to fly to England in order to help him with 'this business opportunity'. He's had some kind of accident and isn't able 'to do, you know, mobility'. He adds, laughing a little, 'It's a big ask, bruv, I'll be real. If you can't come, I'll understand completely.'

'You're hurt?'

'Nah, fam, I'm all right.' As he says this, he texts me a photograph of a leg in a cast. Crutches rest against the couch.

'Jesus. You're really banged up.'

'Yeah, it might be a while before I kick a ball.' He continues, 'Fing is, Markie, I need someone I can absolutely trust. I'm not going to lie, there's a lot riding on this.' He says more, including the assertion that, 'if it comes off, there's going to be a serious – I mean serious, fam – payday down the road for all of us.'

To be polite and for no other reason, I ask him about the time frame.

'We're looking at a week. Tops. I'll take care of your expenses, fam. That's not an issue.' He says this very coolly.

'Let me think about it.'

I'm not going to think about it. A simple rule applies here: no monkey business. An unexplained mission entailing up-front expenditure by me and back-end reimbursement by him? A big payoff that may or may not materialize? That looks a lot like monkey business to me. Geoff is, to the best of my knowledge, a soccer agent. It's a legitimate line of work, but it's not exactly a bishopric. More basically, the whole idea is nuts: I drop everything and set off on an exotic self-financed journey to help him? Who does he think I am – Captain Haddock?

To my astonishment, Sushila takes a very different view. 'You'll get to spend time with your brother,' she says. 'When was the last time that happened? I think you should think it over.'

We've finished dinner. I'm loading the dishwasher. If I have a vocation, it is stacking dishware, glassware and cookware with maximal efficiency.

Her voice goes on: 'Why not go? It'll be an adventure.'

'An adventure?' I've spent years fighting my impulsiveness. Nobody knows this better than Sushila. Now she wants me to fly across the world for an adventure?

When I was ten years old and living in Portland, Oregon, my father announced, 'You have a baby brother,' and little by little further specifics reached me, including the fact that he was in 'England'. This hearsay bore a fabulous geographic tinge that has never completely faded. I came to believe that this baby was born in a land far away from his true home – that is, from my home – and as far as I was concerned, he was a foundling of sorts and it was my duty to track him down and repatriate him. I got out an atlas and discovered where England was. I determined that with a team of huskies I could quite feasibly navigate the frozen surfaces of Canada and Baffin Bay and Greenland, from where I'd hitch a ride on a fishing boat across the Greenland Sea, to Iceland, from where another trawler would transport me across the nameless and terrible body of water between Iceland and the Faroe Islands. From the Faroes it would be a relatively simple matter to get to the Orkney Islands and, finally, mainland Britain. I had no route planned for the return trip. I did, however, foresee that the two brothers (suddenly and miraculously closer in age) would be involved in great perils and great deeds of bravery. To this day I retain several of those visions and can still see, in the flash frames of a child's eye, two boys, on foot in the desert, pausing to share water from a flask; the same two boys riding side by side on white horses; and, vividly, a snowy drama in which our heroes for some reason find themselves bobsledding. Their sled races along a pale and curving track. The two boys are crouched very close to one another in the cockpit, and in spite of everything – the icy chute, the stormy and thundering descent, the obscure, determined pursuers – they are warm and safe.

The next day, I inform the people at work that I will be taking my accrued leave. Then I set off on a journey across the Atlantic. It has occurred to me, at long last, that maybe the brother in difficulty isn't Geoff.

•

The question of dread cannot be left unmentioned. I leave my family and my home with an eerie feeling of things going from bad to worse, and my misgivings are only strengthened on the overnight bus journey through the wintry, seemingly perpetual forests and fields of Pennsylvania. We make only one stop, in the middle of the night, at State College, after which the bus, now loaded up with a boisterous group of students, continues eastward. The passenger body, until that point an assortment of silent and sleepy individuals, is now interspersed with pranksters and hilarious types. Their antics alarm me. It isn't that these kids are a physical threat – they aren't, not for even a second, they're just fooling around – but that they are infected with a terrifying heedlessness. I feel a stormy impulse to rise to my feet and tell them to cut out the bullshit and remove their heads from their asses and take a good look around them for once in their goddamn lives. But of what should they be aware? What danger is at hand? Fearsome, unanswerable mystery! Soon enough, even the newcomers have fallen asleep; but I remain upright and attentive at my window. Earlier, the cabin lighting had made the panes more reflective than transparent, so that any would-be sightseer was foiled by a yellow and shadowy duplicate of the bus's interior; but once the lights are fully dimmed I am offered a view of the outside, which is to say, a charcoal spectacle that mocks the very idea of vision. And yet I maintain my vigil, looking out until the Pocono Mountains, under barely lustrous snow, finally disclose their presence. They loom as immense geological ghouls. I share with almost every member of my species an intuition of Earth as the Planet of the Humans. But as the bus speeds along the I-80 through uplands that once rose as high as the Rockies but which unfathomable erosions have reduced to mere hills, there comes a substitute intuition, as false as the first, of a sullen and resentful terrestrial host. A sense of personal insignificance and doom is inevitable. This is the drawback of vigilance: from your watchtower you finally spy, in your binoculars, your fleeing self; and you release the hounds. There is no outrunning them – grief present and grief foreseen. There is no shelter from the interior outdoors. I speak for myself, of course, on the basis of my experiences and hunches, which is to say, my misconceptions and my stupid fears.

No report needs to be made of our arrival in New York City in the dark of morning, or of my subway ride to John F. Kennedy International, an airport so chaotic, ragged and superfluously authoritarian in character that it contradicts my understanding that this is the First World. Nor need anything be said about the overcrowded, sleepless flight to London, where, when we land, night has already fallen and five hours are instantly stolen from my day. At the arrivals area, I scan the pickup signs. For some reason I always do this, even when I'm not expecting anyone to be waiting for me, and without fail I'm left with an emotion of abandonment when it's confirmed that I am not, in fact, among those who will be picked up. But this time it's different: Geoff has assured me that I will be met at the airport.

My name is nowhere to be seen.

I buy a coffee at a nearby outlet and take a seat at a utility table connected to no particular retailer. At the next table, a young white guy is slowly writing on a sheet of paper. For some reason I continue to watch him – and see that he's scrawled, in infantile lettering, *Mr Wolfe*.

Large headphones enclose his ears, so I touch his arm. He jumps as if I've poured a jug of freezing water over him.

'Yawa?' he says, taking off the headphones.

I identify myself – and soon, towing my little suitcase, I'm following this individual into the parking lot. I don't like the hyperbolic bounce in his step. He unlocks the car with a baroque flourish of the remote key, then hops into the driver's seat with uncalled-for physical joy. On the long drive that follows, my impression of juvenile unprofessionalism is only reinforced. First, the kid wears his headphones while driving, which has to be illegal as well as dangerous. When I ask if he could remove them, he barks something over his shoulder in an English accent or dialect that I can't understand. 'Excuse me?' I say, and he repeats himself in his language, evidently devoid of any conception that, being a foreigner, I might find his speech unintelligible. I sit back helplessly, all too aware that my life is in the hands of a buffoon who, it very soon becomes clear, hits the brakes at traffic lights as if a red signal is something he's never seen before. My intention is to get some sleep. Instead, I spend almost three hours sweating in the cramped back seat as I conduct a pointless supervision of every move this dangerous driver makes at the wheel, which he holds lightly with his right hand while his left hand never moves from the shift stick, with which he incessantly changes gears as if we're racing across the Sahara to Dakar and not motoring at our leisure through the Shakespearean-sounding counties of Buckinghamshire and Oxfordshire and Warwickshire, the countryside almost completely hidden by embankments running alongside the unlit road, the edges of which are discernible only by the shining curves made by the retroreflective pavement markers.

Somewhere near the ergs of Birmingham, we take a wrong turn. Evidently, my driver – navigating by his wits, not by GPS – has been confused by a sudden and extraordinary proliferation of off-ramps and intersections and forks, and for a good twenty minutes we drive ineffectually through built-up suburbs, turning and twisting through narrow streets on which, at frequent intervals, menacing drunken white natives gather on a sidewalk or traffic island seemingly in order to yell and gesture and spill over into the road, more than once fixating on our car and shouting at us with pointless rancor. On two separate occasions, an ambulance followed by police cars yelps past us. When, to my horror, one of the tribespeople, as I think of them, bangs his hand on the roof of the car, the reaction of my driver is to smile. He mutters something to me in his own language. I acoustically replay and reconstitute his statement in mind, and I translate him to be saying, 'It's always like this on a Friday night, Saturday night.' What I'm witnessing, it seems, isn't scenes of civil unrest but the disorderly emptying of bars that routinely occurs on weekends in the English provinces.

We finally find our way back to a large road. Before long we reach Walsall, the town where Geoff is to be found. Walsall, Wolverhampton, Walton-on-Thames, Weilheim an der Teck – it makes no difference to me. Not that long ago, I would have been deeply interested in my whereabouts. I would have researched the locality beforehand and informed myself about its history and its economy and its points of interest, would have come prepared, in short, for the great task of seeing. Not anymore. The great task is precisely that of not seeing – of refusing the whole rotten spectacle. And yet here, as elsewhere, I am my worst enemy. It so happens that I know something about Walsall. Randomly I remember, from certain fruitless research undertaken long ago, during my lost years, that the inspiration for J.R.R. Tolkien's concocted land of Mordor was the so-called Black Country, a region of the English Midlands long notorious as the site of extractive and manufacturing activities (coal, steel, glass, iron ore, chains) that over time transformed a merely dreary and proto-industrialized neck of the woods into a fuming, smoke-blackened inferno of human near-enslavement and environmental ruin horrifying even to the early Victorians. The ruination did not stop there. Further undoing was inflicted, first, by the Luftwaffe and, second, by architects and urban-planning experts who (if I correctly recall), in a spirit of misguided idealism, directed an urbanization of historic brutality. Walsall is in the Black Country.

We stop in front of a large bungalow. I understand the driver to communicate that we have arrived. A light appears at the doorway, and there is my brother, on crutches.

He laughs when he sees me. 'You're looking horrible, bruv.' To the driver he says, 'Good lad, Callum.'

Callum says, I think, 'So you're going to watch me on Saturday?'

'Course, fam,' Geoff says, making a thumbs-up.

Callum drives away with an actual squeal of tires.

'Come inside, fam,' Geoff says. 'And try not to make any noise. Everyone's asleep.'

•

I follow Geoff into an indoor gloom. He makes a sign that I should carry my case rather than squeakily roll it on the wood floor. Geoff's crutches also make a noise, but I guess that's different. At the end of the darkened corridor is a living room with an open kitchen, and beyond that an annex apparently in service as a gym: there are some mats, dumbbells on a rack and a treadmill.

There's also a two-seat leather couch with bedding on it. I drop my bag on it.

'Yeah, that's my bed,' Geoff says, easing himself onto the couch. 'I'm going to sort you out, fam, no worries.' He points at a cooler. 'Go on, get us a couple of bevvies.'

In the cooler, two cans of beer are adrift in melted water. The beer tastes good – but I'm starving. I ask about food.

Geoff hums. 'It's a bit late for a takeaway, bruv.'

I tell him that anything will do. An apple. A hunk of bread.

'Hang on,' he says. He hops over to his jacket and fishes around in the pockets. 'How about this?'

He's holding up what looks like a squashed energy bar. 'I'm good,' I say. I raise my can of beer. 'This'll work fine.' I sit on the treadmill, there being no other seat. 'So', I say, pointing at the crutches, 'what happened?'

One night, Geoff was walking down an unfamiliar set of stairs, carrying a plate of food. It was dark; he couldn't find the light switch; the staircase had a sharp turn; he stepped into thin air. He fractured his tibia and fibula, just above the ankle. Geoff had to have surgery. 'They put in screws and did whatchacallit—'

'Open reduction and internal fixation,' I suggest.

'Exactly, bruv, exactly. Reduction and fixation. So I'm going to be stuck here for a while.'

I say, 'Where are we?'

Geoff informs me – as I listen to him, I translate his words into my own kind of English – that we're in the home of Tony and Julie Atkinson and their seventeen-year-old son, Bobby. Bobby is Geoff's client. Geoff is recuperating in their home because, number one, his North London flat is a third-floor walkup; and, number two, he needs to cement his relationship with Tony and Julie, who are Bobby's influencers. The key to handling any player is handling his influencers. Tony, the dad, sees himself as a football connoisseur, but Julie is the family's psychological arbiter. Both have to be won over by Geoff. The stakes are high, Geoff whispers. Scouts from Premier League teams have begun to take an interest in his boy Bobby. Other agents have started sniffing around. There's even been a rumor that Jolene Ahadi is interested.

'Jolene?'

'Bruv, bruv,' Geoff says, typing into his phone then showing me the image results for Joe Ahadi, evidently an overweight man who at all times wears sunglasses and holds a cell phone. 'He's called Joe, but everyone in the business calls him Jolene, as in, Bro, don't take my man just because you can, bro.'

Jolene has four Premiership players on his books, Geoff is

saying, plus several more in La Liga, the Spanish league. Geoff, who's at the beginning of his agenting career, can't compete with that profile. What he can offer is unique trust and focus. This means that he must make himself emotionally indispensable to Bobby and his parents. Camping out in the family home with a broken leg is one way to make this happen, potentially. Of course, it could backfire. He could end up making a nuisance of himself. Hence the problem with feeding me: the food in the kitchen doesn't belong to Geoff, it belongs to the Atkinson family. That might seem like a small thing, but he's had bad experiences in this area. Once, at a player's home, he helped himself to a glass of grapefruit juice. What he didn't know was that the grapefruit juice was precious to the player's wife. The player got very upset about it. The whole situation took a lot of work to retrieve – flowers, apologies, a crate of grapefruit juice. Two crates, as a matter of fact, because the first crate had been the wrong kind of grapefruit juice.

'You see what I'm saying, fam?' Geoff says. 'I almost lost him. I've got to be careful.'

'Got it.'

'It's all about psychology, Markie, psychology.' Convalescing with the Atkinsons is a canny move, according to Geoff, precisely because it imposes a burden on them. You become an object of care and concern. The family starts to identify with you. You are no longer just an agent, you're a person in need. The relationship becomes emotional as well as professional. That's how human nature works, Geoff explains to me. Jolene might have the star power and the Premiership connections, but he, Geoff, has the emotional bonds. Emotional bonds can be especially valuable in the case of a youngster like Bobby, who's had disciplinary issues and would benefit from a nurturing, even therapeutic, relationship with his agent. Jolene might be a superior deal-maker, but Geoff is the better mentor and caregiver. Bobby's mum will see that, hopefully. Where mums are concerned, emotions beat financial calculations.

I yawn but otherwise don't respond. It's not my job to query or correct my brother.

'It's late,' he says. 'Let's get you to bed.' He opens a closet and brings out a pillow, some sheets and a blanket. They look clean enough. Struggling slightly on one crutch, he drops the bedding on the treadmill track. 'It's very comfortable,' he says. 'Bruv, I'd kip there myself if it wasn't for the leg.'

I look at him.

'Try it,' Geoff says. 'I promise you, fam, it'll be great. It's only for tonight. And maybe tomorrow night.' He gives me directions to the bathroom. 'Just be quiet about it. And don't leave stuff in there.'

When I return, the room is dark and Geoff is stretched out on the couch, his face lit up by his laptop. Without looking up, he says, 'Just relax, fam, get some sleep.'

I lower myself onto the machine. No question about it, it's uncomfortable. The track is slightly cushioned for running purposes, but for reclining purposes it's rock-hard and lacking in support. The longer I lie down, the more aware I am of mechanical obtrusions pressing up against me. In no way is it comparable to being on a mattress or even a carpeted floor. Also, the platform is no more than three feet wide and way too short for a sprawled human body. It's impossible to find a position that doesn't involve a leg dangling over an edge. Whichever way I turn, a metallic post rises inches from my face.

The final obstacle to sleep is my rage. Goddammit, I'm not sixteen anymore. Sleeping on a treadmill? Are you fucking kidding me?

The person being interrogated is none other than myself. I'm not furious at my brother. Nor am I asserting some entitlement to the physical comforts that might reasonably be due a man who has achieved a certain maturity and has shouldered certain responsibilities. It is a question of autonomy – of being in the world on one's own terms. It is a question of my failure, yet again, to ensure that I am where I want to be, in the company of the people I want to be with, in circumstances of my choosing. If there's one thing I have learned over the years, if experience could be reduced to a single bitter apple of knowledge, it's this: self-rule must be exercised with a tyrant's purpose. And yet here I am in a strange home, at the mercy of the toothbrushes and toilet seats of strangers. I brought it on myself. I knew that no good would come of leaving home. I knew, dammit, that it was—

'Markie?'

'Mm?'

'You all right?'

'Mm.'

'Listen up. When you meet Julie and Tony, just tell them that you're just passing by, OK? You're in England on business, and you're just dropping in on your bruv.'

'Why?'

'It's a delicate situation, bruv.'

'Got it,' I say, although I don't get anything.

In this way, tiredly, not out of any real volition on my part, I enter into a conspiracy with my brother to hide from our hosts the true purpose of my presence in their house. That purpose remains hidden from me, too.

•

Evidently the Atkinsons have never seen an American before, not up close. At the breakfast table they gawk at me as if I've walked in with tinkling silver spurs.

An ethos of overt politeness, always unsettling, attends the complex multiparty use of marmalade and teapot and toast. The son – the soccer player, Bobby – gets up to make himself a smoothie involving bananas and berries and protein powder. The blender's loud motorized storm emboldens the father, Tony, to declare, 'That's a professional athlete diet, that is.'

Julie, the mother, is busy in the kitchen, scrubbing a saucepan. Something is bothering her, is my sense. When she finally sits down to join us, she says, 'So you're the half-brother? From America?'

'Yes, ma'am,' I say.

Tony says, 'Watch American football, do you?'

'College basketball,' I say. 'I like soccer, too.'

'Do you support anyone?' Tony asks.

'My team is Man U,' I tell him. It's not entirely inaccurate.

Sushila's father's team is Man U, and he and I have watched a few games together.

The Atkinson males, and my own brother, roar with laughter.

"'Man Yoo,'" Bobby says.

Tony says, 'You ever been there? Old Trafford?'

I reply that I haven't, and again they fall around laughing. Bobby actually slaps the table. 'Just bants, mate, just bants,' Tony says, in case I'm offended, which I am not, although I am a bit mystified.

Julie isn't laughing. She asks, 'You're here for business?' to which I nod affirmatively, to which she replies, 'What sort of business would that be?'

She puts the question with inexplicable aggression. At least, that's my impression. I'm the first to admit that I'm not very good at reading a room, especially if the room is in England.

'Technical writing,' I say. 'Mainly writing grants for corporations. Scientific stuff, usually.'

Tony, making a show of wiping his hands with his napkin, starts to say something in a jolly voice. His wife interrupts. 'They haven't heard of hotels, in this business of yours?'

My mouth full of bacon, I'm speechless. It's rare to encounter rudeness. It always comes as a shock. I'm referring, here, to effrontery – rudeness that's frontal, rudeness that's intended to be received as rudeness. It so happens that I once gave it a lot of thought.

When Fizzy was a baby, I acquired the philosophical conviction that the grand biographical themes, the majuscule motions and the glittering prizes, were a fool's idea of a right and good life, and that it was in the form of small, obscure deeds that one's human potential was properly realized. It followed that the practice of everyday courtesy was of the greatest importance, and I resolved to devote myself to it. I'll admit that this resolution wasn't entirely idealistic. The suspicion had grown in my mind that I was unwittingly ruffling people's feathers and putting their noses out of joint and that it might be in my interest to improve my rapport management, as the experts term it. Once this idea – that maybe I was a communicational imbecile – took hold, it began to haunt me. I consulted Sushila. She said, '"Imbecile" is taking it a bit far. But you're not wrong that people are getting more sensitive. I know that I find myself taking extra care these days. Especially on e-mail.'

This touched a sore spot. For a long time, I'd resisted the culture of digital correspondence in which it was one's job not only to convey relevant information but also to fake affection and friendship, even if one's correspondent was a stranger. I hadn't grasped that a message that would formerly have been understood as concise and helpfully businesslike might now be interpreted as curt and unkind, or that the polite and appropriate 'Dear' greeting in the place of the infantile 'Hi' greeting might be received as cold and dominating. This was an absurd development, but whatever. I adapted. I changed my ways – and what I'd feared would be a humiliating process quickly became gratifying. It felt good to put someone at ease by the simple addition of a pacifying exclamation mark ('Thank you!') or pat on the back ('Nice!'), and sometimes being super-nice made me feel like a courteous bygone stroller who tips his hat at passersby and adds to the pleasantness of the world. And as I said, this was in the context of an all-round effort to bring a more gentlemanly (in the sense of unobtrusively agreeable rather than socially refined) posture to the most innocuous dealings, so that a gratuitous, in the best sense impractical note of tenderness would characterize an encounter with yours truly, and as a side effect my reputation – by which I mean the possible workplace perception that I was something of an oddball and handful – would improve, and people would regard me, to the extent that they regarded me at all, as a nice, co-operative colleague or, at a minimum, a solid non-jerk. That was my thinking and my hope. But the most powerful side effect I could be sure of was that I became more than ever detained by this question of where I stood in the eyes of others. Whereas in the past I'd been barely conscious of those others, in fact would have found bizarre the very notion that to exist in society was to be placed in the dock before a many-eyed jury, I now fretted more than ever about the possibility that during a particular exchange I had failed some secret test of sociability. A loss of confidence will do that to a person.

My reaction to Julie's effrontery, once the first shock has passed, is to presume that the rudeness is chiefly mine. I have somehow abused this family. I have failed to understand something that I ought to have understood. I have messed up.

Geoff speaks up. With great sincerity he says, 'There was a mix-up with the hotel, Julie. I'm very sorry. I should have planned it better, I'm copping to that. It's very good of you to take my bruv in for the one night. We'll both be moving out today.'

Julie is tight-lipped. There is a commotion of chairs and dishes as the men stand up. They look embarrassed.

Later that day, I discover that the nearby Holiday Inn ($72 a night) had plenty of vacancies. Why didn't Geoff book me a room? And if for some reason that wasn't doable, why did he sneak me into the Atkinson home in the dead of night? What is wrong with the guy?

•

The Atkinson debacle has left me very anxious. A former, more youthful self would have found it trivial and funny – but, then again, my former, more youthful self thought it was absolutely normal to live in a house where pizza slices lay on the floor of the kitchen for days at a time and my housemates and I not only would kick the slices out of our way instead of picking them up but, having kicked them, would as an afterthought stoop to pick at the pepperonis. I'm anxious precisely because this pointlessly chaotic, improvised, and childish episode with Geoff has brought back my own history of chaos and immaturity and winging it, a period of my life when I viewed my disorganization, to the extent that I noticed it at all, as a symptom of my powers.

I wasn't entirely wrong. For almost five years, we – I and my three housemates, or 'comrades', as we called one another with only the barest irony – were engaged in a project that would, we were convinced, revolutionize the field of artificial neural networks. All we had to do, to achieve this goal, was to crack the vanishing gradient problem. In addition, we – I, especially – were working on developing a coherent mission statement on the ethics of machine learning, and in particular the foreseeable if (at that time) distant problem of machines acquiring morally wrongful internal representations (racism, say), a mission that somehow got tangled up in the articulation of the collectivist, hobbyistic ethos of our undertaking, which in turn became entwined with the questions of how to finance our research activities in an upright way and how to integrate those activities with the institutional demands of Carnegie Mellon, where we were postgrads. Yes, we were also trying to finish Ph.D. dissertations. Mine was on disambiguation stimuli in image interpretation, or at least that was the plan until my attention was absorbed by a new kind of architecture known as the neural abstraction pyramid, a focus that was itself disturbed by a radical deviation toward semantic rather than visual problems, which led me, erratically, into the world of machine intuition, which led me, predictably, to acquaint myself with Kant and his idea of mathematical intuition, which prompted me to investigate some truly strange philosophical back alleys (most crazily, Hilbert's finitist theories) in a way that felt enlightening and privately glorious but was, I came to see, nothing more than worthless intellectual vagrancy or, to put it more brutally, lostness. All of this was done under the rubric of personal brilliance. Here the comrades were complicit, especially late at night, when we'd hang out in our basement, or 'lab', and drink bottles of Rolling Rock and argue about which Beatle each of us was, the premise that we were a scientific Fab Four being accepted without argument. In the event, I – Paul – produced almost no results, in any field, that were tangible to a third party, except when a grant application deadline was upon us, in which case I was known to pull an ecstatic all-nighter and write a proposal narrative of austere beauty. During the composition process the submission deadline would be lost sight of and, as often as not, missed. My response, after repeated frustrations on this front, was to angrily-cunningly reject the very concept of the deadline and to waste a lot of energy, not to mention time, looking into temporal motivation theory, hyperbolic discounting and suchlike. Time itself – the notion that a clock was ticking and that it might be a good idea to accept what it said – came under my critical scrutiny. I decided that 'the clock', with all of its connotations of commanding power, was a structure of neoliberal control, and in order to resist its domination I conducted a cackling behavioral experiment in which *I* imposed counter-deadlines on my would-be controllers (i.e., our potential funders) and *I* called time when they didn't meet *my* deadlines. I wasn't even on drugs when I did this. This was me at the height of mental clarity. The business with the counter-deadlines caused the first serious quarrel I had with my comrades, who in principle were in favor of revolutionary measures but obviously were concerned that I was fucking everything up. They accused me of self-sabotage and unconscious tailism and other subtle ideological wrongs. Finally, Dan, who was Ringo, said, Bro, money doesn't grow on trees, and it's a measure of my then state of mind that this remark struck me as an eye-opener. Other difficulties, not necessarily of my making, were also besetting us. The vanishing gradient problem had not proved as soluble as we'd hoped; and our guiding principles – to follow our curiosity wherever it might lead, in the amateur spirit, to refuse for-profit and for-prestige incentives, to be relentlessly experimental – maybe weren't the keys to victorious scientific inquiry after all. Maybe becoming a latter-day Watt or Faraday or even Engelbart was trickier than we'd thought. Also, we had to contend with real life, a field that wasn't our strength. Everything started to crumble when the most productive comrade, Nikhil, got himself a serious girlfriend, immediately nicknamed Yoko, who refused to visit our house and got Nikhil to move in with her and focus on his doctorate. He's a professor at Stanford now, which is great; our paths never cross, which is fine. After Nikhil quit, we three remainers soldiered on for over a year, during which things went, in accordance with a law of gravity we didn't understand, downhill. I long ago lost touch with these last two comrades, Dan and Andy, and I haven't done the online detective-work you'd do if you wanted to track down friends who have disappeared.

During the short taxi ride from the Atkinson home to the Holiday Inn, I'm in the back and Geoff is up front, with his seat fully retracted to accommodate the extension of his leg. Once or twice I sneak a look at him, with his absurd disability and his high-tech athletic leisurewear, also absurd, and I uneasily take note of his impassive facial expression, which bears no trace of what I'd call appropriate self-consciousness. I know that look from somewhere.

Where, though? The question coincides with an awareness of the fact that I'm sweating.

When we arrive at the hotel, I help my brother get out of the car. He takes his time to get himself together: backpack on, earbuds in, crutches up. Throughout, he has on that familiar but unplaceable face.

And then I remember: it's the same face of blithering, imperturbable self-absorption that my comrades and I wore while we set fire to our lives. I'm being literal here. There was actually this face that we all had on.

When I approach the hotel front desk, I'm still sweating. Geoff is for some reason nowhere to be seen, even after I've waited for him, because after all he is supposed to be paying for my room. Only after I've handed the desk clerk my credit card does my brother reappear, standing next to me on one leg like Long John Silver. A nauseating fear for my safety passes through me.

He says, 'Bruv, you look, I don't know, pale.'

Something about him tells me that he's not going to be checking into a room of his own. Is he expecting to stay in my room? That's not going to happen. Very firmly I say, 'I'm going up to my room to get some sleep. I didn't get any last night. I'll see you later, Geoff.'

'Yeah, good idea, fam,' he says. 'I'll wake you up in a couple of hours. I'll be right here.'

But there's a hitch: my room isn't quite ready yet, the desk clerk says.

There's nothing to be done. I have to go to the lounge area with Geoff.

He orders a couple of coffees that are charged to my room.

'Listen,' I say, 'I'm going to be straight with you. The coffee's on me, but you owe me for the room. And the taxi. That was the deal.'

'Bruv, that's cool. No worries. I got you covered.'

'Well, could you cover it now?'

'I'm getting a new credit card,' he says. 'You know, a business credit card. So I can keep proper records, for my business. Once I get it, you'll be sorted.'

In my head I'm saying, Don't fuck with me, Geoff, don't make me run after my own fucking money, don't—

'So . . . listen up,' he goes on, adopting a confidential, almost inaudible voice. 'I've got something to show you.' He's pulling an iPad out of his backpack. 'You're going to have to promise me – I mean promise me, fam – that you don't tell no one nothing.'

This is so familiar from my old Beatles days – the paranoia, the fatal secrecy, the conviction that around every corner there lurks an intellectual-property thief.

Geoff is furiously whispering, 'Mum's the fucking word, blud. Like, dassit.'

'You going to show me or what?'

He turns on the iPad. 'This, blud. This is what it's all about.'

•

Geoff opens a video file. He expands the image to fill the screen.

I'm viewing a playing field of orange-red dirt. In the background are some trees and, behind them, brown hills. The video camera – apparently a phone camera – is situated at an elevated vantage point. A youth soccer match is in progress between a team in white and a team in blue. I'm no expert, but they seem to play with skill and intensity. Young spectators in khaki school uniforms are scattered along the side of the field, half following the action. Some of the children watching the game are barefooted. Everybody is black. This has to be somewhere in Africa.

'No audio?' I say.

Geoff touches my arm. The ball has arrived at the feet of a slight figure in blue.

The kid passes the ball back to a defender and runs to receive the return pass. He advances unhurriedly. When two opponents close in, he swerves between them. Suddenly there's a gap ahead of him. He accelerates goalward, just beyond a second pair of furiously chasing opponents, and straightforwardly rolls the ball beyond the keeper into the netless goal.

'Nice,' I say. I don't have my brother's eye for soccer footage. I defer to his knowledge and expertise. But I can't help thinking that this kind of goal is scored every minute of the day somewhere on the planet.

Geoff opens a second video file. This one has much better image quality, even if there is still no audio. It shows a properly marked soccer field of artificial turf, bordered by a clay running track and a tall security fence. Concrete terraces hold a few hundred spectators. In the distant background is the outline of brown hills that resemble those in the first video. The players are grown men. Geoff pauses the film and points. There's that kid again, this time wearing a yellow shirt. He is conspicuously the youngest, skinniest person on the field. 'I'm just going to show you some highlights,' Geoff says, fast-forwarding. 'There's a lot more.'

We watch the kid take a free kick from twenty-five yards out from the goal: for a full minute, he waits for the argumentative positioning of the defensive wall to run its course. Then he takes two steps and whacks the ball over the wall into the top corner of the goal.

'Nice,' I say.

'Yeah,' Geoff says. 'Now watch this.'

How to describe what he shows me? The experience of perceiving a soccer game must be communicated by reference to what has been previously experienced by other members of the perceptual community, i.e., soccer fans. What Geoff shows me is perceptually alien. To put it very basically, the kid scores two solo goals that involve what seem to be fictive spatial and technical powers – an aptitude for drifting at high speed into a pack of opponents and emerging with the ball at his feet and his would-be tacklers decisively, tragicomically sprawled behind him. There is something distinctly asynchronous about the spectacle, and this quality is only heightened by the fact that it's a silent movie. We're offered the illusion that a hidden dimension of human movement, of the relation between gravity and physiology, is being revealed. I'm looking at something that is simultaneously familiar and beyond recognition.

Geoff says, 'I know what you're thinking. You don't want to think it, but you're thinking it. Bruv, I can see it on your face.'

It's true, I'm grinning.

He goes on, without any sign of humor, 'I mean, obviously, I'm not saying he's as good as Messi. I'd never say that. But he's *like* him. What I just showed you? That's different, blud. It's *different*. I've looked at thousands of these clips. I watch clips like this day in, day out. And I've never seen anything like it. Man talk about the X factor: fam, this is the Z factor. Granted, we're not looking at defenders of the highest caliber. But it's not like they're pub teams. Look.' He shows me a random passage of play. 'These are no mugs, bruv. These are proper players – pros, semi-pros. Take a player from the Premiership and throw him in with this lot and he'll look good, 'course he will – but this lad? Bruv, I can't lie, this youth looks like he's playing a different game. You saw him. He's on a level of his own. Usually,' Geoff says, 'usually man's looking for pace and power. That's what the top English clubs want. Man want pace and power. Granted, man want quality, too. But quality, true quality, isn't that easy to identify, bruv. It's not immediately *discernible*. Pace and power you can measure, you can see it; it's right there in front of you. *Quality* is another thing altogether. You're always taking a punt on quality. But every once in a while . . .' Geoff points at the screen. 'That's quality like I've never seen, blud, I can't lie. And there's more. I haven't even shown you the rest of it.'

'Who is he?'

'I'm coming to that,' Geoff says, putting away his tablet computer. 'Markie, this is a special prospect. A mad, mad prospect. I'm talking once in a lifetime. We need to move.'

'"We"?'

He looks around as if the walls of the Holiday Inn have ears. 'Look, it's complex,' he murmurs. 'But it's doable. Very doable.'

At that moment the receptionist approaches with key cards to my room. I accept them with joy. I am exhausted and jet-lagged. In almost two days I've slept only three hours. At long last I will get some rest.

'Let's not talk here', Geoff says.

My brother, crutches thumping, follows me to my hotel room.

It isn't a big room. The full-sized bed consumes most of the floor area. Geoff immediately extends himself on my bed and rearranges three pillows to support his back. The final pillow goes beneath his bad leg. I take a seat in the room's one armchair, which barely fits in the gap between the bed and the window. When I cross my leg, my foot gets caught up in the curtain.

'Now, listen carefully, bruv,' Geoff says. 'Listen very carefully.'

He relates that he received the video file from a 'dodgy' Ivorian named Cyrille who's based in France and makes a living as an intermediary between African players and football clubs in the Far East – Indonesia, Vietnam, Korea. Cyrille acquired the video in Istanbul. For five thousand US dollars, he granted Geoff exclusive access to and use of the video for three months, with an option to renew the term for another five grand. The three-month term will expire in two weeks, and Geoff is not inclined to pay Cyrille another five grand. Geoff asked his mother to help him out with the renewal fee – five grand would be nothing to her, he says – but she refused to lend the money until she first saw the video. It was as if, Geoff says bitterly, she suspected her own son of inventing Godwin to squeeze money from her.

'Godwin?'

That's the kid's name, according to Cyrille. If Cyrille knows more, he isn't telling Geoff. Why would he? It's not in Cyrille's interests for Geoff to locate Godwin. Cyrille's interests are served by prolonging the mystery of Godwin's whereabouts.

'You don't know where Godwin is? You can't tell from the video?'

'Nah, bruv, not without audio.' If Geoff had to guess, it would be somewhere in West Africa. But there's other places it could be. Could be Botswana. Could be Uganda. Could be lots of places.

It doesn't make much sense to me – paying an untrustworthy third party five thousand dollars for a sketchy video of a player whose identity and location are unknown. But it isn't my business.

Nothing that comes out of Cyrille's mouth, Geoff is saying, can be relied on in any way. This isn't a reflection on Cyrille, although Cyrille is basically a criminal. It's a reflection of the world Geoff lives in, my brother says with sudden sourness, a world without rules or loyalties. The players are just kids who want to play football, and their families are only interested in one thing – money.

It's all they think about – money, money, money. The interests of
the player are secondary, even if he's their own son. 'Listen to this,
bruv,' Geoff says. Recently, he landed a young English player a
contract at Sheffield Wednesday, a historic club going through
a hard time, a club that needs new blood. It was the perfect fit.
All that remained, to complete the deal, was a two-day medical –
routine stuff. On the eve of the medical, Geoff and the boy and his
sister and his mum and dad held hands around the dinner table.
The boy's father, some sort of pastor, said a prayer. Thank You,
Lord, for Your servant and shepherd Geoff. Thank You for everything Geoff has done for this family. That was the pastor's actual
prayer. The next day, instead of traveling to Sheffield for the medical, the pastor and his son flew to Germany with another agent
and signed for a 2. Bundesliga club. Talk about a kick in the teeth.
That was two years of unpaid work down the drain. Geoff blamed
himself. He'd been naïve. He should have personally escorted the
boy to Sheffield and not let him out of his sight, not for a second.
Truth be told, Geoff himself once pulled the same trick on another
agent. That's the nature of the business. It turns you into the sort
of person you don't want to be.

I want my bed. 'Geoff—'

He gives the tablet a significant finger-tap. The most difficult
clients of all? Africans. Never mind the logistics – the work permits, the travel arrangements, the passports. The worst thing is the
entourage. You can't talk to an African player without some uncle
or village elder or wizard hanging around, putting stupid ideas into
the player's head. Footballers are famously stupid to begin with;
throw these other clowns into the mix and the decision making
becomes totally insane. Geoff has been burned again and again.
A year ago, he swore never to represent another African prospect,
even though he loves that part of the world, which he's repeatedly
visited. Then Godwin fell into his hands. For Godwin he would
make an exception.

I say, 'You don't even know if Godwin is his actual name.'

'You're right, I don't.'

'You don't even know which country he's in.'

'Bruv,' my brother, smiling, says, 'that's where you come in.

You're the cleverest person I know, fam. If you can't find him, no one can.'

•

The appeal to vanity almost never fails. But what Geoff doesn't know is that I have a long negative history with morbid self-regard, and – I'm aware that this sounds ridiculous – I have fought a successful battle to overcome it.

My vanity manifested as a kind of bigheaded obsession with personal obscurity. So-called failure, it seemed to me, was much more honorable than so-called success; and the loser/winner binary was a falsehood constructed by 'the Man' for his own benefit. Incredible as it might seem, 'the Man' was an unironic and active part of my vocabulary, even after I turned thirty. If it had occurred to me to ask what the binary opposite of 'the Man' might be, I would not have answered 'the Woman', because I viewed the female gender as essentially captive to a reproductive destiny and therefore helplessly implicated in the Man's scheme: women were natural conservatives, would be another way to describe my thinking. I certainly didn't think of 'the Man' in opposition to 'the People', which denoted the hoodwinked masses. Oh no – the Man's opposite number, or enemy, was none other than yours truly. My unspoken fantasy was that I was a furtive ideological hero and that one day I'd come out of hiding and my scorn for riches and recognition would pay off – in recognition and riches, of course. How I lived for years with this garbage is too embarrassing to contemplate. Vanity refers to emptiness, and this conception of myself as a covert winner or dark horse was obviously a way of shoveling dirt into my interior void. But I didn't realize this until I understood myself in archaic terms – understood that nothing less than a monster lived inside me. The monster cannot be slain, I should add. It can only be stilled. When Geoff tries to flatter me into helping him, he is trying to rouse the monster.

'Markie,' my brother is saying. 'Bruv. I can't do this on my own. Help me find this guy. That's all I'm asking.'

I see what's going on. Geoff has seen something in me – that

I'm destroyed by fatigue? That I'm a pushover? That I have sentimental fraternal notions? – that encourages him to believe that I
will do as he asks.

He sits up in my bed. He launches into a story.

Even before he saw the Godwin tape, a rumor had reached
Geoff's ears about a kid in Togo. The kid – the rumor didn't
name him – was said to have turned up at a soccer academy in
Lomé wearing broken plastic football-boots. This happens a lot
in Africa, according to Geoff. You have hopefuls waiting around
the fringes of youth tournaments and trials, trying to make an
impression with ball-juggling tricks, trying to sneak into the pro-
ceedings, even photobombing team pictures. It's pathetic; some
of these kids are well into their twenties and still trying to pass
themselves off as teenagers. It goes without saying that none of
them are anywhere near good enough. Even the legitimate players are no-hopers. Outstanding prospects, the kind you can't keep
your eyes off, are truly rare. On this particular occasion in Lomé,
a scout was present. Not an African scout, Geoff says – a proper
scout, a Frenchman named Jean-Luc Lefebvre. Lefebvre was in
Lomé not to watch anyone but to evaluate the soccer academy
for UEFA. When Lefebvre returned to France, he wasn't thinking
about the academy.

On his final morning in Lomé, Lefebvre observed a practice
match between the academy's A team and B team. Some pickup
players were deployed to fill out the B team. The B team, the second string, destroyed the A team. The upset was all down to one of
the pickup players, an adolescent who scored four times and laid on
two more goals. Lefebvre was enormously impressed – and he had
seen the young Desailly and Deschamps play together at Nantes.
This boy had everything – acceleration, touch, match awareness,
courage.

Football scouts, Geoff says, are a skeptical, cynical bunch. An
old hand like Lefebvre would have been burned a million times.
The problem with the Togo prospect was that normally you scout
a player for months. You guard against the blinder – the anoma-
lously excellent performance – and you guard against the fallibility

of your judgment, of your emotions. With this boy, one performance was enough for Lefebvre. As he watched the game, he had
this crazy vision in his head of a crowd of suitors – trainers, scouts,
club officials – storming the field after the final whistle and mob-
bing the boy with offers and enticements. He resolved to make his
move right away. He would take care of all necessary arrangements
immediately, even it meant personally paying the boy's airfare to
France.

'How do you know all this?' I ask.

'Fam, do I look like a fool to you? I spoke to Lefebvre. This is
straight from the horse's mouth.'

Then something 'African' (Geoff's word) happened. A goat
wandered onto the pitch. Nobody paid the goat any attention until
it stopped near the center circle. What appeared to be a small, hid-
eous ghost began to emerge from the goat. The ghost lengthened
and for a moment was suspended, part inside and part outside the
goat. Then it fell to the ground – and became recognizable as a
white kid, sheathed in a pale amniotic sac. By this point, the game
had stopped. The players were standing around the goat and its
offspring, joking and laughing. The coaches went out to join them.
Out of a habit of decorum, Lefebvre stayed on the touchline. His
biggest error had already been made: in following the drama with
the goat, he'd taken his eye off the boy. By the time it dawned on
Lefebvre that the game had been prematurely terminated, the boy
was nowhere to be seen. Lefebvre ran onto to the field in a panic. It
was as if the boy had evaporated. He hurried over to the academy's
head coach. The coach seemed unconcerned – didn't even seem to
know who Lefebvre was talking about, and couldn't, or wouldn't,
give him the boy's name. It was entirely possible that the coach had
some personal interest, some issue of pride or money, in the boy.
Lefebvre—

'I get it,' I say. 'The kid slipped through his fingers. You're sure
this was Godwin?'

'That's what I'm saying, bruv. It might be. I strongly suspect it
might be.'

'It might be? You suspect?'

'Fam, when Lefebvre described the youth – what he looked like, his playing style – he could have been describing Godwin'.

'That seems a bit tenuous,' I say.

''Course it's tenuous. Hundred percent. That's why I'm asking you for a solid, bruv.'

The solid is that I 'hop on the Eurostar' and go to Le Mans, France, where Lefebvre lives; screen him the video; and either confirm or disconfirm the Godwin identification.

'Why me? Why can't you go?'

Geoff raises his leg an inch from the surface of my bed. 'Can't move, blud. Plus, I've got some stuff to take care of here.'

'Why don't you just send Lefebvre the video and ask him if his boy is Godwin?'

'Blud, that would be insane.' Lefebvre, he explains, is a guy who lives and dies by unearthing new talent. You can't trust a guy like that not to make a copy of the video and go after Godwin himself. That's why Geoff's instructions are that I *show* Lefebvre the video.

'When would I go?'

'I'll be real, bro: there's no time like the present.'

All I can think to say is 'What about my hotel room?' I've just paid for a night that I wouldn't be using.

'No worries,' my brother says. 'I'll take the room. It won't go to waste.' In the same tone of someone doing me a big favor, he continues, 'Your taxis, trains – all on me. Just hang on to the receipts.'

'Let me think about it,' I say. For a few seconds, this is what I do. Then I say, 'OK.'

I say OK not because I want to go to France or want to find Godwin but because my brother frightens me and I want to get away from him.

•

A cab takes me to Birmingham New Street Station; a train delivers me to London Euston; a short walk transports me, eating a hamburger with fries, from Euston to St. Pancras Station. There I board the Eurostar to Paris-Nord.

The Eurostar! I have caught it once before. It was in 1997, immediately after my disastrous visit to Geoff and his mother, en route to Prague. I imagined that a luxurious, deliciously somnolent voyage awaited me, an outing of starched white tablecloths in restaurant cars, coffee poured from silver coffeepots, and one's wagon-lit slipping through a twinkling and civilized continent. What I got was a journey of confusions and stops and transfers – at Brussels, Frankfurt, Leipzig, Dresden – until finally I arrived at Praha Station. The main theme of that Czechia summer was the pauperdom that my college buddies and I inflicted on ourselves, even in a city as marvelously cheap as Prague, out of a basic inability to budget. Eventually, we actually went hungry. I was forced to spend my last month in the City of a Hundred Spires working illegally and shamefully at a pseudo-KFC where the compensation came mainly in pieces of fried chicken and side orders of coleslaw and potato salad. My job was to greet customers in a pseudo–Colonel Sanders outfit, broadcasting my nationality and accent to authenticate the American credentials of the fast food. It was hilarious and ironic for about two days.

This time, in 2015, I'm not a clueless, penniless graduate. I have the wherewithal of an adult, albeit an adult who hasn't exactly hit the jackpot. Money remains a problem, essentially because I have not made enough of it. The good news is that the credit card debts I disastrously incurred during my postgrad-entrepreneurial days – debts that consumed the modest inheritance I received from my dad – have been mostly paid off. Here again, I can thank Sushila and her city employee's salary.

My second Eurostar experience is neither pleasant nor unpleasant, neither interesting nor tedious. The gray and businesslike décor of the train duplicates the gray and businesslike fields through which we coast, a scene interrupted almost twice a second by the outline of a power pole. In northern France, every glimpse of a church spire is accompanied by a glimpse of enormous electricity towers. Thoughtful and acceptable quid pro quos, the beautiful put in the balance with the practical, have gone into making this landscape. In another set-off, I sleep for an hour, but when I wake up at Gare du Nord I find that I'm exhausted to the degree that I'm rested. Fair enough. If the rest of my life is ruled by the same equity, I'll count myself a lucky man. This represents a personal advance. My former, most blundering self was a malcontent. The good-enough wasn't good enough. The humdrum personal outcome was an enraging political injustice. I don't know who planted this nonsensical disaffection in my head. Sushila believes that it is an 'American' thing. She speaks, as do her parents, from a general sense that Americans are fools to be pitied. Pitied for what? For not understanding what family is.

At Gare du Nord there are police officers with machine guns. Paris is still on high alert after the recent massacres. It scares me more than a little, this brush with evil backwardness. Hurriedly, I take the métro to Montparnasse-Bienvenue; scurry from there to Montparnasse Station; and board a third and final train, to Le Mans. (My total travel costs and disbursements, including the aforementioned hamburger and fries: $336). At Le Mans I check into a hotel near the train station for one night ($64, converted from the price in euros). When I awake, at 9:00 a.m., I decide to call Sushila, then decide to e-mail her instead, because in Pittsburgh it is still the middle of the night. I eat a hotel breakfast involving a croissant, raspberry jam and scrambled eggs. This combination of continental and cooked foods triggers a supplementary breakfast fee of $14.

I text Geoff to let him know where I am. He doesn't answer. At 11:00 a.m., I take a taxi ($11) to the home of Jean-Luc Lefebvre. If Geoff can be believed, Lefebvre is expecting me.

The taxi takes me to a dull outskirt of the city and drops me off in front of a semidetached house. The roof is weirdly oversized and pitched at a steep medieval angle, as if attached to a house in a fairy tale. I press the buzzer. Instead of the expected rasping sound, it produces a churchlike chime that I associate with my childhood, which was, now that I think of it, a time of somewhat haunting doorbell sound effects. Lefebvre answers the door. He wears a blue dressing gown over a collared burgundy shirt and a pair of vintage, or old, Adidas tracksuit bottoms. On his feet are tennis socks and plastic slide-on sandals. He greets me in French, a language that I don't understand, then says distastefully, 'Enter'.

Lefebvre leads me through an exceedingly gloomy corridor. His gait is slow and stiff-legged – the result, he tells me, of osteo-arthritis of the knees. We have taken a seat at his dining table. He pours us each a glass of cold water, which he then colors with a fuming measure of pastis. '*Santé*,' he says, taking a sip. Knee trouble is a condition suffered by many former football professionals, Lefebvre claims. He played professionally for only six years, but it was sufficient to ruin the cartilage. He draws my attention to a photograph of himself during his playing days – the late 1960s or early 1970s, to judge from the hairstyles.

My response is to briskly get out my laptop. I have an afternoon train to catch. The plan is to be out of Lefebvre's house within the hour and out of Le Mans before dark.

Lefebvre takes a deep sip of his drink. He tells me, as I fire up my computer, that he's been looking forward to watching this video. When he returned from Togo, nobody listened to him. Why would they? So many of his colleagues in the football world have died or retired. The new generation – the trainers, the directors of football, the recruiters – does not know his work. In a year or two, if not sooner, the name Jean-Luc Lefebvre will mean nothing. He will be completely without influence, without a role. For now, Le Mans FC still gives him some scouting work, mainly on account of his friendship with the great Alain Giresse. Lefebvre is pointing at another photograph. There we are, he says, more than fifty years ago, when Alain was a teenager and Lefebvre, his elder by only a few years but already retired because of injury, was a youth coach at the Girondins de Bordeaux. Lefebvre called Giresse about the Togo sighting. Giresse is nowadays the manager of the Senegal national team, and previously held the same role for Gabon and Mali. Nobody knows more about the football of Africa. Giresse told Lefebvre that he'd heard nothing about a Lomé wunderkind. His advice to his old friend was to let it go, put it down to experience. Experience! Lefebvre did not ask Giresse the question that was passing through his mind, which was: do I have the air of a man in need of more experience? What he, Lefebvre, wanted was the experience of success, of results. That was the genre of experience he wanted.

I indicate that I'm ready to show him the video.

Lefebvre slowly finishes his pastis. 'Before I look, before I give you the information you want, you must pay me correctly.'

'You'll have to speak to Geoff about payment. I'm just a courier.'

'I did speak. I am not reassured.'

I say, maybe a little weakly, 'Geoff will take care of you.' I add, 'I'm in the same position as you. I'm also depending on him to pay me.'

Lefebvre shakes his head. 'You are the brother. I am not the brother.' He points at my phone. 'Me, he never answers. Maybe a call from the brother will work better.'

I ask if I can be connected to his Wi-Fi network. I don't have an international roaming phone plan, I explain.

Lefebvre regards me as if I'm an idiot.

Geoff doesn't answer my call. I leave a voice message. I leave a text, too.

'We will wait,' Lefebvre says. 'When he calls back, maybe we will look at your video.'

As Lefebvre pours himself another drink, I take a sip from my own. And why not? I have checked out of my hotel. There is nowhere else for me to go, nothing else for me to do.

Lefebvre gets ups and shuffles over to a sideboard crowded with soccer memorabilia. He returns with a signed photograph. 'This is my biggest champion. Didier Drogba.'

I think I recognize Drogba. In the picture he jubilantly holds up the huge Champions League trophy. The inscription reads, *Merci pour tout D D.*

The remarkable thing about the young Drogba, Lefebvre tells me, is that at Le Mans, where Lefebvre had been his youth coach, he was very normal. He was a strong, determined boy with good parents, like so many Ivorians. But there was no sign of greatness. The general opinion at Le Mans, then a Second Division club, was that he would turn out to be a solid professional at best. They didn't offer Drogba a contract until he was twenty-one years old. I repeat, Lefebvre says, he was a normal player in terms of talent. Lefebvre always showed him respect, though, which was why they remained on good terms. In this business, Lefebvre says, it is essential to have sympathy for the young ones, to treat them with consideration. Football is such a difficult career, the chance of success is so small. When Drogba was twenty-four, an age by which 99 percent of the top players have already shown their special characteristics, he joined En Avant de Guingamp, a tiny club up in Brittany, Asterix country. He began to score more frequently, earned selection for the Côte D'Ivoire national team, and was bought by Marseille. After that it was goals, more goals, trophies, riches, legends. What I'm telling you, Lefebvre says, is that Drogba was transformed. The African players couldn't believe it. They thought it was the work of a sorcerer. Lefebvre couldn't blame them. When he watched Drogba playing for Chelsea, he couldn't believe his eyes, either. How could a good but not extraordinary player have turned into a monster of the air, a terrorist of shooting? It was as if in Brittany Drogba had drunk the magic potion of Panoramix. That isn't to suggest that Drogba was doped, not at all. One of the great things about our sport, Lefebvre asserts, is precisely that doping is of little use. Of course, if you were to dope a whole team, like the Juventus team of the late nineties – a team that has never been brought to justice, in Lefebvre's opinion – you would gain a clear advantage. But at the end of the day, doping doesn't help you to kick a ball or see a pass or sacrifice for your teammates. The evils of the pharmacy cannot overcome the spirit of football. That is my belief, Lefebvre says. Others think differently.

The winter daylight is starting to fail. Instead of opening the curtains fully, like a normal person, Lefebvre draws the curtains and switches on the recessed ceiling lights, a dozen of which now shine feebly. For a few seconds we contemplate each other from opposite sides of the dining table. He has a fat red face. His gray hair has been lathered in pomade, unless it's naturally greasy, and combed very artificially across the top of his head.

I decline his offer of a cigarillo. Or is it a cheroot? He lights one for himself.

The Drogba phenomenon, Lefebvre suddenly says, was part of the growing supremacy of the African footballer. By 'African' he means not only those born on the African continent, but also those

of African descent – black players, in short. The Brazil teams, of
course, have always contained blacks. The European use of black
players, however, is quite recent, with France at the forefront. It
is nowadays taken for granted that Les Bleus will line up with at
least three or four, sometimes as many as five or six, Africans; but
Lefebvre well remembers the emergence of Trésor and Janvion
and Tigana – respectively from Guadeloupe, Martinique, Mali –
and how remarkable it seemed at the time, in the 1970s and early
1980s. After that, of course, came the deluge: Désailly from Ghana,
Thuram from Guadeloupe, Makélélé from Zaire, Vieira from Senegal, and so many others. What these players had in common was
that they were born overseas and brought to France at a young age.
It is the case, Lefebvre tells me, that youngsters with this immigrant profile became highly desirable in the early 1990s. Lefebvre remembers that technical personnel – scouts, coaches – agreed
between themselves that the white player, the native Frenchman,
was a known quantity and, from the point of view of physiology,
limited and predictable, whereas black players had strength and
explosiveness of an essentially unknown order. The immigrant
footballer represented the ideal, so the thinking went, because in
him were combined the genetic attributes of the African and the
mental discipline and cultural habits of the European. This applied
even to Zinedine Zidane, Lefebvre says, although as one of Berber
provenance he was a special case, from the ethnic point of view.

Lefebvre begins to cough. He raises his hand in apology.
Still coughing, he goes on: but we must not be closed-minded.
We cannot be Francocentric. Other countries, too, took steps
on this front. In England, the Caribbean players appeared. The
name John Barnes is important here. The Dutch of course had
the Surinamese duo, Rijkaard and Gullit. It is unjustly forgotten, Lefebvre says, that these two famous names were preceded
in the orange shirt by players who were, for sentimental reasons,
Lefebvre's personal favorites: the Indonesian magician Simon
Tahamata and the Chinese master dribbler Tscheu La Ling. It
was perhaps true, Lefebvre suggests, that the political uniqueness
of these two artists accounted for their lack of prominence in the
history of football, a history in which there are no chapters about

Indonesia and China. At any rate, after the European Championship of 1988, Dutch clubs very frankly sought out dark boys, to use their own terminology. It was thought that white boys were over-coached whereas dark boys still played the game of the streets, as in the old days, and therefore retained the inventiveness and scrappiness and unpredictability of the street footballer. An Ajax coach, no less, shared with Lefebvre the following concepts of the dark boys: Turks were clumsy, plodding; Moroccans were speedy, imaginative, mentally fragile; and Surinamers were more robust, more Dutch, in their mentality. Your phone is ringing, Lefebvre says.

●

'It's my wife,' I say, getting to my feet.

Lefebvre forms his features into a pleased or amused expression, with the corners of his mouth curved upward and his dark teeth exposed. He raises his glass.

I step through French windows into a shabby little yard. It's cold, blustery. A pair of all-weather chairs have been overturned by the wind and lie around a wet and rusting picnic table.

'I'm a prisoner in a strange Frenchman's house,' I joke. 'Like Harker in Dracula's castle.'

Sushila answers, 'Tell me exactly what's going on.'

I tell her only the essentials: that I am in Le Mans, France, to meet with a guy about a scouting video, at Geoff's request.

'Then what?'

'I'm not sure,' I say. 'I'm waiting for Geoff to answer my calls.' I blurt out, 'It's exactly what I was dreading. This thing is spinning out of control.'

'Here's what I think,' Sushila says. 'You're flying back Thursday. In the meantime, you're totally free to do as you please. That includes changing your flight and coming home sooner. And don't worry about the money. If you want to come home, go to the airport, buy a ticket, and come home.' Lefebvre is spying on me through the dark reflections in the glass. From the next-door house, a figure at the second-floor window also watches me. 'I'll be OK,' I say. 'I'll go back to the hotel tonight, get a good night's sleep, and figure it out in the morning.'

Then Sushila says something surprising. 'You're tougher than the rest, Mark. Never forget it.'

Ten feet tall, I stride back into the house. I declare to Lefebvre that it's time for me to go.

He says, 'My friend, you have come a long way. Wait a little. It's what your brother would like, I think.' He offers me, and I turn down, another pastis. But I do take a seat, because I must counter my impulse to flee the scene. I have fled many scenes in my life. It has gotten me nowhere.

Pouring himself another drink – his fourth, by my count – Lefebvre states, in the manner of a lecturer, that the conception of Africa as a football gold-mine really caught on in the nineties. Which is to say, people began to think that there might be huge quantities of raw talent to be discovered on the continent itself, talent that was potentially more precious than over-processed European talent. In effect, Lefebvre says, the prejudice against Africans was reversed. The original prejudice, it had to be admitted, was not without a factual basis. When African teams began to appear in the World Cup finals – Morocco in 1970, Zaire in 1974 – they made a poor impression. The fans liked them, of course, in the way that they like all underdogs, but professionals saw naïve, undisciplined players. North African, that is to say Arab, teams – Tunisia, Morocco – did much better in the ensuing World Cups; but they were skillful weaklings, lacking the physical power that marks out elite footballers. It was not until Cameroon's exploits in 1990, and until the singular example of the Liberian George Weah, that clubs in Europe began to pay careful attention. They began to send representatives, among them Lefebvre, into Sub-Saharan Africa. I went to Africa for the first time in 1997, Lefebvre declares. They sent me to Senegal with the instruction to look for players with velocity and force, players who could strengthen professional squads with their physical qualities. But of course, in the back of my mind there was the hope of discovering another black pearl.

He looks at me. Do I understand what he means by this phrase, 'black pearl'? Do I understand the reference?

I tell him that, unless he is talking about actual black pearls, the ones that grow in the waters around Tahiti, I do not understand.

Lefebvre affects an expression of despair. What about the black panther? he demands. Does that mean something to me? When I don't answer, he says, Eusébio? What about the name Eusébio?

I say, 'Eusébio? I mean, it sounds familiar.'

Lefebvre chortles. To you, he asserts, 'Eusébio' is just a word. Did you see him play? You did not. You were not even alive in the 1960s. You know nothing, Lefebvre tells me. He, Lefebvre, is cursed to remember the great players of that decade, whose exploits are misrepresented by the unjust fragments of film that one sees on the internet, players whose deeds are being erased by inferior players from our television age. People talk about Messi as if he is without precedent. These people have never seen Jimmy Greaves zigzag through a defense. They have never seen Raymond Kopa. Even Pelé they have not seen!

When Lefebvre heard the news of Eusébio's death, on the evening of the fifth of January 2014, a Sunday, he found himself overcome by a great grief. The deaths, one by one, of the footballers of old was something he didn't like to think about. He preferred to keep looking forward, at the players of tomorrow, and in any case he wasn't emotional about the business. But Eusébio was different. I cry for the death of my brother Eusébio, Pelé declared. Lefebvre, too, wept, at this very table. The next morning, a Monday, he packed a suitcase and flew to Lisbon. He wore a Le Mans FC tie and a blazer with the emblem of Le Mans FC, the red horse, on the heart pocket. It was a gray, rainy afternoon when he landed in Lisbon. From the airport he went directly to the Stadium of Light. Overflowing the famous Eusébio statue were flowers, handwritten messages, and countless red-and-white Benfica scarves and shirts. The statue itself, with Eusébio poised on his left leg and his right leg retracted and ready to shoot, was barely visible beneath the paraphernalia. Nearby, likewise contemplating this pathetic shrine, were other solitary persons who had come to pay respects of their own to the King, as Eusébio was rightly known throughout Portugal. The Black Panther, the Black Pearl: these sobriquets existed only in the minds of foreign journalists. Lefebvre was struck by

how old the mourners were. There were gray heads everywhere, as
at a concert of the Rolling Stones. It's possible, Lefebvre says, that
he was misinterpreting the scene, that his attention privileged the
old men like himself, whose attachment to Eusébio was the stuff
of personal memory rather than of folklore. Lefebvre, as he stood
by the statue, was remembering not the thunderbolt shooting and
lightning speed that had made Eusébio so famous but, rather, his
two Wembley duels with the English assassin, Nobby Stiles, and the
gallantry that Eusébio showed when under physical attack from the
toothless Stiles, who repeatedly tried to injure him with assaults,
masquerading as tackles, that nowadays would be answered by an
instant red card and maybe even police action. In this moment of
mourning, Lefebvre felt at a loss. His guess was that he was not
alone – that those others of his age felt as he did, which was that the
mise en scène did not do justice to their emotions. He approached
a small gentleman who seemed particularly bereft and offered him
his condolences on behalf of Le Mans FC, parting his raincoat as he
did so to reveal the red horse. The gentleman did not understand
Lefebvre. He called over his son, who spoke English. Handshakes
and interpreted messages were exchanged, and the trio stood for
a while in rain and in silence. At the father's prompting, the son
informed Lefebvre that the burial of Eusébio was scheduled to take
place imminently, and he asked Lefebvre if he wished to accompany them to the burial. Lefebvre accepted the invitation. Night
had fallen by the time the party reached the cemetery. Great crowds
of *benfiquistas* were present, chanting Eusébio's name. The rain
was pouring down more heavily than ever, turning the ground to
mud, and the chaotic agglomeration of umbrellas complicated and
obscured the scene further. Lefebvre became separated from his
companions. Then a mêlée broke out. It was caused by the arrival
of the coffin. Lefebvre, swept along by the movement of others,
followed the coffin. On account of his official appearance, perhaps,
he was permitted to walk right up to a deep pit surrounded by fresh
mounds of soil. The coffin was lowered into this pit, along with
a Benfica flag. A pair of gravediggers somewhat frantically shov-
eled dirt into the hole. The chaos intensified. Young men threw
themselves on the grave and kissed it, others hysterically shouted

and sang, and certain fans and yellow-vested police officers became involved in attempts to physically control each other. In this pandemonium, with the rain falling like a cascade, Lefebvre felt an enormous joy. He cannot explain it, even now. But he returned to France very happy and filled with the determination to keep going, in spite of everything.

It's very dark outside. Geoff clearly isn't going to call. I'm about to pull the plug on the meeting when a second intention supersedes the first: I will bide my time. An idea has started to form in my mind; and as Lefebvre keeps talking, I'm falling into a fever of tactical calculations of the kind I've not had since the bad old days, when game theory played a significant role in my thinking and I believed that to master Nash equilibria and tit-for-tat theory was to enter a secret realm of power.

Eusébio, Lefebvre is saying, was from Lourenço Marques, in the days when Mozambique was Portuguese. He grew up in a slum, kicking socks filled with newspapers. His athletic talent – he had prodigious speed and spring – was so remarkable that locally he was known as the Phenomenon of Mafalala. This was the epoch of nicknames, Lefebvre says. The Gentle Giant, the Black Spider, the Sacred Monster, the Galloping Major – everyone knew the identity of such personas. But it was only by a miracle that Eusébio came to Benfica.

Lefebvre pauses to light another cigarillo. He seems very happy to be telling his story, this no doubt lonely man. The room fills with smoke. I would feel extremely trapped if I had not formed a plan.

The Benfica manager, Lefebvre says, was Béla Guttmann, the greatest Jewish coach in history, a man who had led the most extraordinary and mysterious life. Guttmann was at his barber's in Lisbon when into the barbershop walked the Brazilian José Carlos Bauer. Bauer had played in two World Cup finals. Now he was a manager of Ferroviária, a small club in Brazil. We're off to play in Africa, Bauer told Guttmann. Guttmann replied, Bauer, keep an eye out for me for any player you see down there. A month later, Guttmann returned to the barbershop. Who should walk through door, as if in a joke? Bauer! Well? Guttmann said. Did you find me someone? Bauer took a seat next to Guttmann. The barber arrived and

began to lather Bauer, like this, with a brush. Bauer announced that
he had seen someone – an eighteen-year-old so exceptional that
he had tried to recruit the boy for himself, on the spot, but could
not, because the boy's club, Sporting de Lourenço Marques, had
demanded a crazy price. What's the kid's name? Guttmann asked.
Bauer did not immediately answer, because the barber was again
brushing shaving cream onto his cheeks. When at last he spoke, he
uttered a word that would change football: Eusébio.

Lefebvre stops. 'What are you doing?'

I have opened my laptop, the screen of which is not visible
to him.

He says, 'What are you looking at?' He knows very well what I
am looking at.

I turn the screen toward him. He sees the kid, glimpses an
unearthly movement.

He can't help himself. In contradiction of his stated intention
not to view the video before Geoff has paid him, he pulls the computer toward him and takes a better look.

I am closely studying Lefebvre's face. The screen casts a white
glow, so that the cheekbones and forehead loom brightly and the
eye sockets darken. This ghostly visage is the text that I must inter-
pret. It will tell its own story. It will give me my answer. That is my
scheme – to discern, from his facial reaction to the video, whether
or not Lefebvre recognizes the boy.

But his face makes no clear statement. Lefebvre might as well
be looking into a sock drawer.

It is undeniable, however, that he's gripped. His face is blank,
yes; but he keeps watching. He views all of the footage, not just the
very brief highlights that Geoff showed me, and he replays certain
moments. A full thirty-five minutes go by before he shuts the laptop
and pushes it back to me. That tells me something – that, and the
micro-expressions that I once trained myself to recognize.

'Well?' I say. 'Is this your boy?' I am already certain that it is.

Lefebvre rests his elbows on the table and interlocks his hands.
Two index fingers escape and fuse into a single digit that points at
the ceiling. 'Let me call you a taxi,' the syndactyl says.

•

My plan, such as it is, is to get some food and get some sleep. After that I will figure out what to do with myself. I spy a restaurant called Speed Burger and get the taxi ($14) to drop me off there. I eat a speed burger. After that I walk back to the hotel and check in for another night. When I get to my room, I join a Wi-Fi network, then crawl into bed like a castaway crawling onto an island. To sleep, at long last, on cool sheets and ample pillows; to end my agonizing hyposomnia, which not for nothing was used by interrogators as a form of torture—

My phone rings.

'Yeah, I was tied up all day, fam,' Geoff's voice says. 'What did he say? Is it Godwin?'

I tell Geoff what has happened – that Lefebvre refused to view the video until he'd been paid; that I succeeded in overcoming his refusal; that Lefebvre declined to say whether Godwin was or was not the Lomé kid; but that—

Geoff interrupts. 'He didn't tell you?'

'Listen, Geoff. Listen a minute. While he was watching the video, I was watching his face. He recognized Godwin. I saw it in his eyes. His kid is our kid.'

Before I can say more – before I can tell him that, in the course of attempting to develop facial decoding software, I made it my business to study the involuntary signals that a face will emit, and that, even though Lefebvre believed himself to be giving nothing away, I spotted the wrinkling of the eyes that betokens satisfaction, an emotion indicative of happy recognition – Geoff says, 'You saw it in his eyes? Bruv, bruv, what you on about? We need something better than that.'

I think about making a retort, then decide against it. I refuse to be in the retort business, just as I refuse to be in the Godwin business.

'Let me call him,' Geoff mutters.

Ten minutes later, he calls me back. Lefebvre is insisting on payment in full, up front, before he says anything.

'I thought that was the deal,' I say.

'Bro, 'course that's not the deal,' Geoff says. 'I'm not going to get mugged off. I'll pay him a reward, 'course I will, if he leads us to Godwin. A finder's fee. But, fam, we ain't found nothing yet.'

'How much is he asking for?'

'Man wants me to name the price. Which of course I can't do, because it all depends on what man's going to tell me. I mean, what if it isn't Godwin?'

'You don't want to pay for a disconfirmation.'

'Dassit. Why would I pay to know nothing?'

I'm starting to feel an awful, all-too-familiar excitement. This standoff, in which each party has failed to gain a payoff, is very interesting from a game-theory angle. Certain concepts – imperfect information, regret aversion – begin to agitate me. Certain solutions, certain signs pointing to the undisclosed order beneath the surface of things, begin to reveal themselves. I say, 'Is Lefebvre a straight shooter? Does he see himself as a man of honor?'

'What?'

'If he's honorable, the fact that he's bargaining for significant compensation means that he probably has information of significant value. That would mean that his boy is Godwin.'

Geoff laughs. 'Bruv, of course man's not honorable. Man's in it to win it.'

'Are you sure? Maybe he just doesn't trust you to pay him.'

'Why wouldn't he trust me?'

Very awake now, I tell Geoff that this would seem to be a case of two actors – Geoff and Lefebvre – playing a game in which the expected utility is not only apt compensation but fairness inter se. That means that there is a way to identify a mutually acceptable outcome. I explain to Geoff that there are nine possible factual scenarios. One: Lefebvre has recognized Godwin. Two: Lefebvre has not recognized Godwin. Three: he has recognized Godwin and also has acquired some other useful knowledge. Four: he has—

'Markie, Markie,' Geoff says. 'Calm down, bruv. Calm down. Lefebvre is still thinking it over. We need to sit tight.'

Sit tight? That's easy for Geoff to say – he's not stuck in a hotel four thousand miles from home. I try to sleep, but futile mental activity keeps me awake for another two hours. When I regain consciousness, still exhausted, I find myself in a room I don't recognize, a room into which I have been hurled by fate. At the foot of the bed, a gray triangle of natural light is existent, and I stare at it for a while. Then I go to the window. It offers a view of a rail yard. Gleaming brown rails reflect the brown construction aggregate that has been spread on the subgrade of brown dirt. In the leftward distance is the station. No trains. Right below me, as if illustrating a problem of geometry, scores of straight tracks run in parallel. Secondary tracks diverge from the central group and split into further tracks, which terminate at the boundary of a parking lot. A shunting yard, if I'm not mistaken. Suspended above all of it is a fantastically dense canopy of wires that surely would interest a pack of monkeys. The whole scene is soothing, as achieved engineering so often is. It calms me to contemplate the shallow curve assumed by a power cable hanging under its own weight. A catenary is a beautiful thing.

The checkout hour approaches. Rather than extend my stay, I book myself into an Airbnb studio in the *hypercentre* of Le Mans, for two nights, at $27 a night. This selection is purely frugal. Until Geoff's reimbursements come through, I have to be careful with my spending. Cash flow has never not been an issue in my life, not even for five minutes.

I inform Sushila, asleep in the Pittsburgh night, of my new abode. This is done from my private e-mail address, which only very few people have. My work e-mail I neglect out of principle. I am on leave. The boundary between work life and one's own life must be strictly maintained.

The day is another cold and windy one, but I am happy to walk to my new lodgings with my rumbling suitcase and my backpack. To kill time, I take an indirect route. The streets, almost viciously greenless, are bordered by light-brown, downcast nineteenth-century townhouses whose provincial inhabitants I can only imagine as curates, faithless doctors' wives, syphilitic gentlemen, etc. This worthless rumination only reinforces a view that I've long held, which is that there is little to be gained from wandering around just for the hell of it. One strolls; one notices this and that; and one arrives at stupid conclusions. With sour amusement I recall a certain professor's enthusiasm, in my student days, for the flâneur: the aimless, invariably male urban ambler who is alert to things – clues, correspondences, queer wonders – undetectable by the others, the stiffs who hurry purposefully to their for-profit appointments. It made a great impression on our class, especially Baudelaire's idea of the incognito prince, which confirmed our suspicions of our hidden nobility – i.e., that although we might look like ordinary undergrad dumb-dumbs as we slouched around the CMU campus, secretly we were barons of discernment. If, in Le Mans, I were to turn a corner and bump into the same professor, I would take him aside and teach *him* a thing or two. I would point out that bald guy on the sidewalk, heading briskly home with a handful of dry-cleaned shirts; this woman reversing a Peugeot into a parking spot; that other woman, over there, stooping for her child. They're the cryptic aristocrats. They're the ones who are on to something.

Or are they? No sooner have I fantastically corrected my old professor than I begin to self-disagree. A contrarian interior personality tells me that my theory – that the humble errand-runner knows more than the knight-errant – is as useless and pretentious as the theory it opposes. Then a third voice, cutting and controlling, silencing all other arguers, says: Really? I don't have better things to do than conduct debates with the spirits of professors past? And on such a garbage subject? All those years of thinking and reading and growing up amount to this mental junk?

One of the awesome things about Sushila, early on, was her affirmation of my pointless trains of thought. 'You can't stop thinking and daydreaming. It's what you're like. You have all this stuff in your head, and you're sort of helplessly moving it around. It's kind of attractive,' she asserted, perhaps ironically. But I took it. In my whole life, nobody had ever said anything so penetratingly kind about me. And Sushila not only understood 'dark Mark' – her name for the self I most feared, most readily obeyed – but dismissed him as a dolt. 'Anyone can be a cynic. It's the easiest thing in the world. It makes everything so simple. I don't like it. I won't accept it, Mark.' I didn't immediately get why Sushila was so emphatic about it. I did not yet understand the stakes.

Sushila isn't around. Fizzy, my little sunbeam, is not around.

Pearson, my trusty hound, is not around. I am a long way from home. I am vulnerable.

The vulnerability manifests in a strange aversion that must be described.

As I go on with my walk, a hillside offers itself; and my legs automatically accept the invitation to climb, perhaps because they belong to a Pittsburgher who daily walks his dog up and down Polish Hill. Before long I find myself in the old town – or Plantagenet City, as it has been named for tourism – a quarter of narrow, cobbled streets with timber-framed houses and taverns in which, very conceivably, the Three Musketeers are drawing their swords. Every medieval brick and beam has been perfectly preserved or restored; the expulsion of the contemporary has been fully achieved. The sense of sterile time-travel is reinforced by the absence of cars on the pedestrianized roads and by the abnormal character of the street life, which consists of the occasional very small white person, shrunken by old age or afflicted by an inherited miniaturization, scurrying in or out of some doorway. It spooks me. I have been overtaken by a powerful dread, or phobia, of the very old buildings among which I find myself, as if I'm in danger of actual transportation to the Dark Ages. All that's lacking, to complete the experience, is an immense and grotesque old cathedral; and when I turn a corner, exactly such a relic reveals itself.

The encounter with the cathedral is mediated by an information placard. It draws my attention to the gargoyles and to the 'forest of masonry' effect of the flying buttresses; and it describes in detail the building of the cathedral, a nine-hundred-year construction project that started in the sixth century. I stop reading. This decision, to turn my back on the information placard, isn't because I reject the humble standpoint of the tourist. (I used to be that guy – the snob who avoids Times Square and Covent Garden and Charles Bridge out of distaste for the hordes.) It's because the cathedral is exacerbating my historical nausea. This colossal structure preserves a colossal effort – but to what end? The adoring purpose has long since evaporated. All that remains is an eerie latent energy – the storage, in gray stone bulk, of unthinkable joules of labor and unthinkable quantities of false hope. The gigantic proportions provoke a kind of dizziness, as they were designed to; but, rather than looking skyward, one peers into a chasm.

The Gallo-Roman wall only makes things worse.

It, too, offers an information placard, and this time I can't stop myself: I read it. I learn that the wall, which encircled the ancient city and remains mostly intact, was built between A.D. 270 and 310. Cool. The authors of the placard offer a brief account of the invasions and wars that consumed the region for centuries during the so-called Migration Period, as if the protagonists of history were birds or reindeer. In fact, the Migration Period refers to the campaigns of conquest and extermination that were carried out by Ostrogoths, Visigoths, Vandals, Angles, Saxons, Suebis, Slavs, Thuringians, Gepids, Franks and whatever other tribes of plunderers, arsonists, rapists, killers, ethnic cleansers and illiterates emerged from the holes and hinterlands of Europe. They wrecked everything. Classical antiquity was no picnic, but at least it produced permanent treasures. The barbarians left only horror stories. True, they were ill-served by the chroniclers. But what stopped them from writing their own chronicles? They couldn't come up with one Suetonius between them? One theorem? Who was the Euclid of the Jutes? Where are the odes of the Huns?

In my indignation I must have started to mutter, because a passerby looks at me as if I'm deranged. Intending to apologize, I take a step or two toward her. She breaks into a frightened trot. This ghastly mix-up fuses in my mind with other misunderstandings I've had, with Sushila. It sometimes happens that I react heatedly to a disturbing item of news or opinion, and she mistakes my heated reaction to be directed at her when in fact it's wholly directed at the guilty actor or injustice in question, and I have to explain that I wasn't in the slightest bit mad at her but was only being irate in her presence. 'Well, it doesn't feel that way,' she says, and then I have to scramble to make things right, because if there's one thing I can't tolerate it's Sushila being upset with me. Anyhow, I'm sweating by the time I arrive at the 1950s apartment building in which my Airbnb home is located. I enter the access code, hasten up to my second-floor studio, and lock the door behind me.

Once I've succeeded in joining the Wi-Fi network, I see that I have two text messages: one from Sushila, one from my brother. Weirdly, they both say exactly the same thing:

Can you give me a call?

•

There is only one way to describe what happens next: a knock on the door.

The anachronism of the moment is acute. You rarely hear a knock on the door anymore. There are quite simply very few situations in which knocking on someone's door is called for. It is an extraordinary occurrence.

I look for a peephole. There isn't one.

What to do? I am torn between the primeval fear of opening the door to the unknown and the primeval summons of the door knock.

There it is again: the sound of knuckles softly but firmly striking wood.

As if commanded, I advance to the door. I say, 'Who's there?'

A genderless, barely human voice answers, *'Bonjour, monsieur.'* After which I can't understand what is being said, except that it's in French.

'Excuse me?' I say through the closed door. There's no reply.

It used to be that doors had security chains for precisely such a situation: to enable the occupant to open the door just enough to scope out and interact with the visitor while also maintaining the control of ingress and egress that is, after all, the function of a door. But there is no security chain. My only option, aside from cowering in my room, is to open the door fully and expose myself to the unknown party on the other side.

It turns out to be a woman, pleasantly tidy of appearance, of around my age. She has a smile on.

'Yes?' I say. 'I don't speak French. I only speak English.'

The smile intensifies. 'I am your host,' she says, extending her hand, 'Jeanne. I am offering to explain the apartment to you.'

'The apartment explains itself,' I say. 'There is no need for any kind of guided tour. I am very satisfied. Thank you.' Why I speak in such wooden locutions, as if English had suddenly become an alien language, I cannot say. Maybe it's because I'm being forced by this foreigner into a conversation I don't want to have. They say that body language is natural and universal, and in this respect my message is very clear: I am standing my ground. My body says to her, Thou shalt not pass.

Never ceasing to smile, she hands me a folder. 'I give you this information. Have a good stay.' Then she goes up the stairs, presumably to her own living quarters. I lock the door behind her.

My exhaustion spontaneously returns. I fall onto the bed facedown. When I awake it is 4:00 p.m., France time, which means 10:00 a.m., Pennsylvania time, which means that Sushila has already stepped out to work, where she prefers not to be disturbed unless it is an emergency. I have missed the window of communication.

The whole drama of contactability, of being constantly in touch and constantly on call, is weighing on me. In regular life I don't carry a phone around. My whereabouts are not exactly a big mystery. I'm a predictable, straightforward guy. At any given moment I'm most likely to be holding the fort. If I'm out, it'll be because I'm walking the dog or buying food or briefly riding my bike. It won't be because I've put on a wingsuit and thrown myself off a cliff. And if something untoward happens, the kind of hitch or holdup that afflicts countless people every day, I handle it the way grown-ups did in the millennia before portable electronic devices: by figuring it out. The bottom line is that I'm not a package to be tracked and traced.

I must confess that inside me there burns a tiny flame of resentment. Setting off on an international caper wasn't my idea. It was Sushila's idea – that I should have an adventure. If you think about it – which I do, in my Airbnb studio apartment, while looking out the window like a suspect watching out for the police – an adventure boils down to a sequence of uncontrollable, unpleasant and unwanted events. Disaster looms at every turn. If you think about it some more, which I also do, the main difference between a calamity and an adventure is that in the latter case the protagonist makes it home in one piece and lives to tell the tale. What gets my goat is that when this escapade kicked off I was already home. I was already living happily ever after – until it was suggested that I set out once again. Why would Sushila do that? Why did she want me out of the house?

Anger is connected to fear. Even in ordinary life, I cannot open the door of the house without immediately yelling out that I'm home, as if I've returned from a trip to the moon, and there is always a suspenseful pause until someone responds. If there's a fear that tops all the others, it's that one fine day I'll come home to find that everybody's gone.

My phone dings. It's Geoff:

On train to Paris. Meet me at Gare du Nord at 8. Main entrance.

I reply with two question marks. The following comes back:

Change of plan. Will explain.

Protestations congregate in my mind – Why did Geoff send me from England to France if he could so easily make the same journey? What kind of bullshit is he getting me into now? What about the two-night Airbnb booking I've just made? – and almost instantly disperse. I don't want to be in Le Mans. It's no skin off my nose to go to Paris.

On my way out, I run into my host. She is wearing creaturely pink slippers that have furry little ears and bulging, shocked eyes. Her own eyes bear a similar expression. 'You are going? There is a problem with the room?'

She's terrified, and who can blame her? This is a person who lives in the shadow of the single negative review that will destroy her humble home-rental business. For that's all it would take: one vicious person with a keyboard. And who isn't vicious? It's the capacity for viciousness that separates humans from the animals. Historically, the reach of our malice was limited by physical space. You could hurl a spear, or shout an insult, only so far. Now a rotten

tomato can be thrown from any distance, to indelible effect. I assure
my host, as she follows me down the stairs, that the room was excellent, that my plans have unexpectedly changed, and that all is well.
She seems to hear me; but at the doorstep she becomes tearful and
begins to say things in French. I am not sure what to do. 'Madame,'
I hear myself saying, 'madame, please don't be upset.' I consider
touching her shoulder in order to transmit my sympathy but don't
go through with it, because I'm uncertain about French tactility
norms and don't want to distress her any more or get into any kind
of trouble, especially since one or two people have already walked
by with a raised eyebrow. Am I going crazy, or is raising an eyebrow
a French national pastime?

I am seized by a powerful understanding that my Airbnb host
has an opaque and intricate life story for which I bear no responsibility and yet to which I am now very proximate – and this has put
me in a false position. When you leave home, you step right into a
zoo. Everywhere you look, suffering animals demand a liberation
that you cannot deliver. You can only gape. There is nothing to be
done but to leave this woman to her fate.

On my walk down the hill to the train station, I skirt the nause-
ating Plantagenet City and make a stop at my old friend the Speed
Burger. I have time to sit down and enjoy a Speed Burger and fries.
By the time I get to Le Mans Station, I am quite restored.

With no drama, I board a train bound for Paris; and soon after,
the train sets off – except that it doesn't. It is the train on the far
side of the platform that is in motion. The illusion is thrilling; it
returns me to the joyful puzzlement of childhood. All has not yet
been seen through and understood; new mysteries await even this
old Clouseau. When my train actually sets off, zooming nightward
in the twilight, I find myself deciding to stay in Paris during the
few days before my flight home. I will sightsee. I will treat myself
to some good old-fashioned tourism, and to hell with the terrorists
and naysayers, and to hell with Geoff. My brother can take care
of his business himself. Bring on the City of Light. Bring on the
Champs-Élysées and the Eiffel Tower. Roll on, you croissants and
you crèmes brûlées and you croque-monsieurs.

•

The train has Wi-Fi. I am poised to text Geoff to tell him of my change of plan when he texts me:

> Change of plan. Go to Halal Snack Grec, rue de la Goutte d'Or.
> At the corner of rue des Islettes. Easy walk from Gare du Nord!

I think about my reply. I write back:

> OK.

If I'm going to part company with Geoff, it's better to do so in person, on friendly and straightforward terms, instead of texting the guy and leaving things on an unpleasant note. He is, after all, my brother – and merely my brother. He isn't my boss or my captor. I have the freedom to do as I please. And it pleases me to go along with Geoff's request and to keep to myself the fact that our sojourn is at an end and we will very soon go our separate ways. I don't yet have a place to stay in Paris, after all; the smart move would be to spend my first night there on Geoff's tab. Oh yes, I have some tricks up my sleeve, too.

When I text Sushila, she answers:

> Paris? Be careful, love. It's dangerous there right now.

I answer:

> xx

The train draws into Montparnasse exactly on time. I move my body and my luggage through a crappy, pointlessly testing métro ride. At Gare du Nord, as I try to get my bearings among escalators and outlandish signage and gangs of rifle-toting police officers, a succession of impatient pedestrians jostle me. A large bilingual poster warns of pickpockets – and I realize that this station, crowded with aggressive travelers and disoriented visitors, must indeed be a paradise for the practitioners of that ancient, almost magical form of theftcraft, which for some reason lives on in Europe and compares favorably, to my mind, with the unskilled and crudely violent methods of American crooks. On the other hand – when is one hand ever enough? – it also seems to me that maybe there is something to be said for the open criminality of the US mugger or bandit, who at least acts in a spirit of candor, with a certain frankness of wrongdoing . . .

As I occupy my mind with these useless thoughts, my body advances from the train station toward my rendezvous. After a few minutes I become alert to my surroundings. Clearly, I'm in an immigrant neighborhood, but that's about as far as my insight goes, because these are immigrants from Africa, the continent I know the least about. It doesn't matter. I'm not here to do ethnological research or broaden my horizons. I'm here to meet Geoff.

The eatery named Halal Snack Grec is a tiny place with four round metallic tables and a large, dripping cone of meat revolving on a spit. Talkative men, none of whom seem to be eating or drinking, stand directly outside the joint. There is no sign of Geoff. Uh-oh.

Then I'm euphoric. I am home free.

In a spirit of celebration, I buy myself a cup of hot coffee and take a seat at one of the tables. At that exact second, a guy in a tracksuit and a wool hat comes up to me. 'Mark?' he asks. He says something in French and hands me a piece of paper. On it is written, in handwriting I've seen before:

Go with Djibril. See you soon!

Gxo

I look up at the messenger. 'Djibril?' I follow him without so much as a sip of my coffee.

There seems little point in analyzing why I do this.

Riding shotgun in Djibril's Renault Safrane, I see nothing notably Parisian, only the glare of artificial lights, unremarkable urban structures and traffic. We turn onto a freeway and pick up speed. Signs indicate that this is the road to Charles de Gaulle Airport. I consider asking Djibril where he is taking me. I keep quiet, however. Some mysterious mechanism of my volition is at work. I allow myself to be taken into the unknown like an abductee.

Very near the airport, we turn off into a district of industrial buildings, office parks and tidy, drab apartment buildings. The gigantic electricity towers are here, too. When we come to a flood-lit synthetic-turf soccer field, the car stops.

'Where's Geoff?' I ask.

Djibril nods as if we're in agreement about something. 'Fifty euros,' he says.

There's no evidence that this vehicle is a taxi or car service. I look at Djibril with what I hope is an expressively baffled face.

'Fifty euros,' he repeats, eyeing me in his rearview mirror.

My wallet holds seventy euros. I pay the guy. 'Receipt?' I say, making a scribbling motion. Djibril gives a meaningless nod of assent. 'Never mind,' I say.

I make my way to the field. A practice session is under way, involving teenagers in bright bibs. Coaches stand by with folded arms, occasionally shouting. A surprisingly large number of onlookers are present. Geoff is nowhere to be seen – until I spot the one white guy with crutches in a group of men who form a collage of Adidas tracksuit pants, hoodies worn under jackets, and baseball caps. Geoff is dressed exactly the same as the others, except that he wears a new orthopedic boot.

When I approach them, foolishly embarrassed by my backpack and roller suitcase, Geoff makes a great show of limping forward to hug me. 'Bruv, come and meet the lads.'

Patrick, Amadou, John, Bakary and Omar shake my hand. They are friendly. I hear myself being referred to as *l'américain*.

'Let's go to the pub, fam,' Geoff says. 'I bet you could use a drink.'

On our way out, Geoff greets several people who have lined up to shake his hand. When he shouts goodbye to one of the coaches, the guy quits what he's doing and runs over to Geoff, and they solemnly perform a handshake involving a sequence of grips. It is impressive, again, to hear my brother speaking French like a Frenchman. Then we leave as a group. Geoff, Bakary and I squeeze into one of those European cars that feels barely bigger than a bumper car, and with French rap music playing at a high volume we pursue another tiny car, which is being driven at speed by Patrick, at first along a stretch of autoroute, next through the streets of a suburban town. From the front passenger seat Geoff shouts that our companions are friends he's kept from back in the days when he played for a Parisian semipro team called Red Star. These guys are pushing thirty, but they still play at a high level and still are crazy about the game. 'These are proper ballers, blud. Your English players? Bluffers, fam. Bluffers. Don't get me started.' It is not explained where we are going or what is going on, but it doesn't matter. We are headed somewhere, and transcendence is in the air. I quicken with a wild feeling of anticipation that I've not had since the bad old masculine days.

Our mini-convoy stops across the street from a bar. We jump out of the cars with a terrific slamming of doors and roll into the joint like conquerors.

The place is empty. While the staff hurry to join together two tables and drag over extra plastic purple chairs, the proprietor, Mourad, shakes hands with everyone. Geoff introduces us. 'This man here,' he tells me, patting Mourad on the back, 'this man was a real football player.'

Mourad makes a gesture of disclaimer.

'In Thailand,' Geoff, not joking, says, 'he's a legend.'

'Legend, no,' Mourad says. He asks me, 'You live at New York?' Pittsburgh, I tell him. 'I love New York,' Mourad replies. 'I love.'

Mourad instructs the staff to quit preparing tables and chairs for us. We follow him to the rear of the establishment. Heavy black curtains are drawn open to reveal a large oval table, an upholstered black banquette and some wingback club chairs. This is presumably the VIP area, although its separatist logic is somewhat undermined by the absence of non-VIP customers. Nonetheless, I feel a low thrill of gratification. If I have ever been inside a VIP area before, I can't remember it.

A server runs a cloth over the tables. When he leaves, he closes the curtains behind him. This confers a theatrical element to our situation, in which we, the VIPs, keep eyeing the curtains to see who will enter next.

•

Maybe it's the leather wingback armchairs, but when Geoff orders a Scotch on the rocks I do likewise. The other guys, the soccer players, are having soft drinks. Geoff says to me, 'In England, yeah, man would be knocking back the tequilas. Not here. These man look after themselves.'

We are sipping our whiskeys like two old colonels. 'How's Bobby?' I say.

'Bobby?' Geoff says.

'Bobby Atkinson.'

'I lost Bobby, bruv.'

'Lost him?'

'He binned me, didn't he?'

I think I know what he means. I say, 'I'm sorry to hear that. Jolene?'

'Fam, if it was Jolene, I could respect it. Nah, bruv, he's traded me in for his dad. You met him – Tony.'

Tony the limo driver, Geoff says, decided that he could do Geoff's job as well as Geoff could, and keep the money in the family. What a mug. He has no idea what he's getting himself into. This is a complex, cutthroat business. If Tony thinks that football people are not going to take advantage of him, he's even thicker than Geoff already knows him to be. What's interesting, Geoff says, is that Tony's wife is unhappy with his decision. She might not be Geoff's biggest fan, but she knows that he's a pro and her husband is a numpty. And she knows that mixing business with family is almost always a bad idea.

This reminds me: my travel expenses. Geoff must reimburse me. I will mention it when the opportunity arises.

'There's no loyalty in the game anymore,' my brother is saying. 'None.' He continues for a while on this theme – the infidelity of the modern footballer, his wandering eye, his

attraction to the suitor and to the stranger, his absolute sense
of entitlement to fame and riches, his brittleness, his immunity
to advice, his stupidity. Does Geoff blame him? Not really. The
jackpots are real. The TV rights to English football are global
and massive. Every year, the twenty Premiership clubs split
between them a pot worth three billion dollars. 'Billion, blud.'
And that's before gate receipts, shirt sponsorships, merchandis-
ing income, profits on player sales. On top of all that, European
clubs are now owned by very, very rich entities: sovereign wealth
funds, American hedge funds, Russian oligarchs, Arab royals. And
the product – English football – is more popular, more global
than ever. Fans watch Premier League and Champions League
matches in their hundreds of millions. The viewership in China,
Africa, Southeast Asia and South Asia is only growing. The cash is
pouring in from everywhere. A nothing-special Premier League
player makes twenty grand a week easy, fifty grand if he gets
lucky. The top players get ten times that. Geoff is talking sterling
grand, not dollar grand. Footballers in the lower leagues, the kind
Geoff has represented, players who made a grand or two a week,
always feel like they're just a twist of fortune away from the big
time, especially the younger ones. They believe that their true
ability is camouflaged by the mediocrity of the players around
them and that their qualities will be recognized with the right
management, the right exposure. Once upon a time, Geoff used
to be one of these players. He believed himself to be one scouting report away from fame and riches. Why wouldn't he? At Red
Star he shared the field with future professionals – passed the
ball to them, tackled them, dribbled around them. 'Fam, I once
nutmegged Mamadou Sakho.'

These are the players who make up Geoff's clientele – young
lads with stars in their eyes. While they wait for the big time, the
little twerps act as if they're superstars. They want Geoff to hook
them up with free cars, free boots, free drinks, free tickets to fucking Ed Sheeran concerts. Geoff's phone never stops buzzing. They
want add-ons, pay rises, bonuses, lollipops. The more goodies he
gets them, the more grief they give him. All that effort, for what?
For 5 to 10 percent of forty to sixty grand a year. You need a dozen

clients, every one of them greedy and two-faced, just to keep your head above water. 'It's not worth it, blud. They're not worth it. That's why I'm moving on.'

The other guys are lounging around with their phones, not paying attention to us. A few of them huddle together, grin for a selfie, then go back to their respective phones. 'What are you saying, Geoff? You're quitting?'

'Onwards and upwards,' my brother says, flipping his hand. He beckons me to come closer to him, into a zone of even stricter confidentiality. In a voice that's barely but clearly audible – it's amazing how one's hearing improves at the prospect of valuable information – he tells me that he has a project coming together that's 'very different, very promising.'

'I'm listening,' I say.

The project only makes sense, Geoff says, if I understand that the social profile of English professional football has changed. It used to be a working-class sport. The biggest stars – Best, Charlton, Keegan, you name them, Gascoigne, Dalglish – were boys from families where the parents might work in a factory or coal mine or on the docks. The fans were from the same background: working-class lads who loved standing in the terraces, loved singing, didn't mind the odd scrap. That's all gone now. The advent of the all-seater stadium put a stop to surging crowds and cascading streams of piss on the terraces. Aggro waned. The match-day atmosphere became more sedate. Corporate boxes and prawn sandwiches appeared. The game became posher – and even more popular. Middle-class players began coming through, then upper-middle-class. Private schools in England started to take football seriously. The most famous and most traditional of them still favored rugby, but your second- or third-tier schools, the ones that had suffered most from the decline of boarding-school culture, began to raise their profiles by attracting top young footballers.

'This is where my mate Posh Hugh comes in,' Geoff says.

Posh Hugh is a properly posh Englishman. A few years ago, he became interested in an undervalued market in a certain African country too dangerous and too difficult for the scouting establishment, which preferred easy pickings in places like Senegal and

Nigeria, where the academies and clubs had strong connections to established recruiting networks. In the market that interested Posh Hugh, there was just one academy, in the capital, and it was nowhere near ready to deliver the goods.

I interrupt. 'Are you going to tell me which top-secret country this is?'

Geoff says, 'Don't fucking tell anyone,' then murmurs into my ear, 'Mauritania.'

Mauritania is somewhere in the Sahara. That's all I know about it.

Posh Hugh, Geoff continues, wasn't a football man at all. He was a metals broker specializing in iron ore, a notoriously chancy commodity because until recently there were no spot prices for it. Hugh did very well in that business. Using his private-school and university contacts, he built a customer base in India and helped them to break into the booming Chinese iron-ore market at the expense of the Brazilians and the Australians. 'This interesting you, bruv? You getting this?'

While working as an iron-ore intermediary, Posh Hugh became acquainted with a young Mauritanian sheikh. Mauritania's number one industry is iron ore, and the sheikh's family was a big player in iron mining. But the sheikh's true passion was football. He was a Chelsea supporter, on account of the years he'd spent as a student in London; and Posh Hugh, like so many London toffs, was also a fan of Chelsea. Posh Hugh and the sheikh bonded over memories of Stamford Bridge. Soon they realized that they also shared a weariness with the iron-ore business, which had grown much tougher for a broker like Hugh, who'd thrived when the value of iron ore was anyone's guess and the iron-ore game was all about personal relationships and insider information, and not about wide boys trading on electronic platforms. Hugh asked the sheikh about football in Mauritania. The sheikh told him that Mauritanians were as keen on the sport as anyone but lacked the facilities and the know-how to develop the potential of their players. Hugh saw an opening.

The opening was this: English boarding schools were looking to give soccer scholarships to talented overseas soccer players.

With the sheikh's support, Posh Hugh could supply these schools with Mauritanian youngsters, for whom the worst outcome would be a first-class education unavailable in Mauritania.

What was in it for Hugh? Fun – and, potentially, peas. His plan was to form a syndicate of investors to fund the scholarships. The investors would get a cut of the revenue generated by any scholar who went on to succeed as a professional. It was a long shot, but the upside was considerable. If one of the scholarship boys made it in the Premiership, his salary for five years could quite feasibly come to twenty-five million quid. Throw in image rights and the other extras that came with being the first truly famous Mauritanian player, you were looking at twice that amount in total revenue. A 20 percent take on fifty million quid represented a good return for a one-hundred-grand bet spread out over four investors. Then there was the under-the-table payoff – the dosh that was almost always paid on big transfers to the parties who controlled or influenced a player. Posh Hugh would have a lot of control and influence.

The sheikh also stood to coin it. If anything, he got the better part of the deal. In return for his helping Hugh, Hugh would share with him the contacts to the Chinese steel mills that were Hugh's most prized possession. The Chinese were already investing in the port at Nouakchott, and with Hugh greasing the wheels the prospect arose of the sheikh's procuring Chinese preferential loans, repayable in Mauritanian iron ore, for African infrastructure projects. Mauritanian sheikhs weren't loaded, not by oil sheikh standards; but deals on this scale would put serious wonga in the sheikh's pocket. And the fun factor applied to the sheikh, too: a football project was a lot more exciting than an iron-ore project. Sweeter still, the sheikh stood to gain political standing by inserting himself into the world of Mauritanian football, influence over which was viciously contested by the members of the Mauritanian ruling class. The sheikh was from the north of the country, way out in the sticks where the iron mines were. Getting into bed with Posh Hugh would give him clout in Nouakchott.

There was a gypsum angle, too, but that was essentially a side deal. The main deal was letting Hugh corner the market in

Mauritanian football prospects in exchange for broking Chinese iron-ore contracts for his new Mauritanian pal.

Geoff's demeanor does not escape my attention. His distracted, shifty, idiotic air has been replaced by an energized calmness. Telling this story about money and moneymakers has given him a strange kind of moral equilibrium.

'So where do you come in?' I ask.

'Fam, that's where it gets interesting.'

•

The other guys are getting up to leave. This surprises me: I thought it was going to be a big night out. But no – the night out has just happened. Everyone is homeward bound at nine o'clock. Geoff very affectionately makes his farewells, then rejoins me. As far as I can tell, there's no one else in the joint.

'I love these br'ers,' he says. 'I come here, we hang out, I get away from the madness.'

I say, 'They love you. I can see that.' Maybe that's why he's brought me here, to the edge of Paris – to impress me with this fact.

Mourad appears with two more whiskeys. He pulls up a chair to join us, but then Geoff asks him to leave. Mourad complies. 'Now, where was I?'

Posh Hugh and the sheikh got to work right away. This was four years ago – 2011. Hugh spoke to certain schools, rounded up certain investors. He was a salesman; he got the response he was looking for. He also worked the Mauritanian side. The Chinese were brought in, and Hugh helped the sheikh to wangle a jetty project. It wasn't a huge deal in and of itself, but it raised the sheikh's profile. This in turn enabled the sheikh to introduce Hugh to key figures in the Mauritanian football establishment. They lined up five soccer scholars for the 2013 school year. The scholars were fourteen years of age, according to their birth certificates. Three boarding schools agreed to take them. It was all coming off. Except for one rather large detail.

'The players,' I say. 'The players were no good.'

Geoff laughs. 'You get it, bruv. You always get it.'

Three of the scholars were downright overweight. It was embarrassing. Two of them were related to a Mauritanian Cabinet minister, and the other was the son of a senator – who turned out to be sixteen years old, not fourteen. They were out of shape and they were useless at football. The schools were very fucking pissed off with Hugh. Within two weeks, 'the three fatties' (Hugh's term) were back to Mauritania.

'That leaves two good players.'

'It does, bruv. It does. Two cousins who were actual ballers. But there was an even bigger headache with them.' Geoff rubs his face. 'Blud, fasten your seat belt.'

He asks me if I know about the Haratins. I confess that I don't.

Mauritania, Geoff seems delighted to inform me, has always had a slavery problem. It was the last country on Earth to formally abolish slavery – 'in 1981, fam, in nineteen-fucking-eighty-one' – and the abolition was not fully enforced. Slavery persisted in one form or another, especially in the interior of the country.

This rings a very faint bell. Or perhaps I'm imagining things.

The Haratins were the historic slave caste. For centuries they were subjugated by their Arab masters, whose religion and customs they adopted. The master castes, as far as Geoff can gather, were made up of Moors and Berbers. What differentiates a Moor from a Berber from an Arab, Geoff can't say. He's not an expert. Nor can he tell me much about the Haratins, except that they're dark-skinned and, some people say, originate from Sub-Saharan Africa. The important thing is that in Mauritania the Haratins are treated as the lowest of the low. Even after abolition, half of them remained fully or partially enslaved as domestic servants or field laborers. You'd think, Geoff observes, that they would rebel or rise up, especially as they make up a large chunk of the population. But they don't, it seems. How and why Mauritanian society is organized in this way isn't something that Geoff can explain. He's just repeating what he's been told by Posh Hugh.

I'm skeptical. Geoff isn't exactly professor material. But I keep listening. He's telling me a money story. It's very hard not to listen to a money story.

When the cousins arrived at their boarding school, it was

discovered that they didn't know French, which Mauritanian children supposedly learn at school, let alone English. An interpreter who spoke Arabic was brought in.

Then it all kicked off.

The interpreter asked the cousins about themselves. She learned that they were from Haratin families that were still subject to bondage. If the boys were returned to Mauritania, she gathered, there was a real risk of enslavement. She informed the school's headmaster.

The school's headmaster called Posh Hugh and warned him that he'd find himself in a shitstorm of trouble if he didn't fix the situation. The word 'police' was used.

In fact, Hugh was already in a shitstorm. His investors were furious about the three fatties and wanted their money back.

The storm worsened. The interpreter shared her story with a journalist. The journalist was very interested, obviously. He had a scoop about a school saving African slave children, alternatively a scoop about a school sending its pupils back to potential slavery in Africa. Either way, the story was sensational.

'Why do I feel,' I say, 'that this is where Geoff Anibal comes into the picture?'

The journalist had a sister, Pam. Pam happened to be Geoff's then bird. The journalist met Pam and Geoff for a drink and told them about the Mauritanian boys playing football in English boarding schools. He was only a couple of phone calls away from running the story.

Geoff said to the journalist: Hold on. I've got a better idea.

Geoff immediately contacted Posh Hugh. He introduced himself as a football intermediary and suggested a meeting to resolve 'the Mauritanian problem'. Hugh was suspicious as fuck, but he took the meeting. What choice did he have? They met in a quiet pub in Kentish Town in the middle of the afternoon. Geoff explained to Hugh that the way to stop this thing was to buy exclusive rights to the journalist's story. That was something he, Geoff, could make happen. Hugh asked how much. A hundred and fifty grand, Geoff told him. Fuck me, that's a lot, Hugh said. He stepped out and called the sheikh. The sheikh hit the roof.

If the journalist ran his story, it would be an indescribable PR disaster for Mauritania, which already had enough trouble from the human-rights industry. The sheikh himself would be finished. He'd end up living in a fucking tent in the sand dunes. Make the deal, he told Hugh.

The hush agreement was quickly concluded. Geoff collected a 20 percent commission on the contract price.

I express surprise that a journalist would go along with an arrangement of this kind.

'Markie,' Geoff says, 'everyone in football is bent. Everyone.'

My brother settles happily in his wingback chair. After the soccer scholarship debacle, he relates, he and Posh Hugh stayed in touch. Hugh still loved the football business – the colorful characters, the shady deals, the trophies, the money. In his eyes, Geoff represented that world. Hugh and the sheikh, meanwhile, grew closer than ever: their gypsum side deal (exporting Mauritanian gypsum, which is of an unusually pure quality, to Indian construction enterprises) was wildly successful. Soon enough, they were better positioned than ever to re-enter the football market.

Back in November, Geoff pitched them a project.

He proposed a boutique sports agency initially focused on Mauritanian talent. Hughie and the sheikh would bankroll the operation, and Geoff (a French speaker, of course) would bring the football knowledge and attention to detail that were so lacking in their scholarship venture.

'And?'

'Hughie called me yesterday,' Geoff says. 'It's on, bruv. The agency. I'm going to get a salary, a profit share, everything.'

'What about your current clients?' I ask; and as I utter the question I realize that Geoff has no current clients.

'I'll be loyal to them,' Geoff says. 'But the focus is on Mauritania.'

'Wow. Congratulations. That's very exciting.'

'The secret, Markie,' my college-dropout younger brother advises me as he swirls the whiskey in his glass, 'is to keep moving in money circles.' If, like him, I were to stay close to people like Hugh and the sheikh, people who can't help making money, people who practically crap the stuff, my moment would come. It's about being in the right place at the right time. How did Gary Lineker score all those goals? By making a run to the near post again and again and again.

I don't understand that reference. 'What about Godwin?'

'Fam – back burner. I've got to focus on the Mauritania thing. I got bigger fish to fry.' My brother gives me a strange look. 'You're going to find him,' he says.

'I am?'

'He's all yours, bruv.'

•

Geoff has hobbled out, through the curtains. I am now alone in the VIP room – alone, that is, with my thoughts.

There are varieties of thoughts. These ones appear like riders suddenly gathered on the brow of the hill. Their horses stir beneath them. Down they come.

The thoughts in question take the form not of an idea but of a private mental state, centered on Geoff's words 'He's all yours', that envelops me in intense, indefinite rumination. When Geoff returns and announces that we're spending the night at Mourad's place – it would be rude to turn down his hospitality, Geoff claims – I barely hear him. When he suggests that we grab a kebab, I agree without a murmur. When he holds forth, in the kebab shop, on the soccer riches of the Paris suburbs, which allegedly hold the world's deepest, most inexhaustible reserves of raw footballing talent, I pretend to listen. When he goes Dutch on the kebabs, declining even to pay for my skewer of chicken pieces, I don't react. Fuck the kebabs. I'm too busy thinking about Godwin and how to find him.

I remain entranced by an intention to solve the Godwin puzzle, a puzzle I did not fully contemplate when Geoff was the sole proprietor, so to speak, of Godwin's promise. But Godwin is mine now. The strength of the trance is such that, when Mourad drives Geoff and me and my suitcase to his home, which is on the fourth floor of a tower in what looks like a public housing project, and I am informed that the second bedroom is occupied by Mourad's sleeping mother and that Geoff, as the disabled party, has first use of the couch in the living room, and that it is my lot to crash on one of the two armchairs, I am fine with the arrangement. I'm not planning on sleeping. Maniacal experience teaches that the nighttime insights are the most creative. Sushila's window of communication is open, but I don't use it. You could say that I am in a state of disassociation – separating myself from my petty personal situation, with all its profitless distractions, and entering a private kingdom of consciousness. To be emphatic, I have no concrete thoughts as such. I am opening up my faculties of intuition. For the first time in a long time, the premonition of a breakthrough is upon me.

Wearing my shoes and coat, because it is cold in that apartment, resting my feet on my suitcase, I fall very quickly asleep.

It is just before seven when I wake up, and still very dark out. Geoff sleeps. No sound or light comes out of Mourad's bedroom. A light is on in the kitchen.

It is Mourad's mother, I presume. This tiny woman has braved the darkened living room and its pair of sleeping giants and is brewing something in a small copper vessel. There is something folkloric about her presence, attired as she is in a wrinkled cotton gown, a patterned white shawl and a bright, loosely worn kerchief from which unruly orange hair sticks out. I take off my jacket and my shoes and go to introduce myself.

'Mark,' I say, my hand on my sternum. 'The brother of Geoff.'

She smiles and offers me a cup of Turkish coffee. She has a cup of her own, and we sit down together at the small kitchen table. The coffee is lightly sweetened and delicious. I finish it quickly, leaving only a fragrant sludge. For the first time since I left home, I feel rested and refreshed. The euphoria is still upon me.

When the lady has finished her coffee, she demonstratively swirls the residue and turns the cup upside down onto its saucer. I follow her example with my own cup. She goes to a chopping board and swiftly bisects two small cucumbers lengthwise and serves them to me with flatbread and chunks of canned tuna. With a pleasant sound of knife on wood, she begins dicing tomatoes. So efficient and bewitching are her movements, so absolute is her self-possession, that I am mildly hypnotized. When she rejoins me at the table, the hypnosis persists. She turns up my coffee cup and examines the marks left by the coffee grinds. With her pinkie she points at some pattern. '*Voyage*,' she says in French, and after that she loses me. I do understand that she is telling my fortune.

Mourad, in his underwear, pulls up the third stool at the breakfast table and lights a cigarette.

Mourad's mother tells me in Arabic, with Mourad interpreting, that a trip is imminent. A stranger will enter the picture. I am to meet with dangers – her crooked finger hovers and trembles over the pertinent coffee stain – and with rewards.

Mourad extinguishes his cigarette on my saucer. 'Always the same story. Always the voyage.'

Before the fortune-teller can continue, a moan sounds from the living room. It's Geoff, adjusting his body and going back to sleep.

It comes to me how I will find Godwin.

I ask Mourad if he could call me a car. He is happy to, although the telephone conversation he has with the dispatcher is inexplicably contentious. Ten minutes later, a car waits for me outside. Geoff is still sleeping.

I don't wake him. My reunion with my brother is over. Geoff said so himself. His focus is on Mauritania. I am free to go.

'The Eiffel Tower,' I tell the driver. I figure that en route I will have plenty of time to book a place on Airbnb and finalize a true destination. This I do. When I inform the driver that there's a change of plan and we'll be heading to an address in the Quinze-Vingts district, wherever that is, I realize that I'm talking to the same skinny dude who picked me up the night before, Djibril, and that I'm back in his ancient Renault Safrane. There are Kleenexes on the floor of the car that I don't remember. As we wait in traffic, I see that Djibril has nodded off. I touch his shoulder. 'Yo, Djibril.' His eyes open. 'Wake up, man,' I say. 'You want coffee? *Café*?' He gives no response, not even a sign that he has heard me. I hand him my phone, and for several seconds he stares at the address on the screen. He hands the phone back and turns on the radio. I want to spend the journey getting some shut-eye, but instead I'm forced to monitor Djibril, because he keeps shutting *his* eyes. It sounds insane, but the guy is trying both to sleep and to drive.

We pull up at the Airbnb apartment building shortly before ten o'clock – too soon for me to take possession of the rental, which isn't available until 2:00 p.m. 'Seventy euros,' Djibril says, suddenly bilingual.

'Seventy? Yesterday it was fifty.'

He refuses my credit card. It doesn't matter. We drive to an ATM. Then Djibril departs from my life.

I find a café with Wi-Fi that tolerates my presence, suitcase and backpack and all. I order a double espresso and open my laptop in a state of great alertness and anticipation. I open the Godwin video file.

My breakthrough is simple: I will geolocate the stadium where Godwin was filmed – a sizable rural stadium with a backdrop of hills. Geoff obviously doesn't have the know-how to do it himself, and is too secretive, or cheap, to ask someone else do it for him. Like so many breakthroughs, mine is retrospectively obvious. Why didn't it occur to me earlier? Because I was tired, and because Godwin was not yet all mine.

•

But Africa is big and my knowledge of it is small. Where do I start?

According to Geoff, Godwin is probably from West Africa; and according to Lefebvre (to be precise, according to my interpretation of the facial expressions he wore while he viewed the Godwin footage), he is probably somewhere in Togo. Where is Togo?

Online, I find a physical map of Africa derived from cameras photographing Earth from space. Countries and their borders are identified only in very faint print, on a landmass that appears in shades of green and yellow and brown. The colors denote elevations, but I cannot help misinterpreting the yellow and green areas as congruent with certain deserts and jungles of my imagination. I have always been susceptible to the spell of maps, and I came of age academically when 'mapping' was a cool thing and every second grad student was making a choropleth map that revealed the hidden distribution of something – sunflowers, divorces, kidney disease, lawnmowers, anger, country-music listeners. It was the dawn of modern data; newly collectible factual jewels were strewn everywhere.

I'm taken aback: I truly know jack shit about the political geography of this continent. As I visually roam, meeting with one surprise after another, I feel a nonsensical and shameful thrill of discovery. There is a country I've never heard of called South Sudan. Apparently, Niger is huge, the size of two Texases. Angola is for some reason on the Atlantic Seaboard and not on the Pacific. Cameroon seems to have doubled its area and migrated a long way south. Geoff's new favorite place, Mauritania, is roughly where I expected to find it – but who knew that it encloses a coastal territory named Western Sahara?

And there it is – Togo.

The name designates a slender, vertical country hidden among a cluster of states on the Gulf of Guinea. This region of West Africa is lined with countless rivers and appears on the map in dark lowland green. That's not promising: there are highlands in the Godwin video. I zoom in a bit – and from out of the green materializes a pale-brown sierra. It runs along Togo's border with Ghana, then swerves northeastward, growing less marked as it declines and fragments. I'm looking at the Togo Mountains.

I very easily find a list of Togo's principal stadiums. Most are situated in Lomé, the capital. I rule them out right away: Lomé is a low-lying port city, whereas I'm looking for a stadium in a provincial hilly place. At most a dozen stadiums (a quarter-hour of research reveals) meet these criteria.

I'm interrupted by the ringtone of my WhatsApp.

It's Sushila. This surprises me. It's five-thirty in the morning in Pittsburgh. The window of communication – or 'WOC', as I have started to think of it – is to my mind shut. But I am delighted. I want to tell her about my breakthrough.

'Breakthrough? What are you talking about?'

'In the Godwin case,' I say. 'I've got a lead.'

'What Godwin case? Who's Godwin?'

Have I not told her about Godwin? How is that possible? 'Godwin,' I tell her, 'is one of the most valuable soccer talents in Africa. Maybe in the world. He's somewhere in West Africa, probably. Nobody knows exactly where. There's a secret video. It's a long story. It's why Geoff wanted my help – to track him down. Geoff is going to focus on Mauritania now, so finding the kid is my job. Nobody else has the video. The coast is clear. It's just a question of geolocating him from the footage. That's something I can do and guys like Geoff can't do. It's where I have an edge.'

Sushila pauses. She says, 'Mark, where are you?'

I tell her.

'And where's Geoff?'

I explain to Sushila that the Geoff thing has run its course. 'I'm off the hook. I'm a free agent. How's the Fizz? God, I miss you guys.'

That is true. I miss my girls. I miss my home. I am uncomfortable and lonely and filled with loathing for my surroundings. But I've had a breakthrough.

Sushila says, 'Sweetie, I'm confused. You're coming home Thursday, right?'

'Right,' I say. 'That's the plan.'

'What do you mean, "the plan"? What is there to plan? Is there another plan?'

I say, 'I'm going to the airport Thursday and I'm getting on a plane. That's what's going to happen. Wait, is that Fizzy?' I've heard a familiar darling cry. 'Let me talk to her.'

But Fizzy is too sleepy to talk. Sushila has to drop our call and get going on the morning routine of breakfast making and lunchbox prepping and toy fetching and toilette managing that she bravely undertakes early every morning on behalf of our daughter before taking her to the day care and driving to work. What a woman! I overflow with renewed awe of my wife. I had no clue, when I was first drawn to her, that on top of everything else Sushila would turn out to be a maestro of the domestic. I was in the dark about a lot of things, even if in my own mind I had seen through the world. Only recently has it occurred to me that it was precisely Sushila's opaque qualities, which were of course connected to her Sri Lankan origins, that led me to feel a unique curiosity about this straightforwardly beautiful and thoughtful woman whose apolitical disposition would normally have put me off. To my eyes, every woman of my supposed kind, which is to say an American white descended from American whites, suffered from a fatal transparency. Carol or Karen or Sophie might be smart and hot and attractively quirky, but they were like glasses of tap water. Gazing into their eyes, I could see right into their parents' home in some suburb or apartment building or mountain town, could imagine myself trapped by all-too-familiar conversations and hikes and uncles and points of view and breakfasts and jokes and carports. It filled me, I can say without exaggeration, with horror. This was unjust to all concerned, of course; but surely everyone is entitled to romantic biases.

I have a theory about where my bias came from, namely, the structural disappointment of a broken American upbringing in which my father and I, fending for ourselves, treated our home as if it were a continuation of Dad's station wagon, which served as a warehouse for kaput tennis rackets, used food receptacles, old sweaters and family silences – the station wagon that never transported me anywhere I wanted to go. As an adolescent, I distinctly associated this disarray with the mass of white American families in which my father and I were situated, families conditioned and marooned by the same TV shows and equipped, with predictable variants, with the same instincts about the world. Sushila was American-born, too – from Staten Island, no less, and the product of Pittsburgh public schools and Penn State – but to me she emerged from an alluring global gloom. It's embarrassing to think about this stuff. It amazes me that Sushila, who presumably noticed that I was a white fool, somehow fell in love with me. It must be said: she has never wanted to hear much about my misgivings about my childhood. She views the concept of the unsatisfactory childhood (if I may put words in her mouth) as an American neurosis. She doesn't partake (not that she would put it this way) in the indigenous pastime of self-pity and parental resentment. Sushila and her family always struck me as practical, kinetic, somehow nautical. They were immigrants, engaged in an adventure. There was something brave and important about them.

She worked, then as now, for the Allegheny County Health Department. We met because the ACHD was planning a Community Health Assessment – a huge administrative undertaking – and was accepting bids from data-management companies. Among the bidders was a Group client for which I'd already successfully written a grant, and the client asked me to help them with their bid document for the ACHD contract. When the bid succeeded, the client threw a cheap little party to which some ACHD folks were invited. I didn't receive an invitation as such, but I still cycled over to the restaurant. I was in a terrible, volatile mood. My intention wasn't to participate in a crappy corporate celebration but to talk to the client's asshole CEO, this dude Jason, who was trying to stiff me out of my success bonus, which should have been no less than fourteen thousand dollars, the biggest payday of my life, as per our contract for the first grant application, the terms of which obviously remained applicable, under the course-of-dealing doctrine, to my very similar subsequent work on the ACHD bid, for which we'd signed no separate contract. To look at it another way, Jason's position was that, for two weeks' work instrumental in his company's grossing a million and change, I should be compensated two thousand dollars plus a thousand-dollar bonus. Fuck that shit. In a downpour, I bicycled uphill and downhill. I arrived soaked, but I didn't care. I strode into the tapas restaurant like the Count of Monte Cristo.

Retribution isn't easy. It requires planning and follow-through. When I saw Jason, he slapped me on the back and shouted, 'Get this man a drink.' I found myself accepting a glass of wine and a dish of patatas bravas.

'Can I have one of those?' a woman asked me.

That was Sushila.

To repeat, my objective is to find the stadium in the Godwin video. If I had the budget of a government or a corporation, I could pay someone to hover satellites over Togo and to collect and analyze the relevant images. But I'm a guy in a coffee shop with a five-thousand-dollar credit card limit.

What I have to work with is, first, my list of stadiums in or near hilly parts of Togo; second, photographic aerial views of Togo available to anyone with access to the internet; and, third – my ace in the hole – a tool that I own, or to be precise have downloaded, as a consequence of writing a grant for an outfit in Colorado that had created a remote sensing technology that they named 'Roald', in honor of Roald Amundsen. Basically, Roald technology offers LiDAR surveying with some cool features. Crucially, for my purposes, it enables the user to efficiently view orthorectified three-dimensional models of topographic features anywhere on the planet. Google Street View also offers interactive panoramas, but it doesn't function in Lomé, let alone upcountry Togo. With Roald you get an aerial map of anywhere on the planet; you zoom in; and you get a rotating ground-level rendering of the physical lie of the land. My plan is to locate the Godwin stadium by matching the uplands that loom behind it with the uplands I see on Roald. In theory, the process is simple. You trace the ridge line visible on Roald – I know how to do that – and you compare it to the ridge lines in the Godwin video. When you find a match – bingo.

The challenge is a practical one. Even if I limit myself to a dozen stadiums, there are a lot of hills and a lot of ridge formations out there. One man examining all of them on one computer will take time. I must get moving. I must track down Godwin before I catch my plane home on Thursday.

There is a print shop near the café. I print colored still images from the Godwin videos that best capture the stadium and its surroundings. I print a still of Godwin. I print detailed physical and political maps of Togo. Then I buy Swiss cheese, bread, Rice Krispies, milk, instant coffee, a bag of sugar, a six-pack of beer and a jar of pimiento-stuffed green olives – exactly what I would stock up on in the old days when getting ready for an all-nighter. I buy a notepad and a pack of ballpoint pens and Scotch Tape and yellow and blue Post-it Notes. Then I go to my Airbnb abode.

It's a third-floor walk-up studio with a kitchenette, a desk, an armchair and a single window that overlooks the street: perfect for my needs. I attach printouts and Post-it Notes to the bare wall above the desk. A visitor might conclude that I am either a serial killer or someone hunting a serial killer. I remove my sweater, make myself a coffee, and roll up the sleeves of my white shirt. I am anticipating forty-eight hours of nonstop geospatial exploration. Ecstatically, I fire up Roald. Togo, here I come!

It takes me just under one hour to figure out that Godwin has not been filmed at any of the stadiums on my list.

He was not filmed at the Stade Maman N'Danida in Tchamba, or at the Stade Municipal in Kara, or at Stade Municipal in Sokodé, or at Guanha Usdao Pesihu, the home ground of the team known as Ifodje Atakpamé, or at the stadium of Gomido football club in Kpalimé, or at the Stade de Bassar, where Gbikinti FC play, or at Sara Sport's stadium in Bafilo. Not one of these stadiums visually matches the stadium I'm looking for. I didn't need to pull an all-nighter with Roald to figure that out. All it took was a basic Google image search. I feel stupid.

But how stupid can I be? I'm in possession of an actionable world-exclusive video of an athlete with potential career earnings in the hundreds of millions. His representatives would make millions every year. True, I don't know much about the soccer business; but, with all due respect, if someone like Geoff is the competition, how hard can the business be? I can outsmart these people. If and when I need specialized advice, I'll hire specialists – lawyers, image-rights people, subagents. Why would I turn my back on such an opportunity? It's true that becoming a millionaire is something I've never seriously contemplated and in fact have always held in contempt. Money and greed for money are the sources of almost all evil. For years I challenged capitalism; for years I turned my back on personal gain. I've paid my dues, you could say. And I have a family to support. My financial obligations are as real as the next guy's. I have as much right as anyone to a measure of material prosperity – a greater right, arguably, because I would be a conscientious and charitable custodian of my wealth who could be counted on to pay my fair share of taxes.

Also: this kid, Godwin, needs the help of an honest person like me. There are sharks out there. Also: I am at the peak of my powers. It's my time.

I take another look at the map. Many towns – Dapaong and Sotouboua and Mango and Anié and others – are situated within sight of mountains. Any one might have the Godwin stadium. Togo is a small, finite place. I will survey every settlement of note. It is simply a question of systematic perseverance. I make myself another cheese sandwich and crack open my first beer.

Using satellite images and moving from north to south, I swoop down on one place after another. They are clustered like mussels around a single main road, and I am able to determine very quickly the presence or absence of a synthetic-turf soccer field. By midnight, there isn't a community of note that I have not surveyed, in vain.

Could it be that I misread Lefebvre's face? Could it be that Godwin is not the Lomé boy?

I'm not giving up. I'm on my fourth beer and fifth cheese sandwich and more intent than ever. I begin, less systematically but just as single-mindedly, to image-search Togolese soccer teams. I'm looking for the uniform worn by Godwin's team. This grips me for at least an hour. Then a terrifying scream sounds in the street below.

I rush to the window. A group of pedestrians are moving down the sidewalk. What I thought was a scream of horror was a case of laughter.

It's only two in the morning, but my stamina is no longer what it was. Helplessly, I fall asleep.

Early in the morning, I wake up on the bed with my clothes on. That's when I have my actual breakthrough.

It does not take the form of a brainwave. It happens by accident. I'm drowsily eating a bowl of Rice Krispies and navigating with Google Maps like an automaton. The cursor, adrift above the northern extremity of the Togo Mountains, floats toward a name, Natitingou, that I don't remember from the night before. Still eating, I zoom in – and there, right next to the town's main road, is a *stade municipal* containing the dark-green rectangle of a soccer field. Without excitement, I perform an image search for the Natitingou stadium. It produces a picture of a soccer team lined up for a portrait. In the background is a familiar outline of hills. Some trees at the edge of the picture are also familiar. And there's a utility building at the corner of the field that is unmistakable. I have seen this place before. It's where Godwin was filmed.

I fix myself a coffee and write myself a one-word memo: Natitingou. Then I notice something else. Natitingou isn't in Togo. In my tiredness I failed to see that the cursor had crossed the border. Godwin is in Benin.

Who should choose that very instant to call me? Geoff, of course.

Do I answer the call and tell him I've found Godwin? Do I hell. I sit back in my chair, rest my bare feet on the desk, raise my arms in triumph, make two fists, and give the world the double curse finger. The content of my emotions surprises me a little: an obscure, elated sense of vengeance. Exactly what wrong I am avenging is unclear. It makes no difference. My day has come. Justice has been done.

Things keep breaking my way. Air France, I learn, has a nonstop service from Paris to Cotonou, the de facto Benin capital. A round-trip ticket costs less than eight hundred bucks. I can hop on a plane and be there in less than seven hours. The alternative is to take two flights back to western Pennsylvania and then turn around and fly back to West Africa, with stops in New York and Paris. That would be crazy. I will fly on Thursday, yes – but not from England to the United States. I will fly from France to Benin.

•

Sushila's phone call wakes me up.

'Hey,' she says. 'I was worried. You're not answering your texts.'

It's two in the afternoon – 8:00 a.m., Pittsburgh time. I must have fallen asleep. 'I was up late,' I say. 'There's something I need to tell you. It's kind of exciting.'

I explain that I have located Godwin in the north of Benin and that I am the only person in the world with this information.

'Apart from the people who know him, you mean,' she says.

'Well, yes. Apart from them.'

'Tell me you're not thinking of going there,' my wife says. 'Mark?'

'Well, it would make sense. Logistically, I mean. There's a direct flight from Paris to Cotonou. It's cheap, too, compared to the alternative.'

'Cotonou?'

'It's the capital of Benin. On the Gulf of Guinea,' I add authoritatively.

'Isn't there Ebola there?'

'No,' I say, getting excited. Rarely do I get to explain to my wife something about public health, which is her field. I tell her (repeating what I found out the night before, online) that the Ebola outbreak ravaging Liberia, Guinea and Sierra Leone has not yet affected Togo, let alone Benin. To travel, I would still need shots for cholera, yellow fever, rabies, meningitis, typhoid, hepatitis A and B, MMR, tetanus, diphtheria, chicken pox, shingles, pneumonia and influenza – micro-organic life in Africa is very alien and dangerous, evidently – but the good news is that the Air France international vaccination service not only accepts walk-ins but is hundreds of dollars cheaper than any vaccination service in New York. 'That's what I'm trying to tell you. Things are falling into place.'

'What does Geoff say?' Sushila asks, against a background of traffic noise. She's stepped out of the house. Fizz will be holding her hand.

I tell her that Geoff has disclaimed his interest in Godwin and is concentrating on the Mauritanian market.

'You said that yesterday. I don't know what any of that means.'

'It's complicated,' I admit. 'All you need to know is, Geoff has opted out of this. The only thing I need to talk to Geoff about is my expenses.'

My brother owes me $2,243.46, the breakdown of which (including the applicable exchange rates) I sent him the night before, together with my P2P details and copies of supporting documentation. There is an exquisite pleasure to be had in drafting a good invoice.

The traffic sound grows louder. Sushila half shouts, 'Sweetie, I'm not saying that Geoff's not going to pay you, but you have to be ready to write that off. It's not important.' I can hear Fizzy's voice now. They're in the car. 'What I don't understand is what you're going to do once you've found him – Godwin. You're just going to ask him to come with you? Why would he do that? Does he have a passport? Is it legal to travel around the world with a minor? Where will he live? What would you be able to offer this player? Mark, you don't even watch soccer.'

If I've learned one thing from my brief immersion in the soccer world, I tell Sushila, it's that it's a very random business. Most random of all are the agents. Being a soccer agent isn't like being a surgeon or a CPA. Anyone can become one – dads, college dropouts, taxi drivers, dilettantes, rich kids, nerds. These guys aren't expert psychologists or lawyers or seasoned deal-makers. They're fakers and fantasists. Literally, a clown with a red nose could be a player's agent. 'Look at Geoff,' I say. 'I know he's my brother and all, but, babe, he's totally unbusinesslike.' ('Unbusinesslike' doesn't begin to describe it. He is a tornado of unreliability and superfluous scheming. I wouldn't trust him to fetch me a cup of coffee. He'd get the order wrong, or spill it, or drink half of it.) 'If he can be an agent, so can I. Except that I'd be professional and ethical. That's what I have to offer – ethics and professionalism. And the ability to do math and write a grammatical sentence.'

'So that's it? You're going to be a soccer agent now?'

'It's not about having a new career. It's about pursuing a once-in-a-lifetime opportunity.'

'I don't know what that means,' she says. 'Opportunity to do what?'

'To do what?' The question throws me. Do I have to spell it out? Do I have to explain the concept of the bonanza?

Sushila laughs very loudly.

'What's so funny?'

'What language will you use?'

'What language?'

'Yes. With Godwin. What happens when he asks you for an apple?' Before I can respond Sushila continues, 'OK, I've got to head off now. I'll call you later. And charge your phone!' There's that laughter again.

What language will I use? Does nobody in Africa speak English? Babe, I think-speak to a phantasmal Sushila, get real. Since the beginning of time, traders have not let language barriers stop them. Money is a language. Soccer is also a language. People will make it their business to communicate with me.

Or is she saying that I shouldn't go ahead because it would be wrong?

Pacing the tiny apartment, I begin to mutter to myself. Does she know me at all? Does she think I'm the kind of guy who'd malevolently exploit this kid? Who am I, King Leopold of the Belgians? No! – as she well knows. It can only be that I stand accused of some unconscious crime. A soft, bitter sound comes out of my mouth. What does she think – that I'm not aware of the history of the world? I'm the one, not Sushila, who owns a copy of *The Wretched of the Earth*. Benin is one of the world's poorest countries. Half of its population lives off less than two bucks a day. What's the ethical idea here – that I should leave Godwin alone so that he can enjoy an authentic life of poverty? What gives Sushila the right to make that call?

And yet what she said, about the practical difficulties that lie ahead, gives me pause. What Sushila says always gives me pause. Her ability to evaluate what is happening in a real-world, real-time situation has never not been superior to mine.

I make myself an instant coffee and meditatively drink it by the window. It is a gray afternoon made still grayer by the modern apartment building across the street, which has a gray frontage and small black windows.

It comes to me clearly that Sushila is right. I can't go to Africa. At least not alone. Because almost certainly that would not end well. That is all my wife is saying. She's not accusing me of neocolonialism. Sushila? She is the last person to point a political finger.

I am not without inner resources. I have the capacity to accept new information and respond adaptively. Calmly I contemplate the gray building across the street. I need to ascertain the logic of my situation, a process as emotional as it is rational. Very quickly, it feels – in fact, an hour has passed – a new course of action suggests itself to me.

I switch on the electric kettle, then call Geoff. My voice message is short: 'I've found him.'

•

Before the water has boiled, I am once again in the presence of my brother's voice.

'Fam, I knew you'd do it. I knew it.'

'Geoff,' I say, very steadily, 'I need you to pay me my expenses. I sent you all the paperwork. Let's call it twenty-five hundred, to cover me through Thursday. Then we'll be squared away.'

'Yeah, no worries. I told you, bruv, you're good, bruv, you're good. So where is he?'

'No expenses, no information,' I say. 'And there's one more thing.' I stipulate that I want a finder's fee of ten thousand dollars, payable up front, plus a 10 percent commission on Geoff's future income from the management of the player. I'll draft the agreement – all he has to do is sign it. I say, 'We can cap my commission, if you want. Let's say, at one million. That seems fair.'

Geoff laughs. 'Steady on, fam. One step at a time. If the information pans out, you'll get your end, no worries. It's a process, blud. The business is a process. Give me the information and, as I said, if it's worth something, if it produces a result, 'course I'll sort you out. It's like information leading to an arrest, blud. Man don't get the reward until the arrest. A finder's fee before man's been found? Nah, bruv, nah.'

'Geoff? Start with the expenses. Take care of those right away. Meanwhile, I'll draw up the contract for the finder's fee.'

'The expenses is separate, Markie. It's separate. Let's not complicate things.'

I keep quiet. I am very happy. I stir my coffee.

'You're playing me,' he says. 'You're playing me, bruv. How do I even know you got the goods?'

'Here's what needs to happen,' I say. 'You pay me my expenses now – twenty-five hundred. Electronically. It'll take two minutes. Then I'll meet you in London tomorrow. You bring a banker's check for ten thousand to the meeting, you sign the contract, and then I'll show you exactly where those videos were filmed. You'll see it with your own eyes. If you don't want to do that, I'll understand. Your focus is on Mauritania.'

'Fucking hell, Markie, I can't believe you're doing this to me. Godwin is mine. He's my asset. That film is mine. You're fucking ripping me off.'

'The clock's ticking, Geoff.'

'What's that supposed to mean, "the clock's ticking"?' What clock? Bruv, you're my brother. We don't do clocks.'

'You got half an hour to pay my expenses, Geoff. It's very easy.'

I hang up with a feeling of intense gladness and excitement. My days of being pushed around are over. I have stood my ground. I have slapped the hidden face of injustice.

I have never slapped a physical face. It would haunt me if I had.

I step out and eat hungrily at a Burger King – a stroke of luck, in Paris, to find one nearby! When I return, I check my online banking page. There's no sign of any payment of my expenses. It's what I expected. But something else surprises me: a higher-than-anticipated new charge of $214 at the Holiday Inn, Walsall. I booked a room there for myself for one night at just over $70. When I call the hotel for an explanation, they tell me that the room was occupied for a second night, with my credit card still on file. The bill also includes charges for room service, mini-fridge items and sundries.

Geoff! There's no point getting angry about it. I send him a copy of the incurred charge and an amended invoice.

When he calls, I don't answer. He leaves a message. 'Listen, Markie, we got off on the wrong foot there. It's all been a bit less than ideal, fam, I know that, and big-up to you for finding God-win. I don't blame you for asking for payment. 'Course you'll get it. Guaranteed. So come to London and we'll sort it all out. All right? Love you, bruv.'

Will Geoff repay me? Not one cent. He doesn't have the

money; and even if he did, even if I delivered Godwin to him on a silver platter, he'd still find some reason to stiff me out of my train fares and hotel bills and per diems. That's just who he is – a guy who will stiff his own brother without thinking twice about it. He is his mother's son.

There is no point meeting him in London. I take the next logical step.

Jean-Luc Lefebvre is of the old school: he answers his phone. I tell him that I'm in Paris and have located the player he saw on the video and am willing to let him have the information on an exclusive basis.

'I will discuss, but on one condition.' He speaks in a low, growling, almost threatening voice, like a kidnapper. 'We meet here, at my house.'

It's 130 miles to Le Mans. 'No deal,' I say. 'We meet here. And it must be tonight. I leave for London tomorrow. Also, bring five thousand dollars.'

I have never had this kind of power before. It is glorious. Three hours later, Lefebvre is at my door.

My room has two chairs – an armchair and a desk chair. Lefebvre, sweating, takes the armchair. He is wearing a navy blazer with a white shirt and gray pants. His cheeks appear to be covered by red hatching. When he removes his jacket, pale-green patches of armpit sweat show on his shirt. A mysterious, mildly unpleasant smell clings to him. I give him a beer.

He reaches inside his jacket and flashes a bulging brown envelope. 'But, first, you will show me.'

I sit down at the desk. 'One thing at a time,' I say. I hand him a one-page document headed 'JOINT VENTURE AGREEMENT'.

Lefebvre puts on his reading glasses. 'Ah, his name is Godwin.' He reads on slowly. When he is done, he hands me back the document. 'You want to go into business with me? I don't know you.'

'You know me,' I tell him. 'I'm the guy who knows where Godwin is.'

Lefebvre looks me in the eye. 'Who I am, I know. I am the professional – the man of football. Who you are, I don't know. You are not a man of football. You are an American.'

'I'm a businessman,' I say. For the second time, I give him the joint venture agreement.

'Contracts I don't like,' Lefebvre says. 'I like the shake of the hand.'

'This contract isn't complicated,' I say. 'And it's fair.' I'm not lying. The agreement provides, first, that Lefebvre will pay me five thousand dollars in return for receiving accurate and exclusive information about Godwin's location in the video. Second, that Lefebvre and I will form a joint venture partnership for the purpose of managing Godwin's sporting and commercial interests. Gross proceeds will be split fifty-fifty, as will expenditures approved by both parties. That's it.

'What about your brother?'

'He is busy with other things. This is my project now. He doesn't know where Godwin is. Only I know.'

Lefebvre is inspecting me even more closely. Again, I detect his personal smell. 'I will sign the contract. But even more important, I will accept your word of honor.' He places his battered oxblood briefcase on his lap. It opens with a thud of springs and locks. From its interior he extracts a ballpoint pen. He takes up the contract document and writes his signature beneath mine. He does the same on the copy.

'Thank you,' I say. 'Now we're partners.'

Without delay I play him the video.

'See this? And this?' I'm drawing his attention to certain features of the stadium. I'm also opening a Google Maps window. To fool with him a little, I go first to Togo. Starting on the coastline, I slowly move northward. Then I go eastward, across the border.

Lefebvre rests his bottle on his briefcase, which is densely marked with the rings of bygone bottles.

I zoom in on Natitingou. I demonstrate that the Natitingou stadium is where Godwin was filmed. 'This is the place,' I said.

'Yes,' Lefebvre says, 'this is the place.' He mutters, 'Benin. Of course.'

'Why "of course"?'

Lefebvre takes a cheroot from his briefcase. He lights the cheroot with a pink plastic lighter.

'Dude, no smoking. It's not my apartment.'

Lefebvre blows out a smoke cloud of extraordinary proportions. Professional football in Benin, he declares, has collapsed. The Benin *championnat* has been abandoned for this season, 2014–15, and next year the same will probably happen again. It is a problem of corruption, a problem of politics. This is very sad. There used to be a good academy in Cotonou, but it closed four years before. In this moment there is nowhere for a young talent such as Godwin to play, there is no possibility to show his qualities. 'If Godwin is from Togo, he is already playing in France. If he is Nigerian, he is already famous, maybe already playing for the Super Eagles. Lucky for us, he is in Benin.'

'Why isn't he playing for team Benin?'

'My friend, listen to what I say. Benin is a black hole of football. There is no national team. I told you this. The Squirrels do not function.'

'The squirrels?'

African national teams are known by their sobriquets – the Indomitable Lions, the Black Stars, the Super Eagles. The Squirrels are the Benin team. How, Lefebvre asks, did I find Godwin?

I tell him that I examined every stadium in Togo first, then started on Benin. I'm not going to tell him that I looked at Benin accidentally, out of sheer drowsiness.

'Togo?' He seems astonished. 'You think Godwin is the boy that I saw in Lomé?'

'He's not?'

Now I'm astonished. I was certain that Lefebvre had recognized Godwin in Le Mans, that Godwin and the Lomé boy were one and the same. It was purely because of this misconception that I started my search in Togo. I found Godwin by fluke.

Lefebvre makes a sudden movement. I find myself catching a brown envelope.

The envelope contains euros, not dollars. 'Count', Lefebvre says.

After I've counted four thousand three hundred euros, I put the envelope in the desk drawer along with the contract. Lefebvre accepts my hand with his own – damp, soft, red – hand.

•

Toasts and toastmasters are not my thing, but I raise my bottle and declare: 'To Godwin.' I embrace this cliché because the meeting with Lefebvre has progressed in conformity with every fantasy of how a business meeting should go – has conformed, no less, with certain advertisements about how one's life should go.

Lefebvre doesn't reciprocate. 'We must begin now the work. There is no time to lose.'

Something about the light in the room has changed. It is Lefebvre's face, I realize. He has leaned forward into the light of the desk lamp, and his cheeks and nose and brow, previously reddish and dull, now shine ceramically. He says, 'I must go to Benin immediately.'

'*We* must go, you mean.'

The light changes once more as Lefebvre leans back. 'You know Benin?'

'I've never been to Africa,' I tell him – boldly, unapologetically. What does it matter? I've never been to a lot of places.

'Africa? There is no Africa. There is only water or no water, road or no road, hotel or no hotel, language or no language. There is only difficulties and solutions. You, my friend – you will be a difficulty.'

'We have a partnership,' I say, going to the kitchenette. 'I'm going with you.'

'This is not the moment for tourism, my friend,' says Lefebvre. 'You have a wife. You have a child, no? You will leave this to me. You will give me your confidence.' He accepts the saucer I hand him to use as an ashtray. 'Think, my friend. This is an opportunity that comes once in life. We have been lucky. Now we must be professional.'

'How good is Godwin?' I ask the question with a delicious light-headedness. 'Compared to the talent you normally see.'

Lefebvre drinks deeply from his beer bottle. 'To the normal talent, I cannot compare.' Just weeks ago, he says, Real Madrid signed a fifteen-year-old Norwegian named Ødegaard, who has already played for the Norway national team. Lefebvre has not yet seen this boy in action. But it is Lefebvre's expectation that Godwin will be at the level of Ødegaard.

'How about compared to other great soccer players? How about Maradona?'

Lefebvre smirks. 'Maradona the American knows.' Lefebvre first saw him, the god of the round ball, in 1979, when Maradona was eighteen, a little older than Godwin. But Maradona was not playing in Benin. He was playing in Rome, for Argentina against Italy. Therefore, it is impossible to compare. 'Will Godwin become an important player? We cannot know, just as we cannot know if Ødegaard will reach the top. He is young. He must still have evolution. Football is not predictable; life is not predictable. But this one, Godwin, he surprises me. I am not someone that can be very much surprised, my friend. This one makes movements, makes passes, that I do not see in advance. If you watch, you see how he wants the ball, how his teammates always give, give, give him the ball, how he decides the tempo of play. He is like a conductor. He is teaching them how to play. He is teaching me! This is very rare, my friend.' Lefebvre contemplates his cheroot. 'You want to know what I think? You want the truth? I think he is the Black Diamond.'

'Dude,' I say, 'you can't call him that.' I open a window. Cheroot smoke goes out, freezing air comes in.

Lefebvre points at me. 'You – you see only the goals. Not I. I see everything. I analyze all the players – how they move, what their quality is, what their fitness is. I ask myself what it means, that Godwin dominates them. Let me show you.' He joins me at the desk. 'Fast-forward,' he instructs. I do as he asks. 'Now stop. Play here.'

We are watching a passage of play that my brother did not bring to my attention. Godwin receives the ball in defense, facing his own goal while opposition players surround him. From this difficult situation he somehow turns a full circle with the ball at his feet, his opponents centrifugally stumbling in his wake, and then accelerates out of the ruck without seeming to run hard. Lefebvre pauses the video. 'This movement, it is not something you learn on the training ground. It is learned in the streets, it is learned in nature.' The video resumes. Godwin passes to a lone striker, accepts a return pass, then runs forward, drawing the last two defenders to him, before setting up the same striker, now unmarked, with a tap-in goal. Lefebvre stops the video. 'It's not difficult to recognize a genius. Everyone can recognize it, even you. But in order to recognize, you must believe your eyes. You must accept the evidence. The older you are, the more difficult that is.'

In his whole career, Lefebvre says, returning to the one armchair in the room, he was offered only one youth who came close to Godwin. In 2002, he received a phone call from an Austrian trainer named Hofer. Hofer was in Iceland.

Iceland these days is a world leader in the maximization of young footballing talent. Its superb indoor facilities enable boys and girls to play year-round under the guidance of coaches certified by UEFA, and in recent years this country of only three hundred thousand souls has fallen under the spell, in a manner of speaking, Lefebvre says, of football. When Hofer was there, this transformation had not yet occurred. It was precisely in order to train and certify Icelandic coaches that Hofer had gone to this land of volcanoes, an assignment that led to a job as the trainer of a second-division Icelandic team. It was a part-time position. Hofer, aged sixty-six, combined it with informal work as a housepainter. Iceland is an extensive yet sparsely populated country, Lefebvre says, and as a consequence it is not uncommon for Icelanders to hold two jobs; indeed, one of the two coaches of the national team works as a dentist. The labor of Iceland is also unusual, Lefebvre observes, in that you see women on the roadwork crews doing the same work as the men. Evidently, the hostile, in many ways inhuman, environment has blurred the natural difference between man and woman.

When Hofer called him, Lefebvre goes on, ignoring my attempt to interject, Lefebvre had a general scouting mandate from Schalke 04, the famous Gelsenkirchen club. Out of respect for Hofer's knowledge, Schalke authorized Lefebvre to fly to the north. Hofer had been a successful coach in his time, a trusted assistant of the great Ernst Happel, no less. 'Of course, you have no idea who Ernst Happel is,' Lefebvre says.

Hofer drove Lefebvre, who had never visited Iceland, from Reykjavík to Flúðir, a village about one hundred kilometers to the north of the capital. Very little was said in the car. From Hofer Lefebvre learned that the village was famous for its cultivation of gigantic edible mushrooms, but otherwise the drive was spent in silence. Lefebvre was grateful. He was not a man for sightseeing. On the contrary, he had long since exhausted his curiosity about the places where his work took him. Deserts, forests, mountains, ghettos, suburbs, yams, herrings – he had reached the stage where they were all the same to him. Indeed, it was vital to suppress irrelevant sentiments that could interfere with professional judgment. Whether a player is rich or poor, unknown or well known, deserving or undeserving, happy or unhappy, all such matters have to be put to one side. The only thing that matters is to see the football as clearly as possible. Elite football is a business without mercy. It is a zone of objectivity. It is not a zone of sympathy, of equality. There is no room on the football field for the deserving case. A scout must wear blinders, like a horse. And yet in Iceland Lefebvre could not help being impressed by the desolate and unearthly countryside, which resembled nothing he had seen on his many travels, not even in the wilderness of Kazakhstan, and he wondered how the Icelanders of old had managed to survive in a place of ice and wind and lava fields, a place where the meagerest pine tree struggled to grow. But a surprise lay in store. When he came to the village of Flúðir, he saw that it was situated in an exceptionally lush little corner of the country, in a valley that could have belonged to some other nation. Hofer stopped at a football field with intensely green grass and brilliant white goalposts. It was one of the most beautiful fields of football Lefebvre had ever seen, a field that you might encounter in a dream. He was instantly aware of the danger of the charismatic. His mission, as always, was strictly technical: to determine whether a young player named Gabriel Kettilson possessed the characteristics needed for a top-level club like Schalke. Hofer had said little about the boy. He had just said, You need to come. Lefebvre took this as a good sign. Hofer, like Lefebvre, belonged to a generation for whom the less that was said about a player the better. It was no coincidence that Hofer had gotten along so well with Ernst Happel, a man so averse to speech that even during training he would communicate chiefly by grunting, moving his eyes and signaling with his hands, one of which inevitably held a Belga cigarette. This method was in part due to language difficulties: Happel, an Austrian, spent most of his career training teams in Holland and Belgium, and on the rare occasion when he spoke he used an incomprehensible cocktail, of his own invention, of Dutch and German. Even when he spoke German, employing an Austrian version of that language, German players couldn't understand him.

'OK,' I say.

Happel exactly resembled, Lefebvre recalls with a smile, Beethoven. A big block of a head, terrible eyebrows. The players feared him – feared his gaze. He was a moody, brooding, difficult man, a man who had been on the Eastern Front, a man who had been captured by the Americans and escaped. When he entered a room, there would be silence. But what courage he had. As a boy, he refused to sing the Nazi team songs that Rapid Vienna youth players were expected to sing, a refusal that led to his expulsion from the group. Do you think, Lefebvre asks me, that Happel's footballers detected this spirit? They detected. Always his teams fought for him, always he inspired loyalty. Lefebvre will never forget Happel's funeral, which took place on a bright, cold November afternoon, in Vienna. The President of Austria was there; Der Kaiser, Franz Beckenbauer, was there; the clubs that Happel had served so well – Feyenoord, FC Den Haag, Hamburg and others – were represented. But most numerous were wreaths adorned with the blue-and-black ribbons of Club Brugge, which Happel had somehow led to the final of the European Cup itself.

In brief, Lefebvre resumes, Gabriel Kettilson was indeed exceptional – a twelve-year-old whose extraordinary physical and technical qualities allowed him, like an adolescent superman, to control the match even though he was playing with older, bigger boys. Before ten minutes had passed, Lefebvre turned to Hofer and nodded. The boy Kettilson had met with his approval. Hofer smiled. It was a great moment, an unforgettable moment.

What a feeling it is to behold such a marvel, a feeling maybe comparable to that of the man with the metal detector who digs up treasure, a feeling in which elation is combined with a fear of what must be done next, to secure the treasure.

Everyone involved in football, Lefebvre intones, is secretly a scout – the managers, the spectators, the referees, the players themselves. All are implicated in the search for the great player, the future vedette. It is a quest that excludes nobody – the discovery of the immortal one. About Eusébio it was said – by José Mourinho, no less – that he would never die. The parent who does not inspect the child in the hope of seeing the trace of the eternal, that parent does not exist.

The open question with any young talent, Lefebvre says, is whether he has the will, the hunger, to succeed. Without hunger there can be no evolution. All the greats have a strong, almost crazy hunger. No one has more hunger than African footballers. A boy like Godwin, who has no options outside of football, will have the maximum hunger, of this Lefebvre is certain. As in the case of Maradona, it is a choice between football or poverty. With Gabriel Kettilson, it was different. When Lefebvre went to see the parents and explained to them that Schalke, in those days a big force in the Bundesliga, wanted to register their son, they were polite but wary. Lefebvre called the Schalke manager, Huub Stevens. Stevens flew to Iceland in order to offer the Kettilsons every inducement and assurance permitted by the law. All their efforts were in vain. The boy did not want to become a professional player of football – which is to say, want it to the exclusion of everything else. His true passion was horses, the strange little horses of Iceland, famous for their unique ways of running and trotting, which the Kettilson family bred at their farm. 'Benin,' Lefebvre says wisely, 'is not a country of horses.'

Lefebvre gestures for another beer. I grant him his wish.

'What about football is memorable?' he asks. What stays in the mind? For fans, it is specific experiences – the goals, the drinks, the fights, the adventures in distant stadiums. But when football professionals look back on their careers, Lefebvre says, that is not what they dwell on. They always come back to the same topic:

the greats whose paths they crossed. Lefebvre recently had a drink with Youri Djorkaeff, a top, top pro who had won everything in the game, a world champion, a man who had earned his own nickname, the Serpent. Did Djorkaeff want to talk about the contracts he'd signed? No. Did he want to reminisce about the World Cup final? No. He wanted to talk about playing one-twos with Zinedine Zidane, about trying in vain to tackle Ronaldo. 'Not CR7,' Lefebvre, reading my thoughts, says sharply. 'Not Cristiano Ronaldo. The original Ronaldo – O Fenômeno. The Phenomenon.'

The Kettilson defeat was hard to swallow. Real talent was rare; talent that impressed Lefebvre, rarer still; an unknown talent of Kettilson's quality? Well, it was unprecedented in his personal experience. How had he failed? How had he not made the boy understand that the career of a football player is like the career of a dragonfly, that in the blink of an eye he would turn thirty-five, that very soon he would have all the time in the world to play with horses? The setback came at a bad time for Lefebvre. He had already been forced to give up on his true vocation, which was to coach players, and he was finding it harder to find employment as a scout on account of his age and his ever-shrinking network of personal connections. To be a scout is difficult, and Lefebvre, with his old-fashioned habits, made life even more difficult for himself. He refused to fill out the checklists and reports devised by the new powers – the sports scientists. These forms were, to Lefebvre's mind, a waste of time for someone like himself, who knew what he was looking for and understood that scouting was not about counting tackles and passes and touches on the ball. You drove, you stood by the touchline, you watched, you exercised your judgment, you made a phone call, you drove again. That was the work. What was Lefebvre looking for in a player? It was very simple to state: responsibility, fantasy and simplicity. Perceiving these qualities, however, was a much more difficult matter, a question of intuition, a question whose answer lay not only in the repeated observation of the player but in the recollection and application of thousands and thousands of hours spent watching football over many years and through different epochs of the game. It was a question of recognition, not a question of discovery.

Lefebvre's reputation, at that time, was mixed. Some thought he was too picky, too negative, that he overlooked players who would make viable professionals even if they did not have the capacities to perform at the highest level. The criticism was not completely unfair. It was true that he was not as interested as some in the identification of the future journeyman, the merely honest player, the player of limited potential who will competently play lower-division professional football. But others saw him, precisely because he was highly selective, because he did not permit his name to become attached to mediocre players, as a scout of integrity, a scout who could be trusted. If Lefebvre liked a player, you could be sure that the player was worthwhile. Huub Stevens would not have flown to Iceland on the say-so of another scout.

In short, Lefebvre had always held out for the important talent, the big fish – and now Kettilson, the biggest fish he had ever seen, had escaped him. Lefebvre had nothing to show for his integrity.

Of course, Lefebvre says with a smile, this was very stupid – this idea of his integrity. Your integrity, your high standards, your sacrifices, your renunciations – these are noticed only by yourself. Nobody else is keeping track. There was not one person in the world who was giving him credit for his negative decisions. Only the positive was visible, and then only briefly. The reputation that he had imagined for himself, as a man who was hard to please, simply did not exist. Nobody was thinking about Lefebvre, not even God.

•

My new business partner drinks from his bottle of beer, spilling some from his mouth onto his shirt. I have Googled Jean-Luc Lefebvre. His years in the soccer industry have left almost no trace. For all of his yarns, for all of his connections, he has never personally achieved anything of note – never won a trophy, never been a champion. He isn't even a has-been. His career, even at its most successful, was as a mere associate of more successful figures. Yes, he worked with Didier Drogba; but only before Drogba became a star. Now Lefebvre is at the end of his career. He's a washed-up man in his seventies. Godwin is his last throw of the dice. He cannot risk alienating me. I have him exactly where I want him.

Even though it's getting late, I open another bottle.

He says, 'You are thinking, Who is the old man?' He wags his finger as if to indicate that I should not deny it.

I don't deny it.

With a smile, Lefebvre asserts that he can read the visage of a man, that it is a skill he has been forced to develop over the years. What a man is thinking, how he is feeling – it is essential for a coach to answer such questions correctly. In my face he has seen skepticism, he has seen lack of respect. This is not intended as a criticism: I have every justification for skepticism, Lefebvre says. But he, Lefebvre, has the same justification. 'Let me tell you what I see,' he says, pointing at my face and peering down his finger. 'Confidence – true confidence – I do not see. Success, I do not see. What do I see? Only fear.'

He sits back, pleased with himself, sweating more heavily than ever. 'Yes, my friend,' he says. Loss of confidence, fear – perhaps, at the end of the day, this is his real area of expertise. There is no one in football who does not become an expert in fear. Fear of losing matches, fear of losing one's job, but also this fear: of losing one's footballing intuitions. A match of football, Lefebvre pontificates, is a highly complex and unstable event, like the crashing of the sea onto rocks. One minute you understand, you see the harmony; the next minute you cease to understand, you see only chaos. Whether you are a player or a coach or a scout, there is always a bad surprise around the corner, something that you have not previewed, something that makes you doubt your judgment and your conceptions. And without fail, chance will play a role. Chance, Lefebvre says, is the secret player. With good reason did Marcelo Bielsa, that most systematic of coaches, ask the nuns of Guernica to pray for his Bilbao players. Defeats, reverses and deceptions eventually scar everyone in competitive sport. Only those with the strongest mentality are not dominated by their negative experiences. When Lefebvre looks at me, looks at my visage, he does not see the type of the strong mentality. He sees another type, a type he knows very well

– the type of weakness, even of desperation. Why am I in a room with an old man of football, far away from my country and my family? Why am I asking him for cash, like a beggar? Why am I going against my brother? These are not the actions of the winner. This is not the conduct of the man of confidence, the man of control.

'You're right, Lefebvre,' I say with a grin. 'I am not the man of control.'

And why shouldn't I be grinning? I am off to Africa to seek my fortune. Who cares if Lefebvre holds a low opinion of me? I have power, and despite everything I like the guy. We will make a perfectly odd couple of travelers – the wily, grumpy old Gaul and the Yank rookie. I can easily picture us squabbling over the window seat on the plane to Cotonou, poring over road maps in the bar of a hotel, him riding shotgun as I drive a jeep through the bush, the whole thing underwritten by a comic buddy vibe. It is entertaining to listen to the coot. His long-winded old-school sagacity is refreshing to someone like me, who has not fully recovered from a decade spent as an active member of the American intelligentsia, a time of sterility and mediocrity and snark, as I've said, spent mostly with fellow dudes of the left who furtively wanted above all to be famous millionaires and would have caricatured the veteran scout – with his belief in the life lesson and the hard-won insight and the word of honor, with his generalizations about human nature and cultural differences – as a laughable old chump. Then again, almost nobody passed the test of our mockery. Almost anything said or done by anybody was in some way undermined by an unconscious assumption or blind spot or standpoint issue which the speaker or actor suffered from. Everyone was disdained, oneself especially. The performance of kicking in one's own rotten ideological floorboards was something we called 'reflexivity'. This was a cop-out, of course, but it was a smart cop-out. Being smart – which we confused with being knowledgeable – was less about seeing something for what it was than about critically viewing one's act of seeing, and then critically viewing oneself critically viewing one's originally seeing self, and so on infinitely, as in an Escher, without vertigo. In practice, it led to abandoning all attempts to actually absorb anything, and defaulting to an ironic or camp focus on obviously trash TV and comic books and music, and expressing a perverse but real admiration for brazenly rich or crooked or right-wing people, whom we associated with authenticity and transparency, the idea being that human beings purporting to act in good faith were either operators or people who had mistaken their lucky success for merit. It sounds unbelievable, but that's how small-minded and envious we were. That isn't to say that perspectivism doesn't have value, because of course it does. But it does not solve the problem. One remains an American idiot.

Lefebvre and I agree that tomorrow I will get my vaccinations (he already has his) and Lefebvre will make the arrangements for a guide, a hotel, a car. The plan is to fly off on Friday, the only day of the week for flights to Benin.

'Now we must sleep,' Lefebvre says. He looks around the tiny studio apartment. 'You have another bed?'

I tell Lefebvre to take my bed. I find a carpeted floor space near the window and fashion a sleeping nook with a pillow and a bedspread.

When I wake up, Lefebvre is gone. The brown envelope has disappeared from the desk drawer, as has my copy of the contract. There is a handwritten note:

> *Marc I take the money for my air ticket. I am flying today. You must go home to your family. I telephone you after I get back.*

> *J-L Lefebvre*

Is betrayal, like grief, experienced in unavoidable stages? I can report numbness, then disbelief, then fury, then violent shame and self-rage.

I feel more than defeated – I feel doomed. Something about me signaled to Lefebvre that I was prey, that my position in the natural order was that of the mouse, of the snack. I crawl into the bed he vacated, and all day I stay under the blankets in an artificial dark, hiding from the circling raptors. Twice my hand reaches out for Lefebvre's note in the hope that I have misread it. Twice I arrive at the same interpretation: that he has defrauded me of my money, my contract and my exclusive knowledge of Godwin's whereabouts; that his promise to contact me on his return from Africa is obviously false. I think about phoning Sushila and sharing my woes, but I refrain. I cannot expose her to my weakness.

I regain consciousness at the sound of the door opening. A man has entered the room.

He speaks with a raised voice. He seems to be upset with me. He is either unable or unwilling to speak English. He taps an imaginary wristwatch.

This must be the apartment proprietor or lessee or host. My rental expired at noon; it's one o'clock. I am trespassing. He is also angry, unless I'm mistaken, by the odor of smoke that Lefebvre has left behind. It is a squalid encounter: the landlord is a small, overweight, greedy-looking little cartoon capitalist; I am an unshaven, unbathed dude who has slept in his clothes; and the apartment has somehow been trashed and is littered with empty bottles and food containers and the contents of my luggage. The matter is finally resolved when I book the place for another night and give him cash compensation in the sum of fifty euros for the smoking smell. When the small-time capitalist leaves, I sit in the armchair. I am not going to Africa.

I feel a magical relief. It's as if I've been liberated from a hex.

What a near miss! What a reprieve! Canceling my flight back to New York? That would have been like canceling my marriage. What do I care if Lefebvre goes to Benin? Let him go, the poor guy. As for Geoff, it's true that he's cheap, that he's a schemer, that he's not to be trusted, and that he's cheated me. But am I really going to fall out with my brother? Over such a small amount of money?

My armchair is a low-lying leather bucket chair. I'm practically prostrate. The winter sunlight is already dwindling: Paris is at the same latitude as Montreal. Will I explore the wilds of Quebec? Will I lay eyes on Hudson Bay? My life's parts are flying off in every direction. I'm sobbing. I came so close to disaster.

I call my brother. I will tell him what I discovered – that God-win was filmed in Natitingou, Benin. Then I will get ready to fly home.

He doesn't answer. I don't want to leave a message, so I try him again an hour later.

'Yes?'

The voice isn't my brother's. It's my mother's.

I listen to both of us saying nothing. Then I hang up.

L

I am a long-standing member of the American Medical Writers Association. In 2011, I was fortunate to lead a workshop in Sydney, Australia. That remains the only time I have left North America. This year AMWA invited me to run a seminar in Philadelphia. The three days I spent in Philadelphia were fun, if not as exciting as the trip to Sydney. When I returned, I got some bad news.

I was hanging up my coat when Annie asked if we could speak privately. We sat down at the big table in the conference room – the scene of so many meetings between us! Her next words were: 'I'm taking a job in Sacramento. I'll be letting people know this afternoon. You won't see me here next week.'

'Next week?'

Annie said, 'We're going to have to figure out what do about my notice period.'

The *Rules* required one month's notice for termination of membership. In practice, this was treated as a technicality. Strict enforcement was especially inappropriate in Annie's case. She had done so much for so little. I told her not to worry about it. Then I said, 'Well, what's the job?'

She named a pharmaceutical company. They were offering her low six figures, plus excellent benefits.

'Got it,' I said. The Group had solid health insurance, but we couldn't compete with blue-chip corporate perks – the housing supplements, the pension plans, the bonuses, the stock options.

How had I failed to see this coming?

Annie said, 'This feels right for Hazel. And I'd like to see more of my parents.'

It had been ten minutes since Hazel was born, but apparently she was ready to start kindergarten in the fall.

'What I'm going to miss is my colleagues. That means you, Lakesha.'

I appreciated this remark. Annie and I had accomplished so much together. She was my good friend.

'Hey,' she said. 'It's going to be OK. You know that.' She took a Kleenex from the box on the desk and handed it to me. Then she took a Kleenex for herself.

It was dark when I drove home. Snow like ticker tape was falling into the Ohio. Usually, I felt glad to be warm and dry and safe in my apartment. I felt that I had come a long way from Milwaukee. This time, I felt frail and cold. I was extra grateful to be greeted by Cutie.

My wine rack held a dusty, solitary bottle of red wine. Two years before, Annie had given me both the rack and this bottle as a housewarming gift. I opened the bottle.

A storm of questions overwhelmed me. How was the Group going to manage? How was I going to manage? Eventually, I remembered that the Group was a collective of good, smart people. Our governance structures were sound. Our ethos was solid. We were doing well. We would keep going. Annie was right. It would be OK. 'It's going to be fine, Cutie,' I said. I emptied out my glass of wine in the kitchen sink, then did the same with the bottle. Drinking alone has never been my thing.

We held Annie's goodbye party at the office, at five o'clock on Friday. All but three of the members turned up, many of them accompanied by their partners. Some of Annie's clients were present. Then it was time for me to offer remarks. Annie was standing right next to me, plastic cup in hand. It was nerve-racking. I had never addressed such a large gathering of our community, not even at an AGM. Some folks were filming me with their phones. It went as well as it could, bearing in mind my average skills in this area. I'd made sure to write out every word, and the audience laughed even when I wasn't saying anything funny, which I was grateful for. It was a difficult speech to give.

I spoke about the old days. I described how Annie and I met in a shabby office-sharing outfit on Fourth Avenue, and how we hit it off, and how we decided to rent a cheap premises of our own on Baum Boulevard in the days before East Liberty was hip, and how each of us invited a technical-writer friend – Bobbie van Dijk in Annie's case, Linda Phan in mine – to join us, and how the four of us decided that if we were going to share an office we might as well pool our marketing and branding, too, and how out of these chancy beginnings the P4 Group was born, and how it wasn't long before we were joined by others in the same line of work, friends or friends of friends to begin with, and how happily we went about our work, which included physically refurbishing our workspace with our own hands and painting the walls pale blue while singing along to 'Genie in a Bottle' by Christina Aguilera. I spoke about losing an argument with Annie about the décor: I wanted a cozy vibe, she wanted a space with 'no stuff'. That got a big laugh. Annie was the calm, purposeful, clear-sighted member of our quartet, the one who masterminded the move to our current location, the one who stead-ied the ship after Bobbie and Linda left. Now Annie was leaving, and the ship felt unsteady again. (That part was not in my notes.) I paid tribute to Annie's good nature, to her kindness and honesty and dry wit, and I made a toast to 'greener pastures'.

'Greener pastures!' everyone said.

I presented the goodbye gift – a variety box of local beers, because Annie liked beer – and a card signed by all the co-operators. There was a potentially funny story to be told about the beer – about the e-mails that had gone around discussing which kind to buy, and the wires that got crossed – but I decided that I had spo-ken long enough. Also, I could barely speak, I missed her so much already. It was Annie's turn to say something. 'The pith, please,' I joked when I introduced her, and this got a small laugh.

How quickly and completely everyone fell silent for her. She thanked me for my speech ('Thank you, Lakesha') and thanked everyone for the flowers and the beer ('And thanks for these'). After a pause, she declared, 'Greener pastures. I like that. Greener pastures. You're telling me I'm a cow.' Before the laughter had subsided, she added, 'I'm going to miss this pasture, that's for sure. Even if it is a little brown. Pittsburgh, right?' There was soft knowing laughter. 'Anyhow. No more grass metaphors. Thanks, guys. I love you. Goodbye.'

And that was that. We had all been expecting something brief from her, Annie being Annie – but to me it felt cursory. I was thinking, as everyone clapped and Betty Wu handed Annie a big bouquet of flowers, that there was more to be said and that it was Annie's duty, not as a departing Co-Lead but as our friend, to say it. Efficiency has its limits. You can work efficiently. You cannot live efficiently.

Something else made me uneasy. One of our most gregarious and fun members, Richie Forte, appointed himself the photographer of the event. He demanded that Annie and I pose for a picture together, as if it were our wedding, and shouted 'Founders only!' to dispel colleagues who were huddling with us to have their picture taken. Next thing, Richie corralled those of us who had worked at Baum Boulevard with shouts of 'Baum only! Baum only!' and took a picture of that group separately from the others. I didn't like it. A collective like ours could not have hierarchies or factions.

It was during the taking of the Baum picture that I became aware that Wolfe was there. He looked cheerful and shy. His presence had something of an effect on one or two of the members, notably Edil. She whispered into his ear, and what she said made him smile. When Richie called out for everyone to look at the camera, Edil stood next to Wolfe with a hand resting on his shoulder, as if they were old buddies, which they were not.

Shortly before seven o'clock, Annie put on her huge winter coat. It practically doubled her volume. This half-coat, half-person hugged me goodbye and performed the same action with about twenty others. After that, Annie picked up a tote bag she'd filled with her few workplace possessions and pulled up her hood. Then she was gone.

To my surprise, the partying intensified. Dancing, which I had not expected, broke out. I love those rare occasions when the work-place spontaneously blooms into something different and even more valuable. The spectacle of crowded, laughing workmates made me feel hope. When I saw Wolfe at the far side of the room, I gave him a little wave. He responded by coming over like an ant-lered creature, all eyes and straggly hair and brown-and-gold beard.

I said, 'Welcome back. I hope your break was productive and enjoyable.'

He said, more solemnly than seemed necessary, 'It was inter-esting. More instructive than productive. If you'd like, I'll tell you about it over a coffee one of these days.'

His offer felt suggestive – until I realized that it was an entirely appropriate follow-up to our last conversation, which had also involved coffee. I said, 'Sure. That would be nice.'

Here I was applying the advice of my first boss, Dave. Once, when he asked me to perform some chore, I assented with a sigh. Dave stopped what he was doing. He said to me, 'If there's one thing I wish someone had told me early in my career, it's this: if you're going to say yes, never show reluctance or unhappiness. It gets you nothing. You're going to do the work anyway, and roll-ing your eyes gets you no props, creates no goodwill. Whereas if you say "sure" or "you betcha", you're going to build goodwill. And you're going to need that on the day you say no. OK?'

'You betcha,' I said.

We laughed. Dave was like that – someone who encouraged humor. He played an important role in my career. When I needed a reference, Dave came through for me. I needed a lot of references to get my career going, because I wasn't the kind of person folks had in mind when they looked for a medical writer. I never read Dave's reference letter, but it was read back to me, in part, during a job interview once. Sometimes, when I'm feeling doubtful and defeated, I remember his words of commendation. The part they read out was:

Lakesha Williams may be the smartest, most able young person I've ever had the privilege of working with.

I didn't get that job. I now suspect that really the interviewer was expressing his incredulity – mocking me or having fun at my expense. He couldn't believe that I was the recipient of this compliment. It makes me sad, not on my own behalf but on behalf of Dave.

The first reference I ever got was from Miss Gabrielle, who twice a week taught me piano at her home even though she was a science teacher. She was nice. Years later, there was Professor Klaus Mueller, who taught chemical and biological engineering at UW-Milwaukee and was my academic adviser. Wisconsin folks like to think of themselves as German. Mueller was an actual German, with a German accent. After he revealed to the class that he was from the city of Braunschweig, I looked up Braunschweig and learned about Dankwarderode Castle and Henry the Lion and the House of Welf. Braunschweig in English was 'Brunswick'.

It was foreign and intriguing. I found it strange that Professor Mueller went home and spoke in another language. I began to take a secret interest in German words. Later, in Pittsburgh, I took a German intensive and encountered the world of grammar and compound nouns such as *Weltschmertz* and *Vorfreude*. My love of German led me, I believe, to technical writing.

Professor Mueller was very direct – a German trait, I assumed, although I knew nothing about Germany or the traits of the Germans. He wasn't a great adviser in the conventional sense. His knowledge of program requirements was not strong. If I asked him where anything was on campus, he'd have to look at a map. But he did his best, and he wasn't too scared or too friendly to ask me questions about my circumstances – about where I stood with college loans, about my home situation – that the American professors would know not to ask. Why did I accept these questions from him? Because (I can answer in retrospect) it was my intuition that as a foreigner he was not implicated in the American system. 'You Americans,' he would say exasperatedly. It was interesting to be called that – to be naturally grouped with everybody else from my own country.

My intuition would be different now.

The most important cup of coffee I ever drank was bought for me by Professor Mueller at the end of the spring semester of my sophomore year.

We met at the Gasthaus. He got me a cookie with my coffee, because in Germany, he said, you could not have one without the other. 'Lakesha,' he said, 'your grades are a precious resource. You must use them. You must use them now, before it's too late.'

I had no idea what he was talking about.

'What has been happening cannot go on,' he said. 'You know this, Lakesha.'

This part I understood. For the whole semester, I'd been sleeping on the floors of other students, because the situation at home with my big sister and the people she hung out with was unpredictable and dangerous. In the eyes of the Dean's office, I was technically homeless. He continued, 'I asked to meet with you because there is something I must tell you. I have spoken with a colleague at Carnegie Mellon University, in Pittsburgh. His name is Professor Yonatan Abend. He has studied your record. He has seen your grades. He would like to invite you to transfer to CMU. It is a world-famous university, Lakesha, more prestigious than this one. Professor Abend has arranged everything, including an offer of full financial aid.' Professor Mueller handed me an envelope. 'This is the offer.'

Tears came to my eyes, making me feel even more embarrassed. I didn't think that what he was doing was appropriate, ambushing me like this. 'I can't,' I managed to say.

Professor Mueller said, 'In my opinion it is too risky to stay here. You must have a good environment. Environment determines almost everything. You must change your cohort.' I didn't understand exactly what 'cohort' meant, but I got what he was saying. He was saying that bad things tended to happen to people who lived in the North Side, through no fault of their own, and that I was at risk of having bad things happen to me. It was smart of him not to say anything about my sister. Professor Mueller said, 'My advice is that you go right away, Lakesha. You get out. You do not wait for the summer to go by. A summer is long. Anything can happen in one summer. Especially in Milwaukee.'

How was I supposed to go to Pittsburgh? I was nineteen. I had left the state only once, to visit cousins in Chicago. In addition to the hesitancy that is normal and universal, I was affected by a notion that I shared with many other North Siders. Our notion was that we were fated to stay in Milwaukee. We knew how challenging our living conditions were – we didn't need to be taught that at school or to read about it in the newspapers. But we believed, consciously or subconsciously, that to be true to ourselves and to those we loved, maybe even to those we feared, we had to stay put. A life lived someplace else would be a false kind of life. I have since learned that this sort of outlook is not unusual in downtrodden groups. The home environment, because it is harrowing, is a strong source of identity and pride.

There was another notion that was important to us: that nobody knew what our life was like. It was a power we had: the power to say, in particular to those white people who thought that they could help or could offer insight, that they didn't know anything about who we were or what our lives were like. Because they didn't. 'Professor,' I said, 'you don't know who I am. You don't know what my life is like.'

He looked puzzled. 'Did I say that I know what your life is like? I know only statistics, Lakesha. I know only numbers. I believe in the numbers. Your numbers are good in Pittsburgh. In Milwaukee they are not so good.' Professor Mueller said, 'You think about it. Maybe discuss it with your sister. Tell me what you decide. If you agree, we'll take my car to Pittsburgh, and you will stay with Yonatan and his family. They will take care of everything. It won't be easy for you. It will be hard.'

I think that was decisive – when I saw that Professor Mueller wasn't interested in putting himself in my shoes. He was interested in doing what was in my best interests. The measures he took were extreme. Too extreme, some would say. He went too far, they would say – that, by practically forcing a vulnerable young person to separate herself from her family and community, he was misusing his influence. That's not how I felt at the time. It's not how I feel about it now, either, when I'm a busy adult who is about the same age Mueller was when he was my adviser – correction, who is older than he was! It must have taken a lot of work to set up the offer from CMU. It would have been a lot easier for him to put me out of his thoughts, take off on his summer vacation and do nothing. Those who would criticize him – there are many such critics – I would ask them whose corner they are in, exactly. Because, when I look around my corner, I don't see them.

My sister was in my corner – in her heart. She was too over-whelmed by her own life to be more substantially available. She was not available, at that time, to advise me about what Mueller was proposing, not that I wanted to discuss it with her. But I have always attached significance to the fact that she has never said anything reproachful about my move to Pittsburgh.

Professor Mueller wrote down his phone number. 'If you say yes, I will pick you up on Wednesday morning. Bring your most important possessions. I can give you a suitcase if you need.' He added, 'My girlfriend will travel with us. You'll like her.'

I went with him to Pittsburgh. I didn't like the girlfriend.

When nine o'clock came around, so did the job of cleaning up after the party. Varun and Heather were on duty that night, and nobody had been designated to support them with the extra mess. That was an oversight. A few of us stayed behind to help. To my surprise, Wolfe was one of the helpers. During the years I'd known him, he had never put his hand up, never done more or less than his duty. As the saying goes, from each according to his ability, to each according to his needs. When we completed the excess work gener-ated by the party – essentially, putting bottles and paper cups and paper plates into trash bags, and mopping, and folding up and put-ting away tables – we went home. All except for Wolfe, who stayed on to help Varun and Heather with their rostered tasks.

Some people believe that morale is abstract. I think it's real – a question of the actions of molecules. Driving home, I could sense, for the first time since Annie had announced her departure, the inner chemical movement that produces a robust feeling of confi-dence. Our people were stepping up.

•

On the Monday – the Group's first day, ever, without Annie – the Action Committee convened for a ten o'clock meeting. An air of resolve, manifesting as a heightened calmness and orderliness, came from the six members sitting around the table. Our solitary male, Greg Hasler, had shaved. You would never have guessed, if you'd peeked at us through the glass interior wall, that we were scrambling.

Annie's sudden departure left us with two challenges. The immediate challenge was client retention, an issue we had faced many times before and for which we had procedures established by Annie herself. In brief, the departing member, Annie in this instance, took steps to notify her clients of her departure and to assure them that they would remain in excellent hands with the Group.

Then there was the challenge that worried me.

To put it as simply as possible (there are nuances that I won't get into), the Group got two kinds of work: requests for a specific member's services, and generic requests for services. It was the responsibility of the Co-Leads to handle the generic approaches – to connect clients to the appropriate technical writer or, in the Group's jargon, to 'dish out' work, from which came the Co-Leads' nickname, 'the dishwashers,' which I liked, because it captured something true. Newbie co-operators, in particular, relied on the Group's brand and its network of contacts for their work, which, translated into real life, meant relying heavily on me and (before she left) Annie. It usually took members two difficult years to become professionally established and be able to form their own relationships with clients and generate more of their own work. The fee negotiating and billing were handled by Annie and me for years, until we created the position of Fees & Marketing Administrator. Fee agreement was a vital and highly sensitive responsibility, of course. It was unproductive for writers to negotiate their own fees and be consumed by the ups and downs of that process. It is not easy to accept that the value of our work does not always correspond to its worth in the eyes of others.

Why did the co-operators trust Annie and me with these important duties for so many years? Because we were competent. Why were we competent? Because we were experienced. I don't say that boastfully. You don't build up a thriving co-operative like the Group without an effective and evenhanded distribution of professional assignments to our members. All of which left the Committee with the daunting question: who would take over from Annie?

The simple answer was that her successor would be identified in the usual way: by election. But we had never held a substantive election for a Co-Lead Administrator. Nobody had ever contested my or Annie's election to positions that, as I've mentioned, involved a ton of work for less than a ton of compensation. Only one person at the Group, the Fees & Marketing Administrator, Greg, had the know-how to immediately assume some of Annie's duties. But Greg lacked broader experience. I emphasize experience in order to demystify the notion of talent. Impressive personal qualities are not natural. They are developed, over time, by work. If there are shortcuts, I'm not aware of them.

Annie had led Action Committee meetings. Now the responsibility was mine. I was anxious, but I had come prepared. I summarized the Group's situation clearly and calmly enough, emphasizing the need to find a new Co-Lead. Nobody raised any objection to my summary. Nobody offered any solutions, either. I had been anticipating some discussion of our options, but when I asked for everyone's thoughts, there was a procedural response: it was quickly agreed that the most practical course of action would be for Greg to help me out as an Acting Lead until a full-time Co-Lead was elected at the AGM. Greg said that was OK by him. If anybody was interested in running for Annie's position, they didn't mention it.

When I routinely asked if there was any other business, Greg cleared his throat. He said, 'So . . . I want to take this opportunity to make an announcement. I'll be stepping down from this Committee after the AGM.' He had really enjoyed his time of service, he said, but after three years it was someone else's turn. He was looking forward, he joked, to spending more time with his writing, and – this was also intended to be a joke, but I felt it came out a little sourly – 'maybe actually making some money.'

He had a point, in fairness. It isn't easy to combine a well-paid technical-writing practice with tiring administrative work. Serving as a Group officer wasn't supposed to be a career move or even a full-time gig. It was, in theory, a temporary period of part-time community service. In reality, Greg's F & M duties had consumed most of his working hours, all for two thousand dollars a month. The Co-Leads likewise worked on an undercompensated basis. It was only by good luck that Annie had been motivated to do it for so long. The Group was finally being confronted with a flaw in our model that I'd tried not to think about: a lot hinged on the willingness of a few individuals to make financial sacrifices for the greater good.

Greg, for reasons known only to him, had chosen not to forewarn me about his announcement. If he had, it would have enabled me to immediately start planning what to do about it. I would also have had something more suitable to say at the meeting than 'Well, thank you, Greg. Wow. Talk about AOB! I think I can say on behalf of everybody that we feel very grateful for the amazing work you've done for the Group. We thank you for that. We hope you'll change your mind, but we completely respect your decision.'

Afterward, Alison, our Treasurer, came up to me and said, 'It'll be fine, Lakesha. It'll all work out somehow. It always does. Something always turns up.'

I smiled and said, 'Yes, you're right.' Inwardly, I rejected what she was saying. Alison's experience may well have been that things worked out in the end. That was not my experience.

That same day, Wolfe e-mailed me.

Hi Lakesha. I'd love to grab that coffee if you have a moment. Zeke's?

What did he want to talk about, his vacation? He couldn't see how much I had going on? I wrote back:

Sure!

•

An unofficial but essential part of my job was to talk privately with members about their concerns. I listened carefully. When appropriate, I offered counsel. The process benefited me, because it gave me a clearer idea of what a given member needed from the Group. It also gave me a better sense of what kind of people our technical writers were. For example, I learned that not everyone wanted to be kept busy – a new concept to me! Our writers were electively self-employed. They were at the Group not because they couldn't find a job but because they highly valued their autonomy. They tended to be gifted persons who were disinclined to accept a rigid full-time occupation and had personal interests that they wanted to devote time to. This could be parenting, or traveling, or some hobby. Wilderness activities were important: the forest trails of West Virginia are filled with medical editors. At least six members were enthusiasts of kayaking or rafting or whatever it is folks do for days at a time on the Youghiogheny River with no cell-phone reception.

In his early days at the Group, Wolfe was hard to read. He turned down assignments a bit capriciously, it seemed to me. Then Annie and I noticed a pattern: Wolfe responded well to urgent, challenging projects that required him to get started right away and to keep going without stopping. We recognized whom we were dealing with – the person who, for whatever reason, struggles with procrastination and executive function. It was to Wolfe's credit that he had figured out a way to overcome his self-regulation issues, although I also got the sense that he didn't have his heart in his work. He probably didn't respect it. That was his prerogative. My life would have been easier if all our members were strongly motivated – but the point of the co-operative was to enable the members to work on their own terms, not to make my life easier. As long as members paid their dues, kept our clients happy and did not harm the collective, how they managed or viewed their career was their business. The Group existed to serve its members, not the other way around.

Zeke's was the coffee shop nearest to the office. I arrived at the appointed hour – 4:00 p.m. Wolfe was already there. He looked neater than usual. Some kind of haircut or beard trim seemed to have occurred.

He started speaking before I had completed the act of sitting down. He wanted to thank me, he said, for suggesting a period of leave. He wanted to acknowledge again that he'd been out of line, with both Pete and the client, and he wanted me to know that he was now in a much better frame of mind. He told me that he was interested in making a greater contribution to the Group.

'Gosh, that would be much appreciated.' I added with a laugh, 'Your break sure seems to have done the trick.'

'I went to see my brother, in England,' Wolfe said. 'My half-brother.' He placed his head in his hands. What a nightmare it had been, he said. He allowed his brother to drag him into a crazy venture. It was only at the last second, by chance, that he was able to step back – to turn away from the dark side. Wolfe laughed, so I laughed, too. I was curious, despite myself, and I said, The dark side? Wolfe laughed again, but he didn't answer my question. It was a powerful, almost uncanny experience, he said. All his life he had suffered, he said, from a kind self-hostility, a suspicion of his own weakness. The fact that he had been able to resist temptation, that he had made a good decision for maybe the first time in his life – well, to make a long story short, he came home from his leave with a new confidence in his capacities, a new sense of purpose.

He glanced at me as if I'd said something.

'Well, that's great,' I said.

'You have any brothers or sisters? Or fractions of siblings?'

I said, 'Yes.'

He smiled authentically. It was a nice smile, the beginning of pleasantness. I watched him weigh up whether to ask me more, then decide against it. That was correct on his part. Wolfe was self-absorbed, yes, but not without compassion when he escaped the cloud of preoccupation that followed him everywhere. I saw no malice in him. I placed him in that class of sensitive intellectuals who are vulnerable to confusion.

He restricted his follow-up question to asking me where I was from. I was surprised that he did not already know.

'Milwaukee?' He seemed pleased, for some reason. 'Malcolm X lived in Milwaukee for a while,' he said. 'As a young kid.'

'Is that so,' I said. I didn't tell Wolfe that Malcolm's family, the Littles, had lived on the same street as me, West Galena, albeit a few blocks east. I learned about this after I left Milwaukee. When I was there, we didn't talk much about Malcolm X.

Wolfe went on, cautiously, 'Is it true, what they say about Milwaukee? That it's the worst city in the United States to grow up in as an African American?'

'I've read that,' I said.

He was very curious. It fascinates people – the poverty of North Side Milwaukee. They want to hear stories about the ghetto, about everybody gangbanging and going to jail, about nobody graduating from college, about lead in the drinking water, about babies dying of malnutrition, about the possibility of renewal through urban farming. I decided a long time ago that it's not my job to have that conversation.

'Anyhow,' he said in a different tone of voice. 'So I was thinking about serving on the Committee.' He moved in his seat.

'OK!' I said.

'I was thinking that, with Annie gone and Greg standing down, I might, you know, throw my hat into the ring.'

'For which position?'

'Annie's,' Wolfe said, apparently surprised that he needed to spell it out. 'Co-Lead.'

He was talking about running for Co-Lead having never served on the Committee in any capacity, not even for one minute? 'Oh wow,' I said. 'Cool.'

He was embarrassed and yet animated. 'I know I don't have much experience. But I believe I have something to offer.' Wolfe told me that, in addition to serving as Co-Lead, he wanted to recommit to his technical writing. He didn't mean to sound presumptuous, but he was ready to take on as much work as the Group could send his way. He was interested not only in more grant writing but in other stuff that might be a good fit for him. Between him and me and the gatepost, he said, his objective was to break into six figures and double his income.

Six figures, I was thinking, would be closer to tripling, not doubling, his income. I said, 'I'm hopeful that we can do something for you. Your writing is so strong.' This was true. On the page, Wolfe was excellent. I said, 'Doesn't it seem like that might be a lot – taking on a Committee job and also tripling your income?'

'Doubling my income,' Wolfe incorrectly corrected me. 'I think I could manage. I want to be very busy. I want to really throw myself into the Group.'

Did he even know the names of all the members? I heard myself say, 'You seemed to enjoy yourself at Annie's goodbye party.'

'I did. It was good to actually talk to people. There's so much potential in the membership.'

That word, 'potential', has always made me uncomfortable. Some of my professors used to mention my 'potential', and I never liked it.

I said no more. He was obviously headstrong, and my guess was that his motives were obscure even to himself. I was conscious that, as Co-Lead, I had to be careful about weighing in on his candidacy for office. It might be seen as interference.

Making sure to shake his hand, I thanked Wolfe for his commitment to the Group. It was, I told him, very exciting.

Back at the office, I immediately made a lunch date for the next day with Candy Nguyen.

Candy was the Group's Secretary. She had drafted every Committee Minutes and read every Committee e-mail for the best part of a decade. She had participated in countless Committee deliberations and decisions, and she was deeply familiar with the Task Calendar, compiled by her and me. So much of our work was about structure and repetition. Candy was liked by all at the Group. A respected writer with a stable roster of clients in the biotech sector, she would be absolutely trusted as a Co-Lead Administrator by members and clients. She was quiet, yes; but that spoke to her calm temperament and to her discipline. Being a Co-Lead didn't require you to be larger than life. Annie hadn't exactly been the guy at the party with the lampshade on his head.

We ate at a nice falafel place where you can skip the falafel and build your own salad. I was direct, like Professor Mueller. I said, 'Candy, we need you to step up. I would love to have you as Co-Lead.'

Candy looked alarmed, which was to be expected. She had found her groove as Secretary, and she thrived on continuity and predictability. She would need time to get used to the idea of such a big change. I remembered a similar conversation years before, when I'd asked her to run for Secretary. On that occasion, as on this one, she answered, 'I'll have to think about it, Kesha. Talk it over with Ernie.' Ernie was Ernie Drucker, Candy's husband. He taught middle school. I'd always liked Ernie.

'Of course,' I said. We didn't say anything more about it. We didn't need to. That was what was so great about me and Candy. A few days later, she confirmed that she would run for Co-Lead. I thanked her from the bottom of my heart. The system still worked.

By which I mean, any vacant office had always been filled in advance of the AGM by an arrangement such as the one Candy and I had made. These arrangements were necessitated by the chronic difficulty of finding anyone who was prepared to join the Committee. If we waited until the AGM to fill a vacancy, there was a danger that nobody, or somebody random, would be elected.

I didn't tell Candy that Wolfe had expressed an interest in the Co-Lead position. She didn't ask, and I doubted very much that Wolfe would run once he became aware that Candy was in the frame. There was no point in unduly alarming her.

By then I had already gotten Alison Major, our Treasurer, to agree to run for Greg's position, Fees & Marketing. Alison would need me to hold her hand for the first year, but we would make it work. For the Treasurer role I had successfully approached Tommy Szymanski. 'Treasurer' sounds important, but anyone with basic organizational skills could do the job. Tommy was a smart, responsive, enthusiastic younger person who was fun to have around, and he would replace Greg's masculine presence on the Committee. (Greg had briefly been nicknamed 'the Strap-On'. I objected to that, and folks cut it out.) Though the Group's identity as a woman-strong organization was important, it would not be right, or reflective of the Group's gender composition, to have a Committee made up exclusively of women.

That left one more piece of the puzzle. I begged my friend Nadia Minassian to be our new Secretary. She said she would.

Now there was only the question of how to deal with Wolfe.

I got him a contract to write a new-funding grant worth four hundred thousand dollars. It was a lucky break. Wolfe accepted the gig without reservation – and without saying thanks, which made me shake my head, because saying thank you is a vital interpersonal technique for anyone whose livelihood depends on working with people. Next, I forwarded to him a generic query for a writer to urgently collaborate with the client on a fabrication manual for high-precision steel medical products. It was a tricky assignment, and outside of Wolfe's specialization. He said yes. By my calculation, and assuming he did the work, he stood to make around eighteen thousand dollars over the next month. It would keep him very busy – too busy to think about running for the Committee.

There was nothing wrong with having contested elections, of course. Our *Constitution* provided for them. But we had never had a contested election in the history of the Group. Every office was filled by consensus in advance of any vote. And in any case: elections aren't magic, because voters aren't magic. However strong your process and your culture, things can go wrong. Fortunately, our co-operators weren't ordinary voters. They were discriminating and exceptionally educated individuals. Even if Wolfe persisted with his candidacy, Candy's depth of knowledge compared with Wolfe's inexperience would be obvious to all. I had been dreading the transition, but now I was feeling better. The new team – Candy and Alison and Tommy and Nadia and me – had been set up with the 2015 Annual General Meeting still weeks away.

•

The *Constitution* stipulated that the AGM was to be held at the Group's principal place of business at 4:00 p.m. on the first Friday in April. Typically, around half of the membership showed up in person, a number that could comfortably fit into the conference room after you'd moved the table to the corner. The agenda was also prescribed by the *Constitution*: first, officers' reports and the discussion of matters arising therefrom; second, Any Other Business; and, last, the Election of Officers. Immediately after the election, usually at around five-thirty, a low-key office party would kick off. In my opinion, the party was as important as any item on the agenda. It was a celebration, and celebrations are very important.

Annie had presided over all of the AGMs in the history of the Group. Her role now fell to me. That didn't worry me. What worried me was that Wolfe had neither confirmed nor disconfirmed his plan to run for Co-Lead. Candy would prevail against him, obviously, but I didn't want there to be any adversarial energy in the room. I felt bad for Wolfe. He seemed genuinely enthused by the prospect of doing Committee work, and he was making an investment of energy and hope. It's never easy to stick your neck out and ask for approval in the form of votes. It's certainly never easy to run for office and lose. Wolfe might receive his defeat as a personal rejection. The last thing we needed at the AGM was any division or bad feelings.

The scene in the conference room that afternoon was familiar and reassuring. The officers were seated at the table and the members occupied the folding chairs. Everyone was in a good mood. The mood only improved when Scott Morgensen, our AGM master of ceremonies, entered to exaggerated applause.

Scott was a very funny, ironic guy. His shtick, year after year, was that he and the other co-operators were Russian aristocrats who had made a long, irksome journey into Pittsburgh from their dachas and hunting lodges. The Committee members were upstart peasants, crooked and conniving and idle, but nothing could be done about us, because we rigged every election to maintain our corrupt power. This was bizarre and illogical, and I never really got it, but it got laughs. When Scott started to dress the part – he wore a long military-looking overcoat, a long scarf and something he called a Doctor Zhivago hat – the members began to join in, bringing out furry hats, pipes, and monocles as he stood up to do his bit. It made them feel in on the joke in a *Rocky Horror Picture Show* kind of way, so they said. (I haven't seen that movie, or *Doctor Zhivago*.) Scott's nicknames – 'Garbo' for Annie, 'the steaming mess' for Candy, 'the nerdfather' for Greg, and 'Queen Lakesha' for me – had become part of the culture of the Group. Nobody had taken offense yet. A gentle roasting is a healthy thing.

I started the meeting at ten minutes after four. You can't wait for latecomers forever.

Candy, as Secretary, noted who was present and who had sent

their apologies. Very few members had notified the Committee of their absence. It was a slightly lower turnout than usual, which surprised me a little.

I congratulated the members on another good year. We were fortunate to work in a sector that was resilient, even in a sluggish economy. I shared some of the nice things that clients had said about us. People clapped and cheered, and of course it was fun to try to figure out which member was being praised. I paid tribute to Annie; I made special mention of Greg, thanking him for his contribution to the Action Committee; and I extended a particular welcome to the newcomers present. This last portion of my remarks was interrupted by applause. Then Greg and Alison spoke in turn. Greg said his farewells; and Alison, as Treasurer, distributed bound copies of the Group's financial statements. These painted a strong picture, she was pleased to inform the members. We had billed 22 percent more in 2014 than in 2013. Meanwhile, our overheads had not significantly increased. For the benefit of the new members, Alison explained that the Group, as such, only needed to remain solvent. Any revenue increase went into the pockets of the members. There was laughter when she said this, which took Alison by surprise, then made her smile. It was during Alison's remarks that I noticed that Wolfe had entered and taken a seat at the back. He was often late to things.

Candy did not offer remarks. She took the Minutes.

'Y'all have any questions or comments?' I asked. There were two questions for Greg. Then somebody commented that the Committee had done a great job, and there was loud clapping. We on the Committee appreciated that. I thanked the members and declared that we had every reason to approach the future with confidence.

Under Any Other Business, points were raised about the décor of the offices, the need for a new and/or expanded bike rack, and the recycling of coffee capsules. Such things appear trivial but are quite capable of generating strongly held views. Again, these discussions went well. The Group's Annual General Meeting was not one of those events where folks turn up drunk and make trouble.

'The next item on the agenda is Election of Officers,' I announced. I could feel my hands shaking. The Committee members vacated the table and took a seat with everyone else. 'Scott? Mary?'

Mary Golin took a seat at the conference table. By custom she helped Scott to run the election.

Scott paced around with his hands theatrically clasped behind his back. He made a joke about the vulgarity and dreariness of the city, and how he longed to be in the country, beating his serfs. (He made a face that said, Eek, have I gone too far?) He continued, 'So let's get this charade over with.' He folded his arms. 'We have a really cute system here. It's called a duumvirate.' The way he pronounced it made everyone laugh, even though many of us had heard the joke before. 'So we'll start with nominations for our two Co-Lead Administrators. I nominate . . . Queen Lakesha.'

'Second,' someone said.

Alison said, 'I nominate Candy.' I raised my hand to second.

'I nominate Mark Wolfe,' a voice said from one of the rows behind me. Was that Edil's voice? I didn't turn around.

'I second that,' someone said immediately. I didn't recognize this voice at all. This time I turned around to look. The speaker was a girl freshman. What was her name again? I was so flustered I couldn't recall. Candy would know, but I didn't dare look at Candy.

'OK, then!' Scott screamed mock-hysterically. 'A real election! Yay! Three candidates for the two Lead jobs! Let's vote!' With hyperbolic helplessness he demanded, 'What do I do, Lakesha? For God's sakes, tell me what to do!'

I indicated the stack of ballots that the Committee had left on the table.

Scott snatched up the ballots. 'OK, I guess we write down the name of our preferred *two* candidates, fold the ballot paper so it's a secret, and wait for Mary and me to collect them. No write-ins! Then Mary will count the votes and I will make sure she doesn't cheat, because I promise you that she would cheat if she could. Everybody OK with that?'

'What about proxies?' Edil said.

Scott said, 'Proxies? Proxies? Of course! Proxies! Help!'

'Let me check that,' I said. The question of proxy votes had never arisen before. The relevant Rules had been written by Annie, and I needed to familiarize myself with them. The room was quiet as I consulted the copy of the *Constitution, Rules and Guidelines* that I brought to each AGM. Yes, there was a provision dealing with proxies. I passed the booklet to Scott with the relevant page flagged.

Candy was staring at me. She seemed angry. She had not bargained for a contested election. I made a face that suggested that I was as surprised as she was.

Scott read out, 'A Member not in attendance at the AGM may nominate another Member to cast a proxy ballot on behalf of the nonattending Member. The proxy nomination must be in writing.' He asked, 'Do we, um, have any proxy nominations in writing?'

Edil raised a sheaf of papers and dramatically walked up to Mary and deposited the papers in front of her. Mary examined the documents at length, carefully making notes. The room had fallen silent. 'These are printouts of e-mails,' Mary at last declared. 'They all read as follows: "I will not be in attendance at the AGM. I nominate Edil to cast a proxy ballot on my behalf at the AGM in accordance with Rule 26.3."' Mary confirmed that the members represented by proxy were not in attendance.

Scott said, 'That all seems in order. Any objections? No? So where does that leave us, Mary, pray tell?'

'Edil has fourteen proxy votes,' Mary said. 'Any other proxies?'

There were none. Mary created fourteen more ballots and gave them to Edil.

I had a very bad feeling.

We cast our ballots. Mary announced the results. I was re-elected. Candy lost to Wolfe by three votes. Edil's proxy votes had made the difference.

Candy's face was expressionless now. I hoped that mine was, too.

Scott said a little weakly, 'Well, we have our Co-Leads. Congratulations, Queen Lakesha, and, congratulations, um, Lord Wolfe.'

Wolfe looked shocked.

Scott said, 'Who's next?'

'Treasurer?' Mary said.

'Um, nominations?'

I was panicking. Everything was upside down. As matters stood, Candy would not be on the Committee at all. That seemed inconceivable. Candy was an institutional rock. Should I nominate her, and not Tommy, for Treasurer?

Scott said, 'Anyone?'

'Tommy,' I said. I had no choice. I couldn't dump Tommy at the last second. Alison seconded.

'Which Tommy?' Mary asked.

'Tommy Szymanski,' I said.

Scott shouted, 'Tommy Szymanski! Anyone else? No? Tommy, congratulations!'

'F & M next,' Mary said.

Scott did a whirling dervish thing with his coat, turning on the spot and ridiculously clicking his fingers. 'Fees & Marketing! Our favorite! Nominations, please!' He kept spinning around, which made some laugh.

Alison was nominated by me. I was still in a panic about Candy.

"I nominate Edil,' the same girl freshman said.

I was too confused. Edil was running? For F & M, of all jobs? What was happening?

Alison lost to Edil by the same margin that Candy lost to Wolfe. It was the proxy votes again.

'Secretary!' yelled Scott. 'We need a Secretary, dammit! Will nobody nominate a Secretary?'

I had to salvage something. Nadia had been lined up for Secretary, but she would understand that things had not gone according to plan. Candy would stay on in her old position. We would regroup. 'Candy,' I said. I would apologize and explain to Nadia afterward.

Candy shook her head at Scott. 'I don't accept the nomination. Thank you, though.'

The situation was terrible, but I plowed on. 'I nominate Nadia,' I said.

Nadia refused the nomination by waving and crossing her hands. She looked very unhappy that I had nominated Candy. I had breached her trust.

Scott, for the first time ever, was lost for words. Mary said, 'Anybody want to be Secretary?'

Edil exchanged whispers, first, with the freshman girl nominator, then with Wolfe, who said, 'I nominate Betsy,' and, as in a nightmare, Betsy was elected without opposition.

Betsy? That was her name – Betsy.

'That was so much fun!' Scott said. He raised his hands and shouted at the ceiling, 'I want champagne and caviar and I want it now!'

The chairs were removed, the conference table was returned to the center of the room, refreshments were brought out. Scott, now without his coat and hat, muttered into his Coke, 'What the fuck was that?' and I replied, 'That was our AGM.'

I made a point of congratulating Wolfe and Edil and Betsy and shaking their hands. Maybe they noticed that I was in a daze. Maybe they also noticed that the cocktail party was ending earlier than usual. Folks were consternated, I think it is fair to say. Very few of those present had personally voted for Wolfe and Edil. An invisible group of proxies had changed everything. Our livelihoods were suddenly in the hands of two individuals with little relevant experience.

That same night, I sent Wolfe, Edil, Betsy and Tommy an e-mail suggesting that it would be a good idea to get together on Monday, at nine. There was a lot of work to do.

•

The first problem we faced was with Candy and Alison. Previously, every officer who had left the Committee had done so voluntarily. This wasn't the case with Candy and Alison. In effect, their jobs had been terminated against their will. That had never happened at the Group, and it created real-life complications. Committee officers may have been significantly underpaid, but they did receive a salary, which they depended on as they planned their finances and their writing practices. Candy and Alison would suffer an unexpected loss of income that would be challenging for them, at least in the short term. A departing officer usually helped their successor to learn the ropes, but Candy and Alison would undoubtedly find it hard, practically and psychologically, to mentor those who had ambushed them out of their jobs. It was a mess.

I didn't normally make work calls on weekends. I liked to read books, catch up on my own writing, spoil Cutie. The morning after the AGM, I called one of our veteran members, Erica Flood. Erica was a patent lawyer by training. Whenever I needed legal advice, I turned to her.

She took the call at her daughter Isabel's hockey game. 'Honey, let me get home,' she said.

Next, I rang Candy and Alison. Neither answered. I didn't leave messages.

When Erica got back to me, I asked her, 'You've heard about what happened at the AGM?'

'The AGM? Oh, right – the AGM. How did it go?'

I answered her, sticking to the bare facts. As a Co-Lead, I had to suppress my personal feelings of intense disappointment and alarm. My job was to respect the process and move forward.

Erica's only comment, while I was speaking, was to say, 'Who the fuck is Betsy?' When I was done, she said, 'I don't understand.'

I told her about the proxy votes.

'Oh, shit,' Erica said.

A week or so ago, she revealed, Edil had e-mailed her to ask for her proxy vote if she couldn't make it to the AGM. Erica wasn't planning on attending – her girls had activities on Friday afternoons – and out of politeness she complied with Edil's request. She didn't think it was important. 'Lakesha, she never told me she was running for office. Or that Wolfe was.'

That sounded improbable. Not even Edil could be that devious. 'You sure?'

'It was all done by e-mail! We never even spoke. I had no idea it would matter.' The only thing anybody had ever voted on at the AGM, Erica said, was whether to repaint the building, stuff like that. No way would she have given Edil her proxy if she'd known that there would be an active Committee election. 'God, I feel so stupid.'

In response to my specific legal question about Candy and Alison, Erica advised that they would remain employed as officers until the end of their two-week notice period. After that, Edil and Wolfe would go on the payroll.

A walk with Cutie has the effect of suspending the flow of events in my life. It creates a space for reflection. It was sunny. I stepped out.

The Group was imperfect. The Committee was imperfect, and the members were imperfect. Keeping everyone happy, or happy enough, was testing at the best of times and not always possible. Years of being a Co-Lead had made me knowledgeable about complaints and complainants. The real troublemakers were those who, instead of doing their work, poured professional levels of energy and focus into writing prickly, technical e-mails about the Committee's actions or plans. The e-mails read as if they'd been written by a team of litigators. They asked for clarifications and supporting documentation and 'audits' and 'assurances.' Dates were referred to a lot, sometimes in conjunction with the words 'prompt' and, even, 'ultimo'. The e-mails quoted from other e-mails. They frequently mentioned 'accountability' and 'the record'. They demanded that someone in the Committee 'keep their word' about some small, barely rememberable thing. Edil was one of these e-mail writers. Annie had always dealt with her. Annie was an expert at handling this kind of aggression.

Her method was to keep a sense of humor ('I give you my word' was a very dry running joke between her and me); not to respond unless and until it was absolutely necessary (because complaints had a way of going away by themselves); and then only to respond very briefly and very cordially. She never took the particulars seriously. Annie understood that the particulars are almost never the real issue. What is at issue is a certain personality – the unbalanced person convinced that they are suffering at the hands of unfair but always hidden powers. This sort of person only finds their balance in opposition to another. It is in their nature to see threats everywhere. If they don't face real threats, like running out of money – I mean really running out of it – or losing their homes and finding themselves in a shelter, or loved ones dying – they will imagine threats. I have an unscientific thought about this: if you didn't grow up with love, you are always unbalanced. There wasn't a second when I felt that Mom didn't love me. And when my sister began to look after me, she loved me as best she could. Edil had been raised in fortunate circumstances. And yet she'd been upset or suspicious for as long as I'd known her. I've never known what to say to a person like that. It's a type that scares me. Edil scared me.

She scared others, too. Conflict is a frightening prospect. Most of us prefer not to get on the wrong side of someone who has the energy and the will to engage in conflict. When Erica said that she'd agreed out of politeness to let Edil be her proxy, she wasn't being entirely honest with herself. She had agreed out of fear.

Wolfe I didn't get. What was his role in all of this? Should I be scared of him, too?

I liked my corner of the South Side. It was flat, which is a mercy in Pittsburgh. I could take a walk and not be mountaineering up and down hills. At my previous address, in Morningside, it was so quiet that at night I could hear the barking of the seals in the Zoo. Poor seals! This part of the South Side had a human hum. There were places to eat, there were stores, there were others walking around. Yet it was tranquil enough to make a sidewalk phone call. A few blocks from my apartment, I found a bench and called Annie in Sacramento. When I heard her voice, I could barely bring myself to speak.

Annie listened carefully as I related what had happened at the AGM. I didn't ask for advice on anything specific. I wanted to hear what she made of it. She said, 'What do *you* think?'

'I feel terrible for Candy and Alison. I think the transition will be hard. I'm daunted.'

Annie said, 'What are you going to do?'

'I'm meeting with them on Monday morning, the new faces – Edil, Wolfe, Betsy. I'm not sure how to handle it.'

Annie said definitely, 'When the members realize that their proxy vote was used to stage a coup, they're going to be shocked, demoralized and worried. It's going to be on Edil and Co. to regain their trust. You're going to have to have an honest discussion about that on Monday. Even before the transition discussion.'

'Yes,' I said. I wasn't so sure. Adversarial dynamics didn't work out, in my experience.

'It won't be easy,' Annie said. 'But you have to play it straight. You can't outfox crazy.'

'What's the opposite of a fox? A tortoise?'

'A hedgehog. A tortoise is the opposite of a hare.'

'What is a hedgehog, exactly?'

'It's a tiny, cute porcupine.'

Who else could I talk to like this at the Group? Soon Annie would fade away completely. I could feel her fading away already.

She said, 'There's one important thing you have to remember. The members trust you. They love you. That is very powerful. Edil? Wolfe? Nobody really supports them. OK, now I really have to go.'

For a while, I stayed on the bench. Then it got cold, and Cutie and I walked home.

•

The Monday get-together with the officers-elect took place in a coffee shop near the office. It was, as I'd explained to them, just an informal orientation. Wolfe gave me a double thumbs-up when I sat down. He wore a white collared shirt and a dark-blue V-neck sweater. It was a more conservative look than I was expecting. It suited him. Edil wore a vaguely Oriental silk chiffon thing. What Betsy wore didn't interest me. We ordered coffees.

The first thing I mentioned was that Candy and Alison had two weeks left in office, in accordance with their notice periods. This gave us a great opportunity to familiarize ourselves with our new roles. 'It'll be a transition period,' I said.

'It doesn't say anything about a transition in the *Rules*,' Edil said. She appeared to be taking notes.

I took a deep breath. After no one said anything else, I said, 'So maybe we can talk about how we're going to optimally manage the transition – make sure we all hit the ground running.'

'What do you advise?' Wolfe said.

'Well, you and I will have to talk about the Lead stuff. Edil, I'm sure that Greg would be happy to show you the ropes. Betsy, you might want to reach out to Candy.'

Betsy, who was drinking an iced coffee, had a straw lodged in her mouth.

I continued, 'Tommy—'

'Alison's already been in touch,' Tommy said. He seemed ill-at-ease. That made sense. He wasn't one of the conspirators. He hadn't bargained on this lineup. I would have to talk with him.

'There's this, too,' I said. I gave them each a copy of the *Guidelines for Co-Operators*. 'It has a section on officers' responsibilities.'

Edil said, 'I'd like to see the records. Before I start the job, I mean.'

'The records? What records?'

'You know, what every member is working on, what the fees for each job are, which clients the members have. The stuff I need to know if I'm going to do the F & M job.'

I said, 'Greg will have whatever it is that we have.' I felt sick. I was visualizing Edil poring over the numbers, satisfying her greedy curiosity about the income of her fellow co-operators. I heard myself saying, 'All that information is confidential to the Committee.'

'I'm aware of that,' Edil said pleasantly.

'Anyhow,' I said, 'y'all probably have questions that need answering. So fire away. I'm here to help.'

Betsy made a loud sucking noise as she finished her iced coffee. She giggled apologetically. Tommy shook his head. Otherwise, there was no response.

I thought about raising the issue of the proxy voting. I didn't have the strength or courage. The meeting broke up.

I walked to the office, and the others went home or wherever. I was already thinking about Candy and Alison. Monday was one of the two days of the week when they came into the office. They were invariably at their desks by nine. I had to go in and face them.

There was no sign of Alison. Candy was at her desk. I hung up my coat and went over to her, dragging a chair with me. Some members were scattered around the room. It was not a private setting. The open-plan office concept was not designed for the conversation we needed to have.

'Hey,' I said.

'Hey.' She smiled. 'That didn't exactly go as planned.'

I loved Candy Nguyen at that moment. 'Oh, Candy,' I said. I gestured that we should go to my workspace.

We sat down at my desk, and I started crying. It was the first time that I had openly cried at any place that I'd worked at. I apologized to Candy. She got up and gave me a real hug. I took it.

Candy came straight out with it: she was leaving the Group. Immediately after the meeting, she and Ernie had talked things over. The AGM had been a shocking experience. What made it extra painful was that she had not even wanted to run for Co-Lead. Her personal wish had been to keep going as Secretary. She had run for Co-Lead only because I had asked her to. The vote just felt like a slap in the face, an insult for no reason. She hadn't once considered that her job was at risk – that, after her seven years on the Committee, the Group would throw her out.

'The Group didn't throw you out, honey. It was the proxies.'

True, Candy said, but that was how she felt.

After Ernie put the boys to bed, he and Candy ate leftover pizza. Candy took some sips from Ernie's beer. She started feeling better. They found themselves, she and Ernie, thinking about things more deeply. Did Candy want to go back to being a full-time freelance technical writer? What were her options? What were the family's options? Maybe this was an opportunity to rethink a lot of things. Ernie said that they should sleep on it. The following night, Saturday, they talked some more. This time, Ernie bought a nice bottle of wine and cooked his special lemon chicken. The discussion felt amazing. They started talking about Tucson, where Candy's sister and mom lived. There were jobs in Tucson for someone like Candy, it was warm there, and Candy's sister's children went to a great school. By coincidence, a good high school friend of Ernie's now ran a tequila company in Tucson. It was Ernie who said, Why don't we move there? I'll find work. Years of teaching, Candy said, had worn Ernie out. The Pittsburgh winters had worn Ernie out. He was ready for something new. The high desert, he kept saying. A yard with agave and yucca plants. They spent an hour drooling over real estate pictures, then went to bed as excited as they'd been in years. On Sunday morning, they were still excited. That evening, they decided to do it, move to Arizona – in June, after the school year was over. It would be a big adventure. You only live once.

I said, 'Candy, that's so great.'

Candy made a gentle face. She understood how I felt. She said, 'Who's the ringleader? Edil? Wolfe?'

This wasn't the kind of conversation I liked to have. I said, 'Does it matter?'

Candy said, 'I wrote Betsy last night.'

'Thanks,' I said. 'I advised her to reach out to you.'

Candy gave me another hug. 'It'll be fine,' she said. 'You can do this, Lakesha.'

Then I was by myself again. I didn't dare look at my e-mails.

Greg was in the next workspace. He came over.

Greg wasn't someone I'd ever felt close to, even though we worked together well. He was self-contained, with a permanent frown that made him look more displeased than he was. The tattoos of sundry monsters on his neck and arms played a part in this, at least for me. At every social gathering, he held hands with his small, quiet, sweet-looking girlfriend, also heavily tattooed, and he wore a look of happy pride when he was with her, and that was when I liked Greg best. It was his duty to hand over Fees & Marketing to Edil and to train her as best he could in two weeks.

'I have a very crappy feeling about this,' he said. 'Her tweets are . . .' He whirled his finger next to his head and whistled silently.

I'd heard about Edil's social media activities. She supposedly had several thousand followers and posted at all hours about every little thing. That didn't surprise me. I said, as pointedly as I dared, 'I appreciate what you're taking on.'

'I wouldn't have quit if I'd known this would happen.'

'I know,' I said.

'It's insane.'

I didn't say anything.

'I don't get it,' Greg said. 'What do they even want? People who've never done anything for us before? Suddenly they're so desperate to help the members that they do a hostile takeover?'

'The elections were in accordance with the Rules.'

'Were they? So what? Kesha, people are going to leave. They're thinking about it already. I've thought about it. I need to make money – that was the whole reason I stepped down, to secure my future. Now I'm supposed to trust Edil? Trust that kook Wolfe?'

He was hissing, loudly. I murmured, 'I'll take care of you. Don't you worry about that.' I shouldn't have told him that. Work allocation was something I would have to discuss with Wolfe. But I couldn't lose Greg, too.

'What about everyone else? You're going to take care of everyone?'

'Edil and Wolfe are members, just like you and me. They've got competencies. They'll figure it out. We'll get through this.'

'Listen,' he said. 'I'm going to circulate a petition for an EGM. We can take a vote of confidence. We'll win. The proxy thing won't work twice. We'll do the election over.'

'Do the *Rules* allow that?' I knew the answer. The *Rules* were silent on the issue.

Greg looked as if he was controlling himself. 'The *Rules*? This is about people making the rent check.'

'If you feel that there was an irregularity,' I said, 'you would be absolutely within your rights to challenge it. And if you're ready to come back to the Committee, I would be personally supportive.'

'I can't go back,' he said. 'I was thinking Candy and Alison – reinstating them.'

'I guess you'll have to talk it over with them.' There was no point in telling him that Candy was going to Arizona. As for Alison, her absence from work told me that she was quite distressed.

But it was a pointless discussion. Greg wasn't going to do anything. He had the temperament to get mad, but he didn't have the temperament to do anything about it. We had to go forward with what we had. I said to him, 'Give me a few days. I'm going to meet with Wolfe tomorrow. I'll tell him that members are anxious.'

'Angry. Not anxious. Angry. And looking for other jobs.'

'OK,' I said, laughing. 'Angry.'

•

'They're anxious?' Wolfe said.

We were having a drink in a dive bar that he'd picked because it was near my home. He had wanted to meet right away, as if there was something on his mind. It was not yet dark out, but inside it was dark. The other customers were two older, unlucky-looking solitary men who were sitting farther down at the bar, each nursing a Blue Ribbon. Wolfe was wearing a leather jacket and a black-and-red beanie, with locks of hair sticking out behind his ears and neck. It figured that he would appreciate the down-and-out atmosphere, but I felt overdressed. I prefer places that are lit more brightly and where you can eat food at the bar and have fun people-watching. Not that I'm a nightlife expert.

I said, 'I think folks are shocked by the proxy votes.'

Wolfe said, 'I had nothing to do with that. That was fucked up. The whole thing has been a little disturbing, to be honest.' He was intently spinning a coaster on the counter.

Some weeks back, he told me, he happened to mention to Edil that he was interested in becoming active in the Group's administration. Edil was excited. You should run for Annie's old job, she said. Lead? Wolfe said. I was thinking a more junior position. You're too humble, Edil said. Although your humbleness is one of the reasons you're so popular. I'm popular? Wolfe said. He had no idea what she was talking about. The members admire you, Edil said. Wolfe said, The members? They hardly know me. Edil laughed. They know you, she said. Everyone knows you're brilliant. And – I could just see Edil's small colorless eyes looking directly into his – you're charismatic. Clients respond to that. The Committee members are great, don't get me wrong, but I wouldn't call them magnetic. Wolfe didn't know how to respond. Being magnetic isn't the job, he finally said. The job is to do the work well. Of course, Edil said. But the Leads are the faces of the Group. They're the main point of contact with clients. If the Leads make a good impression, the Group obviously benefits. You could add very unique value as a Lead, Wolfe, Edil told him.

Clients would give their work to the Group because Wolfe was hot? I had never heard anything so ridiculous.

Edil said to him, If you decide to run, keep it on the down-low. I'll talk to the members for you. 'It was a very weird conversation,'

Wolfe said. Nonetheless, when he thought about 'the merits' of Edil's idea, he concluded that there would be no harm in giving it a shot. 'I was embracing positivity,' he said. He was sick of shrinking away from things, he wanted to grab hold of ordinary life like a normal human being, take on normal responsibilities, to test himself in normal ways. All that said, he knew that Candy would make a fantastic Lead. He was sure she'd win. He was looking forward to congratulating her and being gracious in defeat. He even had this fantasy of 'raising her hand after the election, you know, like a boxer.' He glanced at me. 'I never counted on Edil turning up with a bunch of proxy votes.'

'I'm confused,' I said. 'You ran for Lead even though you wanted to lose the election?'

'That's what I'm saying. I was all mixed up. It's all been a big mistake. That's what I'm here to tell you. I want to quit. It's Candy's job.'

'Candy's moving to Arizona.'

He seemed startled. 'What about Greg?'

I shook my head. 'He's out. You're stuck with the job.'

Wolfe's response was to assume the drowning-his-sorrows posture of the other two guys at the bar.

'We'll make it work,' I said. I left it at that. I'm happy to offer a shoulder to lean on, but I will not mother a man.

'Edil never told me she was running, you know,' he said.

'She told nobody, as far as I can tell.'

Of course, if Edil had revealed that she was running for office, she would not have gotten her proxies. Wolfe didn't need me to explain that to him.

'But why would Edil want me as a Lead?' he said. 'Why would she go to all that trouble?' He was spinning the coaster again.

I didn't want to analyze a colleague with him. It would have been unprofessional. And I didn't want to give Edil the phantom satisfaction of being the subject of discussion.

I had my private theory. Edil had a sense of herself as being superior to the other members. She had a big, dirty, childish house in Lawrenceville where she liked to hold court to the younger members and their friends. These cliques didn't last long. Almost everyone tired of Edil. It became embarrassing to listen to her moaning about her parents, who had, she would repeat to anyone who would listen, broken their promise to set her up with her own animation company after college. She often boasted – why she did this, I don't know – about how she'd personally paid three months of the Group's rent. Wolfe had not attended her Lawrenceville gatherings. In Edil's eyes, this would only have increased his allure. Nobody at the Group had gotten close to him – but now she and he would be powerful Committee pals. That was how shallow and egotistical Edil was, in my opinion. She saw Wolfe as a catch.

I didn't share any of this with Wolfe. Nor did I tell him that Edil had no scientific training and was granted Group membership only because, on top of offering to pay three months of our rent, she persuaded certain members that her supposed graphic skills would be very useful to an organization like ours, which special-ized in producing scientific documentation. I opposed admitting her to the membership. She occupied the studio next door to the Group's then premises, and I'd never seen her working. It was obvi-ous that she viewed the Group as a hobby and social credential. I saw through her.

Wolfe signaled for two more whiskeys. I didn't want another drink. I wanted to go home. The screen of my phone went blue, and it was a Milwaukee number.

Wolfe watched me putting the phone in my pocket. 'I hate phone calls, too. Unless it's my wife.'

I liked that. You didn't hear that sort of remark very often. If I have a pet peeve, it's co-workers telling me about their disappoint-ing marriages. I don't want to know about it.

Wolfe continued: 'Most of all I hate calls from my brother – my half-brother. And from my mother. My half-mother,' he joked. 'I don't want to hear from my half-mother and I don't want to hear from my half-brother.' He said it rhythmically, like a comic. There was emotion in there, too, which was sad and almost interesting.

'This is the brother in England?' I said.

'The same guy.' Wolfe shook his fine head. He began to tell me the story, which I did not find easy to follow, of his trip to Europe. The whole thing revolved around his brother's business interest in a promising young soccer player from Africa. My impression was that Wolfe was choosing his words carefully, out of a delicate concern for my feelings. Maybe he thought that Africa or Africans would be something I'd feel sensitive about. But I wasn't listening to him carefully enough to be sensitive. The details of the soccer venture weren't relevant to anything I could think of. Wolfe was drawn into the venture, if I understood him correctly, by the brother's promise to reimburse Wolfe's travel and hotel costs. Evidently, the brother broke that promise. Wolfe was left paying for his own expenses. 'The money isn't the issue,' Wolfe said, as if he'd guessed what I was thinking, which was that maybe the brother hadn't committed the biggest crime in the world. 'He set me up. That's what's so hard to accept. He never had any intention of paying me back. My own brother set me up.' Well, Wolfe said, he had learned his lesson – Wolfe, that is. The brother was just like the mother.

'Your mother?' None of it made sense to me. This was the thing about Wolfe – he lived in his head. It was not always easy to understand what he was trying to say.

'We don't speak,' he said. 'Basically, it comes down to being abandoned by her when I was very young, and then discovering, again and again, that she's a very extreme person who will boil her children alive if she needs to. That sounds melodramatic, I know.'

'It sounds painful,' I said.

'So – get this,' Wolfe said. During his first year of grad school, he got a call from the Astrogeology Science Center, which was in Flagstaff, telling him that his dad ('fifty-nine years old') had suddenly died. Wolfe, the dad's only child, drove the two thousand miles from Pittsburgh. The funeral, which had been put together by some of his dad's colleagues and attended by them and a few of Wolfe's childhood friends from Flagstaff High, was the easiest part. The rest of it, for a bereaved twenty-four-year-old with poor administrative skills, was overwhelming. His father was a reclusive, disorganized individual who had not made an estate plan or any other preparations for his unexpected death. Going through his desk drawers and personal effects in search of important documents proved to be immensely frustrating for Wolfe, who also suffered the misfortune of losing the keys to the family home and finding himself locked out for a night and having to crash on a friend's couch. It was the locksmith who put him in touch with an attorney, the locksmith's cousin. She, the attorney, explained to Wolfe that even though Wolfe, Sr., had apparently died without a will, by Arizona law Wolfe would inherit everything – the small ranch house on Swiss Road with the worthless furniture, the ancient Plymouth Reliant, the four thousand seven hundred dollars in the checking account. The lawyer threw around technical terms – probate, affidavit, transfer of title, personal representative, Bureau of Vital Records, death certificate – that only made everything foggier and more daunting. But she did calculate that if, in accordance with Wolfe's intention, everything was sold, he'd be left with about $150,000 after taxes and expenses. Wolfe did not really know what to make of this number. He was financially inexperienced. It sounded both like a lot of money and not a lot of money. There was one more thing, the attorney said: the non-probate assets. The deceased would likely have had a retirement plan and a life-insurance policy under his terms of employment. The attorney advised Wolfe to get in touch with the Astrogeology Science Center about that. The cash value of these products could be significant.

Wolfe called Human Resources at ASC. They referred him to the company that handled their employee benefits. The lady at the employee-benefits company told Wolfe that his father did have a life-insurance policy and a retirement product. There was a problem, however: Wolfe was not the designated beneficiary. The lady would not say who the beneficiary was; that information was private. Wolfe didn't make further inquiries. In some ways, he was relieved. Pension schemes and insurance claims were not things he was into.

Wolfe called his mother, who lived in London, to inform her about his dad's death. She and Wolfe had last been in touch two years before, when Wolfe had visited her and his half-brother on his way to Prague. Wolfe's mother seemed to be aware of his father's death already – how, Wolfe didn't know. When Wolfe mentioned the problem with the life insurance, his mother said, I'm the beneficiary, darling. Oh, Wolfe said. He didn't know what to think. His parents had divorced many years earlier. Wolfe had never learned the details of the split, about which his father had said that his wife had wished to 'spread her wings'. He knew only that his mother, who was from Lakeland, Florida, had decamped to France with some kind of international professor. She and the international professor seemed to do a lot of traveling – every now and then, the child Wolfe would receive a postcard with a picture of London or Biarritz or Australia. Sometimes, at the conclusion of a tense, terse parental phone conversation, the phone would be handed to Wolfe, and he would hear her voice. These interactions became less frequent, although after his brother, Geoff, was born, his mother sometimes sent Wolfe a picture of the little guy. But why would his dad have designated his ex-wife as his beneficiary? The young adult Wolfe had no good answer. There was a lot he didn't understand. His parents still belonged to a mysterious world of grown-up motives and doings.

When Wolfe went to the attorney to sign the papers, she asked about the benefits. Wolfe related the conversation with his mother. The attorney got excited. She said that it was not uncommon for folks who got divorced, like Wolfe's dad, to forget to update their beneficiary designation. The law of Arizona, she said, expressly protected rightful heirs – Wolfe, in this case – from being deprived of their inheritance in such circumstances. The attorney wrote the benefits company, explaining the situation and demanding all relevant information. She attached a copy of the divorce certificate, which, by some miracle, Wolfe had found in his dad's house. Some days later, the benefits people replied that they had already authorized payments to Wolfe's mother. She had received a lump sum of $192,000 in respect of the retirement benefits, and, in respect of the life-insurance policy, one million dollars.

'Huh,' I said.

On the advice of the Flagstaff attorney, Wolfe engaged a fancy Phoenix law firm. There were meetings, there were retainer fees, there were requests for documents, there was correspondence with lawyers representing Wolfe's mother and the benefits company. The case was complex, the Phoenix firm eventually advised Wolfe. It involved multiple parties, multiple jurisdictions, multiple fields of law. Further analysis was required, which they would be glad to undertake once young Wolfe had settled their invoice for $63,000, which had come on top of the Flagstaff's attorney's bill for $16,000.

Wolfe had been deprived of more than half of his remaining inheritance without even receiving it!

I understood, from his passionate tone and his unusual lucidity, that this was Wolfe's day in court. He wanted me to believe him, to adjudicate in his favor, to award him my sympathy. But a story about how Wolfe lost a million bucks in an inheritance feud wasn't the kind of story I could commit to. And I was distracted. I was thinking about the phone call I'd not answered, from my sister.

•

The new Committee's first month was bumpy, but not as bumpy as I'd feared. Our systems were resilient to personnel change. Wolfe and I, the Co-Leads, worked in close consultation. He held a series of one-on-one coffee meetings with the members whose practices had been assigned to him, and he made a careful note of what they said they needed. It was effective, by all accounts. When I congratulated him, he downplayed it with the remark that the meetings were his wife's idea.

'The idea is good,' I said. 'But ideas are overrated. You did the work.'

There is nobody who doesn't feel better after a well-earned compliment – even if they appear to brush it off. Annie was someone like that.

Wolfe had another reason to be congratulated: he had successfully completed the two major writing assignments I'd gotten him in the run-up to the AGM. 'The clients are impressed,' I told him. I shared with him what they had written about his work. I added, 'Always pass on to a member anything nice that a client might have said about them.'

He answered without hesitation, 'There's something you should know, Lakesha. Everyone thinks you're amazing.'

Humor is so important. You can't spend the day together, week in, week out, without it.

If Edil had a sense of humor, I couldn't see it. She sometimes used a jokey, sarcastic intonation, but it wasn't to say anything jokey or sarcastic. It struck me as aggressive. This was my interpretation of her demeanor. Others no doubt interpreted it differently.

And it must be noted that nobody complained to me about her performance as the Fees & Marketing Officer. Edil was fortunate that Greg, a meticulous person, had left her superb spreadsheets of every member's assignment history and fee structure, so she had all the tools she needed.

I confess that I found it very difficult to look over and see Edil sitting at my old desk. (I took over Annie's spot, in the corner.) She was invariably looking at her screen with great intentness, poring over God knew what.

One day in early June, she approached my desk. She held a six-dollar cup of coffee in one hand and a printout in the other. 'So . . . I've been doing an audit?'

'Audit?'

'It's nothing important. Just that I don't see AMWA fees in your earnings numbers?'

'AMWA fees?'

'American Medical Writers Association?' Edil said, and again it sounded as if she'd made a sarcastic remark.

'Those would be separate,' I said. 'Those would be my personal earnings, not the Group's.'

'Yes, of course. But it's just that in the AMWA materials you use the Group's name and Group credentials. Arguably . . . I mean, it looks like you're wearing your Group hat?'

'No, it doesn't look like that. What you're talking about is my bio. My bio mentions my position at the Group. Because it's a bio. AMWA is not a client of the Group. It's an association that I'm a member of. If someone was to invite you to a conference, your bio would mention the Group, too. And your honorarium would be your income, not the Group's.'

Edil smiled. 'It's not a big deal. We'll let it pass.'

'There isn't anything to let pass, Edil.'

'Deal,' she said, as if we'd just struck a bargain. She returned to her space, sipping coffee.

For several minutes, I tried to get back to work. Then I got up and left. I did not feel safe in the building. I went straight home. When I got there, I double-locked the door.

This might seem like an irrational response. But I learned a long time ago that at the first sign of danger you must get away immediately. You do not question your instincts. You do not wait for a second red flag. That is how things go wrong.

I poured myself a glass of water and tried to understand what had just happened. I had fled my place of work. That was a big deal. It had never happened before. But I had to keep things in their correct proportions. I had to think things through as clearly as possible.

It is very useful to have another point of view in these situations. But there was no one at the Group whom I could share this with. I called Annie.

She was driving. A few minutes later, she called back from the side of the road. I kept it brief. She wasn't someone who needed to have things spelled out. She said, 'The AMWA thing is just nothing. You can stop worrying about that right away. I did events like that. It was always separate.'

'Exactly.' It was such a relief to hear this.

Just as decisively, Annie said, 'As for Edil, you don't try to straighten her out or forgive her. That's what she wants – to be the focus. You treat her like the crazy uncle – act friendly, ignore the craziness, focus on your own stuff.'

'OK, good. That's clarifying. Thanks.'

Annie said, 'It's unfair, I know.'

It wasn't the unfairness that worried me. If I let unfairness worry me, I would not be able to get out of bed in the mornings. What worried me was that I was in danger.

I had experience of being in danger – being in a place where folks around me are making bad, very bad, decisions. But none of these folks woke up in the morning wanting to harm me. They were dangerous for complex reasons having to do with their situation. They were situationally dangerous, you could say. Edil was different. She wasn't crashing through a life of obstacles. She was someone who drank expensive coffee. She had elected to use her time and power to cook up an accusation, or a suspicion, of dishonesty against me. That was not situational bad behavior. That was behavior intended to imperil my career and my well-being.

I knew that I would not call Annie again for a long while. The Group was now my burden, not hers. She had moved away. I had this recurrent image of her in Sacramento, a place I've never been to, and in the image Sacramento was lit up by dazzling sunshine, and Annie was always on her way to an outdoor restaurant where everybody was wearing sunglasses and eating a never-ending brunch.

I went back to the office. You keep going.

Wolfe was at his desk, frowning at his screen as though he was finding it difficult to understand what he was looking at. He gave me a smile and a little finger wave. That lifted my spirits.

It doesn't take much. That is what is so tantalizing about the mission of a special collective such as the Group. Small gestures of goodwill, repeated at very little cost to the makers of the gestures, are disproportionately productive.

Every Thursday, the Committee held a 5:00 p.m. meeting. The agenda was always the same: to review the week in progress and to prepare for the week ahead. By tradition, the discussions were cheerful and businesslike. Not long after the AMWA incident, we held one such meeting. Tommy was absent, Wolfe, Edil and Betsy were present. I was alone with the proxy gang.

Early in the meeting, Edil raised her hand – a dramatic gesture that brought conversation to a stop. 'Why,' she asked in that sugary voice, 'did we give the Labs assignment to Ronnie?'

'We' referred to me. Ronnie referred to Ronnie Arelt, whose practice I handled. Labs was a Group client. Everyone knew this, with the possible exception of Betsy, who seemed to have great difficulty retaining facts that were connected to her work as Secretary.

I should not have responded. I should have told Edil that the time to raise a question that was not on the agenda was after the items that were on the agenda had been dealt with. But I could not stop myself. 'What's the issue?' I asked.

'Kyle came to me about it. He believes that Labs should have been his. I made a note of his concerns. I can send it to you, if you like,' Edil said, placing her fingertips on the keys of her laptop.

'No need,' I said, although I was curious-furious, as Annie used to say. I knew Kyle Liu from way back. He had never complained before, not about anything. Edil had been stirring the pot. I said, 'Ronnie's done Labs work before. They wanted to work with him again. Kyle will understand once it's explained to him.'

'What should I tell him, exactly?' Edil said.

'You don't have to tell him anything,' I said. 'Wolfe is responsible for Kyle's practice.'

Wolfe spoke up. 'Yes,' he said.

'If a member has a query about their practice,' I reminded the Committee, 'the responsible person, the person they should discuss it with, is their practice manager. That's always been the procedure.'

'What if they don't want to talk to their practice manager? What's our procedure then?' In a bizarrely emotional tone that suggested that she was discussing something very personal and painful, Edil went on: 'I've been approached by several members who have serious concerns about the fairness of work allocation. They come to me because they don't feel that they can talk to the Leads. They want to talk to someone they trust.' I started to say something, but Edil spoke over me. 'I will not be shut down. Nobody shuts me down. Somebody has to speak for ordinary members.' She seemed to be fighting back tears.

Wolfe looked as if he was trying to catch up with what exactly was going on.

Betsy, her pen hovering over the Minutes book, spoke up. 'Um, so Wolfe's going to talk with Kyle? Is that the decision?'

Edil had flamed out. I felt my power. I said, 'There's nothing to decide. You' – I was addressing Wolfe – 'decide what to do about Kyle. He's your member. The Committee does not get involved unless you think it should.'

Wolfe said, 'Thanks. I will speak with Kyle. And I just want to add: Edil, if there's some issue with work allocation, it has to be referred to the Committee. You can't appoint yourself as a kind of unofficial ombudsman. That would throw everything off kilter. You definitely can't insinuate that Lakesha has done something wrong. It's disruptive. It's disrespectful.'

What Wolfe said was correct. I was surprised and pleased to hear him say it. At the same time, I was thinking that I would have kept quiet if I were him.

•

The real trouble began with the Pexantil job.

Pexantil had been Annie's best client. It was important for the Group to retain the account. Wolfe asked me if he could handle it. He knew someone there – to be accurate, his wife had a good friend whose wife worked at Pexantil – and he was confident that he could manage the outreach. OK, I said. Being entrusted with a big account would give Wolfe confidence. And he was a Co-Lead, after all.

The next day, he came to see me. He looked pleased. 'Pexantil is a go. But they want you, specifically, to take over Annie's writing.'

Writing copy for Pexantil – a booming outfit that specialized in mobility appliances and other products for our older population – would require an extra effort from me, but I could do it. I said, 'Then I guess we'd better give them what they want. Nice job.' I was certain that Annie had quietly set this up when she left, but there was no need to tell Wolfe that.

The Pexantil assignment paid the writer twelve thousand dollars. If I focused on nothing else, I could finish it in a week. This was a big number by Group standards, but it was not atypical of some of the deals that senior members received. Pexantil had a long history of paying well, because Annie had spent years nurturing the commercial relationship on behalf of the Group. Edil of course knew all of this.

A few days later, she rang me at home. It was evening – I was in bed, watching TV with Cutie. When I saw the name light up on my screen, I ignored the call. She left a message. I watched some more TV, then went to sleep. I do not listen to messages last thing at night.

In the morning, I played the message.

'Hi, Lakesha. There's something we need to discuss, and not on the phone. It's not something I *want* to discuss, it's something I feel *duty-bound* to discuss. I'm going to ask for a Committee meeting tomorrow, Wednesday, at ten a.m. OK, bye, thanks.'

I showered, ate breakfast. Shortly before ten, I texted Edil:

2:30 pm works for me. L

I worked for two hours on the Pexantil papers, then changed into the dark-blue pants suit that I keep for certain occasions. I put on lipstick and went in.

It was one-thirty when I got there. Edil was at her desk. She wore several layers of colorful, semitransparent shawls, presumably intended to make her look flowing and natural and not how she in fact looked, which was like someone who had crashed through random flowering bushes. I walked by her and said, 'Hey there, Edil,' and went straight to my desk. Shortly before two-thirty, I observed Edil entering the conference room. Wolfe followed her soon after, and then Betsy, armed with the Minutes book. I let them wait a while. Edil occupied herself by poking around the houseplants. She often made it obvious that she found the plants – which I had donated, and which I watered every day – distasteful or contemptible.

When I took my seat, I immediately said, 'Edil has called this meeting in order to discuss something she believes is important. Edil, please go ahead.'

Edil had sheets of paper set out in front of her. She spread her hands on the table and embarked on her presentation. You would have thought we were in a courtroom.

While she was reviewing her files, she told the Committee, something unusual had caught her eye: Wolfe and I had taken over, for our personal benefit, some of the Group's most remu- nerative accounts, with the consequence that he and I were in line for a 'stunning' increase in our usual earnings. What troubled Edil wasn't that Wolfe and I would prosper – there was nothing wrong with people making money. What troubled her was that Wolfe had procured my new clients, and I had procured his new clients. The optics were very troubling. 'There's no easy way to say this,' Edil said, 'but it looks a lot like self-dealing.' She spoke this last phrase triumphantly.

Edil didn't say so, but she had to be referring to Pexantil in my case, and in Wolfe's case to the two major clients I had passed his way – before the election. Before he and I were the Co-Leads.

'Wait a minute,' Wolfe said.

'I'm not done,' Edil said sharply. 'I will not be interrupted.' She wasn't making accusations, she said. She was just pointing out something that was troubling, something that she'd uncovered—

'Uncovered?' Wolfe interrupted.

'Let her finish,' I said. 'Carry on, Edil.'

Looking me in the eye, she said, 'You don't tell me to carry on, Lakesha. I have the floor. I'm going to carry on with or without your permission.' She would report her concerns, she continued, to the membership. Her only agenda was the well-being of the Group. To this end, she would recommend a full investigation. She had no other option. 'The Group cannot function without complete trust in this Committee. I think we can all agree on that.' Edil stacked up her papers. As far I could tell, they had served no purpose. She said, 'Did you get all of that, Betsy?'

Betsy, still writing, nodded.

'Thank you,' I said. 'Is there anything else you'd like to add?' She shook her head. I raised my hand to stop Wolfe from speaking. I said to Edil: 'If you're going to make this type of serious allegation, you'll have to identify exactly which transactions you believe are potentially corrupt. Because that is what you're saying. You're saying that it looks like Wolfe and I have acted in a corrupt way. But you have not offered any details. Zero. So, before you talk to anyone in the Group, you need to provide the Committee with a detailed written account of what the supposed corruption is. It's not fair to me or Wolfe or anyone else to consider this without a full statement of the alleged facts. Second, I'd like the Minutes to record that I do not accept that there's an appearance of impropriety here, let alone any actual impropriety.'

Edil said, 'You're not going to dictate to me what I should or shouldn't do. I'm going to do what I think is right – what I think is right for the Group.'

Wolfe had been rolling a pencil back and forth on the tabletop. He quit doing this in order to say, 'Can I speak now? For the record?'

'Yes,' I said.

'First off, I reject everything that Edil is insinuating, alleging, proposing, making up. It's all bullshit, it's all bad faith. Second – and

I'd like you to record this, too, Betsy, if you don't mind – I want to say that I do not have confidence in Edil as an officer of the Group. I believe that she is abusing her power to engage in personal vendettas – namely, this bullshit that we're hearing today. How you got elected, Edil – and how I got elected, and Betsy, too – with proxies, that's something that needs to be looked at. My position is that if we're going to start investigations, let's do it properly. Let's investigate everything.'

Edil said, 'This is retaliation. This is textbook retaliation. You're retaliating against a whistle-blower. Betsy, did you get that?'

'Whistle-blower?' Wolfe said, laughing. 'That's what you're calling yourself?'

They started loudly talking over each other. Betsy stopped writing.

'Excuse me,' I said. 'Excuse me!' When everyone was silent, I signaled to Betsy to resume taking Minutes. 'This Committee is bound by the *Rules*, and the *Rules* provide that the Committee acts by resolution. A resolution requires a majority decision. That is not up for argument. Edil, would you like to propose a resolution?'

She became flustered. 'That's wrong. You and Wolfe need to abstain. You can't vote on a resolution that calls for an investigation into your wrongdoing. It's a conflict of interest.'

'Do you have a resolution?'

Again, she just said stuff.

I said, 'Let me help you. How about: "It is resolved that a sub-committee comprising three members who are not on the Action Committee examine the allocation of work by the Co-Leads to each other and determine whether such allocation is appropriate."' I wrote it down as I spoke. 'It is further resolved that the subcommittee shall be organized by Gin Yee with his consent.' Gin Yee was the least objectionable person in the Group. I handed Edil the transcript.

She refused to look at it. 'I don't think a resolution drafted by you is the way forward here,' she said.

Wolfe said, 'I'd like to propose a resolution, too.' He wanted to appoint a second subcommittee to examine the circumstances of the recent election of officers. We voted on Wolfe's resolution. Edil and Betsy were against it. I abstained, on the grounds that it was premature to vote on such an important matter as the election of officers without some advance notice to the Committee. My actual reasons were tactical, not technical. Edil was right – Wolfe's resolution could be viewed as retaliatory. Also, it would magnify the dispute and potentially embroil our members in fighting. That could lead anywhere. Most important of all, there would be another election before long. Edil would almost certainly lose. It was smarter to play the long game and in the meantime avoid unproductive conflict. Storms blow over.

I proposed the resolution to set up a subcommittee to investigate Edil's accusations – for that's what she was doing, making accusations against me and Wolfe. Wolfe voted against it, on the grounds that it was 'total bullshit'. Betsy voted in favor, as did I. Edil suspiciously abstained. She was right to be suspicious. It was certain that the subcommittee would quickly and objectively ascertain that her fantasies of corruption were indeed fantasies. Our members were well aware that the Co-Leads allocated work to each other. They knew me, they knew my character, and they knew my work. The Group would self-correct.

M

Faye is now regularly calling Sushila.

It started with e-mails, after the birth of Fizzy, in the guise of the grandmother. I made it very clear to Sushila that I wanted no part of it. That was my mistake. I should have forbidden it outright.

I'm not sure what prompted the escalation of contact. All I know is that after I returned from Europe, Sushila began to retreat to our bedroom to take the calls – not to hide the fact of their existence from me, but to spare me the trauma of feeling the presence of this harmful person, however indirectly. And yet, I am traumatized. My so-called mother is more than ever disrespecting my wish to separate my life from hers, is pursuing her own objectives even as they lead into my own home. With every phone call she is growing her power at my expense. What are they cooking up?

One evening, I sit down to dinner in a foul, wordless mood. My wife and daughter have just taken another call from England, with the voice of the caller audible on speaker. It's too much to bear – hearing that person's voice, hearing that person talk to Fizzy. When I put Fizzy to bed, I stay with her after she has fallen asleep. Her bed is a warm little boat. Beyond its borders is the dark sea. It's not just this Faye business. At work I suddenly find myself at the center of a stupid, dangerous storm in which my integrity is being questioned. The accusations are a bitter pill to swallow, yes, but swallowing bitter pills I'm an expert at. What torments me is a terror that forms in my consciousness in a series of questions: What next? Where am I headed? Who's with me?

I'm still in Fizzy's bed, holding on to her for dear life, shaking, when the most extraordinary, in every way unprecedented thing happens. At the doorway of the bedroom a person appears in silhouette, a person who pauses to ascertain whether or not I'm asleep; and for the duration of the pause a great strange warmth fills me, and I believe that the silhouette belongs to my mother when she was my mother.

It is my wife, of course. She sits gently on the bed. 'Come down,' she says.

We have a kitchen island. It has a tiny bar area with two stools. In this area Sushila has put out a bowl of freshly chopped radishes and a saucer with salt. This snack signifies that she would like to talk. Good. I'm ready to talk.

She will take care, going forward, Sushila says, to protect me from the calls. But Faye is Fizzy's grandmother. I will have to think about how I am going to manage that fact. Sushila isn't suggesting a reconciliation—

'Reconciliation? We've never had a relationship!'

—but, rather, she's suggesting that I find a way to feel less anguished about the role Faye is assuming in Fizzy's life. 'It might help you to consider the possibility,' Sushila says, 'that Faye is not the person she once was.'

She continues in this vein: that an evolution of my feelings is maybe overdue, that maybe I should consider this person in a revisionist light. Faye has caused me a lot of suffering, Sushila concedes. But, with the wisdom of experience, it is possible to understand that Faye's upbringing did not equip her for conventional family life. She did not know her father. She did not receive much love from her own mother. She—

'I know all those stories.'

Faye's upbringing, Sushila steadily argues, explains her impulsive marriage to my father, an older, responsible, kind man with a good career but otherwise maybe not very suitable for a young woman with—

'Yes, I've already figured that out.'

Was it unforgivable, Sushila asks, that in her twenties she decided to flee marital and parental obligations that overwhelmed her? Look, it was wrong of her to keep for herself the life-insurance moneys that should have been mine. But by then she had my little brother to look after. She wouldn't be the first or last single mother to do whatever was necessary to survive. Maybe, with the passage of time—

'Is she going to pay me back? With the passage of time, I mean. Is she now going to pay me back?'

Sushila says, 'I want a normal, healthy, open family life, Mark. No feuds, no walls, no vendettas—'

She is referring, I realize, not only to the situation with Faye but also to the situation with her own father, Sarva, who has very recently turned against me. 'Is it too much to ask,' I reply furiously, 'that in my house, the one place in the world that is mine, is it too much to ask—'

The door buzzer sounds. The buzz is followed by a loud, vicious knocking.

I peek out from behind the front-window curtain. A stranger stands at the door with his back turned to the house. An SUV with Quebec plates, presumably his, is parked on the far side of the road. The visitor is outfitted in a baseball cap, a black sport coat, khaki cargo shorts and black sneakers with red socks. His very white calves are repulsively bright. He turns to face the house.

'Christ,' I say.

'Who is it?'

'It's Jean-Luc Lefebvre.'

She joins me at the window. 'That's him? I thought he was in Africa, looking for your miraculous Godwin.'

'I guess he's come back.'

'Are you expecting him?'

'Do I look like I'm expecting him?'

'Are you OK? You've actually turned white.'

'Don't answer him. We're not at home.'

Lefebvre removes his cap from his head and waves it in the air like someone from the nineteenth century. He's spotted us.

'Well, you'd better see what he wants,' Sushila says. She seems intrigued.

When I open the door, I'm actually scared. Why? What is it about this man that terrifies me? 'How can I help you?' I hear myself saying.

'Hello, my friend,' he says. 'May I enter? I have some news for you.'

Within minutes, our guest is sitting on the backyard deck with a beer. When I introduce him to my wife, he rises to his feet and disgustingly kisses the back of her hand. He eats greedily from the bowl of potato chips that Sushila has brought out, then empties his beer glass in a long swallow, then helps himself to more chips. Sushila and I sit in our chairs, watching him. The occasion has assumed a premodern quality. Lefebvre is the traveler who appears from beyond the horizon without warning and must be fed and watered and shown hospitality, whatever the cost.

Pouring himself more beer – he insists on drinking from a glass – Lefebvre reports that it's his first time in this country. How many people, he wonders, have traveled to more than sixty nations before traveling to the United States? But in the case of Lefebvre, it is logical: he is a man of football, and the USA is not a nation of football. For the same negative reason, he has never visited India. He looks at Sushila, as if this information might be of special relevance to her. It is a curious fact, Lefebvre continues, that the five most populous countries in the world – China, India, the US, Indonesia, Pakistan – even if combined, would be unable to produce a team that could win the smallest cup in a top European league. The United States has in all of its history produced not a single important player of football. Even its goalkeepers, supposedly the national forte, have been mediocre, certainly by comparison with the great guardians, men like Yashin and Schmeichel, who understood that the keeper, the wearer of the number one, is not a defender of last resort but a player with special powers whose duty is to exude a special, quasi-magical aura. America, Lefebvre gleefully goes on, makes mechanical, mediocre players. They play football in the same the way that he, Lefebvre, speaks English – in translation. Why is it a foreign game to them? Because, Lefebvre asserts, in order to play football naturally you need to play for thousands and thousands of hours as a child, play every single day, play at school during recess and on the street after school until the darkness falls, and then play on, under the streetlights. That is the only way to develop the subtle skills of the foot and eye on which this deceptively simple kickball game insists. American children develop this ability with the basketball, certainly, but with football? No. Lefebvre grunts happily. MLS – Major League Soccer – sounds like a terrible disease, and when one watches the players move slowly and brainlessly around the field, one would think that indeed they suffer from a sickness of movement. Why, then, has he at last come to this country? Lefebvre answers his own question by unfurling a dramatic index finger. The finger points at a flabbergasted Sushila.

The United States, the Frenchman declares, is the producer of the most advanced lady footballers in the world.

Personally, Lefebvre has never been attracted by the football of women. It is not that he holds chauvinistic beliefs but that he is an idealist, someone for whom the beauty of football transcends questions of sex. If a player is good enough, it matters not to Lefebvre whether the player is a man or a woman. Of course, the reverse is also true – if a player isn't good enough, then no special allowance is to be made on account of the sex of the player. Lefebvre has no real opinions about women's sports, nor does he wish to have. Sport is recreational and therefore optional. Nobody is under a duty to like it. Either it interests you or it doesn't. Until recently, Lefebvre had no interest in watching football played by women. He could not get used to the childlike appearance of the players on the field, in particular the goalkeepers, who looked so little when contained by the masculine dimensions of the goals. But this question of the physical was not his fundamental problem. His problem was his unfamiliarity with the culture of the women's game – its history, its myths, its personalities. Who was the Navratilova of football? Who was its Nadia Comăneci? There was Marta, the Brazilian, a very good technical player, certainly. And Mia Hamm, of course, the one who famously removed her shirt. But with all due respect to these sportswomen . . . Lefebvre raises his hands like someone being arrested at gunpoint. He will put it this way: the female Michel Platini has yet to be discovered. This is why he, Lefebvre, is here, in the United States: a certain European club with ambitions relating to the feminine football market has asked him to evaluate certain players from a sporting perspective. His first stop was in Canada, to watch some of the Women's World Cup; and from Canada he drove into the United States. Lefebvre's plan is to acquaint himself with the Women's Soccer League, to learn how to better understand the women's game, and to make certain recommendations. More specific than this he cannot be, for reasons of confidentiality.

'How interesting,' Sushila says. She offers him more potato chips.

As he accepts the chips, first manually and then orally, Lefebvre informs us that after several days in Quebec he crossed the border at New York, near Lac Champlain, from where he headed westward through an endless, truly magnificent forest. To drive for hundreds of kilometers through precipitous mountains densely covered by tall trees – it is a journey that is no longer possible in Europe, perhaps even no longer possible in Africa. Tarzan, Lefebvre jokes, would nowadays be discovered in the jungles of America. Like all Frenchmen of his generation, Lefebvre says, he grew up with stories about the Wild West – cowboys, pioneers, Apaches, horses, canyons, saloons, spittoons – but his imagination had always been drawn to the early 1700s, a snowy, wooded world of canoes, trappers, log cabins, river rapids and redskins. As he drove through the primeval forests of the Adirondacks, Lefebvre claims, he imagined without difficulty the terrible battles that were fought for almost two hundred years by the soldiers of Nouvelle France and the English redcoats and the Indian warriors. It was a tragic story, when all was said and done. The last of the Mohicans! Lefebvre exclaims, and he raises his glass.

Sushila, smiling, joins him in this inexplicable toast. What is the matter with her?

The famous book by James Fenimore Cooper, Lefebvre vigorously continues, was set during the so-called French and Indian War.

Do Sushila and I know that this war began here, in Pittsburgh? A mere mile or two distant from where we sit, at the confluence of the city's great rivers, was the site of Fort Duquesne, control of which offered dominance over the Ohio River Valley and, from there, the Mississippi Valley. It was the fight for Fort Duquesne – eventually won by the British, who promptly built Fort Pitt at the same location – that precipitated the final demise of New France. In recent years, Lefebvre asserts, he has taken a deep interest in the military history of France. For some time, he has wanted to visit Pittsburgh and to see for himself what, if anything, is left of this great landmark of the intercolonial wars.

I say, 'You drove all the way here to see Fort Duquesne?'

Lefebvre licks the last bits of potato chips from his fingers. 'I came, my friend, because you are my business partner. I have important information.'

For the second time that evening, the doorbell buzzes. For the second time, I go to the window. What now?

It's a food delivery guy. I am about to shout down that he's come to the wrong address when Sushila speaks up: 'I thought our guest might want to eat, after his long journey.'

•

'It is not simple,' Lefebvre, his mouth full of rice and chicken, says, 'to go to Africa.' He waves a fork in the direction of that continent. In football, he says, there is the concept of the home and the away. As everyone knows, it is easier to play at home. The conditions are familiar; the stadium is filled with your supporters. But there is no avoiding it – the away game. The road game, as they say in this country. Lefebvre looks at me. 'You say to me, Godwin is in Benin. Therefore, I must go away from home. I must go on the road, to Benin. Even though this is a country I do not like.'

'Why don't you like it?' Sushila says.

Lefebvre nonresponsively discloses that, as he's grown older, his fear of flying has worsened. Flying to Africa, which as a younger man he did many times without a second thought, now fills him with a special trepidation.

This trip to Cotonou he didn't like the look of at all. His original flight was canceled, which was bad luck; and he was not able to get a replacement ticket for another three weeks. In short, he flew out almost a month after our meeting in Paris. The significance of this delay would only later reveal itself.

En route to the airport, Lefebvre had the feeling that something wasn't right. Benin was the only West African land that he had never visited. Usually on trips to that part of the world, he would be met at the airport by a friend, or the friend of a friend. But Lefebvre had no connections in Benin. He had been obliged to make impersonal long-distance arrangements for a local guide. This was far from ideal. To make matters worse, the election season had just started in Benin. Lefebvre was breaking his own rule: never fly into an African country during an election. But he had no choice. He had to find Godwin.

The departure gate was in a remote corner of Charles de Gaulle. At the gate, Lefebvre and the other Cotonou passengers, instead of boarding an airplane, were made to walk out into the freezing rain to waiting buses. In these buses of shit, Lefebvre says, they exited the airport and traveled along a public highway. Lefebvre laughs out of some internal source of amusement. You should have seen, he says to Sushila, the concerned faces of the passengers as they were driven for kilometers past fields and industrial zones. It was as if we had all been tricked and were going to be transported by bus to Benin. In the middle of nowhere, at a locality that bore no resemblance to an aerodrome, they arrived at a row of hangars in front of which Air France jets were stationed. The bus kept going, to the very last of these planes – and only there did they come to a stop and were the Cotonou passengers permitted to get out, into the rain, and to climb another staircase and finally enter the aircraft that was set aside for their transportation to that place formerly known as the Slave Coast.

Looking pleased with this provocation, Lefebvre reaches into the cooler – I brought it out for selfish reasons, in anticipation of precisely this kind of long monologue from our self-invited guest – and extracts another beer. Behind him, beyond rooftops and treetops, the sun is sinking. Mosquitoes have materialized, pestering me but not, for some reason, pestering Lefebvre or his parched, ultra-white bare legs. 'Shall we go indoors?' I say, slapping my neck.

Lefebvre produces a pack of cheroots and lights up. He offers us a cheroot, or maybe it's a cigarillo, with the words, 'The mosquitoes do not like.' We decline his offer.

If she were to fly regularly to Africa, Lefebvre advises my wife, she would know that airlines reserve their most ancient airplanes for the routes to the poorest countries. Lefebvre found himself in an aircraft perhaps a quarter-century old that was equipped with ashtrays in the armrests, tiny primitive screens in the seatbacks, and spacious economy seats in which a passenger could almost fully recline. But he felt more than ever the horror of being irreversibly strapped down, with no option but to wait for the flying machine and its unknown operators to lift him high into the sky.

As if reliving his anxiety, Lefebvre takes a paper napkin and wipes food traces and sweat from his mouth. He who knows about football, he pronounces, knows about its tragic connection to aviation. How well Lefebvre remembers receiving the news of the Munich air crash – the destruction, on a cold, snowy February night, of the brilliant young Manchester United team known everywhere as the Busby Babes. They were not the first. In the eastern outskirts of Turin, Lefebvre says, is a hill named Superga. On the hilltop, which offers a tremendous panorama of the Alps, sits a basilica of great splendor, comparable in its dramatic prominence to the Sacré-Coeur on Montmartre. Almost ten years before the Munich disaster, in 1949, an airplane, lost in fog, flew directly into the base of this famous church. The plane was carrying the invincible Torino team. All were killed – all the players, all the trainers, all the journalists, everyone.

Superga, Munich, Heysel, Copenhagen, Lima – this, Lefebvre says hoarsely, is what he means by the history of football, the spirit of football. Does the football of women have such a spirit? Who are the martyrs of feminine football?

Overruling with a raised finger the objection I'm about to voice – Who are the martyrs? Is he kidding? Every woman who ever breathed, that's who! – Lefebvre instructs us that African football has not been spared disasters of the air – on the contrary. Zambia has suffered like no other. It began, one could say, with Dag Hammarskjöld, whose plane was shot down over that country and for whom a football stadium was built in the city of Ndola. Unfortunately, Dag Hammarskjöld Stadium was long ago erased, along with the memory of the United Nations Secretary-General after whom it was named. Such is the fate of men of power, Lefebvre opines. In 1993, five years after the stadium was destroyed, as if by the operation of a curse there occurred an even greater tragedy. A plane chartered by the Zambia World Cup squad, an old military transporter with large propellers, crashed in the Gulf of Biafra, off the coast of Gabon. Again, there were no survivors. The greatest-ever Zambia team, a team en route, so to speak, to the World Cup finals, was gone, like this. Lefebvre twists his hand in a representation of the twisting of fate.

Whenever such a calamity occurs, he continues, looking at Sushila as if she and he share a special understanding, there is always a footnote concerning this or that person who by chance missed the flight and was saved by some trivial intervention of chance – the lost passport, the traffic jam on the road to the airport, the last-minute change of plans . . . As he sat waiting for takeoff to Cotonou, Lefebvre says, he looked around at his fellow fliers – businessmen, most of them, talking in French or Arabic, people who like him had no choice but to undertake commerce in one of the toughest markets in the world, people of every race, people for whom he had the greatest respect – and superstitiously examined their faces for some sign of destiny.

'So what happened?' I say. 'Your plane crashed?'

'Jean-Luc,' Sushila says, 'can I get you another beer? We also have white wine, if you'd prefer. And maybe a glass of water?' She collects his tableware.

I follow her into the kitchen. 'You can't give him more to drink. He's driving.'

'Why are you so hostile to him?' She gets wineglasses out of the cupboard. 'If you want to throw him out, go ahead. But I'm not going to be rude. Besides,' she adds – and it would feel like a parting shot, if Sushila were someone who goes in for parting shots – 'I'm having fun. When was the last time we had someone over?'

It takes me a few seconds to regroup. Look, am I antisocial? Maybe. Do I overly discourage visits? Yes, arguably. But must I entertain, of all people, Lefebvre? Something brushes my leg.

It is Pearson, pressing himself against me. He does this when I stand next to the kitchen island, in the hope of food. I fetch him a treat, my good, loyal dog. We step out back onto the deck together.

Sushila, looking very relaxed and alert, is asking Lefebvre what the Sahara looks like from high up in the air.

'Ah, the Sahara,' Lefebvre echoes sonorously, significantly, wisely. He states, with no diminution in gravity, that he did not look out of his window because he knew in advance what he would see: the red-and-cardboard-colored ocean of sand and rock of the most arid, most desolate, and most feared region of the Sahara. Even from an airplane it was frightening to contemplate this desert of deserts. In theory, one saw Algeria, one saw Niger. But in reality? A place without people, without roads, without water, without a past or a future – could such a place be called a country? Could Mars be a country? In all of the history of human beings, Lefebvre says, no nation or tribe has successfully inhabited the Tanezrouft, also named the Land of Terror.

In any case, Lefebvre says, apparently losing patience with his own digression, the plane traversed the airspace of Mali and Burkina Faso. At about two o'clock in the morning – Air France always booked the cheapest, least desirable arrival slots for their routes to Africa – the feeble blue electric lights of Cotonou showed in the darkness. Minutes later, Lefebvre landed safely.

Sushila pours Lefebvre a glass of wine.

•

After some visa issues – 'Always it is a drama, the *douane*' – Lefebvre was admitted into the state. At the terminal exit, he joined the hundreds who formed an agitated throng in front of the airport's single large building. Why so many people were gathered at the airport in the middle of the night, and what they were shouting and gesticulating about, was anybody's guess. As is not uncommon in Africa, Lefebvre claims, he was surrounded by a secret emotion, a secret circumstance, a secret energy. Lefebvre needed a taxi. He surveyed the crowd until his eyes settled on a well-dressed, self-possessed man who appeared to be in the private-transportation business. Relying, Lefebvre says, on the intuition developed by long experience of such situations, he approached this man and asked if he could recommend a taxi driver. Without a word, the man escorted the Frenchman to a car. A driver sat behind the wheel, and he agreed to take Lefebvre to his hotel. The driver began to inch the car forward through the crowd. Here the trouble began.

A loud bang sounded. A bespectacled, respectable-looking middle-aged man in a collared white shirt had slammed his hand down on the hood of Lefebvre's car and was shouting at the driver, in French: Am I an animal? Am I chicken? Am I a chicken to be run down on the road? The pedestrian again banged on the hood, then came around and pulled open the driver's door and grabbed the keys from the ignition. Lefebvre's driver – a young, slight, stunned-looking individual, a boy – was paralyzed with fear. The angry man raised the keys to the crowd and shouted that he would keep them until the police came.

The original man, the self-possessed man, reappeared. He calmly spoke with some of the bystanders in an African language; then, in French, he addressed the complainant. The bystanders were by now acting as jurors. Lefebvre took the opportunity to get out of the car. My brother, you are right, he said to the angry man, and he apologized, bowing his head a little. The angry man listened to Lefebvre but did not answer him. He spoke only to the original man. But the car key was returned to the driver. Lefebvre's intervention had done the trick.

'My dad's the same,' Sushila says. 'He can handle any situation.'

Is that what's happening? She's conflating Lefebvre with another old blowhard, Sarva?

Sarva manages a Rite Aid pharmacy up in Homewood and has a lot of stories about his adventures in retail, many of them featuring not-good encounters with Black Americans, a demographic group that he regards with straightforward hostility. I don't argue with him about it. It isn't the place of his white son-in-law to lecture him on the basic tenets of American liberalism. Sarva has tenets of his own, derived not only from his experience as a day-in, day-out dispenser of prescription medication to American real people but also from his experience of immigrating with his wife, Achu, to the United States, under a visa program for medical professionals, in response to the dangerous outlook in Sri Lanka for Tamils such as themselves. After he's drunk a few glasses of red wine, Sarva likes to remind everyone how smart he was to pull off this move and avoid the fate of two cousins shot dead in 1992 by the Colombo authorities. But his long-ago escape from an oppressive island thousands of miles away, estimable though it was, doesn't in my opinion entitle him to limitless deference and respect, and certainly does not make him an expert, or the only expert, on the injustices of his adopted society.

As Lefebvre drones on about how he spent his first day in Cotonou in his hotel room, I am turning over in my mind the argument I had with Sarva a few days ago. In retrospect, the details are petty and embarrassing. What it comes down to is that Sarva made one stupid remark too many over dinner, at my house, about the youth of color whom he perceives or imagines from his side of the pharmacy counter, teenagers whose antics and misdemeanors were not different, it seemed to me, from those of kids in cities all over the world, and (maybe because I was unusually anxious about the tensions at work, who knows) I reacted by impatiently asking how he would like others to jump to prejudiced conclusions about his own granddaughter (Fizzy has her mother's dark skin), a comparison that Sarva rejected out of hand, there being in his opinion no intersection between the situation of his family and that of the local descendants of slaves, to which I responded that maybe he had not learned very much about America if he thought that people here could be counted on to differentiate in Fizzy's favor between African Americans and (from the local perspective) phenotypically not dissimilar South Asians, and whether your average American could be trusted to be negatively disposed toward the former group but not toward the latter, which latter group was, of course, popularly associated with terrorism and religious fanaticism and hostility to America, to which Sarva said that I had no idea what I was talking about, that I knew nothing about the world, that I had done nothing with my life – which prompted Achu to reprimand her husband sharply, and Sushila to command both her father and me to drop it, whereupon I explained – very calmly, I thought – that I would not tolerate bigotry in my own home, whereupon an upset Sarva stood up and, on the grounds that he no longer felt welcome, took his leave, followed by a distressed Achu.

My behavior was combative and pointless. I should have counted to ten, kept my mouth shut, and so on and so forth. I regret the incident. But I don't have it in me to apologize to Sarva. Staging a rapprochement based on the dishonest expression of remorse is simply not within my powers; and as I've pointed out to Sushila, her father is the one instigating the rift. I'm not the one doing the shunning, he is. As far as I'm concerned, her father is as welcome as ever to visit the house. Any bad blood is entirely Sarva's.

Sushila doesn't buy it. She has accused me of alienating her father in retaliation for her rapprochement with Faye. Is Sushila, by encouraging Lefebvre to tell his story at length, herself now retaliating?

Lefebvre is describing his visit, on his second day in Cotonou, to the Stadium of Amity, where he hoped to make general inquiries. Recall, he says, that professional football in Benin had collapsed. The *championnat* had been canceled; all the famous clubs were inactive. At the Amity Stadium, barefooted boys played on the dirt practice ground, but otherwise the place seemed abandoned. Lefebvre crossed the field's coarse, overgrown turf and approached a couple of men who were sitting idly in the shade. Where are the players? Lefebvre asked them. They went away, the men answered – to Gabon or Mali, or to play for a *quartier* team in Cotonou or Porto Novo. Or they had found other work, outside of football. Everyone had disappeared. It was sad, the men said.

'Yes, it was sad, my friend,' Lefebvre repeats to Pearson, who for some reason has left my side and prostrated himself at the stranger's feet.

From the stadium, Lefebvre relates, he returned to his hotel. Its bar-restaurant was named Le Livingstone. Le Livingstone was a clean, pleasant, punishingly expensive joint where Europeans and rich West Africans could find some respite from the local hardships. One sat on the veranda, one drank cold beer, one ate pizza and spaghetti. On the street directly outside, soldiers with machine guns stood guard.

Lefebvre was waiting for a certain Camille Spindler, who ran a Benin tourism operation. He had corresponded with Spindler on the internet but otherwise didn't know him. Yes – his preconception was that Camille Spindler was a man.

A woman approached him and said in English, Mr Lefebvre, I presume?

Lefebvre admits that he did not catch the reference, had no idea (until she explained herself) that she was alluding to a phrase associated with the Dr Livingstone after whom the establishment had been named, a Scotsman of the Victorian era evidently renowned for his ineffectual and deranged explorations of Africa. It mattered not. He was delighted to meet with Camille Spindler. He bought her a drink. He asked how she, a European woman, had ended up on the Gulf of Guinea.

'She was there for love,' Sushila says boldly.

Lefebvre, smiling, tells Sushila that Camille Spindler hailed from Namur, in Belgium, and was a nurse by profession. She had never heard of Benin until, late one night, she mistyped the search word 'Benin' into her computer. The search produced images of children in need of medical care. This occurred years ago, during a crisis in Spindler's life: she was simultaneously dealing with an amorous breakup, looking for a new job, and trying to leave Namur. She took the accidental encounter with Africa as a sign. That very night, she registered for a nine-week tour of service, plus one week of sightseeing, in a country the existence of which she had only just become aware.

Spindler and the other volunteer nurses were put to work in clinics treating young patients seriously ill with malaria, diarrheal diseases and lower-respiratory infections. Spindler was very upset by what she saw. Every night she wept on the shoulder of their guide, who said to her, Spindler, you must toughen up, be less sensitive, you have not even seen the worst things. One night, the nurses went dancing. Spindler and the guide danced together; and they began a passionate romance. When the time came to return to Wallonia, Spindler didn't want to leave. She was in love. Her lover said to her: go back home. If in six months you still feel the same way about me, call me. Spindler returned to Belgium. When she discussed the matter with her parents, they were upset: he wants you for your passport, it won't last, it's a folly, tralala. Who could blame them? And yet, after six months had passed, Spindler's feelings for her Benin lover had not changed. She telephoned him – Fulbert was his name – and three months later, they were married in Cotonou.

That was nine years and two children ago. The couple now operated a tour guide enterprise. They made a good team. She handled marketing and sales; Fulbert went out into the field. It was not an easy business, Spindler admitted with a laugh. Benin was one of the poorest countries in the world. It had not yet been put on the map, touristically speaking. It lacked a profile. Its greatest draw was voodoo, more accurately *vodun*, which had originated in this part of Africa and was of great interest to a small number of tourists (French, most of them). Then there was the fascinating history of the country, which—

With a raised hand, Lefebvre interrupted Spindler. He was not interested in voodoo, he told her, and he was not interested in African history. He was only interested in taking a safari in the little-known wilderness at the very north of Benin, up by the borders with Burkina and Niger.

He didn't reveal his true objective. It was always better that people didn't know his business, and in Africa the need for professional anonymity was especially important. He presented himself to Spindler as a tourist.

She told Lefebvre that he was right to engage a guide. It was a bad idea for a European to travel alone in Benin, and the more north you went, the less it was secure. The staff of the US Embassy were not permitted to travel to the region where Lefebvre was bound.

Lefebvre would be safe with her husband, Fulbert, accompanying him.

At eight o'clock the next morning, Fulbert was waiting outside Le Livingstone in a white Toyota Land Cruiser.

•

It is now dark out, and for some reason even hotter and even more humid. The citronella candles burn brightly and fragrantly. Sushila, who went indoors, comes back out carrying a jug of ice water and a tub of ice cream. 'Bravo!' Lefebvre exclaims.

I welcome the ice cream (the presence of which in our freezer was unknown to me) because it promotes a dessert effect – the sense of a meal achieving its final act. A bowl of chocolate ice cream will symbolize the last course of conversation.

'What does Benin look like?' Sushila asks the guest. 'I can't picture it. Is it green? Is there a rain forest?'

Lefebvre slowly shakes a swollen red index finger. We must not, he lectures, confuse the tropical with the equatorial. Gabon, Cameroon, Congo – these are equatorial. By contrast, the countries of West Africa, from Senegal to Nigeria, are tropical. They extend from the seaside, which is green, to the inland desert – from fertility to sterility. Patches of the old forest survive here and there, but in general the land is either cultivated or it is savanna. There are no jungles in the sense of immense forests filled with wild animals. Any creature that moves is hunted down and eaten. Lefebvre looks upward, as though looking for something to see there. The sky of West Africa, he says, is not like the sky here, the sky of the north. There it is a white sky, the color of tin. It is always a relief to return to the skies of the north.

Lefebvre suddenly announces that he has never liked Africa. He has traveled there only out of necessity, in order to make a living. If he'd been more successful, he would happily have not set foot outside Europe. Whenever he has returned to Africa, it has always been with the sentiment of defeat, of demoralization. It was the same thing this time, hunting for Godwin. Africa was difficult,

from the point of view of Lefebvre's morale and energy, for one
simple reason: he had kept no good memories of his many visits
there. Yes, he had performed his assigned duties; yes, he had helped
a little to grow the sport. But he had not discovered or developed
a single notable talent, not once in all his years of flying backward
and forward. His voyages had made no difference to the life of one
person – not even his own life. In Benin, this was always at the back
of his mind. A lifetime of effort, for what?

Lefebvre raises the palm of his hand to prevent Sushila from
sympathizing with him. It is in the nature of the sensitive European,
he says, to desire to ameliorate the fortune of the African. This
inclination is not moral but economic – which is to say, it arises not
from virtue but from the enormous wealth disparity between the
continent of the whites and the continent of the blacks, a disparity
so stark that every year countless migrant unfortunates set off by
boat from the Maghreb and meet their end in the pitiless depths of
the Mediterranean Sea. Even a man like Lefebvre, an unsentimen-
tal man, is touched by this. Lefebvre cannot deny that he hopes to
leave a mark of construction behind him, a so-called footprint, even
as he recognizes that he is not a missionary or an aid worker. In
some ways, working in professional football is better than working
for a church or a charity. Professional football is not salvation, of
course not – and yet, and yet . . .

Lefebvre gives a troubled shake of the head. The question of
the value of football weighs on him these days, he says. Football is a
diversion, a pastime, something that is extra. It revolves around the
simplest, most childish activity, loved even by dogs: playing with a
ball. This ball game was not supposed to be the difference between
having nothing and having plenty, between having faith and not
having faith, between having life and not having life. A sport is not
supposed to have that importance. Someone like Lefebvre, a func-
tionary of football, is not supposed to have the power of a wizard
– the power to click one's fingers and, abracadabra, in an instant
change the outcomes not only for a young footballer but also for
his mother, who now can have the medical treatment she needs, for
his sister, who can stop walking to the well multiple times a day,
for his brother, who can stay at school and get his diploma, and for

the children in the village, who will have a new schoolhouse . . . Such is the power of the European football man in Africa. And the cliché is correct, Lefebvre asserts. It corrupts, this power – it corrupts not only oneself, but all those who deal with one. Every interaction becomes a calculation, becomes a lie, becomes a manipulation. If Lefebvre had known a single relationship that transcended the corruption of football, if he had enjoyed one true friendship in Africa, he might have felt different in Cotonou. But he had made no such friend – not one!

Lefebvre smiles at Pearson. Yes, old friend, he says to my dog, Lefebvre is cursed to return again and again to that friendless corner of the world, a corner that leaves a man with no illusions except the illusions of the pessimist. Far be it for Lefebvre, Lefebvre allows, to speak about the facts, political and historical and cultural, of foreign peoples. But, guided by a certain idealism and in accordance with a long-standing autodidactic habit, over the years he has read a little about the societies in which he's been forced to operate on the plane of business. This effort of learning ended only in discouragement. One might ask, discouragement from what? Lefebvre pensively refills his wineglass. When one reads about the history of Europe and America, he says, one reads about the horrors – the wars, the massacres, the camps of concentration, et cetera, et cetera – in the knowledge that things turned out well for the West, which in spite of all its difficulties has achieved an inconceivable general prosperity. This consolation – which is to say, the consolation of the happy ending – is not yet applicable to the history of Africa. Its past atrocities and calamities have not assumed the character of a prelude. Madame asked him – Lefebvre gestures at Sushila – why didn't he like Benin. He will tell her why: because he knew about its history. He knew about the Kingdom of Dahomey.

'Dahomey,' Sushila echoes, probably uttering the word for the first time in her life. She is taking the old fart seriously.

Lefebvre narrates that he and Fulbert set off from the coastal zone of lagoons and wetlands and palm trees and drove into a countryside whose rural character was partly disguised by the succession of villages – tiny shantytowns, in truth – that clustered along the road. The country was tranquil. One passed peanut fields, tapioca fields, plantations of palm trees, plantations of teak trees – always, on the Gulf of Guinea, it is the same fields, always it is the same agriculture. It was a relief to be out of the city. Cotonou, Lefebvre says, is unpredictable, hectic, poverty-stricken. If you stop at a traffic light, salesmen crowd around the car and attempt to interest you in windshield wipers, motorcycle inner tubes, tissues, jigsaw puzzles, diary books, soda drinks, steering-wheel covers. If there is bric-a-brac that can be thrust at you, they will thrust it at you, even if their hands and legs are shriveled and deformed by the diseases that unfortunately afflict those who live in this poor part of the world.

What a loathsome, vicious, unacceptable description! I look at Sushila. She gives no sign of sharing my dismay.

The Land Cruiser came to a stop. They had pulled over at a roadside stall displaying the skulls of various animals – goats, monkeys, cats, dogs. Lefebvre had seen this kind of tourist attraction many times before. He said to Fulbert, No voodoo. Continue.

On this question of voodoo, Lefebvre says, it was not that he was opposed to it but, rather, that he already knew enough about it. He had been to Africa many times, had dealt with many African players who practiced a traditional religion. Lefebvre has seen revenants, he has witnessed the ritual slaughter of chickens, he has watched footballers sprinkle juju powder on the goal line, he has found fetishes in their backpacks. None of it is unusual from the perspective of football. African players, Lefebvre says, must be understood like any other players, by reference to the usual psychological concepts – money, family, culture – rather than by reference to voodoo or some other strange concept. The black magic, the sacrifices, the sorcery – in the end these are nothing but superstitions, and, just as all balls are round, all footballers are superstitious.

However . . . Lefebvre raises his finger.

In the theology of Africans, he lectures us without authority, a population of secretly proximate beings – gods, ancestors, spirits – influences the visible world, and the living ask these invisible ones for assistance. What a wise practice this is, Lefebvre says, looking approvingly at my wife, a Roman Catholic from Pittsburgh, as if she's an ancestor worshipper. Traditional religious practices,

Lefebvre claims, must be viewed above all in terms of their psychological efficacy. What could be more helpful to one's mental health than a profound communion with the beloved dead? Lefebvre will confess something to us: he has himself developed the habitude of consulting his departed mother. Yes, it is true: his mother is the one he asks for assistance and encouragement. This is much more calming and comforting than praying to a never-seen God. If there is anything eternal in the world, Lefebvre says, it is the love of a mother.

I make no comment.

We will have observed, he goes on, that players of football commonly cross themselves as they enter the field of play, the Latin Americans and the Africans especially. Some Muslim players raise their hands – Lefebvre demonstrates – to give thanks to Allah, especially after scoring a goal. But these gestures disguise a fact that very few find acceptable. What is this fact? It is this: football is its own religion. It has its own gods and priests, its own traditions and doctrines and churches. It has its own reality. The reality of football is not like the reality of reality. It is not present everywhere. It appears only in certain places, at certain times. But mark well: it is an ancient reality. It is not a reality of the modern.

His face flushing, the old scout refills his glass. He clearly believes himself to be on a roll. Energetically, he reminds us that the purpose of the Benin expedition was to find Godwin. There was no time for voodoo and there was no time for bush game. When, deep in the country, Fulbert again stopped at the stall of a vendor, this time one who specialized in barbecued wild animals, Lefebvre again told Fulbert to drive on. Lefebvre had also seen this before – agoutis with their tails sticking up like rats' tails, a hare, various serpents, an antelope, and, at the center of the display, a large, cooked monkey, lying on its side like a human. Ordinary tourists would find this mesmerizing, of course – it is something they do not see in France or Germany. But not Lefebvre. Without comment, Spindler's husband did as he was told. It was certain, Lefebvre says, that Fulbert had arranged with the roadside vendor to bring tourists to him. Any tourist in Africa finds himself at the center of a network of opaque agreements and secret commissions. It is an unsettling feeling, the sense of an entire society collaborating to separate you from your money. Tourists don't like it. But do the societies of the tourists treat the stranger any better? The traveler of old, Lefebvre says, could count on the hospitality of the villager. Not anymore. These days, people turn their homes into profitable hotels . . . Lefebvre waves his hand contemptuously.

They kept going north. Their destination, on that first day, was the town of Djougou, in the department of Donga. They would complete the journey to Natitingou, in Atacora, the northernmost province, the following morning – two days of driving, all told. In Africa it is not simple, Lefebvre declares, to drive five hundred kilometers. The roads are not like the roads of America. The traffic is not like the traffic of America. There are only two roads to northern Benin – one that goes up to the northeast, to the frontier with Niger; and another that goes northwest, along the border with Togo, into Burkina Faso. Lefebvre was taking the latter road.

'Let me explain,' he says, 'so that you understand something.'

The contrast between the north of Benin and the south, Lefebvre avers, is a contrast of two countries. The languages are different, the religions are different, the history is different, the culture is different. The north is Muslim and rural and conservative. The south is Christian and mercantile and more cosmopolitan. The south is coastal and green and populous; the north, where the savanna is, is more open, more wild. There is the problem of banditry – it isn't safe to drive on country roads after nightfall – and the problem of terrorism. Always there is the threat that the Islamists of Al Qaeda and Boko Haram, active in Burkina and Niger and Nigeria, will bring terror to northern Benin.

'They have Boko Haram in Benin?'

'Not yet, madame,' Lefebvre says. With infuriating self-assurance, he adds, 'But one day it will happen.' The football of Benin, such as it is, Lefebvre continues, is concentrated in Cotonou and Porto-Novo. More you go north, less you encounter the sport. Lefebvre didn't like that. He did not feel comfortable in places where there was not much football.

After they'd been traveling for a few hours – Lefebvre seated drowsily in the passenger seat, the silent Fulbert at the wheel – the proportions of the undertaking, at once delicate and weighty, began to press upon the Frenchman. To find Godwin, to persuade him to sign a contract, to bring him to France, to protect him, to get him a club, to ensure that he realized his potential – none of it was guaranteed. Failure always loomed large. At Lefebvre's age, Lefebvre waffles, one has a different relationship with failure. Whereas a young man can console himself with the prospect of trying again, the older man is aware of the absolute limit of time. One becomes, if anything, more desperate for success – for a sign that one's life has not been lived in vain.

'You don't have children?'

'Madame,' Lefebvre replies magnificently, like the President of France, 'not every man has the destiny of the father.' Some men, he pontificates, are made for the home, for the family, for the life of safety. He opens his hand in my direction. Others, a condemned minority, are made for a life beyond the home, a life of motion and solitude – the life of the sailor, one could say.

I am about to laugh loudly – the life of the sailor! – when I see that Sushila is nodding sympathetically. I can only guess that she understands Lefebvre to be making a coded disclosure of homosexuality – of an old-fashioned ill-starred existence, of trapped longings and unjust suffering. I have a different thought. Lefebvre strikes me as the mail-order-bride type.

The drive north, Lefebvre continues, was hazardous. The interminable potholes, the pedestrians appearing from nowhere, the police checkpoints, the swerving motorbikes on which you might see a dozen feathered chickens suspended from the handlebars – it all added up to a slow, uncomfortable ride. Would we like to know what he, Lefebvre, saw as he looked out of the window of the Toyota? He saw work. He saw men, women, children, working, working, working. Work in the morning, work in the afternoon, work at night. The people one saw on the side of the road, apparently doing nothing, were in reality working or hoping to work. In Africa, Lefebvre says, you have to work hard just to get the opportunity to work hard. You have to wait on the corner, wait at the airport, wait on the side of the road, wait for the tourist, wait for the big man. It is logical that in Benin one does not see happy families. Everybody is working.

Sushila smiles. 'Can that be true? No happy families?'

Were we to go there, Lefebvre says, to Dahomey, we would see for ourselves. The people are cold, cold. We would not see men and women showing affection to one another, we would not see a parent lovingly speaking to its child, we would not encounter families out for a promenade in the evening.

The white of his hand stops Sushila's attempt to talk back. To recapitulate, he says, the drive north was punctuated by delays. The longest of these were of Fulbert's own doing. Without explanation, the guide would make a stop to talk with someone who was standing on the roadside. We have to understand, Lefebvre says tolerantly, that the rendezvous system is different in Africa. Not everyone has a phone. You stand at the side of the road – the only road – and you wait, if necessary for hours, until you see the car you are looking for. Fulbert's Land Cruiser was recognized by all, it seemed, and people would wave it down. Several times Lefebvre watched from the car as Fulbert conducted discussions or small transactions. It was obvious that in these parts Fulbert was a boss man, a mister. Like everyone else, he wore a hard face. He did not hesitate to shout at people. When the Beninois raise their voices, Lefebvre alleges, they don't do it like the Italians, in a manifestly theatrical way. They sound as if they are expressing real disagreement, real anger. This is logical. Italy is a paradise. Benin is a hell.

We may have been wondering, Lefebvre suggests, what was his plan to find the boy Godwin. He had no plan! In this part of the world, planning was useless. You put one foot in front of the other, you looked around, you took another step. You improvised. It was the old way of doing things. Lefebvre knew one thing for sure: he would need to rely on Spindler's husband, Fulbert. But was Fulbert reliable? Was he a man who could be trusted not to take advantage of the situation? Lefebvre gives me a searching look, as if I am the one whose trustworthiness is in question. Sushila, too, looks at me.

I am imagining things? Or are they in league?

'You,' Lefebvre says to me, 'you can be trusted only . . .' He makes a so-so movement with his hand. 'It is not because you are dishonest, my friend – you are not dishonest. It is because you do not know yourself.' He fires up a cheroot and turns confidently toward Sushila. 'I am right, no?'

She does not react to Lefebvre's question. Possibly she thinks it's too ridiculous to answer. But neither does she give me a sign of solidarity.

A numbness enters through my solar plexus – the action of a force I don't recognize, the action of gravity attracting me toward some unknown mass.

•

The hotel in Djougou was a dump, of course. At sunset, Lefebvre and Fulbert took a seat at the white plastic table in the dirt court-yard and drank beer in the shade of a big tree. There were no other customers. A white screen hung from a wall to enable the locals to watch televised football matches, but there was no football to watch. When Lefebvre and Fulbert had finished eating, two chick-ens jumped up onto the table and began to peck at the leftovers. Fulbert asked Lefebvre if he liked his room.

The shower in Lefebvre's room didn't produce water, the air-conditioning unit was broken, and the mosquito net was full of holes. Lefebvre told Fulbert that the room was excellent.

Fulbert had exchanged his Western attire for a chic African suit – a brightly colorful tunic with matching loose-fitting pants. He wore sandals in the place of sneakers. He looked very relaxed. Lefe-bvre said intuitively, You are from here?

Fulbert pointed at the ground: Yes, he was from this place – the north. This, not the big city, was his country.

Lefebvre asked this man, Spindler's husband, if he had any brothers or sisters. Fulbert answered that he had twenty-three brothers and sisters.

Fulbert's mother (Lefebvre learned) was the third of his father's four wives. She had given birth to eight of his children, and Ful-bert was the youngest of these. His mother, Fulbert told Lefebvre, would get up at four in the morning to cook a broth that she would sell at the roadside to people going to work. From the proceeds, she would give the children a few coins with which to buy lunch. Breakfast? They had no breakfast. On the days when Fulbert had no lunch money, he would do another schoolboy's chores and receive payment in the form a mouthful of the schoolboy's food. When Fulbert was nine years old, there was no more school, because Benin's educational system collapsed. This was in the 1980s, during the time of the revolution. For four years, Fulbert told Lefebvre, he lived as an *enfant de la rue* – a child of the street.

Pearson must have absented himself, because now he materializes out of the dark of the yard and approaches Lefebvre. He is looking for food, of course. Lefebvre pats his head. He states that street kids in Europe and South America, and no doubt it is the same in the United States, are either little scoundrels who skip school, or young people with problems: runaways, addicts, the mentally disturbed. In Benin, it's different. In Benin, Lefebvre informs Pearson, it is customary for parents to encourage their children to roam the village and learn to fend for themselves. Frequently, one sees groups of unsupervised kids running around in packs, some of them as young as three years old. These children call any woman who feeds them *maman*. Lefebvre is not passing judgment – not at all. It comes down, like everything else in that part of the world, to money. Why are the babies strapped to their mothers' backs for hours on end? Because it enables the mothers to keep working. Why are babies potty-trained before their first birthday, and slapped and reprimanded even as infants? Because this way they learn independence as quickly as possible, Lefebvre says, giving Pearson something he has pulled from his pocket.

'Could you please not feed the dog?' I say. 'Pearson!' With a click of my fingers, I command him to come to me. Pearson disobeys. That is not like him at all.

'Always dogs like me,' Lefebvre comments.

One day, he resumes, a man by the name of Perrault walked down the street of Fulbert's hometown. He was from Canada. Monsieur Perrault spotted young Fulbert and his friends on the street corner, and he asked the boys for directions to the local orphanage, which was run by the Sisters of the Sacred Heart of

Jesus. Because Fulbert's French was better than that of his friends, Monsieur Perrault invited him to accompany him. They had a conversation. Why aren't you in school? Perrault asked his young guide. Fulbert told him about the implosion of the national school system and explained that his family couldn't afford to send him to a private school. Perrault said nothing to this. A week later, two nuns approached Fulbert on the street and took him by bus to Natitingou. In Nati they went to the bank. Perrault was waiting for them. Fulbert learned that a bank account had been opened for his benefit and that the bank had been instructed to release one hundred US dollars every year to pay for his education. Fulbert went back to school.

'Wow,' Sushila says. 'That's like winning the lottery.'

'That is not the end of the story,' Lefebvre says.

Perrault was in Benin to work on the installation of telecommunications towers. Impressed by the boy Fulbert's ability, Perrault gave him a job on the project. The boy did well. When he turned fourteen, Perrault met with his parents and offered to fly their son to Canada and train him to be a skilled technician in the field of pylons and similar structures. They agreed that the boy should take advantage of this extraordinary opportunity. It involved paperwork, however. Thirty times, Fulbert told Lefebvre, he had to go to Nati to obtain one permit or another. When everything was finally in order, when all the signatures and seals and apostilles and authentications had been effectuated, Fulbert delivered all the original documents to his father, for a final inspection. The father placed everything on the kitchen table and went to the mosque. In his absence, his second wife, Fulbert's stepmother, burned all the papers, even the airplane tickets.

'No!' Sushila screams.

Perrault couldn't fix the situation. *C'est la vie*, he told Fulbert. He returned to Canada and was never heard from again.

How, Lefebvre asks, could the stepmother do such a thing? To a young boy? What kind of perturbation could make someone act in this way?

'She was jealous,' Sushila says.

That was Lefebvre's first thought, too – jealousy. But the truth was much sadder. 'I must warn you,' he says, 'that you may find difficult what I will now tell you.'

The exploitation of children, Lefebvre says, is an old, old problem in Africa – as old as family life, in all probability. In this part of Africa, there is a tradition to entrust boys, boys who might be as young as six years of age, to a master, or *marabout*, on the understanding that the master will teach his so-called apprentice the Koran. In compensation, the master is entitled to put the apprentice to work, whether as a beggar or a domestic servant or a farm laborer. In those parts of Benin where Islam is strong, there are *marabouts* from Niger who go from village to village, looking for apprentices. This was to be the fate of the stepmother's firstborn, a boy: at the insistence of Fulbert's father, he went away with a *marabout* from Niger. He was not seen again.

'My God,' says Sushila.

Children in Benin, alleges Lefebvre, are still sent away by their parents to work in faraway places – for example, the cobalt mines of Congo – in return for money, usually a monthly payment. It is illegal, but the police don't, or can't, do anything about it. Many of these disappeared children have no official identity, because their birth, especially in rural areas, is unregistered. That was why the young Fulbert had such trouble with his Canadian paperwork – because there was no record of his existence.

Now, Lefebvre says, listen well. The stepmother had two sons – half-brothers of Fulbert. After the older boy had been sent away to Niger, Fulbert's father sent away the second son also, to Nigeria, to work in a granite quarry. The stepmother lost both her sons.

Even though he was just a boy, Fulbert told Lefebvre, he understood why his stepmother had torn up his papers. He was not angry with her. And he didn't want to go to Canada. He loved Benin, and he loved school. His good fortune persisted. He became a tour guide, he married Spindler, and together they made a comfortable living. Fulbert was able to have protégés of his own – boys and girls he took under his wing and assisted financially and morally. He claimed to Lefebvre that he had thirty-four such charges, dispersed in the various towns and villages of his home province, Atacora. They included street kids like his youthful self. He'd see them fooling around and he'd call them over and interrogate them about what they wanted to do with their lives. Or he'd talk with one of the mothers and learn about the characteristics of a given child. If Fulbert saw promise, he tried to help.

Fulbert said to Lefebvre, I told you my story. Now you must tell me yours. I know you are not a tourist.

Fulbert was correct: the time had come for Lefebvre to speak truthfully. Yes, I am here on business, the Frenchman admitted. From his briefcase he pulled out a picture – a color still captured from the Godwin video. He showed it to Fulbert. You know this team?

Fulbert carefully examined the image.

Lefebvre was cautious, of course. The African concept of truth, he tells us, does not correspond to the European concept. In Africa, people say whatever is most profitable. The concept of the promise, the concept of the contract – these are not African concepts.

'Always you shake the head,' Lefebvre says. He's talking to me, I realize. 'Always you have the little smile. Tell me what you are thinking, please, inside this shaking head.'

How to answer? Where to start? Indoors, twenty feet away, on the wall that abuts the basement staircase, are plywood shelves crammed with double rows of books about philosophy and politics and theory, books filled with wisdom and uprightness, books that embody my long war against error, books, it must be admitted, that nowadays function not so much as a library as a kind of mausoleum of my mental life, books I haven't opened in years, in part because I cannot face the underscores and the marginalia, made in my neater handwriting of those days, the 1990s, in blue ballpoint pen – which is to say, I can't face the maker of those marks. At any rate, it is painful, the juxtaposition of my so-called library, once a fortress of knowledge, and this guy who has returned from Africa with hunting trophies in the form of stories. He might as well produce the head of a rhinoceros and mount it on our wall.

Yet, for all my scorn, for all the effort of thought and conscience made by the authors whose writings I've earnestly collected, I can't answer Lefebvre appropriately – can't put the guy in his place, can't find the riposte or the rejoinder to justify the smirk on my face. I don't have the necessary equilibrium. I am too confused. I am too lacking in will.

'I'm not thinking anything,' I say. 'I'm listening. Please continue, Jean-Luc.'

Fulbert examined the photograph. He said to Lefebvre, Yes, I know this team.

What is the name of the team? Lefebvre asked.

Fulbert didn't answer him. Pointing at the picture he said, You are looking for this player.

Lefebvre nodded. Yes, I am looking for Godwin.

Fulbert answered, I know his family. I can take you to them if you wish.

•

Benin, Lefebvre teaches us, has a frontier that adjoins Togo, Upper Volta and Niger. (And Nigeria, he adds, but that is not relevant.) This borderland is the site of a large transnational savanna. People don't associate West Africa with wildlife, but in this obscure corner of the continent a vast grassy plain speckled with trees retains small populations of megafauna. The Benin portion of this wilderness is Pendjari National Park. In the interior of the park is a lodge for tourists. It was to this lodge that Fulbert drove Lefebvre from Djougou, a bumpy journey of several hours, past fields of yam and maize and cotton, until the Atacora Mountains, which are lower even than the Vosges, came into view. Lefebvre contrived to fall asleep.

When he awoke, they had come to a stop on a dirt road. A few treetops showed above the tall yellow grass. Fulbert pointed in their direction. Lefebvre looked but saw nothing. Then the ears of elephants emerged from the treetops, and the profiles of several elephants moved briefly but clearly into view.

Soon after, they arrived at the safari lodge. Wait here, Fulbert instructed Lefebvre, meaning that he should stay at the lodge while Fulbert went to consult with Godwin's family, who lived somewhere nearby – exactly where, Fulbert did not reveal. Lefebvre watched

Fulbert drive away in a cloud of red dust. Was Lefebvre nervous? Was he excited? Yes, and yes.

The old scout was shown to his luxurious tent. He took a *sieste*. Lefebvre assures us that he is capable of sleeping anywhere, at any time, like a warrior. He stirred late in the afternoon. After a *douche*, he went to the dining area and helped himself to a delicious cold drink. Then he went out to the terrace. He saw only one other person, a white. Lefebvre sat down at the neighboring table. Before them spread the immense, sparsely forested plain. Before long, it would be dusk, and the roaring of lions would begin.

The white man raised his glass in greeting. Lefebvre invited him to his table.

He was an American, which surprised Lefebvre. Americans were rare in this part of the world. The American told Lefebvre that he was never returning to Africa.

It is not for everyone, Lefebvre acknowledged.

Tell me about it, replied the American.

He was a doctor – an anesthesiologist. He had come to Africa at his own expense, accompanied by his wife, to perform cleft-palate surgery free of charge. They arrived at Cotonou in the middle of the night, exhausted after nearly twenty-four hours of air travel. To their shock, the American doctor was put into an ambulance and taken directly from the airport to a hospital. His wife was meanwhile put in a taxi and taken to their hotel. She was very alarmed and disoriented. It seemed to her that her husband had been detained. She would not stop phoning him as he scrubbed in at the hospital. The American doctor reassured his wife and got down to work. The clinic was chaotic and primitive, naturally. He worked a fourteen-hour day. The patients appeared before him like articles on a conveyor belt, one kid after another with a cleft palate, never stopping. Sometimes a child suffering from noma, a horrifying orofacial gangrene caused by malnutrition, would be presented to him. It was deeply distressing work, even for an old hand like the anesthesiologist. This was how it went on, for two weeks: no days off, no R & R of any kind, no respite from children in need of treatment. When he'd finally make it back to the hotel, at 3:00 a.m., there would be nothing to eat but crackers and canned sardines. His lowest point came when he was trying to open a can of sardines in the middle of the night and the can somehow exploded in his hands and sprayed sardines and oil of sardines all over him. His wife? She had quickly gotten over her anxiety. Every day, she went off on a sightseeing trip with the plus-ones of the other doctors without frontiers – visiting the markets, going to the beach club, going to Lagos, boating around the lagoons, photographing birds, doing fun tourism stuff. Now, at last, the doctor's work was over. This safari was his reward. Never again, the American doctor swore, raising his right hand as if taking an oath in court.

Lefebvre expressed sympathy.

The American said that it wasn't so bad for the other guys – the plastic surgeons and the craniofacial surgeons and the oral maxillofacial surgeons. Those guys were killers – young guns intent on logging surgical experience and building up their résumés. But there was no career benefit for someone like himself, an experienced anesthesiologist with a settled practice. Unlike surgeons, who were gung-ho types accustomed to long shifts, anesthesiologists worked regular hours. The comfortable lifestyle that came with having a predictable daily routine was one of the main attractions of the field. Anesthesiologists, the American said, were known for being calm, witty and contented. It was a shock for someone like him to be forced to work in such extreme conditions. It wasn't what he'd bargained for. He had no pretensions of being an Albert Schweitzer or a Paul Farmer. His only wish had been to combine interesting travel with useful work. It was tremendously foolish and shortsighted of the African authorities, the American anesthesiologist said, to treat visiting world-class medics as if they were servants. The visitors would not return, nor would they recommend the program to their peers. What the Africans needed to understand, the anesthesiologist said, was that there was a lot of competition in the field of charitable medicine. He had been on a similar surgical program in El Salvador – pro bono, of course – and it had been a completely positive experience, with normal working hours, a swimming pool, respect for his labor.

The harshest, most incomprehensible aspect of his ordeal, the American went on, was that at no point was he permitted to see the parents of his young patients. Nothing was more rewarding for a doctor than to be present for that moment when mother and father are reunited with their child after surgery and they see the trans-formational, almost miraculous, effect of the doctor's work. He had been denied this gesture of respect – the opportunity to observe the inscription of joy and gratitude on the parental faces as they beheld their healed or repaired child. Sure, the world-class doctor said to Lefebvre, he was a professional; but he was also a human with feelings. Quite simply, even a medical professional rarely saw faces such as those worn by the happy parents of formerly disfig-ured patients. People could go through whole careers, whole lives, without witnessing such a response to their efforts. The American could not understand why the African authorities would deny him this profound satisfaction and meaning. In all honesty, he confessed to Lefebvre, it made him angry.

To this, Lefebvre could say nothing.

And here they come, the doctor said, indicating in the direction of the low red sun. Two vehicles were approaching in the distance. One of them contained the doctor's wife.

The doctor told Lefebvre that he had declined to go on this sunset wildlife tour, having already participated in such an outing the day before. He'd seen the lionesses sprawled out on the road, he'd taken pictures of the hippos and the antelopes and the ele-phants, he'd contemplated Burkina Faso on the far bank of the Pendjari River. The Pendjari was a tributary of the Volta and sup-posedly teemed with crocodiles, but to the American it looked as unremarkable and artificial as a Hollywood set. There was nothing unknown left to see in Africa, the American mused. The continent had been ruined for the explorer. And, in any case, his curiosity had been exhausted by a disease of the intestines that he'd contracted. Tropical illnesses were no joke. Diarrhea was no joke. Dehydration was no joke. With difficulty, the American doctor rose to his feet, finished his drink, and went down to greet the returning tourists. There was still no sign of Fulbert.

Lefebvre had a decision to make. Either he was going to worry about the husband of Spindler, or he was not going to worry. Lefeb-vre chose the latter.

Meanwhile, night had fallen on the savanna. The elevated stone terrace on which Lefebvre sat encouraged the contemplation of a darkening expanse of land that included, distantly to his right, the dark blank of Upper Volta. Only the sounds of wild animals, grunting and chirping and screeching, could be heard. Lefebvre heard the howl of a hyena. Even a traveler as hardened as himself could not help feeling apprehensive. For as long as he'd visited Africa, there had been stories of fighting in the Sahel – of unrest, of killings, of massacres. He had ignored them. There had always been violence in these lands of sand and rock, it never stopped, it was part of the immemorial history of such places, and no purpose of Lefebvre's was served by concerning himself with these matters, which did not affect him. Or did they? Of late he'd been hearing bad rumors, rumors of a southward movement in jihadist activities, rumors of new threats arriving from beyond the edge of the civilized world. The old Frenchman felt that he was sitting exactly at the edge.

He began to reflect, Lefebvre claims, on what the American doctor had said about the joy on the faces of the parents of the healed. It made Lefebvre think of the happy faces that a goal instantly produces wherever people gather to watch a football game. For why, such joy? A goal was a little thing, with no proper objective value. Why did it matter so much? It was strange: he had spent a lifetime consumed by the activity that goes by the name of football – *le foot*, as they call it in France – yet he had never given a thought to the jubilation caused by a scored goal. He had long been sensible of the seemingly mystical properties of a ball, a sphere that can be kicked or handled or struck with a stick; indeed, he had long believed that to play with a ball was to make a harmonious kind of contact with the universe, itself of course filled with spheres. But he had never succeeded in understanding the potential energy that is released in the form of an explosion of shouting and jumping by celebrating fans when the ball crosses the goal line.

With a painful reorganization of his legs and backside, Lefebvre sits up, dislodging Pearson from his foot as he does so. Making a priestly motion of the hand, he draws our attention upward, to the Pennsylvania darkness. Out there, on that terrace in the African wilderness, he states with the utmost importance, with the lions roaring and big white stars falling into Burkina Faso, it came to him why a scored goal in football produces so much energy, so much ecstasy. The goal, that boxlike zone marked out by the goal posts and the goal net, manifested a hidden dimension of reality. To score a goal, Lefebvre says, is nothing less than to—

Sushila yawns!

Does it matter to Lefebvre? It does not. He goes on talking, this man who is ignorant of his own ignorance, who confuses solipsism with philosophical thought, who privileges his random musings merely because they happen to have occurred to him. Not to be a snob, but who does he think he is? What qualifies him to play on the same field, so to speak, as professional thinkers? His self-absorption, his disappearance up his own ass, is total. When I excuse myself to go the bathroom, he keeps talking as if I haven't gone anywhere. When I return, he is speaking as if I haven't just returned. From his safari tent, Lefebvre is proclaiming, he telephoned Fulbert two times, three times. But Fulbert was not answering his phone. Where was he? Where was Godwin?

Lefebvre is slurring his words. He's drunk. But he seems indefatigable. Sushila looks exhausted. It's almost midnight, two hours past her usual bedtime.

I'm a nocturnal creature. I am wide awake.

•

In the morning, Lefebvre was woken up by a hand on his shoulder. The hand belonged to an employee of the safari lodge. The employee bore a message: Fulbert was waiting for Lefebvre in Natitingou.

The same employee drove the Frenchman through the savanna. It was sunup, and chilly. The driver drew Lefebvre's attention to warthogs, antelope, baboons, et cetera. It was interesting – who among us does not watch the documentaries of nature? – but Lefebvre's mind was not on baboons.

The old man was almost nauseous with climactic anticipation. This was his last chance. After Godwin there would be nothing. He felt at the same time very prepared and very unprepared. Prepared, because he knew the business, knew what needed to be done to get the boy a visa, knew which clubs to call in France and Germany and Holland and Spain and Belgium, knew the medical and fitness requirements, knew how to feed and house and clothe and take care of a lonely and homesick African teenager. Lefebvre waves his phone at Sushila. In this gadget, he tells her, are stored the numbers of more than a dozen *mamans* of football, maternal women whose families can be counted on to give a young professional a good home in France. You, he says, pointing at me, you do not have these numbers. You have none of this knowledge. Zero.

And yet, Lefebvre allows, he was also unprepared. Technical expertise, savoir-faire, connections – they only get you so far. In addition, you need man-management skills. The most difficult, the most unpredictable, the least controllable element of football is the human side. Lefebvre has never possessed, he is the first to admit, a crucial trait possessed by the crème de la crème of agents and managers of footballers – namely, the ability to influence young men to the point of domination. The Svengali, the Rasputin – this type prospers in the sport. Nor has Lefebvre enjoyed that other route to success: chance. Yes, Lefebvre exclaims, chance! Even with the great advances made in the realm of sports science, football remains enigmatic. The mysteries of victory, the mysteries of quality, the mysteries of mentality, are as deep as ever. The game is still surprising, still immeasurable. Still it is ruled by unknown processes. With few exceptions, the greatest coaches have worked unscientifically, almost magically – for example, the Englishman Brian Clough, whose Nottingham Forest rose from the Second Division to win the English championship, then twice won the European Cup, all with a team of drinkers and troublemakers and has-beens. What Clough understood was that the duty of the coach – or manager, or trainer, whatever you want to call this position – is not only to decide on systems, tactics and team selection, but to oversee the project of philosophy and personality that in English goes by the name 'team'. A team, when it functions correctly, is not just a machine for winning. Its function is much more important than that.

But for every crazy genius like Clough, Lefebvre announces,

there are a hundred, a thousand, ordinary coaches who are carried
upward by force of circumstance – an exceptional group of players, for example. They cannot survive very long at the top. It is too
hard. Even able and respected coaches are fired again and again.
Coaches succeed, and fail, for reasons that are not in their control.
Rinus Michels, the godfather of Total Football, benefited from having at his disposal the greatness of Cruyff and Neeskens and van
Hanegem.

Willem van Hanegem, Lefebvre says, was probably the best
opponent it was his privilege to share the field with during his
own short, undistinguished career. Note well, Lefebvre says, that
van Hanegem himself maintained that the best manager of them
all was not Rinus Michels but his predecessor at the helm of the
Holland team, František Fadrhonc, who led the Dutch to qualify
for the 1974 World Cup finals. Dr Fadrhonc was of a nationality
that no longer exists: Czechoslovak. An obsessive on the topic of
athletic education, which he had studied at university, he developed
a football philosophy that was heavily influenced by Sokol. Have
we heard of Sokol? Of course not. Nobody has heard of anything
anymore. Sokol, Lefebvre says, was an idealistic gymnastics movement in which the connection between physical, moral and national
fitness was emphasized. In postwar Czechoslovakia, members of the
Sokol movement were tyrannized by the Communists. Fadrhonc
and his wife fled to the Netherlands, where he had been offered a
job as the trainer of a little club from the town of Tilburg named
Willem II. Six years later, this little club was the national champion.

Dr Fadrhonc was a serious, high-minded, fatherly man who
prized team spirit above all. He was the one who turned the gifted
but fractious collection of Dutch players of the early 1970s into
the unit that under Rinus Michels became famous as Oranje. The
Holland players were notoriously headstrong and difficult, but they
were united in a love of Dr Fadrhonc. When they heard rumors
of his possible termination, they agreed between themselves to do
something about it, and beat Greece five to nothing. Fadrhonc's
team talks could go on forever. He would speak, with tears welling
up in his eyes, about his experiences of oppression and exile, experiences that included a period of slave labor in a Nazi factory. It was

logical that van Hanegem should be receptive to such stories. His own father, sister and two brothers were murdered by the Nazis, and nobody in the game had a greater loathing of the Germans than this sly, tough, dark-browed, shortsighted, bandy-legged midfielder who wandered around the field with the air of a cheerful criminal. Van Hanegem's fervent wish, in the 1974 World Cup final, was not only to defeat the West Germany team but to humiliate them. He played a brilliant, relentless game, driving the Dutch forward with fearless tackles and exquisite passes. The Germans won.

Lefebvre pauses. His own father, too, was killed in the war; or so his mother told him. Was she telling the truth? It was hard to say. She never revealed the father's identity, saying only that he was a soldier. Based on certain things his mother had said and not said, and on certain village whispers that had reached his ears as a boy, and on the shape of his head, a head like a block, a Dummkopf, Lefebvre came to suspect the worst: that his father had been a member of the German army of occupation. The Americans made love to thousands of Frenchwomen, sometimes against their will, producing many babies; but the Americans did not arrive in France until after Lefebvre's conception. I digress, Lefebvre says.

Lefebvre and his driver were traversing the Parc Pendjari when a doglike animal with large ears flashed across the dirt road and disappeared into the grassland. The driver stopped the car and looked back to where the animal had crossed. A second creature, resembling the first, also crossed the road.

You saw that? the driver asked.

Lefebvre answered, I saw two dogs. Or maybe two foxes.

The driver barked something into his walkie-talkie. There was a reply.

We must wait, the driver announced.

Wait for what? Lefebvre said.

For madame. She will arrive here soon.

Which madame? Lefebvre asked. The driver would not say more. Lefebvre felt helpless. There was no way to alert Fulbert about the delay. When he tried to exit the vehicle to stretch his legs, the driver prohibited it. The lions, he said, pointing at the tall, lion-colored grass that obscured the view on both sides of the road.

Almost an hour passed. Then another jeeplike automobile came to a stop behind them. From it emerged two African men and a European woman. Lefebvre surmised the latter to be madame.

He had not met this person before and had every intention of protesting to her about his detention. But when she introduced herself as a conservationist by the name of Emilia Mazzola, Lefebvre fell silent. She took the seat vacated by the driver and opened an illustrated book for Lefebvre's inspection. Did he recognize, she asked in excellent French, the beasts he had seen crossing the dirt road? Lefebvre, bewildered, pointed at two photographs, one of a jackal, the other of a so-called lycaon, or African wild dog. He told her that it could have been either of them.

La Mazzola, as Lefebvre names her, went over to the local men. She was an athletic woman, with a proud forehead and strong thighs. They crouched to examine the tracks. After a brief discussion, Mazzola returned to Lefebvre's vehicle and shut the door with a great slam. My excuses for all this, monsieur, she said. When Lefebvre began to explain that he was late for a meeting in Natitingou, La Mazzola told him not worry, she would herself drive him to Fulbert. You know Fulbert? Lefebvre asked. Of course, Mazzola said. Everybody knows Fulbert.

Did Lefebvre wish to know, she asked, what had just happened?

The lycaon, Emilia explained, was one of the most beautiful and most threatened mammals in Africa. As Lefebvre may have noticed in the photograph, this species had enormous saucerlike ears, lovely delicate legs and sensitive brown snouts. They lived in large, highly social, highly collaborative packs. Their extraordinary efficiency as hunters depended on their famous teamwork, with members of the pack relentlessly taking turns to pursue and harass prey, typically a gazelle or warthog or antelope, much larger than themselves. The painted dog, as it was informally referred to, was also famous for its splendidly mottled coat, the random splotches of brown and white and black truly resembling the handiwork of an abstract expressionist. African wild dogs were not dogs as such. They were descended from the same ancestor as wolves, and, like the wolf, they were unjustly feared, and aggressively hunted, by human beings. The lycaon had not been sighted in Parc Pendjari for five years,

Emilia said. It was hoped against hope that out there, somewhere in the wilderness, most likely across the border in Burkina, a few of these exquisite carnivores somehow survived. Emilia was doing everything in her power to save them. Her job at Pendjari involved more general responsibilities, but finding and protecting the lycaon was her personal obsession. She hoped that monsieur would understand that his sighting had left her with no choice but to investigate immediately. Unfortunately, what Lefebvre had seen was most likely a pair of jackals.

Tell me, Lefebvre asked, are you related to Alessandro Mazzola, better known as Sandro? The captain of the Grande Inter? Who played for the Azzurri in the final of the 1970 World Cup?

She didn't think so, she said, amused. Did she look like Sandro Mazzola?

Lefebvre gallantly denied it. But in truth, Lefebvre tells me and Sushila, with her masculine chin and her tightly curled fair hair and strong nose, Emilia did resemble Sandro; and in Lefebvre's opinion she resembled very much Sandro's father, Valentino, the captain of the Grande Torino. It is a sign of the subtlety and integrity of football, Lefebvre states, that only very rarely at the top level does footballing success pass down from one generation to the next. In the history of the sport, no other father-and-son duo – not the Maldinis, not the Cruyffs, not the Verons – could hold a candle to the two Mazzolas, each of whom independently achieved legendary status in Italian football. Valentino was the footballing superior of his son, according to those old enough to have seen both play, but to Lefebvre's mind it is not only insulting to these great champions but stupid to compare one negatively to the other. Valentino, Valentino, Valentino, Lefebvre says, shaking his head. He was like a Victor Hugo character. He learned football on the streets, kicking tin cans that he'd shaped into balls. When he was ten years old, he dived into the fast-flowing Adda river and saved a little boy from drowning. What became of that little boy? He became a footballer and captained Milan to the championship. At the age of eleven, Valentino was working in a linen mill. At his first professional trial, for Venezia, he played in bare feet. He was fearless, determined, unstoppable. If he rolled up his sleeves, it meant trouble for the other team. Very soon, he became a star with Torino, playing in that strange world of Italian wartime competition, when Serie A continued even as battles were fought all over Europe. Little did that Torino super-team know, Lefebvre says, as they scored goals by the hundred and lifted cup after cup, what fate had in store for them.

Lefebvre pauses. Then, in a whisper, as if he can barely bring himself to speak, he says, Superga.

What is now forgotten, Lefebvre says, is that the doomed Grande Torino were returning from a friendly match in Lisbon against Benfica. Early in 1949, Mazzola had suggested the match to the great Benfica captain, Xico Ferreira. The match would be played in Ferreira's honor, with all receipts going to charity. The two captains immediately agreed, like the gentlemen they were. On the eve of the trip, Valentino fell ill with a high fever, but he insisted on flying to Portugal to participate in the event. Why? Because he had given Ferreira his word, captain to captain, footballer to footballer. Is it possible to imagine modern superstars acting with such humble integrity? Without naming names, he, Lefebvre, is aware of a certain contemporary vedette who committed to appearing at a certain testimonial game. The event was publicized accordingly. At the last minute, the vedette announced his withdrawal, citing a trivial reason. When it was indicated to him that he had promised to attend, what was the vedette's response? He said, I am not a slave to my words.

Lefebvre once met Xico Ferreira. It was on a sunny afternoon in Porto, in 1982. Senhor Ferreira was in a good mood on that day, but it soon became clear to Lefebvre that he had never recovered from the disaster, that he had never ceased to mourn the young men who had honored him with their lives, that in his heart he was, so to speak, forever climbing out of the wreckage of Superga.

Often, over the years, the Frenchman tells us, I have asked myself why, despite all the dangers and discouragements, I kept returning to Africa, even into old age – why I have kept searching, searching. What was I doing? What did I want – money? Respect, recognition? I affirm that these were my motives, and I affirm also that they are good motives, the motives of the professional. But now, looking down from the hilltop of decades, Lefebvre says, he sees that maybe he has been pursuing an impossible spiritual mission. Maybe, in the figure of Godwin, he is trying to resurrect the honorable sport of his youth.

Lefebvre suddenly and loudly expectorates. He spits the product down into the yard. I want to catch the eye of Sushila, who is sensitive to that kind of thing. She has fallen asleep, however. I cover her with a blanket, join her on the couch, and put her bare feet on my lap. That feels good. I am at my most serene when everyone I love is nearby and asleep.

Now it is just me and Lefebvre, man to man. 'Go on,' I tell him.

●

La Mazzola drove Lefebvre to the meeting place in Natitingou. There was no sign of Fulbert. Now we wait, the Italian said.

They were stationed in front of a large, well-preserved colonial building. This building, now a museum, was once the regional headquarters of the French, Emilia Mazzola told Lefebvre. It had quite a history. She looked at Lefebvre, trying to ascertain if he would be interested in hearing more. Lefebvre indicated that he was interested, if only to pass the time. Mazzola told him that his countrymen, the French, used forced labor to construct the building, in accordance with their colonial practices. Men and women were made to carry enormous rônier palms across the Atacora Mountains. This act of cruelty generated native discontent – again, normal in colonial society. But the colonial power had not reckoned on the indomitable nature of the Atacora highlanders, who for centuries had fought off the fearsome slave raiders of the Dahomey kingdom. There was an uprising led by a man named Kaba. For several years the rebels fought a guerrilla campaign against the occupiers, equipped only with spears and arrows, black magic, and baobab trees, in whose hollows they would hide from their enemies. Also, they ate the French. That was what Mazzola had been told, at least. How factually accurate any of the details were, she could not say. Folklore and history were inseparable in this part of the world. When she'd mentioned the cannibalism story to Benin professors, they'd laughed it off. From the point of view of attracting tourism and investment, the last thing they needed were stories that revived the trope of 'darkest Africa'. You want to know what I think, Lefebvre? Emilia Mazzola said. These legends of bloodthirstiness, she thought, were tactical braggadocio, the tactic being to strike fear into the hearts of any potential external aggressor. A reputation for ferocity had its uses even now. The highlanders were still wary of their historic enemies – the richer, more powerful Fon people in the south of Benin – and they were wary of the armed groups in the Sahel countries, who were active not only on the military plane but also on the plane of propaganda directed at poor Muslim youth. Was the propaganda working? It was hard to say, Mazzola said. It was very difficult for a foreigner like her to grasp what was going on.

Lefebvre suggested that working in Africa was complicated.

It isn't easy, Emilia Mazzola confessed. The hardest part was managing her feelings about some of the local attitudes and customs, toward women in particular. There was so much injustice. She was conscious that, as an Italian, as a rich person, as a more or less ignorant outsider, she was not the best person to pass judgment. It was confusing. To tell Lefebvre the truth, she was coming around to the belief that it would be better if she stopped trying to inform herself.

Lefebvre had encountered this genre of distress before. It was common among Westerners in Africa. Yet he had assumed that this strong young woman would be more robust, would have grasped that there was nothing to be done, by her, about the ancient structures that determined the meaning of life in this continent, as they did in any other. Rare is the society, past or present, north or south, Lefebvre intones somberly, that is not characterized by brutality, domination, injustice. Glimmers of light are few. The wrongs of the world are without beginning and without end. It is a folly, Lefebvre declares, to devote one's life to the goal of placating the human conscience. Much better to focus on one's own work, on the private sphere of action, and to play the game to the best of one's ability.

The good news, Lefebvre suggested to Emilia, was that she had found her vocation in the realm of the animal kingdom. She was doing good work. This was all that a person could ask for.

She laughed. The lycaon had almost certainly been extirpated from Benin, she said. She was chasing a phantom. She was no better than the superstitious people who surrounded her, with their belief in ghosts and spirits and enchantments.

It is quite possible that I am drumming my fingers on the wooden arm of the couch, because Lefebvre, who has been addressing the beer in his glass, twitches his head to look at my hand.

He says, 'I believe that madame would like to hear what I will say next.'

'Excuse me?'

'I think she will be interested.'

'Why?'

'You will understand why.'

It is an extraordinary, a sinister, request; but the closer he brings us to Godwin, the greater grows Lefebvre's power. I squeeze Sushila's foot.

My wife is someone who gets embarrassed about sleeping or even appearing to be tired. Guiltily, she withdraws her feet from my hands, gulps down a glass of water and gives Lefebvre her attention.

Lefebvre gives the table three raps. It was with knocking like this, on the passenger window, Lefebvre says, that Fulbert suddenly announced his arrival. The guide chatted with Mazzola for a long time, or so it felt to Lefebvre, before unhurriedly joining his French client in the Land Cruiser.

Did you sleep well? he asked, starting the car. I did, Lefebvre said.

Then Fulbert, driving to an unknown destination, spoke at length. Lefebvre pieced together the following.

Immediately after Fulbert had dropped off Lefebvre at the Pendjari lodge, Fulbert drove to the nearby village of Toucountouna. Like many places in this part of the world, Toucountouna was surrounded by small plots of land on which families grew crops for food and for cash. Godwin's family, the Boubacar family, had such a plot. It was worked by the mother and her two oldest daughters.

The father, Woru, worked in the village, at a motorbike and bicycle repair shop that he co-owned with three others. Fulbert went to see Woru at his workshop.

Fulbert had known Woru for a long time. When one of Fulbert's protégés had expressed the wish to become a *mécanicien deux roues*, a two-wheeler mechanic, Fulbert asked Woru if he could take the boy on as an apprentice. Fulbert would cover the costs (the initiation fee of thirty-five dollars, plus an annual training fee of one hundred dollars) that would normally be borne by the apprentice's family. Woru agreed. Over the course of the three-year apprenticeship, Fulbert regularly stopped by the workshop. He got to know Godwin a little, because the kid loved to hang around his father and work on the *motocyclettes*. Fulbert did not take a pastoral interest in Godwin. The boy already benefited from a lot of attention, not on account of his prowess as a footballer but on account of his prowess as a hunter.

Pearson's sleeping head now rests securely on Lefebvre's foot, I see.

Fulbert was not talking about the kind of hunting that the tourists did in the cynegetic zones near Pendjari – crawling around on their hands and knees to gun down buffalo, antelope, sometimes even lion. He was talking about the communal *chasse sportive*. You put on old shoes and old clothes, you brought along your wooden club and your dog, and you set off into the bush in the company of a few hundred others. The *chef des chasseurs*, equipped with a whistle or a horn, led the way. Males of all ages took part. Fulbert went on his first hunt when he was nine years old. You went out all afternoon and returned before sundown, and nearly everybody killed something – agouti, antelope, rat, francolin, hare. Famous deeds were done, reputations were made and unmade. Football players, because of their fitness and running ability, were good at hunting. But there were holes in the ground, there were hidden roots. Broken bones, leg and ankle injuries especially, were common. Human beings were not designed to run through the bush.

About a year ago, Fulbert advised Woru in Godwin's presence that if he, Fulbert, had Godwin's talent for football, he would not hunt – it was too dangerous. Woru, Fulbert suggested, should forbid his son from hunting. But Woru was very proud of Godwin's hunting ability. Nothing gave the father more pleasure than to watch the son move effortlessly to the front of the pack. It was very gratifying for the father to have the *chef* approach him afterward and compliment him on the boy's exploits. Indeed, the name *Godwin* was a hunting nickname. It had been bestowed by visiting Nigerians who were impressed by the courage and speed of the eleven-year-old whose official name was Boni. Woru said to Fulbert, Hunting is in his blood. It will be fine, inshallah.

'I don't like the sound of that,' Sushila says.

'This is normal. This is what we deal with,' Lefebvre said. 'The stupidity of the family.' Fulbert found Woru at his workshop. He wasted no time: he told Woru that a football scout from France wished to meet him to discuss his son Godwin. Woru was not prepared to give his permission. He told Fulbert to come back in the evening.

They met at sunset in the shade of an immense mango tree. There was tea. Woru was accompanied by a griot.

'What's a griot?'

Griots, Lefebvre answers Sushila, are professional bards. They are found all over West Africa, and there is no shortage of them in Toucountouna. They sing songs, perform various rituals, tell tribal histories. Because of their learning, griots sometimes serve as counselors or arbitrators. A man like Woru, with no literacy and very little knowledge of the world, would listen carefully to what a griot had to say.

Fulbert knew this griot. He was a calm man, more intelligent than Woru.

The griot told Fulbert that Woru did not want his son to leave Toucountouna. Everything that the young man needed – land, work, family, his people, his ancestors – was in Toucountouna. To depart for a football career was to enter a world of strangers and wickedness. It would be haram.

Fulbert understood that this was part of the negotiation. He was also aware, from his own knowledge, that Woru resented Godwin's interest in football. It was a question of jealousy, in Fulbert's opinion. If Woru had been the one with the football talent, he would not have so quickly condemned the world of strangers, the world of riches. He would have been less attached to a hectare of yams, a few chickens, and a workshop filled with broken bicycles. But Woru was vain and small-minded. Fulbert knew many such men in his own village, men who resented the success he, Fulbert, had enjoyed, resented in particular his marriage to Spindler. Fulbert said to Woru: Just listen to what the Frenchman has to say. The monsieur had traveled all the way from Paris. He is a serious, respectable man. He has the power to make good things happen for the Boubacar family.

The griot interjected. He told Fulbert that Woru needed a sign that the Frenchman was serious. When Fulbert said nothing in response, the griot uttered a proverb: Silence is for the dead; the one who is alive speaks.

The negotiation began in earnest.

You will recall, Lefebvre says, that Fulbert had sponsored a boy to serve Woru as an apprentice mechanic. That boy had recently completed his apprenticeship. The griot told Fulbert that if Lefebvre paid for a traditional graduation ceremony, including gifts for Woru, Woru would sign the apprenticeship diploma.

Fulbert was unhappy. The government had banned graduation ceremonies precisely because they enabled masters to take advantage of the apprentice's family. Fulbert pointed out to the griot that there had been no talk of a graduation ceremony when the apprenticeship had been agreed upon.

The griot said: If the Frenchman pays for the graduation, Woru will permit him to speak to his son. Everyone will be happy.

How much? Fulbert asked. Five hundred US, the griot said.

Fulbert looked at Lefebvre. I will pay the five hundred, Lefebvre told Fulbert.

There is one complication, Fulbert said. Godwin is not in Toucountouna.

Where is he, then? Lefebvre asked.

The Land Cruiser unexpectedly slowed down. Ahead, a truck overloaded with cotton had tipped over onto its side. Policemen were stopping and redirecting the traffic. Auxiliary officials, in a different uniform, were also present. Fulbert leaned out of his window to speak to one such official. So sternly did Fulbert address the man, Lefebvre says, so furiously imposing was his advice, that you would have thought that Fulbert was the man's commandant. What the exchange concerned, Lefebvre had no idea. Every instinct he possessed told him that it would end badly, that the police would not tolerate a civilian berating a uniformed officer in such a way. But another policeman approached and waved them through.

Godwin is in Ouidah, Fulbert said. We are going to Ouidah.

There was more.

After the meeting with Woru, the griot and Fulbert met in private. The griot offered Fulbert another piece of information, priced at one hundred dollars.

Yes, Lefebvre said, he would pay the one hundred dollars.

The griot's information was this: Another white man, a football agent, had come looking for Godwin in Toucountouna. This agent also discovered that Godwin was in Ouidah. It happened at the beginning of the rainy season – in March. The griot did not know the agent's name, but if Fulbert agreed to pay a further fifty dollars, the griot would tell him something else of value.

Yes, yes, fifty dollars, Lefebvre said to Fulbert.

The agent, the griot told Fulbert, had been accompanied by his mother.

Lefebvre lights another cheroot.

Sushila covers her mouth with her hands.

I am being slow. I am not catching on.

The griot must have been misinformed, Lefebvre suggested to Fulbert. Or perhaps he was inventing things. Fulbert shook his head. The griot was speaking the truth.

'In this moment,' Lefebvre says to us, 'I am asking, Why is Godwin in Ouidah? Who are these people who are looking for him?' He faces me. 'But very soon, my friend, there will be no more mystery. I will go to Ouidah and I will meet them – your brother and your mother.'

•

From then on, Lefebvre is an auditory presence, a voice that emerges from the depths of a cloud of cheroot smoke. I am inside a cloud of shock. Fulbert's plan, the voice of Lefebvre is saying, was to spend the night at Abomey and to proceed to Ouidah, on the coast, the next day. If Fulbert had any anxiety about locating Godwin in a town of almost one hundred thousand souls, Lefebvre couldn't see it. Lefebvre was encouraged. He had come not only to trust his African companion but also to appreciate what an extraordinary stroke of luck it was to have this man as his guide. His good impression was only reinforced by the way the guide spoke with his wife, Spindler, who would phone her husband several times a day in accordance with the anxious habits of European women, and on every occasion Fulbert would answer patiently and reassuringly. There was, the voice of Lefebvre ventures, something of the nobleman or natural chief about Fulbert, something of the chevalier in his way of traveling up and down that road from Cotonou to Pendjari in his Land Cruiser, which was recognized by all, stopping here and there to be of assistance to whoever needed his help, always wearing an honest, unsmiling face. On the northbound leg of their trip, Fulbert had stopped Lefebvre from throwing away the large plastic bottle he'd been drinking from. The following day, in the Atacora Highlands, Fulbert pulled over to chat with a group of women who were walking barefooted with packages and pots balanced on their heads. They were dressed in blue, in accordance with the custom of their tribe, and one of them wore a light-blue Manchester City shirt bearing the name Tevez. Lefebvre could see how cordially and respectfully the women conversed with Fulbert, and he saw how they accepted his gift of the plastic water bottle with an easy laugh. It was the first time he had seen anyone in Benin laugh, or even smile, in public. It is not a jovial society, says the voice of Lefebvre. The women working in the roadside stores do not engage in badinage or coquetry. The men wear stern, grim faces. Poverty, and the relentless labor of poverty, no doubt has a role to play. The poor, Lefebvre asserts, never stop working, never stop looking for work, never get a moment's relief, always feel tired and fearful and defeated. Lefebvre knows this, he says, from observing his own mother, who could barely write her own name, who spent her life cleaning the clothes and the floors of the rich, who was always terrified of making a mistake or somehow disgusting her employers.

'Disgusting them?' Sushila says.

Yes, Lefebvre insists, disgusting. His mother had once been dismissed because her employer found her, *entre guillemets*, disgusting. But it was not Lefebvre's mother who was disgusting: it was her poverty. To see poverty, to smell it, to be near to it – disgusting! Lefebvre's mother went to great lengths to hide her economic situation, but she bore its signs on her hands and on her face.

Lefebvre tugs at one of Pearson's ears. Lefebvre grew up poor, certainly, but the poverty of France is not the same as the poverty of Africa. The poverty that he and his mother knew, although real, was not poverty without end and without beginning. It was not the final poverty. This type of poverty, with the character of finality, of infinity, was not something he could speak about from his own experiences. Comprehend, his voice demands, that he is referring to rural France in the 1940s and 1950s. Comprehend that his mother was not a member of the peasantry but of the ignoble class of women who belonged nowhere, in neither the city nor the country, an underclass that survived by doing the lowest domestic labor, indoors and outdoors, never accumulating wealth, never leaving a trace of itself, procreating from one generation to the next without legitimacy, living with dignity, yes, but with a dignity that had to be kept secret, a dignity that could not be revealed in the world. But I saw her dignity, Lefebvre says. I saw it every day. She was my mother.

Lefebvre swallows hard. In any case, he continues, he was intrigued and moved by the figure of Fulbert, an authentic specimen of Africa, a boy with tribal scarification on his cheek who had been plucked from the bush and given the opportunity to follow a path in life that was not decided in advance by tradition.

That evening, the two travelers overnighted at an auberge in Abomey. The auberge, a sign informed, had been built by the French colonists as a place where they could safely eat the dishes of France without fear of being poisoned. Lefebvre and Fulbert took an early dinner on the veranda. In the morning, they would set off to Ouidah, but such was Lefebvre's relaxation, such was his confidence in his companion, that he was not even thinking about Godwin. What a pleasure it is, Lefebvre declares to Sushila, to spend an evening in the tropics with a cigar – excellent protection against malaria! – a glass of cold beer, a bowl of peanuts and an interesting companion. It was dusk. Immense bats swarmed in the air above them. Lefebvre asked Fulbert if he had ever been to Europe. Twice, was the answer – once to meet his Spindler in-laws, in Belgium; and before that, before he'd met Spindler, to attend the premiere in Germany of a documentary film made by his Austrian friend and onetime client, Werner. Werner took care of everything – the flights, the hotel, the car service, the sightseeing plans, the living expenses associated with a week of tourism in and around Berlin. The Austrian even offered Fulbert expensive clothing to wear to the premiere. Fulbert declined the offer, just as he declined Werner's suggestion that he wear traditional African attire. In his usual Western clothes, Fulbert occupied the seat of honor next to his friend. He saw his name, Fulbert, in big letters on the screen. The documentary concerned the so-called Somba people of Atacora, who live in mud mansions that foreigners find remarkably interesting. The filmmaking had involved three intense months during which Fulbert never left the side of the Austrian. At the reception in Berlin, many people approached Fulbert and shook his hand and congratulated him. Fulbert was glad when the time came to return to Africa. He was not seduced, Lefebvre pronounces, by the material comforts of Germany; and although Fulbert would not say so, he clearly had not enjoyed being the object of the attention of the Austrian's entourage, ridiculous people of the sort who attend film premieres. In Berlin, Fulbert was a curiosity. In his own country, he had the only role fit for a man – namely, the role of being himself.

A three-vehicle convoy pulled up at the auberge. Tourists stepped out of the cars. Among them, Lefebvre saw, was the American anesthesiologist from Pendjari. He was in conversation with a woman – his wife, Lefebvre correctly guessed. Fulbert got up to welcome the tourists, even though they were not his clients, in essence acting as an ambassador for his country. He offered to carry the bags of the anesthesiologist's wife, who first declined, then accepted, his offer.

Lefebvre retreated to his room. The shower was malfunctioning – he had yet to encounter a functioning shower in Benin – but, experienced traveler that he was, he happily made use of the bucket of water that had been made available for washing. After a short rest, he got dressed and walked in the direction of the terrace, where one could hear the sound, always imbecilic, of Americans chattering. The pro-bono doctors and their spouses had finished their dinner. Lefebvre and the anesthesiologist embraced each other like a pair of old comrades. The doctor introduced the Frenchman to his (second) wife, an American who immediately told Lefebvre that their trip to Africa was only the first part of their honeymoon, with the second part, a trip to the Galápagos Islands, still to come, and that an important factor of their decision to come to Benin had been the prospect of free lodgings and pre-organized sightseeing. She had argued against combining a holiday with work, but her husband had insisted on it. Unfortunately, the work element had turned out to be very challenging for him, as she had predicted, and to cap it all, he had now caught some stomach disease. The second wife glanced sympathetically at her husband, who looked unwell and indeed was excusing himself. She gave an irrelevant laugh. Had Lefebvre noticed, she asked him, how sensitive people in the villages of Benin were to being photographed? She had assumed that it was a religious or superstitious objection. But no! They objected for a different reason, she'd discovered: the villagers believed in the existence of an enormously lucrative postcard industry and thought that the tourists with cameras were making fortunes by taking pictures of them, and they wanted to be paid for the image rights! Had he ever heard of anything so extraordinary? The doctor's second wife and her friends laughed.

It had been a most interesting two weeks, the second wife went on, drinking from her husband's abandoned beer bottle, but candidly, she was looking forward to returning to Atlanta. Was Lefebvre familiar, she asked, with *Things Fall Apart*? No, Lefebvre said.

It was a book about Africa, the anesthesiologist's wife stated, that she had packed though not yet gotten around to reading, so busy had she been since she'd arrived here, but even without opening its pages she felt that she understood the title, because, seemingly, there was no human-made thing in Benin that wasn't dangerous or defective and falling to pieces. Did he know what she most looked forward to, about being back in the States? In addition to electricity and running water and salad and not eating plantain chips? Sidewalks! Asphalt! Lawns! She had developed, she said, a strange, almost indescribable aversion to the blurriness and vagueness of the boundaries between roads and walkways, the crumbling walls and fences of houses and yards and buildings, the general indistinctness between what was public and what was private, the improvised nature of structures and spaces around them. There was red earth everywhere; the buildings and the people and even the trees and bushes were coated in the red earth. Lefebvre had no doubt seen for himself, she suggested, how everything in Abomey was red, how everything was made of dirt the color of meat – the houses, the roads, the shapeless terrain that separated buildings, and of course the palaces. What, she asked him, had he made of the royal palaces of Abomey?

Lefebvre informed her that he had not visited the palaces.

The second wife of the anesthesiologist gave a squeal of astonishment. Lefebvre had come to Abomey without seeing the palaces? How was that even possible? It was the most fascinating, horrifying thing she had ever seen. The name Abomey would forever send a chill down her spine.

Interrupting herself, she revealed that her name was Janice. Enchanted, Lefebvre replied.

The Kingdom of Dahomey dated back to the 1600s, Janice expertly related. Abomey was the capital. The Fon, the ruling nation of Dahomey, believed that the spirit of a deceased king continued to occupy his residence. Every new king, therefore, had to quickly build a palace of his own. Have I got that right? Janice asked her companions, and they nodded in affirmation.

The hastiness of the construction process, Janice said, perhaps explained the primitive design of these so-called palaces. Frankly,

she said, they weren't much to look at – compounds of mud bungalows, basically. A few trees stood here and there in the compounds,
but otherwise not much grew in the red dirt, not even the smallest
bush or decorative shrub. It was a bit puzzling, Janice thought. The
royalty of Dahomey had been very rich for hundreds of years. Had
nobody been interested in landscaping?

Janice had not posed this question to the museum guide, who
had not struck Janice as historian material. His entire shtick, she
suspected, consisted of memorized information that he repeated
like a parrot. His demeanor, as he escorted the Americans around
the palaces, was in Janice's opinion not exactly friendly. The guide
spoke only in French, of course. It was a problem they'd had
throughout their stay, Janice said. People always claimed to speak
English, but in truth they only knew a few words. Fortunately,
there was someone bilingual in their party who was happy to act
as interpreter.

They learned from the guide that the royal grounds at
Abomey had once been the site of enormous public gatherings,
notably the Annual Customs. Had Lefebvre heard of the Annual
Customs?

Lefebvre stated that he had not.

Janice rubbed her face. It was too horrible for words, she said,
but she would give it a go. Every year, she said, the King of Dahomey
oversaw a great ceremonial feast. It took place right here, at the
Abomey palace. As part of the ceremonies, hundreds of slaves were
sacrificed in honor of the royal ancestors. They would chop off the
heads of hundreds of captive human beings in front of everybody.
What a bloodbath! The Dahomey kingdom was obsessed with slaves
and decapitation and skulls, Janice said. Their whole economy was
based on capturing and enslaving their tribal neighbors and selling
them to European traders. According to the guide, warriors who
went off on raids were expected to return with two skulls. If they
failed, the second skull would be their own. If Lefebvre doubted any
part of what she said, he could look it up on Wikipedia. Better still,
he could see for himself the world-famous throne of skulls at the
palace museum, a real throne mounted on real human skulls. Why

on Earth, Janice said, looking at her companions, were they proud of this horrible chair?

Tell him about the wives, one of the ladies said.

Janice said: Basically, when the king died in 1889, his forty-one wives supposedly declared that they wished to accompany him into the afterlife, and in accordance with their wishes they were drugged and then buried alive in an underground chamber that was connected to the king's tomb by a tunnel. The guide showed them the place where they were put under the ground – alive! – the forty-one women and girls. The guide also showed them the walls of the king's tomb – either the same king or another one, she couldn't be sure, it was all so traumatic, her mind was scrambled – and told them that the walls were made of clay mixed with the blood of slaves. It was all too much, Janice said. There was only so much a person could take. She wanted to think about nice things, normal things. She was ready to go home to Georgia.

With a cry of agony, Lefebvre springs to his feet. Pearson jumps up with him. Holding the railing of the deck, the Frenchman straightens one leg, then the other. 'Cramp,' he says. He pours himself a glass of water from the jug, drinks it down in a long gulp, refills his glass, drinks it down again. When he returns to his armchair, he removes a shoe and places a black-socked foot on the table. 'The toes, also, get cramp.' He adds, with a lack of warning that can only be malicious, 'It was not my intention to make the acquaintance of your mother, Mark. But that is what happened.'

I feel Sushila's hand, cool and steadfast, gripping mine.

•

Fulbert and Lefebvre drove down to Ouidah in the morning, a journey of two hours. Fulbert would not reveal to Lefebvre what his plan was for locating Godwin.

At Ouidah, they went to a bank. Lefebvre withdrew the equivalent of one thousand US dollars and paid Fulbert $650, as agreed. The balance of $350 was payable as a bonus if Fulbert found Godwin.

It turned out that Fulbert's plan was to drive to Ouidah's run-down football stadium and ask the people randomly present about Godwin's whereabouts. Lefebvre stayed in the car while these inquiries were made. Fulbert, imperturbable, returned to the car. Without a word, they drove to another football ground, this one with a dirt field as red as Roland Garros. Once again, Lefebvre waited in the car. When Fulbert returned, he was wearing a frown. We will go to the beach, he said, starting the car. *J'aime pas la plage*, he muttered – I do not like the beach.

Normally when people say something like this, Lefebvre tells us, they are talking about parasols and swimming. Fulbert, we will see, was talking about something very different.

The beach at Ouidah, Lefebvre avows, forms part of the sand beach that runs for thousands of kilometers along the Gulf of Guinea. It was once his misfortune, he claims, to fly in a twelve-seater from Abidjan to Port-Gentil. Because of a storm out at sea, their route followed the shoreline of the Gulf at a low altitude, and for three turbulent, terrifying, everlasting hours, Lefebvre peeked out of his window at the edge of the great continent. It was an accursed-looking land, if you could call it a land at all, so submerged was it in lagoons, river deltas, mangrove swamps. The only sign of comfort, to his eyes, was the beach, an interminable pencil line of reddish yellow that separated the green of the water from the green of the watery land. At Ouidah, the beach was exactly like this: a strip of sand that served as a barrier between the Atlantic and an inland lake. But it was not just any beach, Lefebvre says, raising a finger of warning into the air.

Not for the first time, Lefebvre spits into the dark.

They had time to kill. Ouidah, Lefebvre says, is a town of great interest for the tourist – the Vatican of voodoo, they call it. But Lefebvre was not a tourist, and he was not interested in the Temple of Pythons. He asked Fulbert to take him to a place without serpents.

Without further discussion, Fulbert drove Lefebvre to the historic Fort of St. John the Baptist of Ouidah, built by the Portuguese. The English, the Dutch, the French and the Danes had also established fortified trading posts in Ouidah, but this was the only one left standing. There was a handsome, extremely well restored old villa – the residence of the old governor – with outbuildings, also restored, and a courtyard. Every wall and curb was painted a beautiful bright white. Until it passed into Beninese hands in 1961, the fort constituted the smallest colony in the world. Fulbert related all of this to Lefebvre like a teacher.

The forts were built for the slave trade, Lefebvre learned. Only Luanda, in Angola, exported more slaves than Ouidah. More than a million unfortunates were shipped from Dahomey's principal port, many of them destined for sugar and tobacco plantations in Brazil, which did not abolish slavery until 1888. In those bad old days, a moat stocked with crocodiles surrounded the Portuguese fort. The moat was now filled in, and the grand old residence had been turned into a museum. Immense mango trees with white-painted trunks stood as a reminder of the horticultural efforts of the old colonists. Fulbert expressed the opinion that a well-run cafeteria, serving the expensive coffee and cakes that tourists liked, would be successful at this location.

They strolled on.

Fulbert stopped at a gnarled tree. Under this ancient ficus tree, Fulbert taught, men, women and children were auctioned off. Fulbert pointed out an unremarkable but well-preserved building. In there, he said, the captives were branded after their sale.

Lefebvre was annoyed. Why was Fulbert talking to him about this? He was not opposed to history, he was not opposed to remembrance – the museums, the statues, the special holidays, and so on. But he was in the football business, not in the business of commemoration. He was trying to prepare for a decisive encounter with Godwin. It was time to go to the beach, he instructed Fulbert in a voice that was perhaps sterner than it should have been. But he felt the need to impose his will on his guide.

They drove down Rue van Vollenhoven – a name familiar to anyone with some knowledge of French military history, Lefebvre says in a reproachful tone, as if Sushila and I should know about this person – and then followed a dirt road toward the beach. Soon after, Fulbert stopped the car. From here we walk, he told Lefebvre.

The dirt road ahead looked drivable to Lefebvre, but he did not question the guide's decision. He did not yet know that this was the so-named Route des Esclaves, and that they were following in the footsteps of the captives who for centuries had taken this very path to the beach.

With a terrific mechanical effort of knees and arms and elbows, the old soccer player rises to his feet. He begins to shuffle forward – and to my horror I realize that he is, in his own mind, reenacting the gait of the long-gone enslaved persons as they were marched toward the ocean with chains attached to their feet. In the burning heat of the afternoon, says the self-styled man of football, he followed Fulbert through the swamps and lagoons. Lefebvre gestures toward the darkness at the rear of the backyard. Every step they took brought them closer to the ocean. Terrible destination! We have to imagine, Lefebvre insists, the point of view of the captured ones. They came from the interior of the land. They had never perceived the ocean. The pounding of the surf, growing louder and louder as they approached, sounded to them like a monster roaring in anticipation of their arrival. Their terror was already great: the mythic white men, it was believed, acquired slaves in order to eat them. The terror only worsened when they set eyes on the ocean. They had never seen such a thing. They had no comprehension of the marine horizon. They believed that the ships would crash into the sky.

Lefebvre falls back into his chair. The beach, he resumes, was a true ocean beach, a broad belt of yellow-red sand extending without finish in both directions. An imposing and sinister monument, a gigantic arch, rose nearby. It was named the Door of No Return, and it had been built, Lefebvre later learned, to mark the history of this seaside place and provide a dramatic terminus for the Slave Route, which, it transpired, was not a natural historical remnant, so to speak, but an artificial dirt road constructed by UNESCO. Lefebvre felt that there was no need for the Door of No Return. The reality of nonreturn was very easily observable in the infinite and empty body of water that was the true endpoint of the Slave Route. Never before had the ocean terrified him. It was overwhelming, he said. It was like Auschwitz.

Cautiously, Sushila asks, 'What did Fulbert think?'

Lefebvre flings an impatient hand skyward. What Fulbert was thinking was not for him, Lefebvre, to decipher. What was Fulbert supposed to think? What was there to say? Do we suppose that he and Fulbert discussed the matter? For why? To pass the time? If you must know, Lefebvre says, Fulbert walked past the Door of No Return without paying it any attention.

Not long after, they ran into Godwin.

It happened like this. They had walked for a few minutes on the beach when they came upon the dilapidated remains of a beach club. We will wait here, Fulbert said. Wait? Wait for what? Lefebvre asked. Fulbert's response was to hand him a bottle of water. And so – they waited.

For the first time during that trip, Lefebvre felt lost. The beach was like a desert. The sea was like a desert. The white sky was like a desert. He looked east, he looked west – there was no sign of anyone.

A herd of cows materialized out of nowhere. The cows, about forty strong, were pale, thin animals, littler than those you'd see in Europe, their shoulders barely reaching the waists of the two herders. As Lefebvre watched them pass by, he noticed in the distance, where the beach curved slightly into the ocean, a group of runners, in minuscule. He kept looking, to make sure that he was not mistaken. Look, he said to Fulbert. I saw already, Fulbert said. Lefebvre believed him. La Mazzola had told him that there was no guide or ranger at Pendjari who surpassed Fulbert in the matter of spotting animals in the wild, that she had never met anyone with better eyesight or with greater alertness to the irregularities of light and shadow that betray the presence of a far-off elephant or a motionless leopard.

The runners approached in imperceptible increments. A low red cloud followed them. Closer and closer they came, the single mass of their merged silhouettes gradually disintegrating into separate figures. Initially, Lefebvre felt a pure emotion of anticipation. This became mixed with an illogical fear: he had been overtaken by the presentiment that these runners were pursuing him and very soon would catch him. It was a falsehood, of course, a mirage of feeling, and, to be clear, Lefebvre says, it was not that he felt in actual danger. But the timeless, hypnotic spectacle, that of a group of strong, determined young men moving toward him at a speed that he could not possibly hope to outrun, was enough, Lefebvre claims, to make him feel a chill in his bones for the wretches of yesteryear who would have observed the warriors of the slaving parties inescapably closing in on them from afar, across the savanna . . .

Lefebvre's head shudders like a dog's.

When the runners were no more than two hundred meters away, Fulbert stood up and emerged from the shade. Together, he and Lefebvre watched them – about twenty men – come clearly into view. They ran barefooted and chanted as they ran, more like military men than sportsmen. It was a magnificent sight, Lefebvre declares. Far from being jaded by the passing of the years, Lefebvre appreciates more than ever the graceful mobility that is the exclusive possession of the young. Is it possible that Lefebvre, too, once was capable of such physical power? His head shakes again, this time like a human's. Fulbert might have been an expert at spotting crocodiles and monkeys, but when it came to runners it was Lefebvre who had the trained eye. His attention fell on the long-legged boy at the head of the peloton. Whereas the others were more muscular, more like out-and-out sprinters, this one, Lefebvre thought, had a touch of the Sahara in his stride. How effortlessly he raced over the heavy sand!

The runners raced past them.

Fulbert said to Lefebvre, You saw him, yes?

Only then, like a fool, did Lefebvre realize that Godwin, grown taller and stronger and more impressive than ever, was the runner at the head of the pack.

•

Impossibly, the night is getting warmer. I am drenched in sweat. From what body of water have I surfaced? It is truly the early hours. The block's back gardens form a cube without light. Beyond, the darkened city is as silent as a lawn. I feel dislodged, almost adrift.

When Lefebvre briefly falls silent, I hear a faint incessant murmur that I could swear is made by a river, or perhaps by the mingled sounds of the Allegheny and the Monongahela and the Ohio. But is a river audible? Maybe it's dehydration, or the dreaminess of near-sleep, maybe it's the uncanny boatlike dark, but factuality is coming unfastened. As Lefebvre begins again to talk, I feel the secret action of a fourth river, the hidden source of my state and my situation, on which I am afloat, the responsible river, on whose imperceptible current I am being carried away, to a distant confluence perhaps, like that of the Ohio and the Mississippi, and from there to a delta, perhaps, and from there into an ocean, where . . .

After the sighting of Godwin, says the voice of Lefebvre, Fulbert made the following disclosure: Godwin, he had been told, was associating with a European couple who were staying at a certain hotel.

Take me there, the Frenchman instructed the African.

It was a short drive away. The hotel consisted of beach bungalows and a rectangular building that enclosed a swimming pool. Lefebvre checked into a room with a view of the swimming pool. He paid Fulbert his finder's bonus – $350 – and told him to go home to Spindler. Then he went to his room and took a *sieste*.

The sounds of splashing and laughter woke him up. Young men were using the swimming pool. One of them was Godwin.

Lefebvre stayed at the window, watching. There was too much horseplay for his liking – too much running on wet stone, too much pushing, too much foolishness. One slip, and boom, Godwin's career would be over. Lefebvre had seen it happen many times before. He had a strong impulse to shout out the window, *Ça suffit!* That's enough!

A European blonde of a certain age, wearing a bathrobe and large sunglasses and a straw hat, appeared on the scene. She was followed by a waiter carrying a tray of drinks. The boys jumped to their feet and started grabbing the drinks. The lady was very beautiful, very soignée. She handed Godwin a parcel. He unwrapped it, then held up a set of wireless headphones. The friends shouted with excitement. Godwin gave the lady a hug.

If my mother ever gave me a gift, I don't remember it. Maybe that's why Sushila is again squeezing my hand.

Lefebvre went back to his bed. When he rose, all was quiet. Nobody was at the swimming pool. The only object in the Atlantic was the descending sun. Lefebvre went to the reception desk. It was unstaffed. When he called out, a puzzled-looking man appeared. Lefebvre inquired about where to eat, then struck up a broader conversation. He learned two things about the white lady – one useful, one mystifying. The mystifying item was that the madame was not European but American. The useful item was that every night she ate dinner at a beach restaurant called Blue Wave.

Lefebvre lights a fresh cheroot, or cigarillo. He wears an expression of strange intensity.

Blue Wave was busy when Lefebvre arrived. You would have liked it, he tells Pearson, the floor was beach sand. But the situation was not for him. Noisy, badly lit places enervated him; and although in his youth he had scored some romantic victories, he was not one to approach a woman in a bar. Then Lefebvre noticed what he should have noticed earlier: the American lady was already present, sitting alone at a table in the backyard, in a nook obscured by a palm tree. She was dressed as if at Cap-Ferrat – white cotton pants, a blue-and-white striped cotton shirt, and a ribbon knotted elegantly around her blond ponytail. She looked, Lefebvre tells Pearson, like Ann-Margret.

She watched Lefebvre approach her. There was something very calm, very unsurprised about her expression. Either she was expecting him, or she had been approached by men in such a way many times before. Lefebvre understood in that instant that he had to proceed with complete frankness. He introduced himself as a football intermediary who was interested in the prospect Godwin. He asked if he could join madame at her table. Madame said, Of course, and introduced herself: Faye Anibal. Only then did it come to Lefebvre who she was.

He said, I know your son, Geoff.

She corrected him with a smile: I think you know my son Mark, too.

That was when Lefebvre thought to himself, Oho! This lady is a worthy opponent.

The proprietor of the Blue Wave appeared. He told Lefebvre that he was very content to meet a friend of madame's. A waiter also appeared, with complimentary cocktails. Grilled fish for two, Faye told the waiter. She had not consulted Lefebvre.

Facing off like two great adversaries, Lefebvre claims, he and Faye raised their cocktail glasses to one another – a sign, he ventures to say, of mutual respect and recognition. He, like Faye, had refused the path of convention, preferring instead to live by his wits, in accordance with his personal code.

Indignant and useless objections flash through my mind. Personal code? Is that now the explanation for every kind of selfishness – the personal code?

Lefebvre says that out of delicacy he will spare me all the details of his dinner with Madame Anibal, in particular details of the feelings of admiration that she excited in him. He will allow himself to observe that he formed a great esteem for this lady, who was, in his judgment, of a type that one rarely encounters in the modern world, populated as it is, in Lefebvre's opinion, with reproductions of human beings, whereas Faye, if he could be permitted to name her without formality, was possessed of the originality and vitality of the old world. Lefebvre laughs loudly, inexplicably. In short, Faye was, as the English say, a good sport. In accordance with an unspoken but well-understood rule of the game, it fell to her to explain to Lefebvre how she had done it – how she had gotten the better of him and made Godwin hers.

She had two sons, she told Lefebvre. The son in America – Lefebvre acknowledges me – was very private, very self-sufficient, very *bon élève*. The one in England was different – more open, more reckless, less academic. Each son took after his own father, you could say. Geoff was the athletic one. His passion was soccer, and during his teenage years Faye's house served as a kind of youth camp, so frequently did Geoff bring home his teammates, most of them black teenagers from poor London neighborhoods, for cookies and drinks and video games. On weekend mornings she would go downstairs and be met by six or seven young men sleeping like babies on the floor. She felt like a social worker, Faye said. As a mother, she was conventional. She wasn't thrilled when Geoff dropped out of college and disappeared into the shadowy world of Parisian soccer, a venture that ended in predictable failure. But he survived, and that is the most valuable experience of all, is it not? When he decided to become a soccer agent, she did not say anything, even though she knew what would happen: Geoff would quickly burn through the inheritance he'd received from his *papa* and he would ask his *maman* to finance his business. She refused, for her son's own good. The time had come for him to learn how to take care of himself. She would support him, but only as a mother, not as an investor. Geoff took it badly. To punish her, he withdrew from all communication unless it was to ask for money. It was always a worry – where he was and what he might be up to. Her constant impression – this went on for years – was that he was in trouble. She was delighted when his big brother, Mark, flew to England to spend some time with him. That was something she, Faye, had made happen, with the help of Mark's wife.

What?

Sushila says to me, 'I haven't done anything to help Faye. I don't care about what Faye wants. It's just that she and I agreed that it would be nice for you to see Geoff.'

I knew it!

During the time of Mark's visit to Geoff, Faye answered her front door in Winchester to a very handsome, very black man. The monsieur asked if he could speak to Mr Geoff Anibal. She thought about shutting the door, but the gentleman was wearing a tweed jacket and black oxfords. Thugs did not wear tweed jackets, not even in Winchester.

She said, I'm Geoff Anibal's mother. Is he all right? What's happened?

The monsieur reassured her that everything was all right. He introduced himself as Cyrille, a friend of Geoff's from Paris.

Faye said, There must be some mistake. Geoff does not live here. I haven't seen him in a long time. I'm afraid we've fallen out of touch.

In truth, Faye knew where Geoff was – in Paris. She also knew exactly who Cyrille was.

Geoff had called her only three days before. It was their first true conversation in about a year. He was in a fury, as usual, this time about his brother, Mark. It was your idea to have him come over, he shouted at his mother. Faye pieced together that there was a video of a footballer named Godwin which Mark had supposedly double-crossed Geoff about. Double-crossed how? Faye asked, and Geoff shouted that his brother had discovered the whereabouts of Godwin but would not share this (apparently valuable) information with him. Meanwhile, someone called Cyrille was menacing Geoff about the same video. He needed money to get him off his back. She listened to her son without comment. Five thousand US dollars, she was thinking to herself – and she guessed right. When Faye declined to lend him the money, he shouted, All right, then, you deal with him! And that was how Cyrille had ended up knocking on Faye's door.

She said to Cyrille, Would you like a cup of tea? I'm having some. She felt sorry for him, standing helplessly in the street, his jacket of tweed only accentuating his air of financial desperation. Also, an idea had occurred to her.

What sangfroid! Lefebvre comments. What personality!

The visitor, Faye told Lefebvre, was perched on the edge of the chesterfield as if he'd never used furniture before. The teacup looked ridiculous in his huge hands.

Cyrille explained to Faye that in Istanbul he had acquired the exclusive rights to a football scouting video featuring an exciting African prospect known as Godwin. Cyrille brought out a document from his jacket pocket, evidently a bill of sale of some kind. The bill named Cyrille as the buyer.

Never go to Istanbul, Lefebvre warns Pearson. It is a city of cats, not a city of dogs. To Sushila and me he says that in Istanbul there exists an international industry focused on luring unfortunates from Africa with false promises of professional football opportunities. Nigerians, Serbs, Russians, Arabs – every shit from every corner of the world of football converges on the city to exploit these desperate young men. We can be sure that whoever sold Cyrille the

Godwin video had stolen it from an African who had found it on the stolen phone of another African who had downloaded the video from the internet without permission, et cetera, et cetera.

Cyrille explained to Faye that he and Geoff had played on the same team, were old friends. Cyrille had e-mailed Geoff the Godwin video with a view to Geoff's purchasing exclusive rights. Geoff gave his word, as one old teammate to another, that he would not make a copy. Not long after, word reached Cyrille that Geoff not only had made a copy of the video but was trying to locate Godwin. A few days ago, after several months of avoiding him, Geoff finally contacted Cyrille. He told Cyrille to come to this address in Winchester.

Cyrille stood up. He was trying to intimidate her. He looked as if he was going to throw the teacup across the room.

Faye directed Cyrille to sit down. After he had complied, she asked, Where are you from?

Côte d'Ivoire, Cyrille answered.

In this country, Faye told him, we have laws for business problems. We have courts. There is no need for dramatics. She continued: OK, look. You've traveled here from Paris. I'm going to help you. I will buy the video myself. It's the best I can do.

They settled on one thousand dollars. Before she paid him the money – which she kept in a safe in her house – she required that the Ivorian reveal the secret of Godwin's location. He told her that the video had been filmed in Benin. Faye had never heard of Benin, let alone the town that Cyrille also mentioned, and she made him write the place-names down. At her insistence, he also wrote a receipt and amended the worthless bill of sale in her favor. He left looking unhappy.

Faye told Geoff about the encounter with Cyrille. She told him that she had learned Godwin's whereabouts. Where is he? he demanded. She would only tell him, she said, if he agreed to form a partnership with her in the Godwin venture. When Geoff pointed out that it would involve travel to Africa, Faye told him that she would finance the travel. Geoff accepted, of course. He had no option. He was broke. He had no clients. His schemes – the most recent one being to scout footballers in Mauritania, of all places –

were far-fetched, to say the least. Nor could Geoff do anything to keep Faye from accompanying him to Cotonou. He needed her. He didn't have a head for business. He was impulsive, reckless. She was confident that she would be useful to him. And so it proved.

But of course, Faye remarked to Lefebvre, she wasn't traveling with her son as a businesswoman. She was traveling as a mother. Moreover, she had always wanted to visit Africa. From when she was a little girl, it had been her dream to have an African baby.

•

'Pearson,' I say. I click my fingers, loudly. 'Pearson.'

Pearson's rescuers found him chained to a crane tire in Kentucky. Tumors like mushrooms grew out of his abdomen. He had survived by drinking the rainwater collected in the tire. With every justification, he was fearful of humans. It took a year of intense one-on-one training, by me, to cure Pearson of his antisocial habits. This was in the days when I was a dog fosterer, working for nothing out of an animal adoption agency. Most of the dogs I fostered were puppies. Almost all were found a permanent home within a few weeks. Pearson was a hard case. He had trust issues and, as a consequence, aggression issues. Nobody was interested in giving him a home except for two sketchy young guys who liked the idea of owning a pit-bull mix. The agency rightly turned them down. When Sushila became pregnant, she asked me to quit fostering. I did as she asked, but not before I'd signed up to be Pearson's forever parent. This led to a brief domestic quarrel. Sushila wasn't against keeping Pearson at home with our baby, but it disturbed her that I'd acted unilaterally. She had a point. I loved Pearson, however. And I have no regrets about my decision. I saved that dog.

'Pearson,' I repeat. I clap my hands.

Pearson's nearest eye opens. His abdomen briefly inflates. He places his snout more securely against Lefebvre's ankle and goes back to sleep. It is enraging.

It was very good luck for your little brother, Lefebvre is saying to me, that his mother accompanied him to Benin. Without her, he would not have been able to land the fish, so to speak.

When Faye and Geoff met Godwin's parents in Natitingou, they were told by the father, Monsieur Woru, that Godwin did not want to speak with them; but Faye (so she told Lefebvre) discerned in the eyes of Godwin's mother, a simple tribeswoman, a telling silent anguish; and, drawing on her own experience of maternal heartbreak, she concluded (she disclosed to Lefebvre) that there was a rupture between Godwin and his family, and she instructed her guide to investigate the matter further and find out exactly where the boy was. The guide did as he was asked; and he reported that Godwin was in Ouidah and that, just as Faye had suspected, he was not on good terms with his father.

A good guide, Lefebvre affirmed to Faye, was indispensable. He would not be dining with her in Ouidah without the excellent work of his own guide.

Faye smiled. Fulbert is a good man, she said.

Lefebvre was confused. You know Fulbert?

Faye smiled again.

Lefebvre laughed so loudly that their waiter came over to make sure that he was OK. He asked her, Did you pay for the graduation of the apprentice? Faye nodded, then asked, How much? I paid five hundred, Lefebvre said. Faye, who was too lost in mirth to answer verbally, showed three fingers to signal three hundred.

The present-tense, Pittsburgh Lefebvre also begins laughing.

I'm not laughing. I'm feeling a deep, desperate helplessness, a feeling of being outwitted, blindsided, duped and beaten. Will she ever go away? Will I ever be free? I give Sushila a look that says, See? See what I've been up against all my life?

But Sushila is consumed by her own emotions.

Lefebvre raised his glass to Faye. He said, *Bravo, madame. Bien joué.* Well played. He gave this compliment sincerely. He did not have bad sentiments for the lady. As for Fulbert, Lefebvre was more perplexed than disappointed. Why had he deceived Lefebvre with the apprentice-graduation story? If the objective was to reward Woru, why didn't Fulbert simply state that Woru required a reward? Fulbert must have known that Lefebvre would gladly have paid it. There was only one conclusion to be drawn: that his objective was not to make a financial gain but to play a trick on Lefebvre. But for why? Lefebvre throws up his hands.

He produces a dirty-looking burgundy handkerchief and wipes his face with it. Pittsburgh, he says, possibly humorously, is as humid as Ouidah. He offers Pearson the handkerchief . . . to smell? Pearson grabs it and begins to chew it.

Comprehend, the Lefebvre voice says, that we should not mistake his sportsmanship for surrender. Privately, he had not yet conceded defeat to Madame Anibal. Yes, she had succeeded in gaining the confidence of the subject Godwin. Bravo. But the next step was the most difficult: to move from the world of conceptions to the world of realities, of practicalities. The transnational movement of minors was governed by laws. To traffic in a human being remained a crime. Without the official involvement of a football club, it would be very difficult to take Godwin from Benin to Europe; and the Anibals, mother and son, did not benefit from the football relationships that Lefebvre did. If they are not very careful, Lefebvre thought to himself, they will find themselves in trouble.

He said to my mother, as he described her, You have been here at Ouidah for how long – two months? That is a long time. You are having difficulties.

Thank you for your concern, Faye said with a smile. But we are fine.

Where is Geoff? Lefebvre said.

Geoff, she told him, had gone back to England, to arrange for a club for Godwin.

It was Lefebvre's turn to smile. Let us be frank, he said. Geoff is not having success. This is the difference between the professional and, let us say, the amateur. Lefebvre put his telephone on the dining table. With one call, he told Faye, I can find Godwin a club in France.

Faye laughed. There will be no need for that. We have our plan.

And what was the plan? Lefebvre asked.

I am adopting Godwin, she said.

Lefebvre's voice pauses for effect. Even Pearson looks up.

Sushila, suddenly animated and focused, says, 'I'm confused.

There are lots of rules for intercountry adoptions. You need approvals, you need interviews, background checks, immigration clearance . . . And it's not cheap.'

Exactly those thoughts, Lefebvre says to Sushila, passed through his mind. And yet he also had a contrary thought. There exists, Lefebvre claims, in addition to the manifest world of business, a world of bargains and baksheesh, a secret world, a world difficult for a man such as himself to enter. This has always been his limitation – he is a simple man of football. Madame Anibal, on the other hand . . . Truly, Lefebvre says, this is a woman who moves in mysterious ways, in accordance with the knowledge of the ancients. There is more to human life, Lefebvre tells us, than behavior that is good, behavior that is expected. The great prizes are not given to those who behave in accordance with expectations. Faye was not a woman concerned with expectations. Later, she would in complete frankness tell Lefebvre that she had married three times, each time for money. Who else would make such an admission? Who else possessed such freedom of spirit? For such a philosophy Lefebvre has only respect. In former times, Madame Anibal would have been designated an adventuress – ambiguous term! – because there existed a niche for this kind of personality, a specialist in intrigue and feminine courage. But in the modern world, with its obsession with rules, with the correct, with the uniform . . . Lefebvre falls silent with disapproval.

Faye told Lefebvre that, with the assistance of unnamed intermediaries, she had procured the full coöperation of Benin's Ministry of Family Affairs. Even more impressively, she had procured, in her capacity as a citizen of the United States of America, the assistance of the US consular corps. There were bumps in the road, of course. A judicial procedure had to be followed, a procedure complicated by the interference of Godwin's self-described parents, who traveled down from the north to make a scene at the Ministry in Ouidah, wailing and screaming and making demands. They were in no position to make demands, Faye told Lefebvre. They had no paperwork to verify their identities, never mind their parental relation to Godwin. They could not disprove Godwin's sworn assertion that he was an orphan. It was essential—

Sushila, I am suddenly aware, has been listening to Lefebvre with furious carefulness. 'Orphan?' she objects.

—It was essential, Lefebvre repeats, overruling the objection, it was essential for naturalization purposes, according to Faye, that Godwin's age and orphan status be registered. Why? Because, under American law, a fifteen-year-old orphan was immediately eligible for naturalization.

Godwin is fifteen? Lefebvre asked Faye. Born in the year 2000? That's what his papers say, Faye answered.

Sushila says, 'What you're describing isn't an adoption.'

'I agree with you,' Lefebvre says. 'I say to her, "Madame, you go too far. You cannot take the child from the parents."'

Too far? she responded. You think I was too tough with them? Here's what I think, she said. I think that if the parents had really wanted to keep Godwin, if Godwin truly was their son, they would have fought harder. They would have hired a lawyer, they would have gotten testimony supporting their case, they would have bought the judge. They would not so quickly have accepted, in return for withdrawing their objections to the adoption, a donation from Faye. No amount of money, Faye told Lefebvre, could separate a true parent from their child. She brushed a tear from her eye.

A dry, unnatural, bitter sound comes out of my throat – a laugh, you would have to call it.

Lefebvre passed Faye his handkerchief – the very same handkerchief, he claims, that Pearson is now chewing. What Godwin meant to her, Faye told Lefebvre with great emotion, was not something she could find words for, was not a feeling she could share. You needed to be a mother to understand.

Now I emit a true laugh. My hands rise like a preacher's into the dark night. Hallelujah! I feel nothing less than a euphoric sense of vindication. My mother has finally been exposed. I see it in Sushila's eyes, which have fully opened with horrified amazement. At last, she will understand me. At last, I will be rescued from the desert island.

Was she right to think, Faye asked Lefebvre, that he was childless? Lefebvre admitted that she was right. Faye replied that her intuition was nearly infallible in such matters – matters of love, of family, of suffering. These things were more important to her than anything else. There she differed from Lefebvre, and, indeed, from her son Geoff, who perceived Godwin as a valuable athlete. Faye did not see a player of football at all; she did not see fame and riches. She saw a boy who was hungry for love. What drew her to Godwin was not his skill with a ball, which was incomprehensible to her; it was his smile. This beautiful smile had an amazing effect on her, she said, filling her with joy, making her feel an overwhelming desire to take care of him, to put food on the table before him, to watch over him, to do everything in her power to make him happy. Desire, as Lefebvre well knew, Faye said, was never easy. Desire made demands – demands of time, of energy, of money. But in relation to Godwin's demands, Faye felt blessed. In normal circumstances, a prolonged stay in Africa would have been her nightmare. She was a woman who liked luxury, she would make no apologies about that. She liked things to be under her control. But she was on a mission. That made all the difference. Everything she endured was for a higher purpose. Motherhood, she said to Lefebvre, had always been the center of her life. It was very gratifying that the officials in Benin had recognized her vocation.

Lefebvre listened with skepticism to Faye's account of her motives. But he was already in awe of her acumen. The adoption was a brilliant idea. It promised to solve in one stroke all issues of immigration, work permits, welfare of minors, nationality. Over the next few weeks, as Lefebvre and Madame Anibal became, should Lefebvre say, better acquainted, his admiration only grew. Everything came to pass as Faye had foreseen. And the day came when the judge in Cotonou issued the official order that she wanted.

Lefebvre produces a two-page document. After I have unfolded it and read it, I hand it to Sushila. After she has read it, she gives it back to Lefebvre – in a daze, if I'm not mistaken.

'Keep it,' Lefebvre says. 'This is your copy.'

The document certifies, in French and English, the adoptive maternity of Faye Anibal of the person henceforth named Godwin Anibal.

Lefebvre says, Yes, it is an impressive story, a story of courage, determination, fantasy.

'It's a horrible story,' Sushila says.

'From the perspective of Pittsburgh, from the perspective of Paris – maybe,' Lefebvre allows. 'But from the perspective of Benin? From the perspective of Godwin?' Comprehend, he says, that Godwin was content with the adoption. Comprehend that Godwin rejected the destiny of the villager.

'He's a child,' Sushila says. 'His parents have the rights of parents.'

Be that as it may, Lefebvre goes on, there remained a final, central detail. Godwin still needed effective professional representation. Without it, he would be just another African boy in Europe.

At Blue Wave, Lefebvre warned Faye in precisely such terms. Adoption or no adoption, her son Geoff would not be able to secure a professional football contract for Godwin. Geoff Anibal? No disrespect, but nobody knew this name. If they knew, they did not like. Geoff would not be able to market Godwin effectively. Football clubs in Europe, he informed Faye, were always being offered black prodigies. Every day somebody claimed to have discovered the new Yaya Touré, the new Marius Trésor. For a club to take an interest, there had to exist a relationship of confidence. Would Faye like to know how it was constructed, this confidence? By standing in the rain, in the snow, in the heat and humidity, in the jungles and in the deserts and in the ghettos, night after night, year after year, watching and watching football. Lefebvre's method was to be always honest – honest with the coaches, with the players, honest with the mother and father, honest with the man who paints the lines of the goals. It was not easy. Again and again, he said no. No, no, no. He had broken ten thousand dreams. That was his job. It was how he had built the reputation that enabled him to say to a club: Yes. And the club would listen to him. Lefebvre made Faye a prediction: The day would come when she would accept that Geoff was not going to be able to help Godwin – indeed, that Geoff was putting the entire venture at risk. When that day came, she would ask him, Lefebvre, for help.

In my shoes, Faye asked, what would be your next step with Godwin?

Lefebvre said without hesitation, I would remove him from the beach of Ouidah, where he is learning nothing and risking everything, and I would place him in a football academy until his adoption is completed.

A football academy where? Faye asked.

Senegal, Lefebvre answered. I can arrange it like this.

Lefebvre loudly clicks his fingers. My dog jumps to attention.

To shorten a long story, Lefebvre says, the next day he dined again with Faye, again at Blue Wave and at that second dinner she – as Godwin's funder, controller and soon-to-be mother – offered to engage Lefebvre as Godwin's football agent. The offer came with one condition: that Lefebvre agree to work with Geoff, as partners. Naturally, Lefebvre refused the condition. He was a professional. He could only work with professionals. You will teach him, Faye said. No, Lefebvre answered. *Jamais de la vie*.

During the days that followed, Lefebvre confesses with a little smile, Faye changed his mind.

I squawk, 'Wait, are you—'

It would be ungentlemanly, Lefebvre interjects, to say more about the process of persuasion. Suffice it to say, he says, that Faye changed his mind not only in relation to the younger son, but also in relation to the older son. 'Yes, you,' Lefebvre says. 'I am here in Pittsburgh, at your house, on behalf of your mother.' From his briefcase he removed papers. 'I am authorized to give you this.'

I hold a wrinkled page, spotted by droplets of red sauce, with the heading 'Business Proposal'. This subject of the proposal is ANIBAL ASSOCIATES, whose enormous logo – a pair of red intertwined 'A's superimposed on a soccer ball – dominates the top of the cover page. It reads:

> ANIBAL ASSOCIATES is an international SPORTS
> MANAGEMENT AGENCY focused on football but also
> other sports including basketball. ANIBAL ASSOCIATES'S
> experienced team will provide expert personal management

and agent and intermediary services for its clients. ANIBAL
ASSOCIATES is an international organization with offices in
the UNITED KINGDOM, the UNITED STATES and FRANCE.
ANIBAL ASSOCIATES is proud to offer an exceptional family-
based service to its clients and counterparties.

The directors of ANIBAL ASSOCIATES are:
FAYE ANIBAL – Global
JEAN-LUC LEFEBVRE – France
GEOFF ANIBAL – United Kingdom
MARK WOLFE – United States

What is this insanity?

Lefebvre is telling me, if I am understanding him correctly, that
my role in the agency will be communications – letters, contracts,
paperwork, the website. He will manage Godwin and the recruitment of other players. Geoff will focus on his supposed Mauritanian business. Faye will be the investor and managing director, in
charge of the finances. He says, 'This is your mother's dream – a
business that brings the whole family together.'

By way of laughter, I give a croak.

Lefebvre raises his hands, his eyebrows. 'I have done my duty,'
he says. 'To accept or not to accept – this is your decision.'

'You're asking me to join a one-client sports agency. For no
salary.'

'There will be a salary. Faye is a generous woman. And when
Godwin succeeds, we will have many more clients. All of this we can
discuss, if you are open to the project.'

I crumple the proposal page into a ball and toss it over my
shoulder into the yard.

'One more thing.' Lefebvre again reaches inside his briefcase.
He proffers a document of several pages, headed 'Benin Expenses',
which purports to itemize the cost of various meals, hotels, airplane tickets and per diems. From this subtotal he has purported to
subtract the four thousand three hundred he misappropriated from
me in Paris. Lefebvre says, 'You owe me five thousand two hundred
and twelve euros.'

This document, too, I make into a ball that I throw over my shoulder.

Lefebvre fights his way to his feet. 'Come, Mark,' he says. 'No decisions now. It is time for sleep.'

Pearson fights his way up, too.

Lefebvre's last words, before he goes into the house, are to me. 'Be sure,' he says, 'that you do not misunderstand the situation. Godwin is not only a client. He is your brother.'

L

Wolfe told me that he was leaving the Group. This was at the height of the Edil dramas. I didn't want him to leave. Stay on, Wolfe, I told him. Don't let them get to you. The situation was difficult but temporary. Soon everything would be back to normal.

'No, that's not it.' He handed me an unsealed envelope. The letter it contained stated that Wolfe was resigning his position as Co-Lead, effective immediately, to 'pursue a private opportunity.'

'Oh,' I said. It wasn't what I expected. 'Congratulations. Who are you going to?'

'It's not a corporate move. It's very different. More of a family thing.' He was reluctant to say more.

I didn't comment about the complete lack of notice. There was no point. In any case, Wolfe had only been Co-Lead for a few months, too short a time to make himself indispensable. We'd manage.

He said that it would mean a lot to him if he could leave with my blessing.

My blessing? His resignation had been 'effective immediately'. I wasn't his colleague anymore. It wasn't my job to bless him, whatever that meant, or give him a pep talk, or do any more work connected to him. He had no right to ask me to do that.

'You'll be OK,' I said. 'We'll be OK.'

'Good.' He sounded happy, as if I'd blessed him. Then I realized that I had blessed him. He gave me a hug and said, 'They don't deserve you, Lakesha.'

That wasn't a sentiment I liked. He mumbled something about dropping by later in the week. Maybe I misheard. Anyhow, he did not drop by.

In the meantime, Gin Yee had put together his Subcommittee, in accordance with the resolution of the Action Committee proposed by me. Wolfe and I had been scheduled to go before Gin's Subcommittee that same afternoon. I would have to face them on my own.

'Mark's not here?' These were Gin Yee's first words.

I handed him the letter of resignation. Gin read it very deliberately. The two other members of the Subcommittee, Jonathan and Boaz, read it with equal care and gravity. Their vibe was much more judicial than I had expected.

Boaz, shaking the letter, said, 'This is what I'd call unfortunate.'

I couldn't read Boaz. He and Gin had arrived at the Group together, as domestic and business partners. They let it be known that they were involved in an important joint venture, but if anyone expressed curiosity about it, they went all secretive. Apparently their idea was so valuable that even to describe it would have been a risk. Gradually, we heard less and less about the secret project. It had involved, I later heard, some interface improvement. They were, though, extremely successful as a technical-writing team in the computer technology field. Gin provided the technical know-how, Boaz the language. Whereas Gin was friendly and neutral and almost without personality, Boaz was more creative and unorthodox. The blueness of his eyes was produced by blue contact lenses. Annie, when she was the practice manager for the Bee Gees, as the Boaz-Gin team was known, once told me that Boaz had been declared a vexatious litigant in his native California. He and I had always been friendly, in a collegial way. Was it possible that he didn't like me? Was it significant that he and Gin had not invited me to their wedding, which had taken place several months before? It was quite the party, to judge from the pictures. Edil had attended.

Jonathan I had no worries about. I managed his practice. He knew me well.

But it didn't matter who was on the Subcommittee. The facts were clear. I had written down all the relevant particulars in numbered paragraphs, copied and collated all supporting documents, and organized my work into three binders, one for each Subcommittee member. Nobody had asked me to write this presentation. I did it voluntarily, to assist the Subcommittee; and I hand delivered each binder a week before our meeting. It was important to convey in correct detail the circumstances of every piece of work that I had given Wolfe, and vice versa. I gave special attention to the Pexantil contract to which Edil had objected, even obtaining a statement from my counterpart at Pexantil confirming that it was Pexantil, and not Wolfe, that came up with the idea of engaging my services after Annie's exit. I made a bar graph showing that my increase in earnings after Wolfe became Co-Lead was within the fluctuations of my historical earnings. As for Wolfe, it was true that his earnings had spiked; but the assignments (from me) that produced the spike predated his election as Co-Lead – in a candidacy that I had opposed at the AGM! (I appended the AGM Minutes.)

Presenting information with accuracy and clarity was my job. My presentation demonstrated clearly and accurately that there was no reasonable basis for believing that the Co-Leads had corruptly conspired to favor each other with work assignments. The Subcommittee would be grateful for my work. I wasn't anticipating a long meeting.

'When did you, ah, first become aware that Mark was leaving?' Boaz asked.

'This morning. When he gave me this letter.'

'Is he willing to cooperate with this inquiry?'

'You'd have to ask him,' I said.

Boaz handed the letter back to me. To Gin and Jonathan, he said, 'I guess he's bolted.'

'Bolted' was a strange word to use. But I said nothing about it. A colleague's departure was not my business.

We were all seated around the same conference table. I brought out my own copy of my presentation. 'Do you have this?'

Nobody answered immediately. Then Jonathan said, 'Not *to hand*,' and Gin said, 'I *believe* we received this,' and Boaz said, 'Do you have any copies *extra*?'

We adjourned to enable Jonathan, the junior member of the Subcommittee, to make more copies of my presentation and staple the pages together. When he came back from the copy room, the Subcommittee asked me to step outside. They lowered the blinds of the conference room for privacy. It was not easy for me to wait outside, in full view of other members, but it was vital that the Subcommittee read my work. It was only twenty-three pages, including the appendices. After fifteen minutes – it felt longer – Gin opened the door and called me in. When I entered, Boaz was looking at his phone.

'Thank you for this document,' Gin said.

'You're welcome,' I said. 'I hope it was useful.'

'It was super-useful,' Jonathan said.

I sat there, waiting.

Boaz said, 'I appreciate the great detail here, Lakesha. It's very, um, apt. But, ah, help me with this. There may be those who say that the problem is one of, ah, one of *perception*.' He seemed very pleased with this concept. 'What are your thoughts on that?'

'Perception of what?' I said. Boaz did not even try to answer my question, so I continued: 'The whole point of having this Subcommittee is that the Subcommittee determines what the perception is. The Subcommittee looks into the situation, it finds out the facts, it reports the facts, and that's the end of any perceptions.'

Boaz said, 'But how do we put out the fire? What if there's still smoke?'

'Smoke? You mean gossip?'

He made a face like a Supreme Court judge's face, puzzled and smug at the same time. 'What I can't figure out, exactly, is why Wolfe got so much work right before the election.'

I said, 'I explain it in my presentation. Wolfe asked for more work. I was able to help him. It would be the same for anyone.'

'If I asked you for more work, you'd give me more work?' Boaz asked. 'Say Jonathan asked for more work. You'd turn on the faucet for Jonathan?'

'There is no faucet,' I said. I looked at Gin and Jonathan,

searching for some help in their faces. 'Here's what I can tell you: I do my best. I do my best for the Group; I do my best for the members.'

'Would it be fair to say that you and Wolfe have a special relationship?'

'No, Gin, that would not be fair. We had a normal professional relationship.'

'Thank you,' Gin said, with that polite smile of his. Boaz, meanwhile, was highlighting a passage in my presentation. Was it possible that he still had not read it?

Jonathan poured himself a glass of water. He held up the carafe. 'Water, Lakesha?'

'I'm good, thanks.' I didn't have a glass. They hadn't given me one.

I'd thought these men were conscientious. I'd thought they were capable. They were my colleagues, after all. I had misjudged them. It wasn't easy to accept. And I wasn't prepared for it.

Boaz said, 'Who's going to replace Wolfe as Co-Lead?'

What did that have to do with anything? 'I haven't thought about it,' I said. 'We'll figure it out. The Group, I mean.'

'So, as of now, nobody's managing my practice? Nobody's managing Gin's practice?'

'The question of the new Co-Lead is not on the agenda for this meeting,' I said. 'But I can tell you that I'll be handling all of Wolfe's work until he's replaced. Members managed by Wolfe don't need to worry.'

I was expecting Boaz to be reassured – maybe even grateful. But he sat up, dramatically put down his highlighter, and looked at Gin.

'The problem,' Gin explained to me, 'is that if you control the practices of all three members of the Subcommittee, there's a conflict of interest. We're not in a position to find against you without putting our practices at risk. I'm not saying that we will find against you. I'm talking about the optics.' He smiled.

'It won't look good,' Boaz said. 'They'll say that it's not a coincidence that Wolfe resigned on the morning of the hearing, leaving you as the sole Lead.'

Calmly, I said, '"They" will say that? Who's "they"? This isn't the internet. This is the Group. This is real people. Who know me. Our people.' I was pleased to have found the words I needed.

'It just smells bad,' Boaz said.

I looked in the direction of Jonathan. All I saw there was weakness and confusion. Same when I looked at Gin.

I said, 'Look, what difference does it make that Wolfe resigned? The Subcommittee members were always going to be investigating their practice managers. The conflict of interest, if that's what you want to call it, existed from the beginning.'

'That's what we were discussing during the short adjournment,' Gin said. 'We think that this Subcommittee isn't the right way to proceed. There needs to be an independent investigation, not an internal investigation by members with conflicts of interest. Either that, or . . .'

'Or what?'

Gin looked at Boaz. Boaz said, 'The conflict of interest would go away if you stood down as Co-Lead. We're not recommending that. We're just saying.'

Resign as Co-Lead? Had they lost their minds? The members were relying on me. They had rent checks to write, medical bills to pay. How dare they!

I said, 'The Group is a small, good-faith organization. We've always managed things as a community. We've never brought in an outsider to settle our issues. We have a culture of trust. If we don't have that, I don't know what we have.' I stood up. 'Y'all can decide whatever you want. I've got work to do.'

When I got to my desk, I couldn't work. I could barely catch my breath.

I thought about calling Wolfe. That would not be a good idea, I decided. In some ways, it benefited me that he was out of the picture. Wolfe was a qualitative variable, a wild card. Also, I was still too mad to speak with him. He had left a mess behind him. I had to clean it up. Next time I saw him, I would share my thoughts about that.

There would be no next time. I would not lay eyes on Mark Wolfe again.

•

Gin Yee's Subcommittee informed the Action Committee that it would be potentially unethical for the Subcommittee, as constituted, to investigate possible improprieties by their own practice manager(s). They recommended an investigation by persons independent of the Group. The Action Committee thanked the Subcommittee and stated that its recommendation would be considered at the next Action meeting.

Normally, I would have strolled over to my Co-Lead – Wolfe, or Annie – and had a face-to-face chat about what do next. But I had no Co-Lead. I only had Edil.

Our respective desks were separated by thirty feet. Each of us had already decided not to talk with the other unless it was necessary. Outside of Action meetings, I had not found it necessary.

I thought to myself that if Boaz and Gin felt so conflicted about me managing their practices, it was only right that they should have Edil. She was, after all, the next most senior member of the Action Committee.

I wrote the Committee members:

Hi! Can I suggest that Edil take over Wolfe's members until our next meeting, as Acting Co-Lead? It would also alleviate the conflict-of-interest issues that Gin's Subcommittee has mentioned. Would that be OK with you, Edil?

Edil replied to all:

Yes, OK. We'll need to discuss compensation for the extra workload.

I knew she would find her new title irresistible. I replied to all:

Wonderful! Annie bequeathed most of her work to me, so, thankfully, Wolfe's workload is quite manageable. We can talk about a more permanent arrangement at the meeting!

By separate text to me, Edil wrote:

Please stay away from me and stay out of my business.

For about a minute, I took satisfaction at the thought of Edil and Boaz and Gin dealing with each other. Boaz and Gin were not in league with Edil, but they shared her foolishness.

After that, I felt bad. The practices of Boaz and Gin would be OK with Edil, but that didn't change the fact that I had acted with a kind of malice in my heart. I had acted without the best interests of the Group as my motive. It was a painful realization. I had never done such a thing before.

The stressor, the thing that caused me to suffer from hour to hour, was that I was alone. My friends in the Group did not reach out to me. Nobody invited me out for a coffee or took me out for lunch, nobody checked in with me to make sure I was OK. Nobody took my side. I sensed that they were embarrassed about the allegations against me, even if – especially if! – they did not know exactly what the allegations were. They were keeping away from the disturbance. I'm not saying that, in their position, I would have acted very differently. Taking a stand isn't just about aligning yourself with right and wrong. It is about making a commitment of energy. Edil's craving for intrigue and litigation and controversy was inexhaustible. Everyone was frightened by it. I don't know what I would have done without Cutie.

That was the state of play when I received a message on my work phone from someone whose voice I had not heard in more than twenty years. How happy that voice made me! As soon as I'd heard 'Hallow, Lakesha,' I knew who it was.

His message said that he was in Pittsburgh for a conference and that he would like nothing better than to have coffee with me. The next day, he and I met at the La Gourmandine, on Butler Street.

Professor Klaus Mueller looked at me intently from across the table – examined my face, my shoulders, my breasts, my hair. 'You look exactly the same, Lakesha,' he declared.

I answered, 'You look good, Professor.' I meant it, even though his hair was gray and thinning, and he'd gone from skinny to stocky.

'Please, not "Professor,"' he said. 'Klaus.' He explained that he had left academia soon after his return to Germany from Milwaukee. He had always been interested in optical isomers, and when the opportunity arose to head up a team in Stuttgart specializing in the manufacture of chiral ligands, he seized it with both hands. It was satisfying and rewarding work. He gave me a happy, apologetic smile. The years had treated him well, he admitted. He had two children in high school, a good wife, a good life. 'And what about you?' he asked. 'Tell me your story, Lakesha.'

Your story depends on your listener. The story I told Klaus was about my career. I described my brief stint at grad school, my short-lived corporate jobs, the founding of the Group. I was fighting guilt as I spoke. Klaus had expected better of me. I should have become a scientist.

'Tell me more about your Group,' he said.

I did as he asked. I finished by saying, 'It's a never-ending project.'

Klaus said, 'It is a beautiful achievement, Lakesha. A cooperative like this is rare in this day and age.'

We drank coffee and ate pastries. Klaus did not ask any more questions about me – about my private life, for example. That was respectful but in some ways regrettable. I had planned to tell him that I'd studied German at CMU; I was ready to recite the unforgettable prepositions of the dative case: *aus, bei, mit, nach, seit, von, zu* and *gegenüber*. But the conversation moved on, to other subjects. We talked about Pittsburgh, a city with which Klaus had until this visit been unfamiliar and whose tall, dramatic riverbanks reminded him, he said, of the Rhineland; about Professor Yonatan Abend, who'd left CMU many years ago and was back in Tel Aviv; about the cinchona tree, the bark of which was used by Klaus's company to manufacture quinine and other medicinal alkaloids; and about the four-day trip Klaus had recently taken to the eastern highlands of the Democratic Republic of Congo, where his employer owned plantations of these precious trees.

He'd traveled there out of curiosity, essentially, to see with his own eyes the fabled forests that produced the tree bark to which he had devoted so many years. The trip was the experience of a lifetime, you could say, Klaus said. He was filled with admiration and pity for the farmworkers, men and women who were fated to live in one of the most war-torn regions on Earth. For many years, he told me, this region of the DRC had been the site of never-ending conflict between Hutu and Tutsi forces. Troops from Rwanda, Burundi, Angola and Uganda were also intermittently present in the region, and most destructive of all, perhaps, were the activities of terror of the Congolese warlords and rebel militias, who, working with corrupt government elements, controlled by force most of the mines in the area. Eastern Congo was very rich in precious minerals – tin, tungsten, tantalum, gold. The United Nations had stationed peacekeeping troops in the region, but of course there was a limit to what they could do. 'You know me. I am someone who is positive, who looks to fix what can be fixed. I came back from Africa not at all optimistic about the future, Lakesha,' Klaus Mueller said.

You will of course be aware, Klaus went on, of the refugee crisis we are having in Germany. Stuttgart, his current hometown, was one of the most severely affected cities. Thousands, maybe tens of thousands, of Syrian families had descended on the city center. They could not look more like refugees if they tried, Klaus said, with their shawls and blankets and headscarves, with their inevitable children, with their standing in interminable lines for food and social services. You would think, Klaus said, that they were actors in a movie about refugees. Stuttgart had been transformed by the newcomers. It was impossible to go anywhere without seeing them. They blocked up the sidewalks. They filled the parks. The stadium by the Neckar River was filled with tents. You saw people on their hands and knees, praying to Allah. Everywhere you heard Arabic. How was Germany supposed to take care of these people? Germany was not like the United States. It did not have large empty regions. It did not have an economy that depended on the exploitation of illegal workers. It was not a melting pot. The most worrying thing, Klaus said, was how quickly and unstoppably this enormous migration had occurred in response to a civil war more than two thousand miles away. What will happen, Klaus asked, when the climatic change of Africa, already destructive, leads to agricultural failure on a scale never seen before? The instability, the political violence, could only increase; economic productivity could only worsen; the movement north of desperate families, first to North Africa and from there to Europe, would reach proportions beyond the scope of modern human experience. Returning to Germany from Congo, Klaus said, he had what was called in German a *Vorahnung*—

'A premonition,' I said.

—exactly so, Klaus Mueller said, not pausing to acknowledge or wonder about my ability to translate the word from the German, a premonition that initially took the form of unease but then, during his drive from Frankfurt Airport to Stuttgart, the form of terrifying mental images of what lay in store for Europe unless something was done: cities overrun by Africans, crime rampant, schools collapsing, culture collapsing, the sweet life of civilization gone forever and replaced by a violent struggle for survival from which no family would be exempt. Terrorists, jihadists, criminal gangs – in short, backward types from the world over – would disfigure the gentle streets of Germany. Had I read about what just happened in Palmyra?

'No,' I said.

At Palmyra, in Syria, the Islamic State occupiers had captured the leading scholar of that place, a gentleman in his eighties who had devoted his life to the legendary ancient city. His captors demanded that he disclose where were hidden the treasures of Palmyra. He held firm. He told the barbarians nothing. Klaus paused to fight off his tears. Anyway, they beheaded him. They hung his body from the Roman ruins. After that they blew up an ancient temple, in order to nullify the effect of his act of courage.

Klaus said that it was unlike him to think in visionary terms. He was a man of data, of analysis. But how often have we seen, Klaus stated, that data analysis is useless without an original spark of intuition, of imagination? Lakesha, he said, what became apparent to him, on that drive home from Frankfurt Airport, was that in the bloody hills of Congo he had seen the future of the West.

'Global warming is a serious problem,' I said.

'It is not global warming per se,' he said. 'It is the movement of people – of entire peoples. It is the movement of disorder and desperation. Already we have thousands and thousands coming every year to Germany from the East – from Romania, from Albania. These are not climate refugees. These are settlers. They are coming because they are poor and Germany is rich. It will affect the US, too. You have a very big southern border. There are a lot of poor people, a lot of wars, on the other side of the border.'

'Yes, it's true,' I said.

Klaus said, 'There is no time to lose. The time to act is now. There must be strong, commanding leadership. New leaders for the new challenges.'

I wasn't sure what he meant. I said, 'Yes.'

Klaus continued talking about his vision of the apocalypse. It occurred to me that he was an extreme character. It was strange that I, of all people, had not seen this earlier. Then it was time to go. We had an argument over the check, which I quickly won. He gave me a big hug. 'Till the next time, Lakesha,' he said, and I answered '*Auf Wiedersehen*, Klaus,' and away he walked, his hair white and shining in the sunlight. When I got home, I held Cutie and cried a little.

•

The Action Committee usually met every Thursday. In August we met less frequently. Folks were away. Edil was famous for her vacations. This year it was Morocco. The first available Thursday was on August 27, almost two weeks after my interview with Gin's Subcommittee. At Edil's insistence, the first item on the agenda was the Subcommittee's recommendation that external investigators be appointed to look into the dealings between me and Wolfe.

My hair stylist, Jackie, had wanted for a long time to give me shoulder-length Fulani braids with beads. You have got a beautiful brow, she always said. I always said no. It felt too bold. It was easier just to flat iron my hair and keep things low key. But this time I called up the salon and said to Tamara, who answered the phone, 'Tell Jackie I surrender.' Tamara passed on the message right away. I heard Jackie whoop in the background. We made an appointment for the following Thursday, at 10:00 a.m. The Action Committee would meet on the same day, at 5:00 p.m. I booked the appointment with Jackie because I did not want to spend the day at my desk, in suspense. I wanted Edil to be the one in a state of suspense, wondering about where I might be.

I love the tranquil morning atmosphere in a hair salon; it can be a bit boisterous for me in the afternoon. They made me a cup of herbal tea. Jackie herself shampooed and moisturized my hair to prep for the braiding. Two chairs down, Tamara's client was questioning the choice of the first-dance song at a wedding she'd just been to. The song was 'How Deep Is Your Love'.

'It's a classic,' Tamara said firmly.

Right, the client said. She liked the song. It *was* a classic. But if you listened to the words, you realized that it was about two people in love, but also asking about how deep their love was. That wasn't right for a wedding. 'It's your first dance,' Tamara's client said, 'and it's how deep is your love? On your first dance? Already? Really?'

Jackie laughed. 'You want to ask how deep is your love *before* you get married.'

'I like "Stayin' Alive,"' Tamara said. 'But not for a first dance. For a first dance I'd want "All of Me".'

'Mm-hmm,' Jackie said. 'Too late for that for now.'

There was laughter.

It was very soothing. I closed my eyes and let the chatter wash over me. My eyes were mostly closed while the braiding and extending was going on, too. It was just what I needed to gather my thoughts for the Action meeting.

My Subcommittee idea hadn't worked out. It had prolonged the drama, maybe even worsened it. I had outsmarted myself. But I still had faith in my presentation. It explained everything anyone could possibly want to know about the dealings between me and Wolfe. I would take the Action members through the presentation in detail, paragraph by paragraph, line by line, point by point, for as long as it took, and finally demonstrate that I had acted honestly and appropriately. By the time I was done, there would be no more talk of outside investigators.

Jackie did a fantastic job. I could not believe how good I looked.

The last time I'd had braids was when I was thirteen years old. Mom did those. She had fast, deft fingers, just like Jackie. I left the salon feeling calm, prepared and stronger than ever. Pete, the front-desk agent, did a double take when he saw me. Hair has power.

There was a strange atmosphere in the office. Normally, only a handful of members would be present on a Thursday afternoon, but I counted eleven members. They weren't working, either. They were standing around, talking, some with hands in pockets. Edil was among them, with a vacation tan and a blazing yellow caftan that she must have bought in Morocco. They all turned to look at me. A single expression – of astonishment, maybe, or of shock – was distributed among their faces. 'Good afternoon,' I said, making my way to my desk. I strode with my chin up. They would not detect any self-doubt.

Through the glass wall I could see Edil and the others conferring. One or two of them looked in my direction. Tommy Szymanski was there, and Betsy, too. What was Edil up to now? Whatever it was, I would handle it. I turned on my desktop.

Before I could do any reading, Edil came in. 'You've heard?' she said.

I wasn't ready to speak to her.

'Wolfe died,' Edil said. Her face reddened. She began to cough and cry. Because I didn't answer, Edil said, 'It's true. It's on Facebook.'

Nothing she was saying made sense. I went out to the others. One member, Nicky Caffo, gave me his phone. It showed a Facebook post.

Devastated to hear the news about Mark Wolfe. A deep soul. My thoughts and prayers go to Sushila and Fizzy.

There was a picture of Wolfe as young man. With him was the guy whose post it was. The two of them were comically crawling on their hands and knees across a lawn.

I gave Nicky back his phone. 'This is reliable?' I didn't understand.

There were posts by other people confirming it, Nicky said.

Somebody standing next to Nicky stated that the cause of death was unclear.

Another voice, trembling and brave, spoke out. 'He was an unusual man.'

It was Edil. She had taken a seat on the wall bench, ensuring that we all had to turn to look at her. She made no attempt to brush away her tears. She announced, 'I was fortunate to know him well. Very well. We had special times together. We—'

She started crying again. Betsy went over and comforted her.

I objected to this performance of bereavement. A person who didn't know better might gain the impression that she had been intimate with Wolfe, a family man. She was a disgrace.

Tommy Szymanski whispered, 'What about the Action meeting?'

We went ahead with the meeting – Edil, Tommy, Betsy and I. It was over very quickly. Betsy wrote in the Minutes:

The Committee was informed that longtime Group member and former Co-Lead Mark Wolfe had passed. The Committee noted his service to the Group with deep gratitude. It was resolved to offer the Group's sympathies and assistance to his family. It was further resolved to hold an Extraordinary General Meeting to elect a successor to Mark. In view of the sad news, the meeting was adjourned.

'This is an excellent Minute,' I told Betsy. 'Thank you.'

'I'll write to his partner,' Edil said.

'Thank you for offering, Edil,' I said. 'But writing to the next of kin is the responsibility of the most senior officer in the Group. It communicates maximum respect. That's the etiquette. We established it after Alex Remy died. Plus, you have lost a dear friend. Everyone can see how upset you are. It wouldn't be right to burden you.'

I had to protect Wolfe's family from this woman.

When I stepped out of the conference room, the atmosphere had changed. I knew what this meant: a new fact was in circulation.

It was horrible to see the excitement in the faces of my co-workers. It's not an exaggeration to say that it changed my perception of them, for the worse. It changed my self-perception, too. Why had I committed so much of my life to these people?

There is more to work than labor and compensation and being of service and achieving a state of flow. There is also the day-to-day human element. You want to look into the faces of your co-workers and like what you see there.

The exciting news was this: Wolfe had died in an airplane crash. It had come out on the internet somewhere. Further research dug up a report in a French-language news site. From this it was learned that the crash involved a small aircraft in The Gambia, Africa. None of the seven travelers survived.

That night I wrote a condolence letter to Sushila Rasiah – an actual letter, in my handwriting – on Group official notepaper. In addition to offering the Group's condolences, I informed her about the life insurance that the Group offered its members. Wolfe had resigned from the Group, but his death occurred within his notice period. Sushila would be entitled to the sum of nine thousand dollars, irrespective of his resignation. It embarrassed me to write this, but those were the facts. I assured her of the Group's continuing support, and I strongly encouraged her to be in touch with me personally, for any reason.

Then I held Cutie. Poor beautiful Wolfe!

•

Eight weeks went by before I heard back from Sushila, by e-mail. She apologized for not writing sooner. She had been out of the country, 'taking care of things'. To my surprise, she asked to meet for coffee. We agreed on Lili Café, where Wolfe and I had met back in January. Now it was October.

At the Group, meanwhile, a lot had happened.

It was Betsy's responsibility to inform the membership about the Extraordinary General Meeting. I was surprised, therefore, to receive the announcement e-mail from the Acting Co-Lead, Edil. After explaining that the purpose of the EGM was to elect a new

Co-Lead, Edil stated that she would be 'honored' to 'serve' in this
position. The e-mail went on, as if she'd already won the election:

> It won't be easy to detach myself from F & M. But I have every
> faith that Betsy will do just great as my successor. I strongly
> endorse her. For Secretary, I encourage you to consider Eddie
> Verrucci. Our brilliant new members must be empowered if the
> Group is to move forward into the future.

> I would like to take this opportunity to mention our departed
> Co-Lead Mark Wolfe. Mark was a dear personal friend. His
> passing leaves us heartbroken. I promise to uphold his legacy.

Normally, I would have been outraged – about the wholly
improper use of an official e-mail to push the candidacies of Edil
and her cronies, about the obvious insincerity of her supposed
thoughts about Wolfe. I wasn't outraged, though. The situation felt
too false for that.

Within minutes, the members got another e-mail. This one was
from Betsy. She invited each of us to confirm our attendance or
nonattendance at the EGM.

I saw what was going on. Betsy would tell Edil who was not
attending, and Edil would write them asking for their proxy. A significant number would comply. Compliance is so often the path of
least resistance.

The path of resistance was to find and promote a candidate
to do battle against Edil. This prospect overwhelmed me with the
same feeling of falseness.

Either way: when I looked ahead, it was like I was about to perform in a play. I have never wanted my life to be a play. I have always
wanted it to be real. Anything else would be intolerable.

I don't make decisions impulsively. It wasn't until the next
day, in the early afternoon, that I wrote the members that I was
resigning as Co-Lead, effective twenty-one days' hence, i.e., a week
before the EGM, to enable the orderly and timeous election of my
successor. I added:

I am proud of the work I have done for the Group during these
last eleven years. It has been very rewarding for me. I have every
confidence in the Group's future and intend to remain a working
member. I would like to thank each and every one of you for
your kindness and, yes, cooperation!

I was aware that what I had written was illogical and boilerplate
– a rough first draft, in ordinary circumstances. I didn't care. I sent
it off.

The next day, I wrote the members again. I informed them
that, on reflection, my membership would be coterminous with my
Co-Leadership. This language was passive aggressive, but I did
not amend it. I could not contain my anger and disappointment. I
somewhat regret that.

Greg kindly organized my leave-taking drinks. I wrote out
upbeat remarks in which I made sure to mention everyone I needed
to thank, even if that person was not present. The event was under-
attended, in my opinion. If I'd been more motivated, I would have
organized it myself, just as I had organized Annie's goodbye gathering. Edil wasn't there, of course. In my remarks I said nothing
about her or her stupid discontinued investigation into Wolfe and
me. I did mention Wolfe, but only in passing, because my focus was
on those who had made a notable contribution to the Group. I had
earned the right to reminisce as I pleased.

After several minutes, I noticed that some folks in the audience were chattering amongst themselves. That only made me
more determined to complete my remarks. It was a boring, lengthy
speech, and I enjoyed giving it.

Sushila was reading, or at least holding, a thick book when I
arrived at Lili. She was enviably beautiful, with long straight hair
and skin that was darker and smoother than mine. There were bold
strands of gray in her hair. That showed a strength I would like to
have one day.

The first thing I told Sushila was that I was no longer at the
Group and would, unfortunately, only be able to offer her my personal help.

Sushila said, 'I heard that.' She asked me why I had left.

It wasn't my intention to make myself the subject of conversation. But I had a statement ready, as you do when you change jobs. I told her that working at the Group had been very rewarding, but after many years the time had come for me to do something different. I wasn't yet sure what my new direction would be, but meanwhile I was very fortunate to be able to keep working as a freelance technical writer.

She said, 'It must have been hard for you to leave.'

'Yes, it was,' I said. It wasn't the occasion to explain my crisis of faith. Disillusionment is such a hard state of mind to confess to, and folks don't want to hear about it. I said, 'The office politics helped me to make up my mind.'

'Office politics? I always thought it was a place of harmony,' Sushila said.

I was surprised to discover, as we talked, that she knew nothing about the outrageous accusations leveled by Edil against her husband and me. She had never even heard of Edil.

'He basically refused to discuss his work,' Sushila said. 'It was frustrating. It still frustrates me.'

I said with a smile, 'I don't think that he saw himself as a technical writer. Not many people do! But we liked him.'

'He did tell me,' Sushila said, 'that he'd been elected to a leadership position. He was proud.'

'He was right to be proud.' There was no point telling her about the proxy-vote scandal. 'He was elected Co-Lead. I was the other Co-Lead.'

She said, 'OK, Co-Lead. That makes sense.'

I explained as briefly as I could what a Co-Lead did. I made sure, too, to tell her what an outstanding writer Wolfe had been and how much good he'd done for his clients. She seemed passive and maybe a little bewildered. It wasn't an easy conversation for either of us. I'd thought that she wanted to meet for a specific purpose; but it appeared that she just wanted to talk with someone who knew her husband. If Wolfe had ever mentioned me to his wife, there was no sign of it.

My phone briefly glowed. Sushila pointed at the screen and said, 'Oh, is that your dog?'

'This is Cutie,' I said. Sushila seemed interested, so I showed her more pictures.

'How adorable,' she said.

I told her that I'd met Pearson. 'He's a real little gentleman,' I said. 'He must be distraught.'

'He is,' Sushila said. Pearson, she said, was very much Wolfe's dog. Last year, she related, their daughter, Fiza, had developed asthma caused by an allergic reaction to the dog. Sushila had felt that they had no option but to give Pearson a new home. Wolfe had ruled it out, however. It had been a source of strong disagreement. 'So stubborn,' she said. Pearson still slept by the front door, awaiting the return of his absent master. Whenever the doorbell rang, he dashed to see if it was him. It was heartbreaking.

I found this topic of conversation painful. I asked her about the book she was holding, on the cover of which was a photograph of a man lighting a cigarette.

She turned the book over and revealed its title: *The Collected Poems*. The author was named Zbigniew Herbert.

I said, 'That looks amazing.' Had I ever met anyone, after college, holding a book of poetry?

When she had first met Wolfe, Sushila said, he was for some reason very impressed that she owned this book. She had never admitted to him that she had not read it, and that it was a graduation gift from a teacher at her high school, here in Pittsburgh. She was only now reading it – or trying to. The poems seemed dark and difficult to her. And it was too late.

She stopped talking, I think for fear of crying.

'Are you getting the help you need for your daughter?' I asked.

She said vaguely, 'My parents have been supportive.'

I mentioned the life insurance again.

After a hesitation, she told me that Wolfe's mother's money was keeping them afloat.

'That's nice of her,' I said.

'Well, not exactly,' she said. That was when I learned that Wolfe's mother, Faye, had been on the plane with him. Her other son, too – Geoff. They were flying from Dakar to Ziguinchor. These were cities in Senegal, Africa. The small plane encountered difficulties.

An emergency landing on the Gambia River was attempted. The maneuver was unsuccessful. They crashed. 'It's this huge river,' Sushila said. 'And, you know, the currents . . .' Only the remains of the mother had been recovered.

My hands covered my mouth. I was able to say, 'Was it – a safari?'

It wasn't. They – the two brothers and their mother – flew to the south of Senegal 'for business reasons, essentially.'

'I believe Wolfe once told me something about a soccer player in Africa?'

'Yes, that would be it.'

'So that's why he left the Group? To get into this soccer business?'

She drank from her water glass, summoning the energy to tell me the story. I was right, Sushila said, about Wolfe not being satisfied with technical writing as a career. It did not fulfill his potential. He always carried inside him a yearning to do something more consuming, exciting. Sushila had done her best to encourage him, in this regard – to make him aware that there was no need, as far as she was concerned, to do a job that he didn't want to do. Follow your dream, right? But what was Wolfe's dream? He had tried so many things, without success. Then along came this bizarre, unlikely project – to launch a sports agency with his mother and brother, on the back of a prodigy they'd recruited out of Benin, Africa. Sushila had 'serious reservations' about the scheme, which had crazy and disturbing aspects. She advised her husband to think carefully before committing to anything. At the same time, 'I didn't want to be the one standing in his way. And it was an opportunity to repair his relationship with his mom, which had brought him a lot of suffering. And he was unhappy about work, which, now that you're telling me that there was a lot of office politics, in retrospect makes a lot of sense.' Sushila gripped her warm coffee mug without drinking from it. 'Anyway, he decided to go in on the Africa venture.'

I said firmly, 'You can't blame yourself for that.'

Sushila said, 'I'm not blaming myself.'

'That's good,' I said.

Then Sushila said, in an outburst, 'He knew it was wrong, what his mother was doing. Taking that boy from his family. He knew better than anyone what she was like. But it in the end, he couldn't help himself. It was the money. He saw a chance to make a fortune. He couldn't help himself.'

I wasn't sure what she was referring to, exactly. I said peaceably, 'Wolfe didn't really strike me as a fortune-hunter type of guy.'

Sushila smiled. 'I love how you call him Wolfe.'

She had just returned from five 'surreal' weeks of unpaid leave in England, trying to deal with the financial and legal fallout. She and her parents and her daughter checked into a hotel in Winchester, where Faye's house was situated. Sushila walked into the office of a random small law firm in the town and asked if anyone could help her. She got lucky: she found an experienced and businesslike lawyer who thought of everything and took care of everything, even the burial of Faye's remains in a Protestant graveyard in The Gambia. When the parents returned to the United States, the lawyer – what would Sushila have done without her? – pointed out that she was free to stay at Faye's house; and the move turned out to be strangely comforting to Sushila, who discovered many photographs of Wolfe as a boy with long gold hair. She also discovered a safe in Faye's bedroom. After a technician opened it with a drill, she found gold jewelry and sixty-three thousand euros in bills. Her first instinct was to tell Wolfe about it: he had always claimed that Faye had a stash of money – and he had been proved right! But Wolfe was nowhere to be found. 'I could look for him everywhere, in every corner of the universe, for eternity, and I would never find him.' She smiled. 'It makes no sense.'

I touched her hand. I was asking myself, Who was looking after Pearson while Sushila was in England?

The legal process in England was still ongoing, Sushila said. Even after Faye's probate was settled, she would have to go back to take care of the affairs of Wolfe's brother, Geoff. Then there was Mark's estate, here in Pennsylvania.

I said, 'It's your job to take care of this stuff?'

'I'm Fiza's mom.' Fiza, she said, was the biological next of kin of both Faye and Geoff.

'Biological?'

Sushila closed, then opened, then closed her eyes. There was a complication, she said. A non-biological next of kin. It was too overwhelming to think about, let alone explain.

That night, I discussed the Pearson situation with Cutie. After sleeping on it, I wrote to Sushila suggesting a doggy play date. Cutie was a ferocious, somewhat picky little guy, I warned her, but maybe she and Pearson would hit it off, and maybe Sushila would consider me as a possible pet parent for Pearson? Without calling it an ulterior motive, I wanted to see Sushila again. I, too, was lonely.

The basic cause of my loneliness was not my exit from the Group as such but, rather, the isolation resulting from an interior drama that I could not discuss with anyone. These secret feelings seemed maybe a little laughable. They centered on certain high-minded notions of community that I had projected onto the Group. I had always been a practical, down-to-earth person, and never a leftist in the way of some people I knew – full of theoretical passions, full of abstract anger and hope, seeing themselves as protagonists in a drama of ideals. Wolfe was something like that. But I did respond idealistically to the co-operative movement. It was exciting to learn and affirm its principles – solidarity, self-responsibility, equity, and so on – and to put them, or discover them, at the center of my identity. I was a co-operator.

And now I wasn't.

Sushila agreed to the doggy play date. As far as the adoption of Pearson was concerned, she told me she'd had a change of heart. She and Fiza would keep him, allergenic as he was. The dog was old. He seemed to carry within him the spirit of his master. They would cherish him for the rest of his days.

I was very happy to hear it.

It's funny how things work out. Sushila canceled the doggy play date; then she was forced to travel to England again, to deal with the riches that had come her daughter's way. We did not become friends. In early December, I rented out my place in Pittsburgh and moved back to Milwaukee, to a rental in the Lower East Side, which is a fancy, dog-friendly neighborhood. I felt strong enough to see my sister again, but I didn't want her dropping by my place unannounced. Her home was in the North Side, near the cemetery, not too far from where we grew up. She would have no reason to find herself in the Lower East Side, across the Milwaukee River.

You can be sure that some will find a way to criticize. That is a person's right, to criticize. But I have a right to live where I want to live, in a lifestyle of my choosing. If I do not have a view of Lake Michigan, it's not because I would be ashamed if I did, or because I cannot afford it; I just don't like looking at that big cold lake.

My new job – a real job, terminable by firing – kept me busy. I didn't think about Sushila until she called me in January 2016. She was in Milwaukee. She asked if we could meet up.

I was delighted. 'Come to my place,' I said. 'Come for dinner.'

•

Sushila was the first guest I had in my Milwaukee home. She brought two bottles of wine – one pink, one white – and, as a house-warming gift, a nice framed black-and-white photograph of Pitts-burgh in the old days. I hung it up right away, on a nail left in the wall by the apartment's previous occupant.

'This place is so cozy,' she said. 'I think I might get something like this – more modern. With doormen. When we're ready to move. We're not ready yet.'

I set out the nice Korean food I'd pre-ordered. We opened the bottle of pink wine and sat down for dinner. Something in the atmosphere, a feeling of trust, told me that Sushila had something important to share. It's funny how you have confidence in some people right away.

She asked about my move to Milwaukee. When I answered one question, she asked another – and I answered again. I told her the usual things (regarding my new job she said, 'That sounds amaz-ing'), as well as things that I've spoken about so rarely that you'd call them secrets were it not for the fact that they're not secrets. They're just private. Privacy is unfashionable, I know. Not every-body values it. I do.

When she asked about my family, I responded easily. I told

her about my mother, who died when I was thirteen years old, and about my sister, Genevieve, who took care of me after Mom died. Genevieve was nineteen. Very soon she had problems with drugs, problems with unreliable, unsafe men in her life. (I was thinking in particular of one man, whom I did not tell Sushila about, and who in any case is dead.) My sister made a real effort to raise me, I told Sushila, and never stopped encouraging me with my schoolwork. There was a lot of conflict and mayhem, too, as one might expect. After I left Milwaukee for Pittsburgh (I saw no reason to tell Sushila about Professor Mueller), Genevieve's issues worsened. I told Sushila something I'd not told anyone, which was that for many years I paid my sister – paid her landlord, to be accurate – no less than three hundred bucks every month. In return for these payments I was exempted, in my mind, from having further contact with her. It was a painful, unnatural arrangement. The alternative, though, would have been a relationship in which Genevieve would never stop calling me to ask for money. That wouldn't have been tenable.

Things changed for the better. In the last two years, Genevieve had been in a solvent and stable relationship. (They met at church; he was the bishop; there was a brief scandal, his wife having died only weeks earlier.) The bond between her and me was still complex. We certainly needed more practice at getting along. But money was no longer changing hands. I could not have returned to Milwaukee otherwise.

'What about you?' I asked. 'What brings you here?'

'I don't know where to begin,' Sushila said. Then she told me the story of Godwin.

I emphasize this: Godwin, not poor Wolfe, was her focus, her central character. The other, I guess entertaining, parts of her story – Wolfe's unusual mother, her sons' bizarre attempts to track down the boy prodigy, the French soccer veteran Jean-Luc Lefebvre, the extraordinary and unlikely business partnership between Wolfe and his mother and brother, the bizarre scheme to relocate Godwin to England and 'launch' him there and make millions out of him, the small-aircraft flight to retrieve Godwin and Lefebvre from the Senegal soccer academy, the flight's tragic ending – these parts were not the point of Sushila's story. The point was to explain the situation of Godwin Anibal. I don't think I could have listened if the point had been anything else.

Godwin was currently in Senegal, at the soccer academy. But with the death of his adoptive mother, the fifteen-year-old no longer had a home. He had no legal right to live in France or in England, and he apparently had no wish to return to Benin, where he had been totally disowned by his father. The youngster had two things in his favor. There was Jean-Luc Lefebvre, his agent and mentor; and there was Godwin's (naturalized) citizenship of the United States. It came down to this: Jean-Luc had secured Godwin's admission, with a full ride, to a top soccer academy in the United States. The boy would learn English, continue his general education, and, of course, keep developing as a soccer player. Jean-Luc was sure that scouts from the top clubs would quickly appear.

'When is this supposed to happen?'

Godwin was due to arrive in the country within a month.

I could see where this was going. 'You're not responsible for him, Sushila,' I said.

'When they turn up at your doorstep,' Sushila said, 'you're responsible.'

I didn't have an answer for that.

Sushila clasped her hands. 'The soccer academy is in Wisconsin,' she said. 'Just west of here. That's why I'm in town. To check it out.'

'Oh,' I said. So that was it. 'You want me to pick him up at the airport? Take him to his new school?'

'"I was thinkin",' Sushila said slowly, 'of something bigger. Something crazy.' Godwin needed a guardian, she explained. A guardian was someone who—

'I know what a guardian is,' I said. My sister had been my guardian for four and a half years. Then I turned eighteen.

'Right,' Sushila said. It was my offer to look after Pearson, she quickly explained, that got her thinking of me. After that came the realization that Godwin's school was close to Milwaukee.

'What's the ask, exactly?' I was confused.

The ask was that I consider becoming Godwin's guardian, Sushila said. 'Just think about it. Whether it's something you'd consider seriously. If you think it's conceivable, we could go more deeply into the details.' In an ideal world, she said, Godwin's guardian would eventually adopt him. He needed family. 'I think you would be wonderful.'

'Wow,' I said.

As far as finances were concerned, Sushila explained, Godwin (along with Fiza) had inherited Faye's estate. His guardian, whoever that was, would have to serve as the trustee of that money.

I couldn't speak.

'I can't do it myself, Lakesha. I'm not in any kind of shape to look after him. I'd do a bad job. I'd resent it. He doesn't deserve that. He deserves a real parent.' To her credit, she did not go all tearful on me. She was holding up her phone. 'This is him. If you don't want to look, I'll understand.'

It wasn't a great photograph. It showed Godwin sitting down for dinner with other kids. He was the one with the goofy grin on his face.

'What's he like?' I heard myself asking.

According to Jean-Luc, Sushila said, he was a good kid.

'Why doesn't Jean-Luc become his guardian?'

Sushila said, 'He's too old. And he's not parent material. And I don't trust him with the money.'

I handed Sushila back her phone. As I did so, I felt myself going through a strange neurological storm. My face and neck and hands were suddenly hot. I felt an intensification of reality so strong that I had a touch of vertigo.

Godwin was fascinated by the United States, Sushila was saying. He much preferred to come here over going to a school in Europe.

I said, 'What about me? I mean, as his guardian?'

'He would be so excited,' Sushila said.

I picked up Cutie. 'What do you think, Cutie? Would you like a little brother?'

Cutie gave me a very doubtful look.

I decided to talk it over with Genevieve. It would do us good if, for once, I was the one asking for her sister's help and advice. I was also interested in her point of view. She had never been a physical mom (a complicated, sad story), but I suspected that she had practical wisdom I didn't have; and because her partner had two children in their twenties, I thought that maybe she had access to the special knowledge of parents.

Genevieve enjoys talking on the phone. She insisted on a blow-by-blow account. I told her what I could. When I was done, her first question was, 'Why you? You the only black woman they know?'

I laughed.

She made some comment about the expense of having a child.

'I haven't contemplated the financials yet,' I said. I had no intention of telling her about Godwin's wealth. 'The stage I'm at is wondering, Am I crazy to be even thinking about this?'

'Mm,' Genevieve said. 'You want my opinion?'

'Yes, please.'

Genevieve's opinion was that guardianship made sense – for me. I would get personal satisfaction out of it, and I would get money out of it.

'Now, hold on,' I said.

She wasn't a fool, Genevieve said. She wasn't blind. I had tried to hide it from her, to obscure it from her, but the kid came with an inheritance. A big one, would be Genevieve's guess. He probably had no clue how rich he was. He was just a little African boy, taken from his kin. That's what I was party to, Genevieve said. I was party to the taking of an African child away from his African family.

'I'm not *party* to anything,' I said.

'No, but you *contemplating* it,' Genevieve said with poisonous emphasis. What I had to think on, she said, while I was contemplating *helping* the kid, giving him *opportunities*, *saving* him, was my motives. Only a selfish—

I said, 'I'm going to stop you there, Genevieve. You have a good day.'

The conversation left me with a desolate feeling. I felt more strongly than ever the urge to have Godwin in my life.

The next day, I told Sushila I was interested. She gave me more details. I made further inquiries. I didn't talk with Godwin, because his English wasn't good enough yet. But I sent him pictures of me and Cutie and of the building where we live, and then, after he'd asked, Cutie videos. I did talk on the phone with Mr Lefebvre. I insisted that Lefebvre inform Godwin that if, in the future, Godwin wanted to return to Benin or otherwise reconnect with his family of origin, I would do whatever I could to grant his wish.

When I was satisfied that it would be ethical for me to go ahead, I petitioned Wisconsin to appoint me as a Guardian for a Child Without a Living Parent.

Three weeks later, pending the hearing of my petition, I was made Godwin's Temporary Guardian. It was that fast.

•

Cutie is not a great one for the outdoors, but if it's dry out and not too cold, she will make her way around the block. The winter in Milwaukee is colder and snowier than the one in Pittsburgh, and Cutie has a new wardrobe of canine apparel. On this day, she is wearing booties and a classic green parka. When we return from our walk, one of the front-desk guys – they are so polite and kind – says, 'Your guests are here, Miss Lakesha.' I turn back toward the waiting area in the lobby, and there he is – Godwin.

He has on a voluminous puffy jacket, shiny silver, that comes down below his knees, and a red baseball hat. Sushila is here, and there is a third person – an older man in an old-fashioned wool overcoat. That must be Jean-Luc Lefebvre.

I'm holding Cutie in my arms. She growls when they approach. Godwin stops. He is apprehensive. We will have to take care of that right away. They will have to learn to get along.

My apartment is comfortable but compact. The bedroom I've got ready for Godwin is on the small side. I didn't know what a boy's bedroom looked like, so I gave him exactly the bedroom I saw in the IKEA catalogue. I was concerned that he would be disappointed. But he immediately falls onto the twin bed and looks quite happy about it. I show him the pull-out storage drawers under the bed, and his closet, and his study desk. It is dark out. In the morning he will see a quiet, pleasant street.

I ask Godwin if he would like to eat pizza for dinner – there is an excellent pizzeria nearby – and Mr Lefebvre repeats my question to him in French. Godwin nods. Mr Lefebvre declares, 'Tonight we eat pizza. After that, *madame*, no more American food. No more hamburgers, no more fast food . . .' He is wagging his finger at me.

Sushila, horrified, says, 'Jean-Luc!'

There is no need for her intervention. I have learned to manage overly direct individuals. 'I agree with you, Jean-Luc,' I tell him. 'An athlete must eat good food. I'm not good at cooking, but I'm excited to learn.'

Jean-Luc wags his finger again, this time to indicate exaggerated approval. He says something in French that makes Godwin smile.

I say, 'No more French. English is the language of the house. In this house, English,' I repeat to Godwin, making sure to sound extra friendly.

'*English*,' Godwin echoes. With his jacket off, he looks very slight.

The pizzas are chosen, ordered and delivered. We eat almost without speaking. Everything has already been discussed in detail and worked out. I would never accept such a responsibility without thinking about it very carefully and considering every possible arrangement. At nine-thirty, Sushila and Jean-Luc leave for their hotel.

I give the young man toothpaste, a toothbrush, two towels and a ticking alarm clock. I set the red alarm needle to six-thirty and point it out to him. I tell him that *breakfast* will be at *seven o'clock*. I make him repeat the emphasized words. Then Cutie and I go to bed.

After lying there for a few minutes, I get out of bed. I lock the door of my bedroom. For many years, I've enjoyed a quiet, safe home of my own and on my own. No shouting, no strangers coming and going, no surprises, no sounds that are not mine or Cutie's. I'm not afraid of Godwin. It feels good to have him under my roof. But his presence has the effect of filling me with suspense and fear.

I'm grateful to him for this. It enables me to start fixing a problem that I now feel ready to fix.

This was an important part of my thinking – that becoming

Godwin's caretaker, or American mom, would benefit me, too. Pure benevolence is not sustainable. Mutually beneficial arrangements are the most durable and do the most good. I wasn't being ironic with Jean-Luc: I have long wanted to learn how to cook properly. I could do with eating better, too. That will only happen with another person to cook for. Loss cannot be avoided, but maybe you can counteract it by letting something into your life.

In the morning, I find him sprawled fully dressed on the bedspread, with one foot still wearing a laced-up sneaker. I am so ignorant of the behavior of male teenagers that my first thought is to wonder if bedding is new to him. After breakfast – scrambled egg whites with slices of apple; the boy barely touches it – we drive to the hotel where Jean-Luc and Sushila are waiting for us. Sushila hugs Godwin, then hugs me, then receives a kiss on each cheek from Jean-Luc. She leaves. She looks simultaneously destroyed and relieved. Godwin is no longer her responsibility.

The academy is a forty-minute drive away. Jean-Luc rides shotgun. '*Snow*,' I say to Godwin, pointing at the fields. I look in the rearview mirror. He is sleeping.

The Principal, Dr Grulke, greets us in his office. Next to him stands the Head Coach, Mr Raul Martinez, whose bio states that he is a former professional soccer player who played for Real Zaragoza, the Los Angeles Salsa, the Fort Lauderdale Strikers and the Rochester Raging Rhinos. It is an old-fashioned office, with a large executive desk dominating the row of chairs reserved for visitors. At Dr Grulke's invitation, I sit in one of these chairs. I indicate to Godwin to do likewise. Jean-Luc and Coach Martinez remain on their feet, over in the corner.

Consulting his desktop screen, Dr Grulke asks me to confirm that Godwin's permanent address is mine. He says, 'You're happy to be Godwin's person of recourse?'

I say, 'Yes. You call me if there's any problem.'

Dr Grulke asks for and receives my driver's license. 'Can you officially confirm to me that you are the legal guardian of Godwin Anibal?'

I can and do give him this confirmation.

Dr Grulke explains the administrative fees that are payable

to the academy, even though Godwin is on a full scholarship, and hands me the invoice. This includes a school bus fee, because Godwin, this semester, has elected to be a day student and not a boarder. I insisted on that. I pay by check and keep the invoice for my guardianship records. I sign papers that Dr Grulke gives me.

He seems very satisfied. 'You will be happy here,' he says to Godwin, and shakes his hand. In answer to a question I have not voiced, he says, 'We have students from various educational backgrounds here – various cultures, languages, scholastic levels. They all benefit from their time here. I always say, education is a process. It is an environment. And there is no better environment than football. Isn't that so, Mr Lefebvre?'

Jean-Luc says, 'I learn English, I learn psychology, I learn history, I learn geography, I learn business, all on the football field. Not in the classroom.'

Dr Grulke smiles. 'Well, we hope to teach our students something in the classroom, too.'

Coach Martinez puts a hand on Godwin's shoulder.

'I will be here at six p.m.,' I say to Godwin. He will not be taking the school bus until he has settled in.

I don't hug him, even though I want to. That will come later.

He is taken away. It's sudden – he is in the room, and then he isn't. Am I already missing him? How is that possible?

On the drive back, after a minute or two, Jean-Luc says, 'You have a man? A boyfriend?'

I don't look at him.

'A woman friend?'

'The forecast is for more snow,' I say, peering out at the charcoal sky.

I drive Jean-Luc to the train station. He is going to Chicago. From there he'll fly back to France. His plan is to return to Milwaukee frequently, for the purpose of managing Godwin's soccer career. I'm grateful to him, because I have very little knowledge about that side of things. That will change. I will inform myself, and I will keep an eye on Lefebvre. Whatever happens, I will take care of my boy.

At the station, Jean-Luc bangs the rooftop as a thank-you. I wave to him, then drive the few blocks to my new place of work. The excitement I feel as I stride away from my car is almost overwhelming. Things can change for the better as well as for the worse. Who would have foreseen, a mere few months ago, that I would find myself back in my home city, with a fine young man in my care, working for the Hillary for America campaign? President Hillary Clinton! Mr Godwin Anibal! There is so much to look forward to.